Diamond Love

S.C. Miotto

Dedicated to my wonderful family. I love you so much Robert and my little gems: Dominik, Carla and Leah Rain!!

iv

DIAMOND LOVE

Diamond: The symbol of purity and innocence.
It embraces the prospects of love and fidelity.
It encourages faithfulness.

A diamond represents the perfect love...

CHAPTER 1

It was a very dark, weak and confusing time in my life to be alone. Regardless of how nice Dr. Bailey and Myra Santana were to me at the hospital, when I walked out on Aug. 18, 2012, I would have been happy to see anyone – ecstatic to see any familiar face.

But I wasn't exactly expecting John to be standing there in the waiting room, nor did I expect to find so much comfort in his company. I was determined to not fall back into my pre hospital routine or bad habits. And even though I was feeling incredibly heartbroken -- and broken in general -- the determination to be a stronger person kept me moving forward. *Well, most days.*

John drove me home that day but it was difficult to find comfort in my own house again. There were too many traumatizing memories. The empty house reminded me that I truly was all alone. I couldn't sleep there. From all the times that I've ever spent with John it was obvious that he was lonely so it wasn't a huge surprise when he asked me if I needed a place to stay. Not wanting him to get the wrong idea, my initial instinct was to decline his offer. But also being in a position where I didn't want to be alone either, I second guessed myself.

Thankfully, John informed me that he was newly involved with a woman from his firm named Judy. My focus was towards anything to keep from getting into a dark place again. So there I slept, every night in a guest bedroom in John's house. Somewhat missing my old life and grateful that a new one was slowly, or eventually, beginning.

I still managed to have my good days and my bad ones, but didn't everyone? Even though I didn't hear from Frank once since the night of the fire, it wasn't wise to pretend that he disappeared forever. One of these days he would pop back into my life, and it would probably be at the worst time, but I would be ready. That was a promise I made to myself. My children were the only good that came from my relationship with Frank. I didn't want that man anywhere near me, ruining my progress, messing with my head.

I hadn't seen Brooke who randomly decided to go

upstate New York to finish the classes she needed to complete her bachelor's degree. She and I agreed, through email, to split the work from "Little Treasures," which she had been running by herself from home while I was in the hospital. I made sure to bring my desktop to John's house and this kept me actively working and busy for at least some of the days.

My other days consisted of tea, talks, and dinner with John. The nights were very different from the composed person I pretended to be during the day. Late night crying sessions when I was by myself were something that just didn't stop. Of course I missed Collin the most when I was all alone with nothing but the distant lull of the night to keep me company. Even when several more weeks had past and I thought time would erase the memory of us.

It was one night early October and as I lay in my bed the emptiness set deep in my belly as my throat tightened and eyes tinged with the familiar sting, but I couldn't cry. I was all cried out. And exhausted as my endless turning and position switching began early that particular night.

I closed my eyes tight and there it was. His arm draped across my body, as each other's warmth comforted both of us. His face nestled into my hair as he breathed steadily against my neck and all I felt was serenity. But of course it wasn't real. I was at a stand-still of the interaction of past, present, and future. Too immobilized to walk in either direction. But I knew that the haunting sheet of emotions that enveloped me daily wasn't going to disappear on its own.

The next morning I felt different. As if I knew what I needed to do. I contemplated all day but wasn't sure if I was making the right decision. When John was home I sat in my favorite spot in his kitchen -- on the barstool where I had a great view of the aquarium in the dining room.

He had the most elegant salt water fish with green, pink, teal, and purple rocks and plants strewn about. Canary yellow, fire orange, electric blue, and multicolored striped beauties graced through the water. I usually really enjoyed watching them but my mind was somewhere else.

There I was sitting with my phone in my hand and all I could think about is what he's doing. *What is Collin doing?* I

10

could picture him, so cute, so responsible, taking charge on some movie set, just like he did when he and his friends were working on their project. *What exactly is a production coordinator?* I wondered. Whatever it was it sounded important and despite Collin's carefree ways he knew when to put all nonsense aside and get serious. He's was so amicable. *I really can't stop thinking about him! And it's been so bad these last few days especially.* Would it be selfish if I disrupted his life, just for a moment? Would it be wrong of me since I was there with John? No. That wasn't an issue. We're just friends anyway.

My biggest setback was that I didn't know what to say. And it would crush me if I didn't get the response I was looking for. I glanced over at John who was making some boring fish platter. Even if John was available he was too boring for me. The truth was that I wanted to be with Collin and *only* Collin. I would never think twice about it again. If he wanted me in California, well then that was where I would be. Because it was all I wanted.

"What's going on?" John asked breaking my thoughts. "You seem stressed."

"I am. A lot actually."

"Anything I could do to help?"

I talked to John so much and because he was right there. He knew so much about what brought me to my breaking point that led to my hospital admittance. I was able to tell him all about my affair with Collin, my history with Frank, and everything that happened between me and Brooke. John had surprisingly become my go-to person when it came to advice, but I was nervous about telling him how I had been feeling lately.

"Oh, you've already done so much John. And I really appreciate it. This is more of an internal battle. A decision that I am trying to make," I said, sort of hoping that he would ask me to elaborate anyway.

"Well you should know by now that I am a great listener," he said looking up at me before turning the fish with a spatula.

That he was. And he was my only true friend at that point. *I guess there shouldn't be any hard feelings if I told him about what was on my mind.*

"I've just been thinking a lot. And part of me is wondering if I should just put myself out there rather than wondering 'what if?'?"

"Is this about that young man?" he asked, as he raised an eyebrow. His tone sounded slightly judgmental. He never criticized me for cheating, but he did for the fact that it wasn't with someone who could offer me more. John was a bit materialistic. He wanted to see me with a man who was financially stable and mature. I was so over being that way though worrying about what didn't really matter.

"Yes. It is," I said quietly.

"Oh. I see."

"I don't know if I should call him. Find out where he stands. I just … I think I'll regret it if I don't."

"The real question is; has he tried to get in touch with you?"

"I … I'm not sure," I said sheepishly but the real answer was "no." Noticing John's scowl I felt the need to defend the situation. Or I guess to defend him.

"I didn't have my phone while I was in the hospital. Maybe he did call but gave up when I didn't respond," I said defensively.

"Victoria, you would know. You already know that I left you several voice messages, and when you never got back to me that's when I became concerned enough to find out that you were in the hospital. I'm sure that a text message would have come through once you turned your phone back on, if he actually did try to get in touch with you."

"I know. But at the same time I do understand why he didn't. He's probably trying to move on."

"Then why get in contact with him?"

"I just have to. If he rejects me …well then I'll figure it out from there. I just need … well …"

"Closure?"

I looked at John with a frown. Of course that wasn't the word I was looking for. "I surely hope not," I said. "But if that's what it's come to then, I guess so."

"He's across the country. Isn't that enough of a ..."

"It doesn't matter," I said shaking my head. "It's just distance."

He looked at me skeptically.

"Wouldn't you have done the same?" I asked trying desperately to get him to agree with me. He's told me so many times how much he loved Susan why couldn't he understand me?

"Of course," he said and sighed.

Then John and I were both quiet for a minute before he surprised me by saying, "If you really want to get in touch with him then may I suggest sending him a text message? You could carefully map out what you would like to say. It's less pushy and will give him the opportunity to respond without being put on the spot."

"You're right," I said. Then I looked at my phone and felt my heart race a little. My nerves stood tall as I stared at the empty message box. *Here goes nothing.* It was just like the first time I ever messaged Collin from Sean's phone, except this time I had so much more to lose. It took me a while to figure out something appropriate enough to say after the gap since the last time we spoke. John was right and thank heaven for modern technology because otherwise I would have been completely tongue tied.

Then I also unfortunately considered for a moment if he was seeing someone else. And if so, I wanted to make sure that I respected that. So ultimately after several versions my final message read:

"Hi. It's Victoria. I know that it's been a while but I just wanted to say hello. I hope all is well."

Short, simple, sweet. It was good, so after I sent it I placed my phone down feeling better. It hurt a little to have to send such a casual message to him, but I tried to brush those feelings aside and hoped for the best.

"So what did you say?" John asked.

13

I picked it up again, read the message that I sent aloud, and then returned it to the counter.

"Not bad," he said seeming impressed.

I helped John in the kitchen and made our plates while he set the table. He poured each of us a glass of Pinot Grigio and we took our places at the table – the super long table I referred to as "The Godfather table." At least six chairs were on each side, with a head seat at each end. I always wondered if he ever entertained this many people? Other than his lady friend, he never mentioned friends at all!

Like his dining room, his kitchen was extremely spacious. And in the kitchen everything white. White, like those pants he wore on his yacht last February. White, white and more white. The counter tops, the curtains, the cabinets, the stove, the leather kitchen chairs. And perfectly flawless.

I eyeballed the teal colored mini bar that was near the kitchen entrance and contemplated suggesting we sit there instead of this absurd table. I mean, really, why dirty a little spot just for two people? Everything was so pristine, it just didn't seem right.

I turned my thoughts to Collin again and several minutes after my message remained unanswered I sat quietly at the table, my stomach in a complete knot. I pushed the food around and took tiny bites.

John looked up at me. "Victoria … it's his loss," he said trying to be kind.

But it really was mine. Collin was my other half and I was the one who took too long to realize it. I messed up. I didn't say all that to John though. I just gave him a fake smile and nod, pretending to agree. "Definitely his loss," I said.

"You're a beautiful woman, and you're too good to play these silly games with him. Hell, if he doesn't realize that then …"

His words were interrupted by my phone's famous ding sound. I could have sprinted from my seat but I kept my composure in front of John. Then dabbed my mouth with my napkin and stood up slowly. "Excuse me," I said then walked over to the counter where my phone sat still lit up, with the envelope icon on the screen.

I opened it to find a message from Collin. *A long one.* I sighed and turned my phone over. Was I ready to read what his response was? This was it. The moment where he either told me to go to hell or we could possibly be one step closer to reuniting. Turning my phone over *again*, there was no more stalling. His message read:

> Hey stranger. It definitely has been a while. Funny thing is that I was just thinking about you today. Everything is okay. VERY busy... but it's all good. Long days, even longer nights. Work, school, sleep (hardly) that's about all I have time for. I hope you're taking care of yourself. So nice to hear from you. Would love to catch up. Take care.

Oh it was absolutely wonderful to hear from him. Even if it was all electronic, it was still him. The last time we saw each other it was under such terrible circumstances. Although, I suddenly had mixed feelings about the message. It was written so matter-of-fact. There were no cute nick names that he usually used for me. It didn't end with a question, so was I even supposed to respond? He was thinking about me *today*? Only *today*? Has it been a while since I crossed his mind? What the hell do longer nights mean? For me "longer nights" were when I couldn't sleep and was staring at the ceiling thinking about him incessantly.

John glanced over at me. "I'm assuming that was him?"

"Yes," I said quietly, feeling confused.

"You don't sound too thrilled."

"I'm not sure if I should be or not." And as I always did I needed someone else to help me figure things out. Didn't everyone do that anyway -- get a second opinion? I showed him my phone to let him help me analyze the message.

"So?" I asked John after I knew he finished reading it and still had no response.

"Victoria, do you want my honest opinion?"

I nodded reluctantly.

"I still stand by what I've said to you before. You're

too good for this," he said rubbing my arm sympathetically then returning to the table.

"What do you mean? He took the time to write back. He said it was nice to hear from me …"

"He was being polite, I'll give him that, but he has no interest. Trust me."

"I don't know," I said trying to contemplate all possibilities.

"He only talked about himself. He didn't ask you how you're doing. He didn't really sound all that excited to hear from you. And how long has it been?"

John was really raining on my parade. This was the first time Collin and I exchanged words in almost three months. The thought made me queasy. Even if John made some good points, it wasn't enough for me to really go by. Couldn't I just enjoy the exchange in general? Did it have to turn so negative?

"John, can't you see where I'm coming from? You've been in love."

"Yes I have. But I don't think you're in love. The idea of being with someone… trust me I do understand. I've felt that way at one point too."

He really didn't get it. "I suppose," I said, annoyed, then added, "I'm turning in early," while clearing my plate. I washed my dish before escaping to the room away from John's pessimism. In my night table was the picture that I looked at every single night before bed. It was so early, only 7 p.m., and all I wanted to do was sleep. I closed my eyes and fled to the only world where I could see Collin again.

CHAPTER 2

Not even remembering when I fell asleep, my phone woke me up. It was 2:15 a.m. I stretched and squinted my eyes trying to focus. It was absolutely pitch black in the bedroom. There were so many trees in Alpine and not many street lights. And it wasn't like John had any neighbors close enough for their light to reflect through the windows. Where he lived really was woodsy and desolate.

Then I remembered that it was the phone that woke me up. I reached across the bed lazily and felt for it on the night table. There was that envelope icon again.

I opened it to find a message from Collin. Which was really surprising.

Collin: Are you up?

Well, now I am, I thought. I started to click at the keyboard on the screen then stopped. Where was this going? When I first messaged him I was so adamant about it but now I wasn't sure what I wanted out of it. But again what John said – closure -- if that's what it's come to.

Me: Hey

Collin: Did I wake you?

Yes, but I'm so glad you did. And I probably could have written this if it were a few months prior. But now everything was so awkward. It's like we were back to square one.

Me: It's okay. What's up?

Collin: Sorry I couldn't talk earlier. I was working. And to be honest I was really surprised to hear from you.

Oh. Okay good he was being very straight forward. That's

what we needed. No dancing around things.

Me: I know. It was out of the blue. I just wanted to say hi and see how you're doing.

Collin: I ended up taking that job in Cali. I'm actually on my second project now. It's a lot of work but I love it.

He really was only talking about himself. I wondered if there was a possibility that he really had completely moved on. Or maybe he just changed. But it was just me being paranoid because while those thoughts crossed my mind he sent another message.

Collin: But enough about me... how are you? How's everything?

Should I tell him the truth? Seemed a bit like we were still doing the weird small talk thing. I was doing a great job taking care of myself. I stopped drinking with exception to the occasional glass of wine. I hadn't touched one prescription drug since I left the hospital. I was eating and sleeping regularly. Everything was good for me too, but no matter what I wasn't whole. Not without him. How could I say that? I couldn't.

Me: Congratulations. I'm happy for you. You deserve it. And I'm doing well.

Collin: That's great to hear.

I was a bit disappointed about the way the conversation was going. It really was dragging out and part of me wanted to just call him. But remembering John's advice I decided against it. *Why can't I have enough courage to tell him the truth?* It was probably because of all the other times that things didn't turn out the way I was hoping. One great thing that I always admired about Collin was that he was much bolder than I was. He was usually less hesitant to tell me how he felt.

Collin: I'm just a little curious as to what made you message me.

And now the spotlight was on me and I could give him another dumb generic answer or I could take this chance. If he didn't already know, through Britney or Brooke or some other means, how do I let him know that I was completely single? Well -- almost. He didn't know anything about my impending divorce. And he probably didn't know that I wasn't with John either. But I couldn't just throw it out there. Would it be completely crazy to tell him that I still wanted to be with him? My heart was always his and that never changed. Hell. No more games! That's what got us into this mess -- *games*. I took a moment to gather my thoughts and with that familiar erratic thumping in my chest, I typed the most honest and straightforward answer to his question.

Me: Because I couldn't go another day not messaging you. A lot has changed since you and I last saw each other. I know that the timing is a little off but I wanted to tell you that I'm not committed to anyone right now... I don't know if you are.... But I've really missed you.

After I sent and reread it I decided to write one more message.

Me: And I don't know what's going on in your life but after everything we've been through no matter what the circumstance are I was hoping we could at least be friends.

And of course that last part was a lie. I could never be friends with him if he was with someone else, but I didn't want to back him into a corner either.

Collin: I miss you too.

Collin: But I am still in California...

That's all he had to say? I know he's there... he told me that already. *But he misses me too.* These words brought a little comfort. And again he didn't address the questions. Was he with somebody else? Was he back with Vanessa? This was starting to become draining and I didn't know what to say again.

Me: I know

Collin: I would love to talk more but I have to be up in four hours. Crazy schedule.

I looked at the time. He had to be up at 3:30 a.m.? That seemed far-fetched. Was he leaving me hanging? Damn. *Maybe I did say too much.*

Me: Okay. It was really nice talking to you.

Collin: Goodnight sweetie

Me: Good night

And now that I was up at 2:30 a.m., after seven hours of sleep, not tired at all, and with my mind racing. Rather than staring at the ceiling it seemed better to go into the kitchen for some water and maybe a small snack. John's house was dark and quiet and eerie.

As I neared the kitchen I was startled as I could overhear the sound of talking coming from a distance. I was about to turn the kitchen light on then realized that John was outside on his phone. *That's so strange.* Not wanting to invade on his privacy I decided to skip the snack and figured a water bottle would do. Then his words caught my attention.

"You have to be more careful we can't keep moving because of your careless mistake... If you get caught you already know that I can't bail you out... No of course she doesn't know and she can't find out... You'd better not ruin this..."

It sounded pretty serious, but definitely not something I wanted to get involved in so I turned around and quickly kept it moving before he could notice me. Most likely just trouble with his son anyway. So I headed back to my room and put all my efforts into clearing my mind and getting back to sleep.

In the morning John was making his coffee and already had his briefcase, new paper, and to-go coffee cup together. I was surprised to be up so early, after spending hours thinking and watching the sun rise as I fell asleep, but it was a habit that was hard to break.

"Good morning!" he said cheerfully.

I was curious about the conversation that I had overheard, but of course I didn't ask him about it. He didn't seem the least bit daunted by it though, so maybe it was no big deal. He probably just stepped outside so he wouldn't wake me.

"Are you feeling any better?" John asked, breaking my thoughts.

"Huh?"

"You were pretty upset after dinner," he said.

"Oh yeah. I'm sorry. I forgot about that."

"Honestly, Victoria, I wouldn't worry about it. Like I said he's just a kid, and he's probably just moved on, that's all. It happens. He didn't realize what he had. You definitely dodged a bullet, that wouldn't have worked out."

Yup there goes John Montgomery with his super positive outlooks to start off my day.

"Well actually, he did eventually respond to me," I said correcting him.

"Oh?"

"Yes. He was working the first time I messaged him. But we talked, well texted, for a bit last night."

"I see."

"I'm still a bit conflicted, but I'm not giving up."

He nodded but obviously didn't agree with me.

"What?"

"I must say that I'm a little disappointed."

I looked at him confused and thought for a few seconds.

"I'm sorry John, I don't know if you thought that maybe you and I…"

"No. No, that's not it at all," he said then laughed a little. "I already mentioned to you that I started seeing someone."

"I know. I'm sorry. I thought that's why you were so unsupportive about my decision. I even felt a little guilty for involving you."

"No, I was being unsupportive because I am your friend, I care about you, and I wanted to give you honest advice. I'm not going to encourage you to do something that isn't in your best interest."

"You really don't think it's a good idea?"

"Well let me ask you this. What did you end up saying to him?"

"Um…" I tried to recall the conversation. "It's too much for me to remember," I said then took out my phone and scrolled to the messages. "Here, I don't mind if you read it," I said and handed it to him.

"Who has work at three in the morning?" was all John had to say.

"That's what I was thinking!" I said.

"You poured your heart out and he didn't even have the decency to answer your question. End it now before you get hurt again. And, in my opinion, that last message from you sounded a bit desperate. Maybe that's what turned him off."

Desperate? I didn't agree with that one. But maybe from the male perspective I did?

Thank goodness John needed to leave because I've already had about enough of him for the morning. I was about to start up with the computer when my phone went off again. Compared to the previous weeks I felt so popular. I had another incoming text message.

Britney: "Well hello there!"

Me: "Hey Britney. How are you?"

Britney: "Good. And I have to ask what did I ever do to you?"

I knew where she was going with this. At first, when I left the hospital I responded to a message from Britney to let her know that I was fine. She never received the full details as to what happened but we ended up meeting for lunch twice in New York. I promised to keep in touch with her but slowly started to distance myself from her as well as everything else from my past.

Me: Sorry I've been busy

Britney: You don't call. You don't text. And what happened to having lunch every week?

Me: The whole going into the city thing. I love hanging out with you but too many memories, you know?"

Britney: You already know if that's the problem I could always meet you."

Me: You're right. When are you free?

Britney: I'm actually doing a photo shoot in Jersey at 10:30. I could meet you after.

I probably could have declined her invitation and glued myself to my computer until John returned to entertain me more with his mundane conversations and anti-Collin comments but I opted towards a change of scenery. I needed some female interaction. And of course there was a small part of me that was hoping she could give me some insight. She had more information. It was almost as good as going directly to the source. We made plans for lunch at noon then I shut everything off again and headed to my room to get dressed.

CHAPTER 3

I met with Britney at Cuisine 16 in Rutherford for lunch. I arrived first and pulled my Audi into the parking lot across the street. There weren't many people there for lunch yet which was nice. I locked my car then went inside to get us a table. My waiter, a young red haired skinny young man, came up to take my order. In a very professional manner he began to tell me about the specials but I let him know that I was still waiting for someone and simply ordered an iced tea.

It was a nice place with a unique menu. Cozy and cute with artwork from different parts of the world. It was definitely a hidden gem.

About five minutes later Britney came strolling in wearing a long navy blue tube dress with white stripes and lime green high heels. When she spotted me her face immediately lit up into her huge smile and she waved to me excitedly.

"How are you?" Britney asked while leaning forward to hug me. "It's been forever," she said as if we were long lost friends that haven't seen each other in years.

"I know! Sorry. I've been a little busy with running the business from home, or well my friend's house, and every so often my time is occupied by trying to sell the house."

"How's that going?" she asked then picked up the menu glancing at it and looking up at me every so often to let me know that she's still listening.

"We've had a few offers but nothing solid yet. What have you been up to?"

"I've been traveling again. I just got back from London."

"Wow what were you doing over there?"

"I was part of a fashion show."

"That's really cool. Congrats."

"Thank you. It was awesome. Everything is so different there."

"I can imagine," I said then our waiter returned.

This time around he seemed so nervous compared to earlier. It was obvious that he was intimidated by Britney as he started to forget the specials and his perfectly polished speech now had gaps, pauses, and stutters.

"And the soup of the day is… I think we have chicken… no I'm sorry that's tomorrow…" He was so frazzled

"It's okay. We already know what we want," I said unable to see the waiter embarrass himself anymore. We placed our orders and when he scurried away I couldn't help but laugh a little. "Poor kid," I said to Britney.

She also laughed then changed the subject by suddenly giving me a funny, inferring look. "So…" she said. It was as if she was waiting for the opportunity to talk about something in particular.

"What?" I asked but already knew.

"Anything *else* new in your life?"

"Not much," I said looking at my glass.

"That's not what I heard," she said.

I looked at her inquisitively. It was such a bonus to have a way to know what was going on inside Collin's head because I sure had no idea.

"Hm. So he mentioned me?" I asked casually.

"Yes! I'm so excited that the two of you started talking again!"

We started talking? Really? This was news to me. "We did?" I asked confused. It wasn't like we spoke on the phone yet. And we exchanged very casual messages, unfortunately that was all so far.

"Yeah… Didn't you?"

"Define talking."

"You went months without saying one word to each other. Even if it hasn't been a whole lot yet it's a start, right?"

"You're right. I just had to break the ice. And I wanted to do it through him. I could have easily asked you what was going on in his life but I feel like it wouldn't have gotten us anywhere."

"I'm glad you did. Look, don't tell him that I'm telling you this but…"

"What is it?" By then I had become such a good actress. I

spent my entire life faking my emotions while I was with Frank. I could casually smile and nod while crying on the inside, or in this instance acting so nonchalant with Britney when anticipation was actually gnawing at me.

"You know that Collin and I speak to each other like every day. He hasn't been the same without you. He was so happy that you messaged him. I think he was like speechless. He spent all day trying to think of what to say to you," she said.

"Really?" I asked, feeling a little choked up.

"Yes. I just knew that you two would end up back together."

I needed to hang out with Britney more often. Every time I was with her I felt better about life. About everything really. She never seemed to be in a bad mood either.

"You think so?" I asked.

"Is that what you want?"

"Hm. I would consider it," I said, still trying to act modest.

"Oh my God shut up," she said and laughed. "You forget that I know the whole story!"

I couldn't help but to laugh too. "Well it was a stupid question. Of course I do."

"Aw you guys are in love, that's so cute," she said teasingly.

I felt my face flush but couldn't help smiling. That was no secret. *I definitely was.*

Our food arrived and I had the shrimp teriyaki and Britney ordered the duck au poivre. We each had a few drinks. I couldn't remember the last time I was able to enjoy my afternoon. As much as I appreciated that John was letting me stay with him, he was so boring and negative that I almost dreaded returning to the house.

"This was nice," Britney said as we stood outside by our cars.

"Definitely. Let's do this again."

"I'm free next Tuesday. Same time?"

"Sounds like a plan. You pick the place." I hugged her and returned to my car, then thought about anything I could do before going back to John's house. Unfortunately my errands were cut significantly once I no longer had the entire family to take care of. I called to check on Ashley and Nick but as usual Ashley was in class and Nick was out with Debra's kids. Before the Route 17 Jersey traffic started I decided to head back up to the house.

I arrived about an hour before John did so I sat on my bed with the laptop. I quickly checked my business emails and figured I could let the personal ones pile up for another day or so. No worries.

I was startled by a knock on the door. I didn't even realize that John was home already. I opened the door to greet John and his dark tan Ralph Lauren suit.

"Hey, hope I'm not bothering you. I was wondering if you would be interested in having dinner outside tonight," he said. "We may as well relish these last few warm evenings, as colder days are amongst us."

"That sounds nice. Thank you," I said cheerfully.

He looked at me surprised. "Okay. Great. I'm glad to see that you're back to your old self."

"I had lunch with a friend and got some fresh air," I said deciding to leave out the details of the real reason to my newfound happiness. The truth was I just couldn't stop smiling, both inside and out. "Let me just log out of my email and I'll meet you in a few."

John set up the patio outside and lit a few tall citronella candles to keep bugs away. I tried to help too but John never let me do much so I just set the steaks that he grilled onto a plate. He also made ratatouille and grilled asparagus.

The deck was very high rise and we had a magnificent view of the yard. We sat perched above the grass and shrubs overlooking an acre of land on that tepid fall evening. It felt so good to be outside. It was so peaceful, with just the sound of a few birds chirping as they made their way to their evening rest area. A few squirrels ran across his lawn chasing each other. I breathed in the fresh air and smiled softly to myself. Life was beautiful, once again.

"So tell me about Judy," I said to John while we sat on the comfortable Allegro Classics white and burgundy outdoor wicker sofa set. I ate very carefully to not get one drop of steak sauce on the white cushions. A huge red umbrella shaded us, even though the sun had pretty much set for the evening.

"Well," he said, then took a sip of his merlot. He seemed to be caught off guard. "She's tall, has red hair, green eyes... Very smart... Funny... You would like her," he said simply.

It was nice that John found somebody that he could relate to. The two of us were definitely too opposite to date, but we made great friends to one another. And with Judy keeping his interest, I didn't have to feel so guilty that I was going to be with Collin again. But for some strange reason I still felt unsure about updating John with this information. Maybe because he was a glass-half-empty type of guy. He was too much of a realist for my dreamlike personality. Me and my fantasies; always imagining a perfect life, always holding on to that true love feeling, still imagining my Tahitian get away with my love.

Just as I was thinking about him my phone went off and I held it to my side and glanced quickly at it.

Collin: Hi beautiful

I could feel my face blush a little but before I made a fool of myself in front of John I turned briefly to him and said, "Would you give me a minute?" Then I casually disappeared into my room before writing back to him.

Me: how are you? ☺

Collin: Good now that I'm talking to you.

Me: home early tonight?

Collin: No I'm actually on my break I just wanted to say hi

Me: I'm glad you did. Why don't you call me...

Collin: too noisy here

Me: Oh

Collin: Look, last night you were honest with me so I thought I should do the same. I'm sorry about the way things ended and I wanted to let you know that I'm also not with anybody

Me: I already told you how I feel. So where are we going with this?

Collin: hopefully somewhere good...

Me: I think so

Collin: I really do miss you

Me: I miss you too

Collin: I wanted to ask you something

Me: Sure

Collin: Maybe this is a lot to ask but I was wondering if you would consider coming here for a few days. I'm off on Thursdays n Fridays. I'll show you around. We could spend some time together.

Me: I would love to. I guess I should rent a really good car...

Collin: why?

Me: I'm not getting on an airplane!

Collin: You're nuts you can't drive here alone. Just fly you'll be fine

Me: Fine. Only for you. I'll do it

Collin: awesome... You'll love it here.

I couldn't care less about California. I really just wanted to see him. But what exactly was it that we were doing? We've established that we both miss each other, and now I'm going to visit him? *Were we an item again?* Not wanting to jump to conclusions I diplomatically addressed my concerns.

Me: I really wish you could call me. I don't want to get back together through text

Collin: Me too. Can I call you tomorrow night? I have to go back now but I'll call you. I promise. We'll talk about everything and figure out which dates will work best

Me: What time?

Collin: 7 pm your time

I was a little disappointed to let him go but was so excited at the same time. For two months since the second we broke up right up until then there was only one thing that I wanted and that was Collin. I knew John didn't know what he was talking about. *Oh no! John!* I quickly typed up my good-bye to Collin, as I remembered John sitting all alone on the deck.

Me: Okay, that works. Bye. Don't work too hard.

Collin: I'll talk to you tomorrow

Me: okay xoxoxo

Collin: @}--}--

Me: what's that?

Collin: A rose, silly

Me: Aw you're soo sweet.

I was back to my happy self. *Poor John.* I was gone for a while. I hurried outside to find him still sitting on the deck with one leg crossed over the other, still starting out at the grassy scenery.

"I'm so sorry. That was my sister. I haven't spoken to her in a while."

"No worries. I was actually just about to head in. I brought home some work that I need to get started on," he said.

"Oh okay."

"Maybe next time," John said seeming hurt. He was so overly sensitive sometimes. I didn't mean to ditch him. And I did feel bad, but at the same time I couldn't let his mood ruin mine. I was on cloud nine. I couldn't wait to get through one more day then I could finally hear Collin's voice again. Finally, that night was one night where my sleep was uninterrupted and sweet and I was looking forward to a brighter tomorrow.

CHAPTER 4

I knew it was 5:30 p.m. because John walked into the house. He was so predictable. Headed to work every morning at 7:30 on the dot and left work at 5, took exactly a half hour to drive home every day. There was really nothing spontaneous about him at all.

John changed out of his suit which I was surprised that he didn't cook in as well. His comfortable clothes consisted of a polo shirt and khakis. He started to take out and season chicken breasts and potatoes to begin his dinner creation.

"Do you need any help?" I asked hoping he could give me some task to keep my mind busy.

"No thank you, I couldn't ask you to get your hands dirty."

"I do cook too you know!" I objected.

"I'm sure you can. But I still consider you a guest here."

"Okay," I said then looked at the clock again. One more hour. *I feel like such a little kid*, I thought.

"Is something wrong? You keep looking at the clock," John asked while he started to also pull vegetables from the refrigerator.

"Oh," I said feeling a little abash that he noticed. "I'm just excited, I guess. Waiting for a call at seven."

"I see," John said but didn't ask any details. He probably put two and two together. He quietly returned to his cooking and I sat on the barstool zoned out.

He glanced over at me then broke my trance when he said, "Actually, I just ran out of garlic powder, could you get more from the pantry for me please?"

"Of course," I said hopping off the stool.

In the garage John may as well have had his own store. With exception to meat and dairy he had what looked like years' worth of groceries. Everything, from paper towels and toilet paper to canned goods and seasonings, neatly stacked and organized on metal shelved racks. I found the garlic powder and grabbed it from the shelf. When I returned to the kitchen John had stopped cooking and he had my phone in his hand. I had a flashback of me and Collin and that one argument we had, but in this case the tables were turned.

"Um, did I get a call or something?" I asked John, putting my hand out for my phone and trying hard not to snap at him.

He looked up at me but didn't seem fazed by my annoyance. "No," he said then handed it to me and casually took the garlic powder.

"Then what the hell were you doing?"

"I just figured that you might want some advice before your conversation tonight," he said unpretentiously.

I narrowed my eyes at him. "Were you going through my messages John?" I asked more annoyed at the fact that he didn't grasp that there was a problem.

"Victoria, I don't understand. Every day you've been asking me what to do and what to say. Just yesterday you said you didn't mind if I read them and handed me your phone yourself... remember?"

I put my guard down realizing that John meant well and as usual it was me who was overreacting. "You know what... you're right. But for future reference I meant that only when I'm *asking* for help."

"I apologize then, it was my mistake."

"It's okay, I guess," I said returning to my usual spot at the bar stool. It was now 6:20. I fiddled with my phone and sat quietly while John continued to cook. I felt a little bad for snapping at him. I was always so paranoid about everything because of the people I've had in my life in the past. One goal to change about myself was my tendency to assume that everyone was like Frank or my father. *There definitely are still some good people out there.*

Now feeling somewhat guilty I looked up at John. "So how did you know that I was waiting for a call from Collin?" I asked him, breaking the silence with intensions to lighten the mood.

"It was pretty obvious," he said. "I wanted to ask if you knew what the two of you intended to discuss. But it seems as if you have that figured out already."

"I do. I think we're going to give it another shot. This is definitely what I want. Or apparently what we both want. I didn't mean to snap at you. I know you were just trying to help," I said, then added, "As usual," while smiling at him.

"No problem. And good for you guys. It's always nice to see when things work out."

"Thank you," I said then stood up again. "I'm going to head to the room. I should probably have an idea of what flights to California look like so we could talk about it when he calls."

"Okay," John said and I left him to his cooking.

I went to my room, or the room where I had been staying for the past seven weeks, and shut the door behind me. Then started up my laptop and tried to remember the popular travel websites. Browsing distracted me for a while and it didn't help that I had no idea what I was doing while searching for different flights for the next upcoming weeks. It wasn't rocket science but at the same time I wasn't sure exactly where I was supposed to be flying to. Just to have an idea I searched options that were leaving from Newark and flying into Los Angeles. The prices seemed to be the most reasonable on a Wednesday, which was perfect since he would be off the next two days afterwards. *Did he want me to come in a week or further out?* I wondered as I looked at the drop down calendar on Jetblue.com.

I was so into what I was doing that when I glanced at the clock again it was 7:15. I was a bit annoyed because I was hoping that we would start off on a better note. *No big deal maybe he lost track of time.* I couldn't be too compulsive about it. I decided to check my emails and de-clutter my inbox for a while but by 8:30 I was actually getting irritated and even considered calling him instead, but of course decided against it. When 10:00 came around I couldn't make sense of what happened. There was a possibility that he got caught up at work and would eventually get around to calling me.

Well that was a waste of an evening, I thought while I got ready for bed around midnight. My emotions were all over the place at that point. Angry, sad, foolish, worried. *Is he okay? Maybe he lost his phone? What if he got into an accident?* These different scenarios and excuses played through my mind as I lay sleeplessly hoping that John's initial suspicions weren't right. Was Collin having second thoughts about getting back together? Britney said he was so happy about it. What if there was someone else? Should I try to get in touch with him? *No.* I already put my heart on the line; the ball was in his court so if he never got back to me then that's how it was going to have to be. *If anything I could figure it out tomorrow.*

But by the next morning I didn't feel any better about the situation. Part of me was hoping he would message or call me, even if it was at 3 a.m. No matter how much I wanted to consider my pride and dignity it wasn't that simple. Collin wasn't just some random guy that I didn't care about. I needed to know why he made such a commitment to call me then broke it with no explanation what-so-ever. And because I obviously cared so much for him I messaged Britney to make sure that nothing bad happened.

Me: Hey Britney

Britney was usually very quick at messaging back. The girl had the phone attached to her hip and she was always so excited to talk to me. But during the few minutes it took her to respond I was on edge. I started to have a really bad feeling that maybe something did happen. When the text alert came through I quickly checked my phone.

Britney: What's up?

Me: Not much. I was wondering if you've heard from Collin at all. Is he okay? I'm a bit concerned.

Britney: Yup

Okay. That was weird for her to give me such a bland answer. What was going on? Was I missing something here?

Me: Sorry... is that yes you heard from him or yes he's okay?

35

Britney: Yes to both

Relief was my immediate feeling but it was quickly followed by anger. *What? There isn't something life threateningly wrong with him? Wow so he just stood me up then.* He realized that he didn't want to be in a relationship? Or my other fear: he was already in one and couldn't just let me know. Figures. It was too good to be true. He probably didn't want to hurt me. Well this wasn't the way to do *that.*

Me: Oh. Okay. Well are we still on for next Tuesday?

Britney: Actually something came up. We'll reschedule.

Me: Alright no problem, just let me know

Britney: Ok

I didn't mind not seeing Britney the following week. Whatever the reason, Collin obviously changed his mind, so the details didn't matter. I couldn't dwell on it because it was a long shot to begin with. For us to rekindle after all the drama, after not speaking to each other. Could I really blame him? Now to start the process of moving on all over again.

Again it was easy to primarily tell myself to let go. To return to the routine at John's house. And at first I tried to act like nothing ever happened. It took several days but I found myself in a strange place again. Back in robot mode. Heartache was something I was becoming all too familiar with. And always with him. It was seriously time for me to accept that it was never going to work. The age, the distance, the obstacles, it was all too much. Our ship had sailed a long time ago. I was so sick and tired of crying but unfortunately I couldn't control my feelings. Then I was back to my "time healing all wounds" theory.

A week after no contact with Collin, or even Britney, I decided to really try to get motivated into another direction. Desperately wanting to focus on something else. Anything else.

I was so consumed with my own issues that I had completely neglected my manners as a guest. During my entire stay I hadn't done anything to help John at all. So I shut down my computer a little early and cleaned his house for him. Not that there was much to clean, everything was always so tidy. But that wasn't the only reason. He was there for me from the second we left the hospital. I wanted him to know that I appreciated everything that he'd done for me up to that point.

I also cooked dinner for the two of us. Poured two glasses of white wine and had everything ready on the deck at 5:25 p.m. John could tell me that he was dating Linda, but I knew he was still interested in me. It was obvious. And he was definitely upset that I bailed on him several nights earlier. It definitely wasn't a nice feeling to be ditched, so I decided to make it up to him – and act like the friend I should.

Of course at 5:30 John strolled in. He was very pleased to see all my efforts.

"You've been busy," he said. He smiled as he looked around.

I smiled back and said, "Yes I have." Then my smile quickly faded and I became more serious for a moment. "But I've also been very selfish. I haven't helped you around the house at all. You've done everything for me since I've been here. I'm sorry about that. I cleaned the kitchen, living room and bathrooms today."

"You didn't have to do that. I told you, you're a guest not a maid."

"Well I guess I'm also a chef today. I told you I could cook!" I said. I smiled again as lifted the top of the pan.

"I'm impressed!" he said when I revealed my chicken parmesan and baked ziti.

"Change into something more comfortable and meet me out back," I said while making our plates.

John disappeared to his room then met me outside several minutes later. He and I finally shared a good time together. No hard feelings, no phones interrupting us, just a nice dinner outside as the sun set and cool breeze took over.

We talked about where we grew up and got to know each other more. He was from Colorado which I didn't know.

His oldest son also went to the same college that Brooke was enrolled in. But even after he shared numerous stories I still didn't feel like I learned much more than what I already knew about him. Maybe he was more reserved then I thought. Either way he managed to keep me distracted for several hours. At the end of the night I kissed John on the cheek and thanked him again for everything again. It was only when I was by myself again, in my bed, when all the buried real emotions erupted at once. Tears fell into my pillow like a tidal wave as my dreams moved further from reach as my heart continued to break.

CHAPTER 5

My favorite time of the week became the weekend because I had time to myself as John always disappeared. He left early in the morning on Saturday and Sunday and returned late both evenings. I ventured off, visiting Nick and the kids at Paul and Debra's house. The following weekend I drove up to get a manicure and pedicure with Ashley then took her shopping. I was starting to think that maybe being single for a while was best for me. They were growing up so fast and I really wanted to continue to make efforts towards being a better parent. I even made plans to take Nick to Fright Fest at Six Flags since Halloween was around the corner.

I also started to spend more time with John. Every day we took turns cooking for each other and even cooked together on occasion. I food shopped with him, continued to help him clean, and spent evenings watching the wildlife from his deck.

It was Friday afternoon and John had taken the day off. I was trying to get some work done but found myself staring at the wall. I shut my computer off and decided to bother John instead.

John was sitting in the living room sorting through some papers while music filled the room. He must have heard me walk in and looked up at me.

"Hey there. How's work going?"

"I can't concentrate," I said then sat on the arm of the sofa.

"Maybe you should sit outside for a bit," he said. "It's beautiful out."

Why would John bother to take a day off to sort through papers in the house all day? Especially if he knew that the weather was nice. There was still so much to do. He needed to get out more as did I.

"John you're off from work today. Why are you sitting in the house?"

He looked at me confused. "Where am I supposed to go?"

"I don't know. *Anywhere.* Take me somewhere interesting. Please. I'm in this house way too much."

"Well, I do have one place in mind. I was going to wait until next weekend to show you but, hey why not."

Now this caught me off guard. John and I never spent a weekend together and suddenly we had plans? "Next weekend? Really?"

"Yes. Sorry. I was going to run it by you first. I don't want you thinking that I am planning your days out for you."

"No, it's fine. But you said we could go today?" I asked.

"I don't see why not."

"Sounds good, let's go. You want to show me something? What is it?" I asked inquisitively.

"It's a surprise," he said.

John had a surprise for me? This was interesting. "Now you have me curious. Well okay. What should I wear?"

"Anything will do. Bring a sweater it may get chilly."

I went into my room and looked through my dresser before throwing on my dark denim jeans and a white top. Should I wear make-up? Why not? I rummaged through my jewelry and began to miss the accessories that I left behind at my house. How long would I be staying with John? Not much thought had been put into it before. While the gears turned in my head as usual, I managed to apply my concealer, lip stick and eye shadow to look less plain, but still subtle. My hair flowed bouncy and wavy down my back. I finished off with an olive green cardigan and the only pair of fall shoes that I brought with me to John's house; maroon knee-high boots.

Just as I searched for a purse that matched my outfit I received a text message. *Wonder who that is.* Why is it that every single time that familiar sound went off my heart always jumped a little?

I grabbed the phone to read the message. It was from Brooke. She was just checking in since we hadn't spoken in a while. I responded to her letting her know that everything was fine and that I was still staying at John's. She suggested that we do something the following weekend and I mentioned Six Flags. We made tentative plans and ended our short conversation. I returned to my outfit, picking out a cute brown purse to complete the ensemble. *One more thing.* Before heading out I made sure to change the sound alert for my incoming text messages. Maybe erasing even the smallest reminders might help this process.

John waited for me outside with the car pulled up to the front door. When I walked out of the house the autumn breeze was cool and refreshing. It was a bright sunny afternoon. John stepped out of the car and walked up to me. "You look absolutely stunning!" he said taking my hand.

"Thank you," I said smiling as he quickly locked the front door to the house behind us and led me to the car, holding the passenger door open for me, and again I thanked him as he shut the door gently after me. He was always such a gentleman. I sat in that very red Jaguar that I hit from behind one year ago. John probably had eyes for me since that day because I was dressed so nicely, in my teal dress, for my date with Collin. Oh yeah... *Collin*. I sighed aloud as he crossed my mind *yet again*.

"What's wrong?" John asked as he began to cruise down the right lane of the Palisades Parkway. Driving slowly in a fast car. Only John Montgomery.

"Nothing. Just thinking."

"About?"

"The same thing I keep wondering for what seems like the longest time. Is there something wrong with me? I'm always told that I'm beautiful and stunning, yet my husband left me for another woman and the one person I thought really loved me doesn't care about me at all."

"There is absolutely nothing wrong with you aside from your own insecurity. I don't think you realize how much you intimidate men," he said glancing over at me and smiling warmly before returning his eyes to the road.

"I don't know if that's it," I said and sighed again staring out the window as the view of trees kept me occupied. Contemporary jazz play from John's Sirius car radio. I wasn't big on Nora Jones, so I turned the volume down to a softer level as we drove silently for a few miles. My mind never actually shifted from where it was when the car ride began.

Still wondering to myself I decided to ask the expert. "Can I ask you a question?" I said turning my focus to John again.

"Sure."

"Why do you think Collin completely cut me off?"

"There could be a number of reasons."

A number of reason? Jeez. "You think so? Well you know everything that happened up until that point so what do you think it was?"

"I think he thought about it and realized what it would mean to invest into a relationship, a long distance one at that. You seem to forget how young he is. And you did say that he's now back in the area where he's from? So he's home with this new job. He's probably thinks he's living the life. Where is there room for a committed relationship?"

"Everything he and I always talked about boiled down to one thing. Us being together. And we finally have that opportunity. I can't imagine that those other things would be so important. Not to him. It just doesn't seem right."

"People change, Victoria, or have you ever considered that maybe you never knew him at all?"

I shook my head. Of course not. Collin and I were so connected that it never crossed my mind at all. "I want to ask him myself. I think I need to hear him say it… whatever it is," I said. I was so determined to get an answer that maybe I was becoming a tad obsessed. "I'm thinking about calling him. What do you think?"

"Don't take this the wrong way but why bother to ask me? You're not going to take my advice anyway," he said almost bitterly. He was right though, I did do the exact opposite of everything that he suggested up to that point, and it got me nowhere.

"I know I tend to ask for someone's opinion and do what I want anyway," I said and laughed. "Sorry, I'm not great at making decisions. The ones I've made in the past were the wrong ones. But not this time. I'm really stuck and you were obviously right about everything else you said. Whatever you think is best I'll really take to heart."

"I know that this might be hard to hear, but I think you need to let him go once and for all. You're too smart for these games and to be wasting your time. And haven't you ever heard the saying that if you love something to let it go, if it's meant to be it'll come back?"

"Okay. And yes, that makes sense," I said disappointed with his answer. "But how do you get over someone you love?"

"It's not easy, but as the days go by and you realize that your heart is still beating you will only get stronger."

"You're so right John. You see things in ways I've never thought of."

"I've been here much longer than you have. And I've been through a lot."

The truth was I was happy to have John. He was my only real friend at the moment. Brooke was going through such a weird and distant phase. Britney was sweet, but in all reality she was Collin's friend, not mine. I trusted John and felt like I could talk to him about anything. Even if he did come off as jealous and unsupportive at first, that didn't really matter. He was there for me when it did matter.

After a 40 minute drive we arrived at a boat dock in Edgewater, New Jersey. We pulled into the designated parking spots then stepped out. It definitely was getting chillier. I put on my cardigan and walked with John to the where the line of boats were anchored. *Figures. John's surprise would involve boats.*

"I told you that I have a surprise for you," he said with an animated grin as we walked on the wooded bridge. This was the most excited I think I'd ever seen John. Being that we were at the local marina just the two of us this didn't surprise me. "Last weekend I went to a boat show. Well it was more of an auction. I was determined to add something smaller but faster to my collection."

I wanted to say pardon my unenthusiastic glare, but instead I just forced a smile, "I can't wait to see which one it is," I said faking my excitement. Oh, was this going to be another long boat date with John? At least he was dressed semi-decently this time, in a blue button down and casual black slacks. His hair was short, neat and tidy and he was completely clean shaven. But he sported his usual dorky look and I just shook my head and laughed on the inside.

The air held the strong scent of the river which could be equally pleasant or unpleasant. The wonderful traces of the natural trees and nearby flowers were breathtaking, but when the wind occasionally held the odor of sea life, moss, and algae it reminded me why I didn't really care for anything that wasn't on land. The sea and the air were not my things.

"I found the most gorgeous fifty-one Navigator Pilothouse," John continued. "I had to have her. Several bids were placed... it was quite a tight race!"

"So did you end up winning?"

"Victoria, of course! One thing about me is that I always get what I want," he said. "I paid ten thousand over what it's worth."

"Not a great marketing strategy," I teased.

"It's okay. It was all very well worth it," he said then stopped walking. "Well here we are!"

"Okay," I said waiting for the big reveal. "Well, where is this fabulous boat?"

"Turn around," he said.

I spun my body slowly trying to figure out which one it was but I knew right away. It was obvious. On my right side was a white yacht with tinted black windows. It had a top and bottom deck and was in mint condition. What caught my attention was apparently the big "surprise." Written across the side of the boat in huge black capital *bold* letters was "Victoria." I could have died. *This man is insane!*

"What a coincidence. Me and your boat share the same name." I decided to play dumb. I could only hope that it was a coincidence, but I wasn't that lucky.

"She didn't have a name when I bought her. I didn't even have to think twice though! It's a perfect fit don't you think?"

"Wow... I don't know what to say!" I wasn't lying. *I really didn't know what to say.*

"I know you've been feeling down lately. And you told me that you want to travel. Well now we could do it. Together! She's great on gas. There is plenty of space inside, it comes complete with a bar, kitchenette, lounge area..." He stopped his child-like ecstatic rambling and took my hand. "Why am I telling you all this? Just come inside! See for yourself." He practically ran ahead pulling me behind him and seemed so young and alive for once.

It still seemed ridiculous yet who was I to rain on his parade? Oh yeah, I was the person whose name was splashed across his boat which made me completely uncomfortable especially considering that our relationship was supposed to be platonic -- wasn't it? But instead of saying something, I quietly followed him onto the boat.

We walked down a set of narrow stairs to get to the lower level. The inside was clean and shiny with pine shudders with a matching table, wine cabinet, refrigerator, and counter. A chocolate brown leather sofa sat in front of a large window. It was fully equipped with a microwave, counter, bar stools, and a radio.

"This is incredible John. You really did all this for me?"

"All for you," he said.

"I don't know what I would do without you!" I gave him a hug and a friendly kiss on the cheek. It probably wasn't what he wanted, but the gentleman that he was he didn't protest either.

"Where are we headed to first?" he asked.

"Oh. Uh. What would you recommend?"

"Anywhere you want! Depends what you're looking for. Do you want tropical or historical? Warm or cool climate? We could cruise the Atlantic. We could go down to the Caribbean islands. I hear that Barbados should be amazing this time of the year."

"I'm not sure yet. I will definitely think about it and let you know," I said smiling but knowing that I couldn't go on a private cruise with him without it leading to something else. Something I was completely not ready for yet. Not with John, anyway.

I looked through everything, all the appliances looked brand new. Of course it was impeccably spotless. It smelled nice as if it had been freshly cleaned. John was also exploring buttons and switches trying to figure out what each one controlled. He turned on the radio then dimmed the lights.

"May I have this dance?" John asked extending his hand out to me as a waltz song played softly through the speakers."

"I'm not sure about that," I said. I knew it wasn't a big deal but I really didn't want John to get the wrong idea again.

"I can dance very well," he insisted.

"Maybe next time."

"Then would you like to go for a quick ride around the

Hudson?"

"Not tonight."

"Are you sure?"

"I wasn't expecting this. Next time I promise we could dance, cruise...do the whole boat thing. Let's just head back to the house."

"If that's what you want," he said sounding rejected. My plan to not hurt his feelings wasn't working.

"I didn't mean it like that," I said then thought of a quick excuse. "I'm just hungry." I lied but felt better that he looked less upset. "How about we do dinner and a movie?" I suggested. *Damn, why did I just say that?*

But it was too late to take it back because his eyes lit up and he accepted without hesitation. "Really? Okay," he said then started to shut off the radio and lights as we walked up the little set of stairs back out to the main deck.

I took John's hand to step off of his boat. Or was it *our* boat? Either way it was overwhelming and I needed to get out of there ASAP. We were headed back to his house and the entire drive he continued to plan our impending traveling adventures. I stared out the window, my mind somewhere distant. Every so often I would nod, smile, and agree, but deep down I was a little annoyed at him. My wounds were still very fresh from my recent breakup. I was still very much hung up over Collin; didn't we just talk about that on our way out here? For the first time it seemed like John wasn't being very understanding of my feelings and -- did I just agree to a date night with him? *Great.* What was I getting myself into?

CHAPTER 6

When John and I arrived back to the house it was already after 7 p.m. I told him not to cook and convinced him to order Chinese food instead. It was so out of his element but I was proud to see him step out of his comfort zone for once. I still set the table nicely with the good plates and silverware despite the fact that we were having take-out.

The food arrived within 20 minutes. We ordered a little of everything; steamed chicken and broccoli, white rice, vegetable Lo Mein, wonton soup, and steamed vegetables. I was so happy that John didn't mention anything else about traveling or about the boat while we sat for dinner. After we ate I decided to let him choose the movie. I wasn't very picky and I figured he should know my taste already.

John started up the surround sound and turned on the 60 inch flat screen. He decided on a classic movie "Citizen Kane," which I had never seen. *This movie actually is in black and white*, I thought as it started. And I could usually enjoy a good old movie. But it had to be something like Alfred Hitchcock or "It's a Wonderful Life." Why couldn't we have more in common? John really was a great guy. But he wasn't the right one. I already had someone who shared the same interests as me. We could watch a new comedy, cheesy romance or suspenseful action and have a great time all the same. And as nice as John was he didn't keep me excited. In any way possible. Yes, part of me wanted to give him a chance, but the financial security just didn't seem all that appealing anymore. There had to be something special going on for me to consider dating another man. *Is this what our life would be like?* Watching old classic movies on a Friday night, discussing the irony and theme; then going to bed at 10 p.m.?

As the movie started John stood up and grabbed a tray of snacks from the counter then placed it onto the coffee table in front of me before sitting down again -- very close to me. Suddenly I felt stiff and shifted nervously in my seat. He didn't seem to notice as he reached for a cracker that was accompanied by a small bowl of caviar.

"You have to try this," he said to me spreading a small amount of the slimy black jelly looking orbs onto the cracker. *Hmm classic movies and caviar.* Whatever happened to microwavable popcorn?

"No, thank you," I said trying not to make a face.

"I'm sure you've tried it before," he said questioningly.

I nodded. "Yes, but I'll pass. I'm still full from dinner."

"Okay," he said leaning back into the sofa, sitting even closer to me. He casually stretched and nonchalantly placed his arm across my back, resting his hand gently on my shoulder. I felt even stiffer and *so uncomfortable.* I leaned forward a bit and John retracted his arm.

"I'm sorry," he said sheepishly.

What am I doing? Here I am with this good guy who has everything going on for him and I'm really acting like this? What happened to trying? "It's okay," I said then thought quickly. "I just need to use the restroom," I said then stood up and swiftly escaped.

Why couldn't I see myself with John? The man named his yacht after me! And I couldn't even give him the time of day. It wasn't like I ever had to worry about not being treated well. But even as much time that had passed since we saw each other I still couldn't shake the feeling that I was supposed to be with Collin. I couldn't get the kid off my mind. And the worst part was that he obviously wasn't thinking twice about me. *Why can't I just let go like he did?* Three months without him. Three long months with that empty feeling. But also -- three months of not drugging myself to get through the day. Three months of eating healthy. Three months drama-free and focusing on myself. Was I better without him then? It was the illusion that I was holding onto. The fear to move forward. The fear of every night hurting as much as the last 90 ones did. It was fear and illusion tying me to Collin, nothing more.

Still staring at myself in the mirror of the bathroom, I wondered what could make me feel better. Dabbing some water on my face, hoping it would help, didn't do much. It wasn't quite refreshing me the way I'd hoped. Not sure how else to get through this date I wondered if I should turn to one of my old tricks. Just for that one night. Not touching alcohol during these three emotional months, with exception to an occasional glass of wine, was difficult. It singularly had gotten me into so much trouble in the past. But this was different. I had complete control over myself. I wasn't dependent anymore. Just one drink or two- to loosen up a bit couldn't hurt. Maybe then I wouldn't feel so nervous. Heaven knows that there was no reason to feel that way around John.

Looking up into the mirror again I made sure my makeup wasn't running then reapplied my pink lipstick and a bit of blush. *Out there is a man that adores me. Why not enjoy that?* It's not like I was getting engaged or anything. If I was ever going to move on the best way would be to find someone to move forward with. So for the first time I embraced the possibility that there might be some hope for John and me.

Now, feeling somewhat different about the way I would approach the evening, I returned to John greeting him with a smile.

"You feeling okay?" he asked, concerned.

"Yes." I nodded then sat. "But there is one thing," I said.

"Sure. What is it? Did you need something?"

"I was thinking. It *is* technically the weekend. Right?"

"Yes."

"I know I said dinner and a movie but... why don't we make that dinner, movie, and a few drinks?"

"Okay. That's not a problem at all. Why didn't you say something earlier?" he said standing up and walking over to the bar.

I shrugged. "I didn't really think about it."

John stopped at the wine cabinet and grabbed a bottle of red wine. "There's always room in the evening for a glass of wine," he said cheerfully.

I grimaced and disapprovingly shook my head. Not exactly what I had in mind.

"No?" He looked around puzzled then stopped over a bottle of white wine. "This is a dessert wine..."

I shook my head again.

He headed over to the fancier selection and held up a crystal decanter. "This is Jenssen Arcana it's a delightful aged cognac."

"Yes. I'm familiar. It's aged ninety-eight years in oak

barrels," I said and John's mouth almost dropped to the floor. Little did he know; that his $6,000 bottle of cognac wasn't *that* impressive. If there was one thing I did know about it was finer wines, whiskeys, and cognacs. Frank had quite the collection -- that was something I could say about him. And I knew the whole collection inside and out. So now at least John and I had one common interest.

"Wow," John said still shocked.

"Well am I right?" I asked. I waited for his response with a smirk on my face.

"Yes," he said taking two heavy looking short crystal glasses that matched the decanter from the bar. "Now, are you sure you're okay with this?" he asked before pouring my glass. "I don't want to be a bad influence."

"Not at all," I said giving my approval. "It was my suggestion, remember?" I took the glass from him then took a small sip. It was strong, but smooth, and exactly what I needed.

As we drank a little and I snacked on the crackers that were on the table. For a few minutes I was actually enjoying myself but then my eyes wandered away from the screen and the digital clock caught my attention. The time seemed to scream at me. Ten-thirty p.m.? Dinner and a movie didn't seem to be that uncommon of a date night. Not to mention that we were drinking. *Why did I still feel so old?* It was something about John's company. This just wasn't how I wanted to be spending my Friday night. I randomly craved the night club, colorful cocktails, and the gorgeous young man that came with that life. *Damn. There goes my mind wandering again.* I was mad at myself for going there, but how could I not -- with that terribly boring movie that John had on? Quickly I grabbed the remote control from the end table.

"Okay. That's it. Turn this off," I said abruptly, trying to figure out which one of the hundreds of buttons on the fancy universal remote control worked for the movie player.

"Wait. Why?" I seemed to have broken John's deep concentration. He was so into the movie that he had obviously seen 100 times anyway. "You're going to miss the best part," he protested.

"I don't care about the movie John!" I said and pushed his

arm playfully. "Come on what are we like eighty years old!"

"Hey! What do you have against Citizen Kane?"

"*Nothing*. But it's a Friday night and look at us!" I pressed several more buttons until I found the radio then scanned through the stations stopping on one that was playing Pitbull's "Give Me Everything."

"Come on!" I said pulling him up. "You wanted to dance before. Now all I want to do is dance." *I could thank Jenssen Arcana for that.*

"I don't know about this…" he said once I had him on his two feet.

"I thought you said you could dance," I teased.

"Not to this."

"Oh have a little fun," I insisted trying to get him to loosen up a bit. He tried a little but seemed completely uninterested at the same time. But at least he was trying. He reminded me of a time not that long ago when I used to have two left feet... And before any more thoughts beyond that could creep into my mind I stepped aside and grabbed my glass then filled it up to the top. *Try not to down this one.* I reminded myself.

"Slow down there. You're going to make yourself sick," John warned.

"I'm okay," I reassured him.

"So is this is what you listen to?" John asked sounding surprised.

"I listen to everything," I said still urging him to dance.

"I have no idea what I'm doing but okay," John said shrugging. Then he took my hand and twirled me around. I lost my balance falling into him.

"Clearly!" I said then we both smiled and laughed. After the stresses I had been through, I so desperately wanted nothing more than to have a carefree, fun night. Joking and dancing and drinking. As we were. And John was so cute trying with his idea of a two-step to some throw-back '90s songs that started playing. I guess he didn't mind those. He knew I was so entertained by him so he went with it and kept dancing even as hip hop played. I was laughing hysterically for the first time with him as we did the robot and other dances that weren't, and probably never will be, invented. And finally for those few moments I forgot everything else. But it didn't last long. Maybe this was meant to be a sign but as the song by Chris Brown, "Turn up the Music" ended and new song began I recognized it immediately and my heart dropped. The good feeling was gone. Suddenly it felt like I was going to be sick. John was so clueless, but I was no longer there with him. I floated back away to the haunting memories that seemed impossible to block. When John finally noticed me he stopped and looked concerned.

"What's wrong?"

"Uh…" I said, almost feeling like I was in numb mind state.

"Victoria?"

"Um. Nothing," I said shaking my head then sitting down. "Can you grab me some water please," thinking of the first thing I could say to shoo him away," I wanted to break down in tears but held it back as "DJ Got Us Falling in Love," continued to blare through the radio.

John walked over to the bar and conveniently had chilled water bottles available. He grabbed one then returned to me. "Here," he said handing it to me. I felt so detached, as my stomach knotted up. I really wasn't ready to let go if something this simple affected me so immensely. *Why was I being forced to move on? It wasn't fair. Weren't we just getting back together? What the hell happened?*

"What's wrong?" John asked again. I wished he would go away. Let me breathe for a minute.

"Nothing. Maybe I did drink too fast," I lied.

"Oh okay. I think we should take it easy," he said then reached over me to grab the remote and unknowingly saved me by changing the radio station again. And what did he put on? *Jazz.* Of course. Was he really trying to set a mood? He was trying too hard. But at the same time I was sick and tired of moping around over Collin. *He's* not moping around for me. I gathered myself together and stood up.

"I'm fine now," I said taking his hand and placing my other one on his shoulder. John then planted his hand on my waist and we proceeded into a dance. *This* he was really good at, but I couldn't seem to bring myself back to my previously more cheerful mood.

"One second," I said stepping away from John and taking my whiskey glass again.

"I thought you just said you don't feel well…"

"I'm okay," I said brushing him off before quickly finishing my third drink. "Okay where were we?" I asked placing my hand into John's again. As we moved the room began its slight sideways tilt that I was all too familiar with, and in fact, missed a little.

"Oh John, you're too nice," I said, resting my head on his shoulder. It was true though. And that might have been part of the problem. He didn't grab my attention. And then I wondered as we were there slow dancing, our bodies close together; *is this a connection I'm feeling? I've had feelings for two people at the same time before. So is there something here? Or am I a bit tipsy?* Unable to decide I ignored my questioning thoughts instead and tuned into the dim room that was filled with the sounds of soothing saxophones and strings.

"I think you worry too much, Victoria." John said, "Just go with the flow." He held me a bit closer and I then believed that maybe, just maybe, we could be more than friends. I looked up at him for a moment and he looked back at me, deeply into my eyes. We stood motionless for a few seconds before he unexpectedly leaned forward to kiss me. A little curious, I leaned in too with my eyes halfway closed. Our lips almost met until our foreheads bumped into one another.

"I'm sorry…" he said and I also mirrored the same words but then we chuckled it off sheepishly as I rubbed my head. He took my hand and gently moved it out of the way and again attempted to kiss me. This time I tilted my head a bit to the right but he did the same, tilting to the left. Our noses were in the way, each of us wasn't sure what the other was doing. We were so uncoordinated with each other. *Forget it.*

"This isn't working," I sighed, disappointed, before releasing from our dance-stance-like position and returned to the sofa again. "We shouldn't force this."

He sat next to me and took my hands into his. "No. I don't think we are. Or at least I know that I'm not." He was so sure of himself, so certain that he had my absolute undivided attention as I turned my body slightly to face him. "There's something about you," he continued. "It's hard to explain but it's as if everything that happened to us brought us to this point in our lives. As if it was all supposed to happen, good and bad. And here we are. I've never felt this way about anyone. Not about Judy. And I hate to say it but not even about Susan. With you it's... different. And I don't think this isn't working because we're forcing it. It's not working because I'm just so nervous with you. You're the most amazing person I've ever met."

I stared at him but didn't know what to say. It was the sweetest thing John had ever said to me. I found myself suddenly so drawn to him. Maybe I was a sucker but I was sold. My hand rested lightly on his cheek as I brought my lips to his. Without stumbling this time we kissed. I wish I could say that it was super romantic and that sparks were flying in every direction. Unfortunately, that just wasn't the case. It was an attempt and regardless of the initial hesitation on my part, I really was trying now. But it was terrible. He was hasty and greedy and I thought at any second he would swallow my face whole. Did he not know what he was doing? Who has time for tutoring? I pushed him away gently to slow him down a bit but mostly to breathe. Not to mention that he smelled like he took a bath in Old Spice Cologne.

"Let's slow down. I'm not going anywhere," I said hoping he would take the hint. Maybe he needed another drink. I sure did! I refilled his glass, and mine too, while I was at it. I sat next to him again, brushed my hair back with my hand and smiled softly at him as he leaned close to me again.

And it would seem that a third attempt would have been better. Three's a charm is the saying? Well it sure wasn't for us! There was no chemistry. It was like trying to make a hermit crab seem entertaining. His hands sat awkwardly on my thighs and it felt like I was kissing a hungry zombie.

Then it dawned on me. I was doing it again. Purposely being too hard on him. Trying to find any excuse as to why it wouldn't work out. I needed to stop being so judgmental and go with the flow like he said. Even if the flow needed to be brought down from a tsunami to a stream, but I could do that. The poor guy did just pour his heart out to me. And he was honest enough to confess that he was nervous. Thankfully the radio was on my side again and playing Spandau Ballet, "True." It was a nice melody for us and with the room still dim I tried to relax a bit as the fourth glass of cognac kicked in. I cleared my head to focus only on me and John and Spandau. It was so obvious that he hadn't been with a woman in a while. Finally I decided to take over.

Adjusting myself upward, I shifted my body and moved over to John's lap. His hands were then wrapped around my waist which was a good start. The kiss still wasn't working, though, so I pulled away from him again and pointed my chin up hoping he would get the hint. Thankfully he wasn't completely dense as he lowered his lips to kiss my neck. Okay this could work, I thought closing my eyes. It was fine until he whispered, "You smell amazing." He then successfully managed to remind me of Collin again. "You're so beautiful…" he went on. *Even worse!*

"John…"

"Yes."

I wanted to tell him to shut up but instead I calmly and sweetly said, "Please don't talk."

"Oh. Okay," he said and I had to resist laughing.

He continued to kiss my neck then lowered his focus to my chest. I closed my eyes again and found a place where I could imagine me and John together. Transcended into a world where we could be intimate and romantic and a couple. I painted a picture of us walking through the park. But the thought of me in a summer dress and him in a suit in Central Park was irking me. We would probably just spend most of our evenings on the SS Victoria drinking wine, eating fish, and discussing boring old movies.

Realizing that I was day dreaming again, and bored, with John still kissing on me, I took it up a notch and thought of the most random and drastic thing I could do to excite the mood. I leaned away from him and peeled my shirt over my head then dropped it off to the side. John slid his hands up my back and even if he took forever to do so, he eventually unfastened the hook to my bra and let it fall off my body. I liked the fact that he was showing some initiative. Not being as hasty now but dominating enough to intrigue my senses I actually started to respond to him physically as he caressed my breasts and drew a line of kisses up my neck and across my jaw line. He brought his lips back to mine. One thing ran through my mind: If this kiss doesn't work I'm going to throw in the towel.

I pulled John closer as his lips pressed into mine again. Finally he got the hint and followed my lead. He ran his hands through my hair and chills flowed through my body. Unfortunately it came with unwelcomed familiar memories. "Please don't do that either…" I whispered. So he just continued to run his hands down my upper body as I leaned back and again he trailed a line of kisses, but this time down my stomach.

John pulled his shirt off then proceeded to unbutton my pants he slowed down and looked at me for approval, since I seemed to be so particular about everything, but I actually didn't mind. It had been a while and as my unfulfilled needs became apparent and began to rise, it was hard to fight the urge. Then I wondered what his size was like. Feeling drunk and bold I decided to reach down to find out. He was completely taken aback by my advances. At least it was definitely not an issue whether he was turned on by me or not. I helped him unbutton his pants before he added them to the growing pile of clothes on the floor.

He actually did this right as he slid the remainder of my clothes slowly down my legs and they too dropped to the floor. It all seemed to be happening really fast. He held himself over me then kissed me deeply. I closed my eyes and entered another dimension mentally. Surprisingly I actually felt happy. Happy and loopy and a little dizzy, all in a good way. I wrapped my legs around him waiting for his next move. *Are we really about to do this?* My heart was beating faster and my breathing hitched. He lowered his lips to my ear and whispered "I love you, Victoria," before trailing kisses sensually along the side of my neck.

I was so lost in the moment. Somewhere in liquor and romance fuelled space. Completely naked wrapped up in John's hold about to take whatever our relationship was to another level. It was nice to feel the warmth of another body next against mine again. That sweet anticipation just before making love. And hearing another person tell me they love me. Yes, I felt so incredibly happy again and with my eyes still closed and my arms around him I held him tight and whispered back "I love you too, Collin…" It wasn't until a millisecond after the words left my lips that I realized it and wished they hadn't, but it was regrettably just a millisecond too late.

CHAPTER 7

It felt like a bucket of ice water was poured over us. *Shit*. Did I really just do that? I was so scared to open my eyes but when I did the expression on John's face was indescribable. *I can't talk my way out of this one.* This had to be the most embarrassing thing that could possibly happen to either of us. *Say something Victoria... do some damage control, quick!*

"Oh my God. I am so sorry!" I said once I found my voice. I pushed him away and wanted to hide under a rock as I gathered my clothes.

"Well... um..." he said, also at a loss for words. "That was rather unexpected."

"I'm sorry John," I said again then quickly stepped to the side of the sofa to finish dressing while he was respectful enough to turn away as he did the same. "Wow I can't do this," I said realizing that I should have stuck with my true feelings. "I thought I could... I thought that maybe we could but... Not yet. It's too soon. I'm not over him...well you knew that..." I was so back and forth, trying to explain myself but at the same time realizing that he was also at fault. "I know you don't want to be some rebound," I added, rambling and trying to make sense. He wasn't even responding. Was he hurt? Mad? Indifferent?

"Are you mad?" My voice was now small again with shame.

"I'm not mad. You obviously didn't know what you were saying," he said giving me the benefit of the doubt.

"I'm really am sorry." *I should probably stop apologizing.* It wasn't undoing what happened. Thankfully we hadn't actually done anything yet because I would have definitely regretted it. "This is so embarrassing. I knew I shouldn't have jumped into this," I said unable to look John in the eyes.

"Jumped into? Victoria we've known each other for well over a year. You've been staying here. I've done everything to make you comfortable and feel at home. I don't understand why you still think that this isn't right," his tone started to intensify and he sounded annoyed.

"John. Are you serious?" I said as the feelings of

embarrassment quickly transformed to irritation. "*Why do I think this isn't right?* I just called you by the wrong name!"

John sighed then finally said. "I'm not happy about it. But it's okay. I think I could forgive you for that."

Unsure if I felt shocked or insulted or both, I took a deep breath and waited a few seconds before speaking again. And even when I did it was clear that I was still floored by John's last comment.

"Excuse me? Did you just say '*forgive*'?"

"Yes. I'm sure it was an honest mistake," he said sticking to his statement.

"No. This, *me and you,* was a mistake. And I'm not looking for your *forgiveness.* Are you kidding? You already know what I'm going through, if anything you're the one who took advantage of the situation," I said.

"I did? That's funny because you were the one with your hands down my pants five minutes ago!"

Ew. Please don't remind me. I must be drunker than I thought. "Look, we're both wrong here. But *I'm in love with someone else.* That's something I have no control over. I can't start something with you or anyone else for that matter until that's no longer true."

John sat quietly and very still with his glass of whiskey in his hand. At this point he was either angry or upset, but it was very hard to decipher between the two with him. He calmly took a sip but was staring straight out, a little dazed. As annoyed as I was at the whole situation and his insensitive remarks, I did feel bad so I calmed my tone and sat next to him again. "John. I'm not saying that you and I could never try to make it work. I just need more time."

He didn't look at me. He continued to stare straight ahead but scoffed at what I said. "More time..." he said very dryly and almost to himself.

"Yes. I'm just having a very hard time moving on."

"You're so pathetic," he said under his breath.

Wait did he just say that? I didn't say anything because it was extremely unexpected. *Was he was saying it to himself?*

"Isn't that just fucking convenient..." he said bitterly but this was definitely intended towards me.

Did John just curse at me now? That's it – now he was definitely starting with the wrong woman. The person who took that shit was long gone.

"What did you just say?" I asked.

He ignored me and stood up abruptly, yet a little shaky as he was obviously also fairly intoxicated. I was surprised to see him appear so different. All of a sudden he gave me this cocky, smirking face, as if to say, "I'll show her." It was so out of character and strange.

He suddenly spoke sarcastically to the empty room as if there was an audience. "Ladies and gentlemen you hear that? Victoria needs more time! What a big fucking surprise!"

Not wanting to argue with him while he was in this intoxicated state, I tried reasoning first. "I'm sorry I thought you of all people would understand."

My words didn't help. He continued on, his attitude and tone continuing to grow harsh. And I just stood there with my mouth open, in total shock of his performance. This didn't make sense. This was *John*. My *friend*.

"Of course you thought I'd understand! Everything is all about you in your perfect little world isn't it?"

Shot down again Victoria. So now I actually had nothing to say so I just bravely raised my eyebrows at him, almost challenging him to continue, a subtle reminder that John needed to come back to earth.

But he didn't. "So, Miss Diva Princess," he said, getting right up in my face. Spit flew out of his mouth as he spoke. So gross, and when he turned around again I quickly wiped my face.

He continued, in the nastiest tone I ever heard him speak. "Do you know how long I've just sat on the sideline and waited for you to realize that you were wasting your time with your fucking husband? Then I find out about this fucking kid and again, I had to wait until he was out of the damn picture. Now, I finally think you've snapped out of this stupid bullshit fairytale land, we have an amazing evening, *and now you're telling me you need more time!*"

I waited to see if he had anything more to say. It was dead silence as he stared at my face for what seemed eternity.

"You make me sick," he said, dragging the words out, slowly and incredibly stern. He then let out a big huff and as he furiously walked away from me he knocked a bunch of things off the shelf, throwing a mini tantrum, screaming out choice words like "whore!" "slut!" and "fuckin' bitch!"

So that was it -- this whole time John had a hidden agenda. No matter how convinced I was that we were just friends. Convinced or convincing myself? It was definitely the latter. I would have told myself anything so that staying at his place would seem like such a bad idea. This could have been avoided I should have never spend so much time with him. And this "date" was a terrible idea! *Come on Victoria, get with the program. You need to learn you can't use stupidity as a matter of convenience. I definitely need to use more street smarts.* Why I thought I could actually have a male friend was beyond me. He wasn't a friend at all if he thought he could demean me the way he was. Still angry myself, but trying to be a better person I spoke to him calmly but firmly and this would be his last warning.

"John. You need to calm down. And I don't know who you think you are, speaking to me that way, but it's unacceptable."

"Who am I?" he yelled throwing his hands up outraged. "I'm the only person who cares about you," he said. "Look at your life Victoria. Your kids, your sister, your husband, and even your precious Collin all abandoned you. But me? I gave you a place to stay. I cook for you. Hell, I'm all you have!"

"First of all," I said calmly, "you know nothing about me. And if you really think you can talk to me however you want because I've been staying here then you have another thing coming. I'd rather sleep in my car then be disrespected by you."

John really didn't know anything about me, and definitely not about my anger that could turn up full-force especially when I was drinking and being provoked.

Fortunately my calm demeanor calmed John down as well. Now he sounded pouty, like a little boy. "Why can't you think about me the way you do about him? From everything you've told me it's obvious that he was only after one thing. I actually *want* to be with you ... and ..."

61

Ew, a softer tone now, but still a jackass! I'll fix him. Cutting him off I said, "I'm going to stop you right there... don't talk about him because all you're doing is pissing me the fuck off right now."

Now John looked at me shocked not realizing how fast I could switch up my attitude too when the wrong buttons are pushed.

He started getting loud again. "You know what? You're insane! If you were with me I would give you the world," he said grabbing me desperately, "Are you that blind that you can't see that!" he said shaking my arm.

"Don't touch me!" I shouted peeling my arm free and pushing him away. "Right now that's so far from ever happening!" More like *never* happening.

"Goddammit! All you care about is this fucking loser who doesn't give a shit about you! So that's what you want, to spend your life struggling with a 'nobody'? While he probably cheats on you because, newsflash, Victoria, he doesn't love you! He's nothing but an ignorant, mediocre, piece of shit!"

I said absolutely nothing. Instead with my reaction as fast as a boomerang my anger radiated through my hand which smacked across the face. Fuming couldn't come close to describing my emotions. I was also tired of him raising his voice at me and more so because he was badmouthing Collin again. I did warn him! *Nobody talks about him like that.*

John grabbed my arm again, pulled me to him and suddenly tried to kiss me. I leaned away and with my free hand reached for my drink then in one swift jerk of my wrist I emptied the contents of the glass all over John. His face and hair were drenched with whiskey. I knew some of it got in his eyes as well, and he looked furious. He grabbed my other wrist and snatched the glass from my grasp. I froze from the confrontation. It was so unexpected. Us arguing, me slapping him, and now this, as he stood towering over me ominously as Frank used to; now I was more than a *little* frightened. The heavy crystal glass was clenched tightly in his grip over his head and out of habit I braced myself for the worst.

"So you're gonna hit me too?" I challenged him trying not to let my voice crack. Trying to be brave – no matter how frightened I was on the inside I would never let him know it.

Instead he stepped away from me and heaved the glass against the wall sending it shattering into a million directions. Then he turned around and had both hands on his head as if he had a massive migraine.

"Why are you doing this, Victoria? You're making me crazy! All I want is to make you happy! Is that so much to ask? Why are you treating me like the bad guy?" He was freaking out, yelling, and sounding like he was going to cry all at the same time.

Now I only had one mission. To get the hell out of that room. And next - out of that house. "Sorry that you got the wrong idea, John. I'll give you your space now," I said, speaking softly and sympathetically, then found an opportunity to slowly back away from John who stood dumbfounded. Once I felt that it was far enough I stopped in the doorframe then said, "It's probably best if I go back to my house tomorrow."

"Victoria...wait..." he called behind me frantically.

"Good night, John," I said and quickly walked out of the room before giving him a chance to say or do anything else. Luckily he didn't follow me as I marched upstairs and headed for the shower.

I made sure to scrub every inch of my body clean, focusing on any area that John touched or kissed. Then changed into my night gown and despite still being intoxicated I felt somewhat better physically. Mentally I couldn't get over the episode that occurred between John and me. What a nightmare! He did a good job of hiding his true colors from me for a while. Now it made sense that he was still single. *Victoria, you sure attract some real winners!* Frank was nothing more than a drunken, abusive, asshole. John turned out to be Dr. Jekyll. But Collin? He ended up being the worst one. I really thought he was someone I could trust. I always thought that even if he didn't want to be with me that he would have the decency to tell me. *What an asshole.* By that point I was completely hating all men in general again. *But you don't hate him, you love him,* I reminded myself during the never-ending internal battle. It was entirely draining.

No matter how much abuse I've taken in the past the

emotional damage that Collin caused burned the deepest scar. How could I ever be with anyone else if I can't even let someone call me "beautiful," or run their fingers through my hair? In one year this was the affect he had on me? I was with Frank for 18 and he never once crossed my mind after the day he left.

There I was lying in bed, hating Collin, or trying to after another exhausting night. Starting to feel a little nauseous as the liquor's strong effects on me continued and resentment built in my heart I rolled to my side and impulsively grabbed my phone. It was probably the stupidest thing I could do, but unable to listen to my voice of reason I started to write a text message. Angry and drunk I typed up some kind of mess of a paragraph. I wanted to just get it out of my system then erase it but somewhere during my decision making process I sent the most ridiculous message in the world – full of misspellings and bad grammar.

I hope your happy that you ruined my life. I gave u everything youre so ungrateful. I hate you and love you at the same time I guesits like tht song. I hate how much I love yuo. I can relate. How could u never think of me? whatever. its fine. onee day I will let you go too. And onedayyouwont ever cross my mind when that day comes itll be the happiest day of my life. I cant believe I ever wasted my time. Turns out that r u the one who deserves the emmy. goodbye

I felt a little better after I sent it. But if I was really honest with myself that was a lie. Holding onto the pillow I couldn't stop the tears that spilled out. Somewhere in the back of my mind my fears haunted me. John sure was doing a number to me emotionally, with everything that he planted in my head. He brought most of my biggest worries to life, things I would have never thought of otherwise. And when he said that I had nobody left that was true too. But either way I needed to move on and go back to my house. Being alone over there was better than being anywhere near John. He wasn't what he seemed to be at all.

I knew that I would dream about Collin that night.

Just as I always did. I had a real problem. Like an addiction that had no cure. Except that night was different because it almost seemed as if I could feel his presence. I was asleep, but not deeply, when a gentle touch grazed against my cheek. A familiar caressing touch. And when I felt my hair brush gently back I awoke with butterflies and hope. *Wake up*, I told myself. *It's him. He's here.*

I could feel the excitement build as I came back from my light slumber. Groggy, and feeling a little disoriented I reached out for Collin but felt nothing but cold, crinkled, empty sheets. *But I did feel a touch. I wasn't imagining it.* I rubbed my eyes to look around and once they were opened and focusing in the dark I jumped, startled, finding a tall dark figure at my presence. As my eyes adjusted to the darkness I could now recognize the figure.

"John?" I squinted.

"It's okay. You were having a bad dream," John said sweetly as if he were trying to comfort a 7-year-old.

No I wasn't.

"I don't think I was..." I started to say but now awake and alert and quickly remembering the events of the evening I turned my defenses on full force. *"Why are you in my room?"* My voice escaladed as the hairs on my arms did as well. *I should have locked the door but I never thought to do so before. I invested way too much trust in John! Has he ever done this before? The thought made me sick.*

"I just wanted to check on you."

Feeling very vulnerable I pulled the comforter up, over my exposed nightgown.

"I'm fine," I said through clenched teeth, my tone bitter.

"Are you sure?" He reached forward and brushed my hair back. But it wasn't sweet or sensual. In fact it was just creepy. I leaned my head away and adjust myself, sitting upright and less vulnerable. I reached over and turned on the night lamp.

"John I'm fine," I said firmly. "Honestly I really just need to rest. Is there something you need?" I snapped.

"No," he said at first then changed his mind. "Well, yes…"

I gave him a look hoping that he understood that I was not feeling very conversational. In fact I was being nice. Another minute and I would be cursing him out. "Look, if this is about earlier we could talk about it tomorrow morning."

"Okay," he said. "Good night."

When he didn't receive a response he quietly vanished from room. I waited a minute before I walked over and locked the door behind him. After climbing back into the bed I remembered the mistake I made right before going to sleep. *I'm such an idiot!* I hesitantly reached for my phone to see if Collin responded to me. But there was nothing. Finding John in my room was bad enough. And the fact that nothing I said to Collin even fazed him anymore hurt. Yes, it was a terrible message, but he had *nothing* to say? Nothing at all? With those thoughts heavy on my mind I couldn't get back to sleep until the sun's rays started to peer through the window. I closed my eyes determined to sleep for an hour or two because first thing in the morning I needed to make some serious changes.

CHAPTER 8

The insisting beeping of my alarm went off at 7 a.m.

Worn out, I reached over to shut it off and then dragged myself out of bed. Groggy, head spinning, running on no sleep, and emotionally overwhelmed -- what a way to start the day!

Regardless to how I felt I forced myself to get up and gather my belongings. All I wanted to do was pack and go home, but at the same time it seemed like the mature, adult thing to do was talk to John about what happened.

I threw on my dark jeans, found a purple top, and then slipped on my Nikes before following the welcoming aroma of coffee brewing in the kitchen.

"Morning," I said awkwardly to John who was casually filling two mugs.

"Good morning, Victoria," John said then placed a yellow mug filled with fresh Arabic coffee in front of me as I took a seat at the counter. "How are you feeling?"

"Hung over," I said.

"Great for hangovers," he said and smiled slightly while nodding towards the coffee.

I responded with a half-smile. I didn't know if he was trying to act like nothing happened to avoid an uncomfortable situation, or if he was going to mention it eventually. Either way the events from the previous night were a lesson learned. What was I thinking staying in his house -- I barely knew the man! I just needed to get through the morning then I could head back to my house.

John poured his coffee into his travel mug. Guess he was going somewhere again this Saturday morning. Even better for me.

"I owe you an apology for last night," John said suddenly. "I'm not usually one to get overly intoxicated. With everything that was going on I really let my emotions get the better of me. But my behavior was unacceptable."

I nodded and took a sip of the coffee and hoped it wasn't poisoned. And being that I had nothing to add, I waited for him to continue.

"I should have respected that you were being honest with me. But at the same time I felt a little ... led on," he said.

I almost choked on the hot beverage!

I coughed and cleared my throat then looked up at him with my eyebrows raised. "Led on? By *me*?" If there was anything I was certain of it was the fact that I made it very clear to John that I saw him as a friend – nothing more.

"I did. At first," he said quickly to reassure me then added, "but then I realized that it wasn't you at all. You told me that we should slow down. I pushed you too hard."

It sure as hell wasn't me! Thankfully he did make a note of that or this might have been another ugly argument.

"It's fine John. I think we both had too much to drink," I said remembering everything that happened. *Ew. I can't believe I made out with him.*

"You really don't have to go. You're still more than welcome to stay here. I don't want you to think that this will be an issue anymore. In fact I am spending the day with Judy. She called me this morning and invited me, last minute, to the Greenwood Lake Air Show. I am hoping that it will go somewhere."

"That's good. She's probably a better fit for you," I said then my eyes were lost in the contents of my cup for a few moments of silence before I looked back up at John. "We would have never worked out," I added just to emphasize it one more time. Maybe then he'll really pursue Judy instead. Still feeling too detached to make eye contact with him I began to watch my favorite tropical fish glide around.

"You're probably right. But you won't have to worry -- I promise to completely respect my boundaries," he said.

"Thank you. But I still think I've overstayed my welcome. I really should be heading home. There are things I have been avoiding that I really need to take care of."

"Okay. I understand," he said then casually turned to the stove where something was already sizzling in a pan. "Would you care for some eggs or turkey bacon?"

"I'm fine, thanks." It actually sounded really tempting, but I didn't want to accept anything else from him, even the simplest thing, as petty as it sounded.

We sat quietly again while John added two eggs to the stainless steel pan. Then removed a few pieces of toast from the toaster, spread jelly on them, and offered one to me. I finally gave in and took one slice then nonchalantly continued to sip my coffee and watch the fish until John spoke again.

"I know I am in no position to ask you this but … Well … Do you think you could just do me the huge favor of staying for a few more nights?"

I looked at him puzzled. *Why would that be a favor?*

He noticed my confusion and took it upon himself to explain. "See my son, Jacob, is coming next week with his girlfriend and I was going to ask you if you could help me set up for them. The other guest room is so outdated and I don't think I'll have enough time to do it myself. Besides I think it really needs a feminine touch."

So now I'm an interior designer? I didn't mind helping since I didn't have much else to do but I cringed at the thought of staying there another night. Were the showers safe to use or were there little hidden cameras in the shower heads? Was the mirror in my room double sided? How many times had John crept into my room while I was sleeping?

"Uh… I don't know…" I said while completely freaking myself out but also failing to find a better excuse to leave.

"Just one week. That's all I ask."

"How about this -- I'll go home today, but I'll still come help you out with the room, whichever day you need."

"Okay. No problem," he said but obviously didn't mean it. He was sulking, yet again, like Eeyore from Winnie the Pooh. "Just remind me to call Raymore and Flannigan to cancel the deliveries that are arranged for Tuesday and Wednesday since nobody will be here."

Unfair! He definitely wasn't a happy camper when he didn't get his way. *Did I not just say that I'd still help?*

Then I figured that he was making excuses so he wouldn't have to be alone. It was understandable. I mean, just a few weeks ago I opted to stay with him because *I* didn't want to stay alone, so saying that I couldn't relate would be a lie.

And should the man be condemned for his mistakes if

he wasn't holding mine against me? I still sort of owed him one.

I sighed, too tired to protest anyway. "You win. But just one more week." The last part was emphasized by my "I'm-serious" tone that I used whenever my kids were trying to pull a fast one on me.

"Of course," John said nodding in agreement. "Thank you, I appreciate it," he added, then cleared his plate and proceeded to wash the coffee mug and other dishes. This was yet another man whose place was always spotless. But I'm not sure why it was creepy with John. Everything he did seemed to weird me out lately. An immaculate house but nobody ever came over? *Nobody*. And he wasn't a loner. He was almost desperate for attention. Why didn't things quite add up with him? I wondered as I watched him dry each dish and return them to their previous places.

Just then an unfamiliar sound broke my thoughts. It was a text message with its new bell chime alert tone. I told myself not to get all worked up though. That habit would need to be broken because any excitement to hear my phone was always proven to be let down anyway. And good thing I didn't expect anything more because it was in fact only Britney.

Britney: Hey. How are you?

How am I? Basically a mess but what else is new? Of course I wasn't going to write that though.

Me: Hey. I'm good.

Britney: Are you okay?

Why would she ask me that? *Oh yeah, I almost forgot.* Of course she must have talked to Collin and learned all about the wonderful friendly message I sent him before bed. I reluctantly reread it from my sent box and grimaced. More embarrassment has come out of my drinking and emotions. Although some of it was exactly how I felt, I should have kept it to myself. I sounded like such a jerk. Not to mention dumber than a box of raisins. Hearing from Britney several hours after sending him a

70

message like that wasn't surprising. *Should I mention that I wasn't exactly myself last night?* No, there was no point anyway.

Me: I'm okay

Britney: Ok. Just making sure.

Before my temptations to begin to go in depth with her kicked in I ended it there, putting my phone away.

"How's everything else going?" John said with an insinuating tone. Maybe he was making assumptions about my messaging. I was so over him being my shoulder to cry on though.

"In time everything in my life will be on the right track and back to normal," I said sounding more confident than I felt.

"Of course it will," he said. "That's a great attitude to have!" He took his keys, wallet, and phone from the counter and placed the latter two items in his pocket then grabbed the coffee with the other hand. "Well I'd better head out. Feel free to call me if you need anything."

"Sure thing," I said then returned to my phone that never let me breathe.

Britney: So … I'll actually be in Jersey at the Fiesta hall setting up for an event all day. You really should come by so we could talk.

Me: I have a few things to do today. I'll try.

Britney: I really think you should come. Even if it's only for 5 minutes…

When I didn't write back she continued to insist.

Britney: I gotta go. Hopefully I'll see you later. Oh and dress nice.

It's not like I didn't consider meeting with Britney to talk. She had my curiosity peaked since she was so convincing and persistent. And being that she knew more than I did some of my million questions could finally be answered. But instead of following old habits I didn't give in and hang out with her this time. However I decided to send Collin one simple message. A sober one. Just so there was nothing left ill-mannered or unresolved on my end:

"Sorry about last night. I've had a lot on my mind. Didn't mean to bother you."

Afterwards I followed John's lead and got out of the house nice and early to meet up with Ashley and Terrance. The several hours I spent with them was fun and occupied with Halloween themed activities. We ventured off to our usual October trip, a haunted hay ride in Sleepy Hollow New York, then through corn mazes and haunted houses in Long Island. It was always a great time since both of them were such good kids. I was happy that Ashley was with a guy who treated her well and also respected me. I dropped them off at the campus which was an hour away so I didn't get back until after midnight.

When I returned to John's house it was quiet. And my mind was back to wandering. I hadn't checked my messages all day, which I was proud of myself for. Maybe I was actually moving on? It wasn't until I was in my pajamas under the covers that I opened my phone's in-box.

Not much. A check-in from Brooke, which was becoming normal to us, not talking for weeks then updating each other. Britney sent three different messages asking where I was and if I was still coming. And no reply from Collin. But was that a big surprise anymore? I don't know why I was expecting something else. I felt it deep down that we should be talking and couldn't let it go. Talking about something. Anything. Finding a resolution once and for all. Again that word I dreaded but was the right one -- *closure*. But he had been ignoring me since the day he realized that a relationship with me wasn't what he wanted. *Whatever*. If he wanted to be immature about it than that was on him. That's what I get for getting involved with a kid.

Realizing I was too good for the nonsense I finally took control of my own emotions and didn't let it cross my mind again. I was able to sleep that night and for the first time in months my pillow stayed dry.

CHAPTER 9

I tried to keep my promise to John, to stay just one more week until Friday, but it became a grueling task when Tuesday rolled around and I was already beginning to count down the days. It was as if I was serving time. *Three more days then I'm free!* I reminded myself as each day dragged.

Tuesday. 5:30. I automatically assumed John would walk through the door. But nothing. So I continued about starting a simple dinner. Time escaped me as preparing a vegetable lasagna distracted me. When the timer went off and I pulled it out of the oven I was surprised to see that it was 6:45 and John still wasn't home.

I cut the dish into nine pieces, left one on a plate for John and covered it, put the rest in the refrigerator, wiped up the kitchen counters, then disappeared to my room.

Almost everything was all packed and ready to go; three suitcases, a lap top bag, purse and duffle bag were lined up neatly against the wall. I couldn't even believe how much stuff had accumulated during my stay. Just a few articles of clothing were still hanging in the closet, a few shoes, and my toiletries were in the bathroom. Not to mention a few things that I must have misplaced and needed to find. *Should I make a trip and bring some of these things home now?* I guess it could wait. I didn't really feel like driving to my house anyway. But not sure what else to do with myself, I sat and stared blankly and the suitcases. The familiar feelings of sadness began to sprout. The same ones that existed when it was quiet and lonely. Then "ah there it is!" -- That urge again. Bored. Nothing to do. Emotions bubbling. And wanting to randomly turn to the bottle. With no one there to object and a diminishing will power, I decided to fulfill my impulses.

I strolled into the living room and remembered that I hadn't been in there since that night with John. There wasn't even the slightest evidence of the scuffle. Everything was on the shelf as if it never happened. The crystal decanter was right in its place. The glass that didn't make it through the battle was all swept up. Again that one word came to mind -- creepy.

I shook my head at the thought and hoped that John

wouldn't mind that I was helping myself to a bottle of vodka that was already open. But while watching the glass fill with the debilitating liquid, the sad heavy feeling that was building resurfaced and only grew stronger. *This isn't right. Why am I trying to drink away reality?* Cleaning. Cooking. Drinking. *Distracting* is what it was. All of it was a front but I was only lying to myself. Pretending that I was okay. Pretending that my heart wasn't still beating for Collin every single second that added onto my days like heavy weights. *What do I do?*

It was ridiculous but in those moments I remembered something Ashley did with her best friend Morgan Summer in our back yard years ago after her boyfriend broke up with her. She was devastated for weeks so one night they lit our fire pit and threw every memento of their relationship into the fire. Afterwards she never looked back and met Terrance months later.

Are you really thinking about this Victoria? You're 33-years-old! When it came to matters of the heart, though, age was irrelevant. I returned the bottle back into its spot on the bar then moved over by the fire place. It wasn't hard to start up since it was similar to the one we had at my house. Then I realized I didn't have many actual tangible mementos. *My phone,* I thought rolling my eyes at myself. But of course there was one thing, the only thing -- our Valentine's Day picture, which I now held in my hand as I sat in front of the dancing orange flames. I meditated on all of the emotions that had been buried as the warm air made a serene feeling wash over me.

While lost in the yellow and orange muddle of heat and light, different thoughts crossed my mind. *How did I get here? Why are Collin and I not together?* Then my mind went elsewhere. *What do I want for my future? Why are Frank and I still married? God, what am I doing? This doesn't feel right. Nothing feels right any more. What's wrong with me?*

As I held my head as if it weighed a thousand pounds I wished I had some idea as to what to do, not only about Collin, but about life in general. Lost in my deep thoughts and sorrow and confusion I didn't even hear that John was home until he walked into the room. From my peripheral vision I saw as he sat on the chaise adjacent to me but I didn't turn my head to face him.

"Victoria? What's going on? You alright?" John asked in a low voice filled with concern.

"I started up the fireplace. Hope you don't mind," I said robotically still staring straight, feeling hypnotized.

"Not a problem. Was it chilly in here?"

"No," I said then laughed at myself sheepishly snapping out of my daze a bit. "Yeah. Let's just say that I was cold. You'll probably think I'm crazy if I tell you the real reason why I turned it on."

"I don't think I will," he said.

Feeling foolish as usual and being coaxed into sharing my woes with John yet again I exhaled slowly then handed him the picture. "I can't look at this anymore," I said.

"Oh. I see…" John understood my insinuation. "Are you sure that's what you want to do?"

"It's haunting me, John. The memories. My fear of moving on. I know this'll sound dumb but I feel like if I get rid of it maybe it'll help."

"You consider it a symbol of your estranged relationship," he said then handed the picture back to me. "You feel like by burning that photograph you, in turn, are burning the relationship and hopefully some of the memories of it."

Wow. So he does understand. That was a pleasant surprise for a change. I still felt like an explanation was necessary but not sure if it was warranted. "I need to do this for myself."

Ready to toss in my last memory, well not really, but I was going to do it anyway. The symbol of the happy couple from the past. That's where it needed to stay. *In the past.* Then it seemed like it was so long ago that Collin and I kissed and laughed infectiously together. We fought but always made up. We made love for hours and felt like we traveled to a passionate perfect planet. We took on the city together, we've cried in each other's arms, and no matter what ever happened all we both truly wanted was nothing more than to be together.

Getting myself all worked up, thinking way too much, my eyes began to water and I realized I was still holding that damn picture. "Okay… okay… I'm going to do it now…" I said aloud. It wasn't meant for John as much as it was for me. *Just let it go! The picture. The relationship that is no more. All of it!*

I extended my arm and could feel the waves of heat spread over my hand and I sat close, quiet, eyes closed -- because I didn't really want to watch it burn but I wanted it gone already. Just as I released my grip and "let go" I felt John take it from my hand. I opened my eyes and looked at him inquisitively. *Maybe he wants to throw it in?*

But instead he placed it onto the end table then genuinely said, "Don't do something now that you may regret later."

What? That was extremely unexpected! But maybe he was right. I wiped my eyes and nodded solemnly.

"It's funny Victoria, you and I may not agree on everything, but we sure have more in common than you think."

"I guess so," I said then we were both quiet. Just staring as the brazen orange and yellow flames as they blended and danced haphazardly.

John sighed and now he too suddenly looked stressed out. "Victoria, I have something I need to tell you," he said in a serious tone.

"Okay," I said a bit taken a back. *What is this about?*

He sat quietly for a while then I got nervous. What is he going to say? But he wasn't talking, he was just... thinking. "Well, what is it?" I pressed when he seemed to float off to outer space for too long.

When he finally seemed to return he spoke softly. "I know we discussed this already but, you're such a good person and well a really good... friend. And I still feel absolutely terrible about ever mistreating you."

What the hell? That's it? Jeez he's so melodramatic. "John, I already told you not to worry about it," I said reassuringly.

"Okay. And I was actually also wondering if you would mind joining me in the kitchen for a moment," he said while standing up.

"Oh. Well, okay," I said indifferently and also stood up.

John led the way. "By the way thank you for preparing dinner," he said. "I ate earlier, but I'll definitely be taking it for lunch tomorrow."

"No problem," I said as we entered the dining room. On the table was a red velvet cake, which was my favorite, a bottle of white wine, also my favorite, and a fresh bunch of red tulips. Three for three. He definitely paid attention to everything I've ever said to him. The table was set with two dessert plates.

"I didn't know you were expecting company," I said and even I knew how stupid of a comment it was after I said it.

"Actually I don't have anyone coming over."

"Oh…"

"This is for me and you."

I couldn't hide my scowl, "I don't know if this is the best idea…"

"Victoria … it's only dessert. Sort of my way of thanking you… for everything."

"Thanking me?"

"You didn't have to help me with the room. It looks great now. And you have been so kind and understanding."

Not really. But this man saw things the way he wanted to so who was I to argue?

"Okay, fine," I agreed, walking over to the table. "Just one thing," I took the bottle and moved it to the counter then stopped to look at the assembly which was now just dessert and flowers. "Better," I said as I took my seat.

The cake was big, way too big, in fact, for two people. It had a pale yellow icing designed fancily into a gridded pattern, with crumbs of burgundy cake sprinkled over the top. John cut each of us a slice and placed mine in front of me then he cut a slice for himself and sat across from me. We were only five minutes into dessert when I remembered his unusual disrupted daily routine. I didn't really care but just curious enough to mention it.

"Did you drive far for the cake? You came in pretty late today."

"Not too far. I did make another stop though," he said.

"Where to?" I asked then took another small bite of cake.

He reached into his pocket and pulled out a small, mint green, white flower printed jewelry box. "I picked something up for you." He looked at me with that admiring smile.

Oh no, not this. "You don't have to give me anything. The flowers and cake; that was more than enough. Too much in fact."

He discarded my comment and said, "It's nothing, really. Just open it."

Okay, maybe it's "nothing" as he said. I was hopeful, but when I opened the box I should have also remembered that he referred to his jaguar as "just a car." This "nothing" that was in the box also happened to be the sapphire necklace that I was admiring at Zales around Valentine's Day; the $2,500 necklace! No. Absolutely *not* doing this with John.

I replaced the lid and slowly pushed the box across the table until it was by John's plate. "I can't accept this," I said simply.

"Why not? I don't understand."

Here we go again. I sighed really not having the energy.

"John. You already know why."

"Victoria, you don't have to be in an intimate relationship to appreciate somebody. I'm sure you've gotten gifts for your sister or your children. I remember how much you loved the necklace. And, well, I think you … absolutely deserve it." Then he put his hand up as if he were taking an oath and added, "No strings attached."

"Thank you, John, I appreciate it. I really do. But when I get something for Brooke it's a simple pair of shoes or a hand bag. Not an expensive piece of jewelry. I'm sorry."

He looked troubled and annoyed as he squinted slightly at me. "You really can't just accept it? I went out of my way to get it for you. You mentioned that you adore it. I don't see what the big fuss is about."

"No, I'm sorry, I just don't feel comfortable." I was sticking to my guns.

He sat back in his chair, disappointed, and sulking as usual, probably trying to think of the right thing to say to change my mind. Just the way a lawyer would. He treated everything like a case and wanted to win them all.

"Well now this is quite an inconvenience," he said. "Can't imagine when I'll be able to head back out that way." He frowned as if he really had taken on a huge burden now.

I would offer to return it for him but how tacky would that be? Should I just take the stupid thing? It was gorgeous… and he did go through all that trouble to get it for me. *No!* He wasn't guilt-tripping me into this one!

"I don't know what to tell you. You should have asked me first." After it was said I felt like I deserved a gold medal. Standing up for myself was becoming second nature. And when he finally gave up and realized that I wasn't budging, we quietly finished dessert and yet another awkward, long, emotionally draining day and night ended.

On Wednesday I woke up a little later than usual, 7:45, so John was already gone for the day. I did my usual morning routine, checked company e-mails, checked personal ones, and then ran a few quick errands since we were expecting the final furniture delivery between 11 a.m. and 5p.m. When they arrived it was 4:30 of course.

Two young men stood at the door with two large boxes, which should be one dresser and one chest. They guys were both in their mid-20s and not bad looking if I do say so myself. Ugh! What is it with me and cute, young delivery boys! I shook my head and decided to keep the friendly chatter to a minimum.

"Where's it going Miss?" the blonde one asked while they started to walk inside carrying one of the apparently heavy boxes.

"Upstairs then down the hall, it's the second door on the left side..." I said pointing toward the stairs.

I waited at the bottom as the men brought the second piece up. Then one of them called down sounding confused, "Where exactly do you want them?" I jogged up the stairs to find both guys and both dressers in the wrong room. John's room. Oops I had forgotten to count the bathroom door which was also on the left side.

"I'm sorry guys, it's the next room over," I said. "It's pretty empty already. You could put them wherever, thanks. We'll fix it later. Sorry about that."

"No problem at all," the dark haired kid said while smiling at me as they began to move the long dresser to the guest bedroom first. Again I decided to completely ignore him especially since he reminded me of someone I didn't want to be reminded of.

I now found myself standing alone in the room. Hmm,

interesting. *John's bedroom.* I had never been in there nor did I ever plan to. It was dim, plain, and completely lacking life of any sort. For such a beautiful house maybe he did need an interior decorator, at least for the bedrooms. There was a king size bed with black sheets, one black dresser, and one mismatched pinewood night table. It looked like he had just moved in even though he told me that he's been there for several years. Then I remembered Susan and felt bad, maybe he threw away the old furniture before moving in? But it wasn't like he couldn't afford to furnish his room. After the guest bedroom I needed to help him with his room. I was about to walk out when a hardcover book in a pink and white cover on the night stand caught my eye. I leaned closer and the name of the author was Judy Goldstein. *Is John dating an author?*

"Okay ma'am. We're all set," the blonde delivery man said.

I went into the guest bedroom, where I spent Monday afternoon painting the walls tan, and was happy with the way the new mahogany furniture complimented it. The chocolate and Prussian blue curtains, new table lamps, floor plants, circle mirrors and contemporary wall art looked amazing. The room was complete and I was pleased. The guys were even nice enough to place the dressers against the walls where they fit.

"Perfect. Thank you so much," I said and proceeded to walk down with them. I handed them each a $20 tip then they were on their way. And now it was a little after five and I was curious to check out that book on John's night table. I quickly looked around even though I knew that nobody was there. I snuck into his room and snooped a little, first looking at the inside jacket to read about the author. *Yes, I'm being nosey yet again.*

This was the strange thing -- Judy Goldstein wasn't some young stunning lawyer as John had claimed. She was an elderly lady with red hair and green eyes. Her biography said that she lived in Minnesota with her husband and college aged son. *This is too weird,* I thought as I closed the book. Even if John had some strange thing for older women he wasn't traveling to Minnesota to spend time with her. *Was this yet another lie?*

81

Ugh… Why do I always find myself investigating something? But between the conversation I overheard in the middle of the night, John's strange behavior, and now this, I was becoming even more suspicious of him. I opened his night table drawer to see if there was anything else but there were just a few papers, some coins, and a bible. Cautious not to disrupt anything from its place I rummaged around carefully. Deep down I was hoping not to find anything and was hoping I was just a paranoid fool, but I knew that was wishful thinking. Once I got to his dresser it only took one drawer to put me in disbelief. My mouth dropped open upon discovering the contents: underwear, bras, hair ties, lip gloss…It might have not been that strange, maybe some guys have a collection of things from the women they were with. But no that wasn't the case here. *These things were all mine!* He even had one of my lotions, a pair of my earrings, and a bottle of my Amber Romance spray. There were at least a dozen of my belongings. Wondering what else he took I opened the next few drawers but these were all filled with his clothes. Then I revisited the top drawer and noticed something I hadn't before, peering up from the corner, under everything else, was a picture, *my picture of me and Collin!*

Okay this is too much. I need to get out of here, I thought, feeling a bit light-headed as I rubbed my temples. I quickly closed the drawer, did a quick onceover to make sure there was nothing out of place because I was sure he would notice, shut the door behind me, and rushed into my room. It was already 5:15! Could I pack everything and go home before he arrived? Or should I just leave -- forget the stuff. No, I got this! Most of my things being packed already I grabbed everything I could carry and ran the bags out to my car in two trips.

The car was loaded but another hurdle surfaced. Shit, where did I put my keys? 5:24… Not wanting to end up with my head in some closet as a shrine, or with my body decaying in a basement while John sat next to it while wearing one of my dresses, I moved faster than I ever did in my life. *Yes!* Keys were on the bar stool. Grabbed them and was about to run out. 5:26 now. Damn one more thing! I stopped to scribble John a quick note. It sounded like a stupid thing to do but if I left suddenly with no explanation he might think that something was up.

Where does he keep the damn note pads? I started to frantically search through the kitchen. Not this drawer... not this one... not this cabinet. On the fridge? Got it! And now a pen? I sighed and tried to stay calm as my heart continued to beat hard and fast. But I was saved as I found one then jotted something quickly.

"Furniture arrived safe and sound. Room looks great! Sorry I had to run. Thank you again for everything. We'll do lunch some time.
-Victoria"

The note was left on the counter. And that necklace was still there in its mint green flower printed housing. Maybe he was hoping I'd take it? *That's not happening* was my last thought as I placed the spare key John gave me next to the note and practically ran out of there.

Relief wasn't the word as I pulled out of the driveway and drove off at 5:29. I never thought I would be so happy to head back to my house on Lilac Lane but being free never felt better. And I thought that by leaving John behind me that I was leaving a large part of my problems behind me... I was wrong.

CHAPTER 10

It was so strange being "home" again. Somehow, I could breathe in this place that I once saw as a confinement chamber. At least I wouldn't have to worry about someone creeping into my bedroom in the middle of the night. That recollection made me shudder as I sat in what was once Ashley's room. Entering the master bedroom still summoned up too much anxiety in me as there wasn't enough incense in the world to eliminate the smell of burnt wood and the stench of charred dreams.

It seemed better being home. Sometimes. But, realistically I wondered how long I could stay by myself. I hoped that the house would sell soon and I could get a much smaller place. Contacting the real estate company was on my extensive divorce-process to-do list.

No matter how long I managed to keep the thought from entering my mind, it always snuck its way back in and deep down it bothered me that I was still alone. *How the hell did I end up alone?* Wasn't there a point when I had options? Yes, there was but of course I always made the wrong decisions. If I could do it all over again I would never second guess love.

Every day I kept telling myself that it was going to be okay, and every day that's what I believed, even if I wasn't quite sure what "okay" meant anymore.

On a positive note, the tide of heartache was slowly starting to recede. Or maybe it seemed that way because of the recent distractions. John only called exactly 18 times in the last three days; once before work, once on his lunch break, once after work, and three times in the evening; every single day. And despite the annoying number of voice mails and text messages, I still gave him some credit because I actually anticipated it would be double that amount. Being that I had absolutely nothing - or nothing nice - to say to him, I let him continue a relationship with my voicemail.

I tried to ignore the fact that my house, at night, was just plain creepy. There was something weird about the absence of sound. *How do some people do this? Maybe I should get a roommate.* It wasn't that there was much creaking or cracking. It could have been the sheer silence that was getting to me. But then again there was still the occasional random sound. Things rustling around outside. And there was, of course, the signature sound of crickets chirping in the night. *I definitely need to move out.* These were the things that continued to swim through my mind at night as I tried to get some sleep.

I didn't think much about my paranoia. Wasn't it somewhat to be expected since it was the first time I was ever living alone in 33 years? It wasn't until I was asleep on the third night when a sound from down the hall woke me up. *What was that?*

Night noises from a tree outside or a settling house could masquerade footsteps or other human activity. And couldn't my sleep deprivation make me a bit more susceptible toward painting a sinister stroke over a harmless sound?

Trying to find my grounds I rubbed my eyes and slowly clambered out of bed at 1:30 in the morning. I followed a faint sound in the darkness of the house. Then I realized that I was able to place the sound. The shower was on. A tension seized me as if my fear was substantiating into tangible form in the cold air of the empty house. *Maybe Ashley or Thomas is here?* For all I knew they could have been going to the house while I was staying at John's. *But Ashley wouldn't be this far from school at this time.* It was already too late when I realized that maybe I should have approached the bathroom door with a weapon.

No, I can't keep being paranoid and won't keep living like this! After I made a futile attempt to knock, hoping someone would answer, I stood there convincing myself that it was just a burst pipe or faulty plumbing. I flung the door open and hoped that I wasn't walking in on anyone. But I wasn't. Then I sort of wished I had. No relief came from finding the room empty if the cost of that knowledge was to question my own sanity. The room was a cloud of steam that started to disseminate slowly. Only a steamy, wet haze, fear, and I were in the room. *Am I going crazy?* Then I had a terrible realization. *What if it isn't paranoia or faulty plumbing? What if I'm not alone? If that's the case, then, who is here with me?*

I searched carefully and slowly through each room upstairs, but found nothing. I was too scared to check downstairs so I continued to camp out in the room that was now just an airbed and a set of Venetian blinds. I waited for either another noise or the sun to come up; whichever happened first, as I had no hope of sleep finding me. Not tonight. Thankfully that strange occurrence was the only disturbance of the night.

I groggily searched for breakfast then realized that there was no food in the house. I made a quick cup of coffee but had to take it black since there also was no milk. I decided that I needed to spend the day out. With the events from the previous night still lingering in my mind, just sitting home then became even more intolerable. My goal to be out of that house of broken dreams was now priority. Far away from that town, and settled into a place I could call my own by the end of the year. I needed to get those divorce papers signed and out of the way, then I could begin focusing on other things. I still needed to post classifieds to sell everything that we didn't want. It was going to be a much longer process than I wanted or cared to deal with. The New Year was around the corner and 2013 could be my fresh start. *The best year ever. Hopefully.*

So working towards it, I decided to start with phone calls. The first call of my day was answered by someone I didn't care for; Wendy Summer. Wendy a/k/a Morgan's mom, a/k/a Dragon Lady. She was one woman I never got along with. I thought sometimes she resented me because she felt I had a life she was entitled to.

"Thank you for calling Re-Max, Wendy speaking, how can I help you?"

"Hi Wendy. It's Victoria Carlisle."

"Oh. Victoria. Sorry, Diane's not t here."

"It's alright I was actually calling to ask..."

She quickly cut me off saying, "Still nothing yet on your house. I'm sure she'll let you know when there is an offer or whatever."

"Actually, that's not why I'm calling."

"Okay. So, what can I do for you?"

"It's obviously taking a little longer than I had hoped to sell. I'm looking into possibly buying something that I can get into sooner, rather than waiting for the sale."

"Uh huh… I see…" Wendy said, again giving me half of her attention as I could hear papers, typing, and other calls going off in the background.

"Well, like I said, Diane isn't here."

"Yes, I got that part. But you do work there too, correct? Is that something you can help me with?" I snapped, losing my patience.

They certainly were not the only real estate company in the area and Diane would hate to find out that I took my business elsewhere because of Wendy's incompetence.

"Um. I'm kind of swamped," she said. "Have you considered renting? I could connect you with Valerie Smith, she specializes in rentals…"

"No." *Rentals? Why would I?* The house hopping was getting old. I wasn't some drifter in my 20s. I needed something stable. Something permanent.

"Actually that's the exact opposite of what I'm looking to do," I retorted.

"What areas do you have in mind?" she asked.

"Not too far. But not too close either." I was definitely tired of Alpine and the thin walls of the suburbs.

"May I suggest that you look in Passaic County?" she asked, and then began to name towns that weren't exactly the best locations.

"Actually, I was thinking the Old Tappan or Norwood area."

"Victoria, given your current situation don't you think…"

And there it was. She was dying to use that card. Regardless to how unprofessional it was she wanted to throw my failed marriage in my face. She *would* be the one to make the assumption that I was financially impaired without Frank.

"And what situation would you be referring to?" I challenged.

"We all know that you're going through a… rough patch…" she said with thinly veiled condescension.

"Wendy…. I'm looking to buy a house. I have numbers to companies that won't judge me or my personal life."

"Look, all I'm trying to say is that maybe you need to consider your budget," she said changing her tone.

"Why don't you let me worry about *my budget?* Correct me if I'm wrong but you're not exactly a financial advisor … Are you?"

"I didn't mean to offend you. How about you meet with an agent at one of our locations?"

She was so eager to pawn me off to someone else. Better for me.

"That's fine. Do you have anything that I could see today?"

"Actually… there is one house on Kinderkamack that you could see in an hour. It's a two bedroom house."

"Right now I'm not interested in moving to a town that I'm completely unfamiliar with."

She sighed. "Well in that case I have a six bedroom mansion on Alpine Drive. Do you want me to set you up to see that?" she said with a sarcastic I-told-you-so tone.

"No. I guess not."

"And there is a two bedroom in Emerson and one in Oradell; both are around three hundred thousand."

Maybe I did need to look much further than the outskirts of Alpine. This was supposed to be my fresh start.

"Fine," I said with slight disdain in my voice and while gritting my teeth added, "I guess it wouldn't hurt to look." Even if it was like downgrading from a penthouse to a hole in the wall. *Suck it up,* I had to remind myself. *Change is good.*

"I think this will be good for you. I'll have Preston meet you at eleven," she said then proceeded to give me an address. I scribbled it on a notepad but was a bit distracted. *Hmm Preston;* that name brought back a fond memory of my childhood best friend, Preston James, who I hadn't thought of for ages. He was around when my life was still simple and innocent enough to allow good people to get close. That seemed so long ago. I wondered what ever happened to him.

"Victoria? You still there? Did you get the address?" Wendy's voice pierced through the phone, breaking my thoughts.

"Oh. Yes, I got it," I said, then verified that I had it

correct before thanking her and hanging up. It was only 9:30 so I took a shower in the guest bathroom. I threw my blue cardigan over a beige tank top that went well with my dark blue jeans and knee high camel boots.

The constant reminder that I needed to stay on top of my disregarded and ever growing to-do list was when my car wouldn't start. One of the many responsibilities I would have to learn to take on. Thankfully, my car eventually did start after a few attempts and buying a new battery was bumped up to number two on said list.

I still managed to arrive early and pulled up to a quaint country looking white house. It needed some work but overall was… nice. I guess. Simple, looked like one, maybe two floors. Or one floor with an attic. Great; back to creepy. *And still alone.* My hopes weren't exactly high as I waited and stared at what was my new future: a plain, colorless, small house. It may as well have had a white picket fence and a lone standing mailbox with… *what*… written on it? As I continued to feel conflicted about single life and returning to my maiden name a black truck pulled up.

The hum of the engine softly faded off as my real estate agent stepped from the vehicle. I was quickly astonished. It *was* in fact the very Preston James that I was just thinking about earlier that morning. But he was not the grade school boy that I knew then. Though he'd always been cute, the dark skinned and fresh faced boy I'd known had matured into a man with refined features. He shaved his head since I last saw him, but it worked for him. Though not quite my type, I didn't think for a moment Preston had any trouble meeting a lady if he wanted to, and I'm sure his appearance helped him in his real estate career as well. Despite the changes he was still easy to recognize with his distinct yearbook award smile.

"I'm so sorry I'm late," he said and seemed too frazzled to even recognize me. "Hello," he said then flashed me that very smile as he extended his hand, "My name is…"

"*Preston James,*" I said for him then laughed a little. "I know."

He looked at me and seemed to desperately fish through his memory. "Yes…Hi… Have we met before?" he asked and smiled nervously.

Have we met before? In the past that wasn't a question either of us would have ever imagined we'd be asking one another today. Before Brooke was old enough to fill the title, when she was busy watching *Sesame Street* and my only concerns were my lip gloss and sticker collections, Preston was my absolute closest friend in the world. I spent all my time with him especially when there was turmoil at home, or basically any time my father drank. He and his mother lived across the street from us. Our mothers were very close so while they were having girl talk and wine he and I were curled up in a homemade fort on the couch while watching things like *Nightmare on Elm Street.* Then of course we complained that we couldn't sleep at night. Those were the good times.

"Victoria Car-... *Soto*," I said correcting myself when I realized that he would only recognize me by my maiden name. Okay, good thing. That helped my previous concerns.

"Victoria? No way! Oh my God. How are you?" he said excitedly then hesitated to give me a hug until I gave him the okay by also extending out my arms. It was a quick hug but long enough for me to take in his pleasant cologne. The fresh notes of citrus and woods were strong yet still discreet enough to not be overwhelming.

"I'm good," I said remembering where I was for a moment; reuniting with an old friend but also house hunting. "And you? How have you been?"

"Life's great. Can't complain," Preston said and led the way. We approached the front of the house as I followed behind him. He grabbed the lock box that was attached to the handle of the door knob and entered the code to remove the key which he then used to unlock the front door.

"I can't believe I almost didn't recognize you!" he said suddenly as we stepped into the house.

"Almost?" I asked and raised my eyebrows teasingly.

A look of something just short of actual remorse crossed his face. "Alright. You got me. But... you've changed a lot... in a good way!"

"In twenty years? Nah... not *that* much right?"

He laughed then said, "Well then, what does that say

90

about me? You recognized me right away."

"I have a great memory. Besides all those days of seeing the same smile, how could I forget?" I said and smiled reminiscently.

"Of course," he said as we entered the cozy living room. *I hated houses that led directly into the living room.* And the closed floor plan wasn't helping.

"What have you been up to?" I asked.

"After school I went to Kean University for two years, but it wasn't quite my thing. I enrolled in the military for a few years and don't ask me how I ended up back in Jersey and in real estate..." he said then trailed off for a moment.

We continued to walk through the house into a small carpeted area. I peered into a simple 12x12 or so, dining room that was off to the left. There was no fireplace. No extra room for a home theatre. No marble floors. Nothing that was my normal habitat.

"Wow. This would take some getting used to," I said and even felt a little spoiled as I said it.

"Why? Where are you moving from?"

"I'm selling my home in Alpine. You might have seen the listing. It's Diane's."

"Alpine?" he asked then thought for a moment. "Wait, don't tell me... Seven-two-oh-nine Lilac Lane?"

"Jeez, how'd you know?" I asked.

"That's one of the best listings we have right now. I tried to take it off Diane's hands since she doesn't seem to be doing much to sell it anyway. The funny thing is I actually was going to show it to a customer yesterday."

"Really?" I asked then remembered what happened. That could possibly be an explanation... sort of. "Do you think you might have left the lock box open by any chance?"

"No, I didn't even get as far as the lock box because I saw a car in the driveway."

"Oh..."

"The original instructions stated that nobody was living there anymore, that's why we went." he said.

"Yes. That was the original plan. But do you think maybe you or Diane ever forgot to close it in the past?"

"No. I doubt it, we've both been doing this for years," he said, and I believed him.

"Do you think anyone else could get the combination?" I asked, desperately fishing for answers.

"No, I really don't think so. Why? What's going on? Did something happen?"

"Nothing. Don't worry about it… It's stupid anyway."

"If you're this concerned I'm sure it's not," he said with genuine concern.

"I think I'm just being paranoid. But I could have sworn someone was in my house last night."

"Maybe someone was," he suggested.

I shot him a nervous look.

He noted my anxiety about the situation then elaborated by saying, "No, I meant maybe a family member or friend stopped by?"

"I doubt it," I said, knowing that I already thought of every possible person it could be. "Just forget it," I continued, wanting to let it go as I followed him down a hallway to glance at the bedroom and kitchen.

"You do know that this one is a two bedroom," he said turning the subject back to the house tour. "Is this going to be enough space for you and your family?" he asked, glancing briefly in the folder.

"Yup. That's fine. It'll just be me."

"Oh. You and your man?"

"Nope. *Just me*," I repeated, this time more convincingly.

"Really?" he asked. That fact obviously got his attention.

"You sound surprised," I said and couldn't help but to laugh a little.

"So, you're single?"

"Yes. Well… almost."

"I see. So do I get the liberty to say that I was right or is it too soon?"

"Nope. I'll go ahead and say that you were *very* right. You earned an 'I-told-you-so.'"

"Well, I wish I hadn't been right," he said.

I responded only with a resigned facial expression.

We walked through the kitchen which had black knobs on

the farmer-looking white cupboards. The counters were beige and the tiles black and white. The bathroom was tiny and it was painted baby pink with emerald green tiles. I didn't like anything. I tried to not complain aloud but my body language must have given me away.

Preston stopped in his tracks and turned to me. "You're not crazy about this one. I can show you something else if you want."

"I honestly don't know if I'll be *crazy* about anything."

"Why not... the being alone thing?"

"That would be one of the many things."

"Are you sure you don't want me to show you some apartments instead?" he asked.

"No. I'm too used to living in a house."

"I think you're brave for that." he said.

"Why do you say that?" I asked.

"Well you said it yourself that you felt like someone was in your house. And there are too many crazies out there. But you're still standing firm for what you really want."

"Oh trust me, I know," I said. "But I think I'm at the point where I need to take care of myself anyway. You can't live your life in fear, right?"

We walked out of the house as it was an unsuccessful showing.

"Okay," Preston said then locked the door behind him. "Let me know if you change your mind. We have tons of apartments available for rent in Emerson."

"Why Emerson?"

"That's where I live and I wouldn't mind having you for a neighbor."

"Again, you mean..."

"Yes."

"I'll be sure to call Diane and scratch Emerson from my towns of interest!" I said jokingly.

"You do that then I'll change your file to Emerson only!" he responded.

We laughed and stood by our cars while we continued our conversation.

"How's Willow-Brooke?" he asked and his brown eyes

lit up as we felt completely comfortable around each other again.

"Oh, wow! I forgot about that," I said referring to the nickname we gave my sister after one of the malls in New Jersey that we all spent a lot of amount of time at.

"What happened to your great memory?" he asked and smirked.

"I just haven't thought about that nickname in so long," I said then remembered his question. "But, yeah, my sister... She's good, I guess. I haven't seen her in a while."

"Really? That's surprising. You two were super close."

"A lot has changed."

"Sure has," he said, then filled the silence before it was long enough to be awkward. "Do you remember our names for each other?"

"Wow. Yes of course, but don't even say it," I warned pointing my finger at him jokingly.

He laughed. "We can travel down that road anther time," he said while glancing at his watch. "I have another house to show in Oradell. Victoria, I need to get going."

"Okay. Let me know if another listing comes up."

"I will," he said, lingering a moment longer, before continuing, "It was so great to see you."

"Same here."

"We should do this again," he said.

"Well since Wendy pawned me off to you, I think we'll be doing this again."

"Yes, of course. But maybe aside from the house hunt we could grab lunch... catch up a little bit?"

I didn't even have a chance to respond because I wasn't sure what to say. It sounded so much like a date request which was nice but strange at the same time.

"What does your week look like next week?" he asked.

"I would have to look." I knew my schedule was wide open, but I didn't need Preston or his charming smile distracting me from my goals.

"Well you have my number so if anything comes up about a house you would like to see... or for anything else... let me know."

"I will. Thank you," I said as I hugged him.

He got into his car as I went to mine and we both went our own ways just like we did several years ago when we lost contact. I hoped that this time would be different. It was my call as he was obviously interested in spending time together. Maybe someday I would take him up on the offer. Preston was a good person and although he was exactly what I needed in my life I just wasn't quite there yet. What's that they say? Relationships knock on your door when you aren't looking and never come when you ask. Par for the course lately.

CHAPTER 11

After seeing Preston I continued remembering all the things we used to do together as kids. Really thinking about it, we'd made a ton of memories. Thinking about having a real friend, no problems, and days with our innocence still intact made me realize how long ago and far away that time felt. I thought of those days when you did something just to do it, on no schedule, with no focus on the outcome. How long had it been since I had just done something for no reason other than simply doing it?

I would have been sitting there wondering why we lost touch, but that was definitely no mystery to either of us.

My thoughts were rerouted as I arrived at my house. The instant angst I always used to feel upon pulling into my driveway was back, except the dread was different. Back then my fear was fueled by Frank's abusive behavior and never knowing what I was coming home to, but these days I was dreading being alone in what felt like an old vacant hotel. Aside from still being uneasy about the strange things that happened, I was nervous about talk of a huge hurricane that was making its way up north.

I approached the front door when my own little red alert system shifted from the memories that haunted that house to feeling a person entering my space to the left. I jumped a little when I realized it was not my imagination. It was the mailman. Not the usual guy either. Before I could excuse myself, he spoke and said there was something I needed to sign for. He wasn't concerned with my jumpiness, just with getting his job done. Nothing good ever came by certified mail. I wasn't really expecting or waiting for anything.

It was divorce papers. I knew these were coming. My feelings about getting them couldn't have been more mixed. Although they were on some level only a technicality, I felt like a page had just been turned.

I threw them onto the bare counter in the kitchen and then tore open the large envelope. *Great. This is exactly what I need right now.* A letter that read:

SUPERIOR COURT OF NEW JERSEY
CHANCERY DIVISION
Bergen County
FAMILY PART – CIVIL ACTION

I got that far and saw November 21, 2012 elsewhere on the page as the date of the scheduled appearance. It mentioned to contact my lawyer and that failure to appear will result in contempt of court. I didn't feel like reading any further.

Seriously? I thought and rolled my eyes. I sighed and then haphazardly tossed the papers to the mess of envelopes on the counter. I always knew that we were eventually going to finalize the divorce but the fact that he went ahead and filed before me was a bit insulting. But no complaints on my end, the sooner the better. The summons reminded me of a few things that needed to be done anyway.

I was then motivated to spend a few hours going through the dining room where some bins and boxes were piled up and needed sorting. The time alone was helpful, as I obviously needed to get used to it, and I started to go through the empty mess of the place. I managed to spend the rest of the day filling black trash bags with items and objects I didn't want or need. It wasn't that bad with the company of music playing from my phone. I also made a box filled with clothing and household donations. The photo albums, jewelry, and other vestiges of my marriage were where I got stuck, not knowing what to do with some of them.

Time seemed to fly and before I knew it the room grew colder and darker as autumn's earlier nights loomed.

Then I really missed when Ashley would come home with Morgan and Terrance and clear out the contents of the kitchen cabinets before submerging into the computer. I missed Galina and the background noise she created between cleaning, cooking, and chatting in her heavy Russian accent with me and the kids.

If I wasn't already rattled enough the windows shook as the wind gusted by. Hurricane Sandy was announcing her approach. It wouldn't have been so bad if Brooke was around, but she had really committed herself to the wall she'd recently built. I made a mental note to check on her as well as the kids to make sure they were all prepared for the storm.

I decided to bring the black bags out since it was garbage night. I grabbed two of the four bags then opened the front door. The curb seemed so far away. It was dark. Suburban dark. I stepped out and was taken aback by how windy it was. I quickly pulled the door behind me, took a deep breath, and walked as fast as I could with one bag in each hand. I dropped them gently onto the grass and could feel my chest suddenly surging with nervousness. The strangest feeling came over me as if there were eyes on me. *But from where?* I thought and glanced around the street; empty except for leaves being blown by the wind. It was the eeriest feeling. Just wanting to get back inside I quickly spun around.

When I was facing the house again, the front door, which I was sure I shut, was wide open. The walk back towards my house felt slow and dreadful; my feet felt heavier each step closer. *It had to be the strong wind that blew it open, right?* I practically tiptoed through the door, but when I made it past the threshold I was too scared to close the front door and end up in an even more vulnerable position than I already was.

I glanced at the kitchen table and saw the mail was piled up. I had tossed it chaotically as in the moment I just didn't want to deal with that. Not only that, but the divorce papers I was sure I left on top of the pile were folded back up, and placed back inside the envelope .*The wind doesn't organize things. Did I do that? I must have? But, no, I definitely didn't! And I absolutely am not crazy.*

I hesitantly called the local police station and Officer Betsy Harris answered. She was with the precinct for over 20 years, and knew my family and me both for the length of our residency in town and, unfortunately, I was a familiar face.

"How are you, Victoria? Everything alright?"

"Hi Betsy. I'm getting by."

"You don't sound too good. What's going on?"

How would I sound if I told her my shower turned on mysteriously or that it felt like someone was watching me all the time? The same way the word of my impending divorce spread through town like a flu, everyone must have heard about my recent hospital incident. I didn't want to add fuel to the fire but I needed some peace of mind. I knew it wasn't all in my head and I had to find a way to explain it.

"Actually, between you and me, I'm calling because I've had a few strange things happening around the house," I said and felt the embarrassment build as the words poured out. So she wouldn't disregard my call altogether I made sure to add, "I think someone has been inside."

"And you're sure it's not Frank or the kids?"

"I'm pretty sure."

"Well, there have been a few burglaries in the area," she said.

"Really?"

"Just be sure to always set your alarm. I'll let Eugene and Daryl know what's going on. They'll pass your block a few times during their shift."

"Thank you so much, that makes me feel better," I said feeling somewhat relieved but there was still one more thing. Something that was irking me ever since my undergarment became a stolen prize.

"I'm sorry to be a nuisance, but do you think you could check into something for me? Whenever you have a chance, of course."

"Sure. What is it?"

"I have a feeling I might know who's been lurking around. Can you run a search on a man named John Montgomery? He lives right here in town."

"Hold on just a moment," she said. There were a few seconds of silence before she came back. "Victoria, you still there?"

"Still here..."

"I don't have access to that database from my computer right now and I have a ton of paperwork but Daryl just walked in and said he'll run a full background check for you."

"Okay. Thank you."

"No problem. Be sure to call if you see or hear anything fishy."

"I will. "I thanked her again and hung up before I began to search around my kitchen. Most of it was packed up already and in storage but I knew there had to be a knife or something sharp still floating around somewhere. I rummaged through several drawers and found a small steak knife in a mix of loose utensils and spatulas. I made note of where it was and also knew that I had my handgun upstairs buried in my duffle bag.

If someone was in the house I wouldn't know where to begin to look but I did my best to thoroughly scan through bedrooms and closets. Nothing. So after looking through the rest of the mail, ordering pizza, and running a load of laundry with no other strange disturbances I was ready to call it a night.

There were two lights on in the hallway as well as one in the foyer. I wasn't sure how I was going to sleep but I stood my ground. No one was going to scare me out of my own house. I didn't forget to set the alarm before heading upstairs.

I would be spending the rest of the night locked in Ashley's old room. I wished there was someone else I could call so I wouldn't have to be alone. Unfortunately, everyone was entwined in their own lives. *Collin would have never let me feel unsafe.* As usual he crossed my mind randomly, but I knew over time it would happen less often. But when I really lingered on the subject, I still missed him so much. Shaking my head quickly as my mind wandered again I pulled out my phone to check on everyone.

I first made calls to Debra, Michelle, and Sue. Then I sent text messages to Brooke, Thomas and Ashley to make sure they were ready for the storm. Thankfully everyone was; except for me. While I was responding to Thomas, who wasn't worried about the hurricane since he was in Texas, I randomly received a text message from Britney.

Britney: Hey. Just wanted to say hi and see how ur doing w/this crazy storm everyone's been talking about

Me: I'm okay. What about you? Are you all prepared?

Britney: No not at all! I didn't buy any food. My car isn't parked on a high street. I'm here by myself... omg I'm kinda freaking out

Me: Don't worry too much. It'll be fine. It's only rain and heavy winds that's all. But def move your car if you can...

I tried my best to be positive and reassuring. The previous year they made such a big deal about Hurricane Irene which hardly did any damage to my area.

Britney: I will n I hope ur right!

I was in the middle of sending a response when our conversation ended because I heard a noise downstairs. *Now what?*

CHAPTER 12

I found myself waiting for footsteps or more sounds to occur. I was already nervous to go down, then, there it was again. *Someone was in the house.* This time I was ready with my gun now clutched in my hand. I reminded myself to be extra careful considering that as much as it could be an intruder it could also be a family member. When I opened the bedroom door to find every single light shut off I was shaken and almost certain that it wasn't the latter. *What do I do now?* With my back tightly glued to the wall I slowly made my way down the stairs using my phone as a flashlight.

My hand wasn't steady but my grip wasn't letting off the handle of that gun. I could feel and hear my breath fill my lungs as, from inside my head, it seemed like the loudest noise in the house. I managed to make it to the bottom of the stairs. *It's so dark! Now what? What's my plan?* I was determined not to walk around the house like an idiot and say "hello" as if the person was going to answer me. It never seemed to make sense when people did that in horror movies. That's exactly what these days were starting to feel like; a real life horror film. *I could try to get to my keys and flee. But flee to where? A hotel?*

My slow motion home inspection continued. The little bulb over the microwave was the only light that was on and gave a mild orange glow to the room. I tried, again, to go to a positive place, hoping that it was someone I knew that came into the house but the likelihood of that seemed more and more unrealistic with every step and every breathe.

A new noise, which was a scratching sound, started as I entered the kitchen slowly. None of the light switches worked.

"Hello?" I asked aloud finally giving in, not knowing what else to do. "Frank? Ashley? Tommy? Someone there?" I asked cautiously. I circled slowly around the kitchen island and heard the sound again. It was coming from behind the backdoor. All the hairs on my arm lifted as cold chills surged through my body.

What definitely sounded like a small animal scratching

around continued. Why was I panicking about what was probably just a raccoon or possum outside? It didn't feel right. I knew there was more to it.

Then my fright justified itself when the doorbell rang. It was almost 1 o'clock in the morning. I never thought the sound of my doorbell could cause every ounce of my fear to flood through my veins. I lowered my body from sight and crouched close to the ground with my back against the cabinets. It felt like someone was going to come out from around any dark corner of the house. My cell phone was still clenched tight in my hand. *But, who would I call at this time?* I had no intention of opening the door or even entertaining the idea. The scratching noise by the back door seized, and then I heard a familiar dog bark.

There was little doubt in my mind that it was my dog that was out there. *But how would she have gotten here? Is Ashley outside?* As my mother's instinct kicked in, the fear I felt earlier was replaced with adrenaline and concern as I hurried over to the door.

"Ashley? Is that you?" I called from the other side but no answer other than that from the excited dog, who I was now 100 percent sure was mine. I grabbed the door handle and opened it so slowly, so carefully, and only slightly enough to peer outside. It was so windy I was surprised that my five pound Yorkie, Kiwi, didn't blow away. I scooped her into my arms and looked around again but there was no one. No car. *Nothing.*

I shut the door and locked it before setting the alarm. *Wait, didn't I set this earlier?* I didn't even have a chance to address the thought because the large white note attached to her collar caught my attention. The handwritten note read:

You should keep a better eye on your loved ones. Wouldn't want anyone getting hurt.

It was a subtle and equally sinister threat. Anger overtook me and momentarily replaced the fear. Harassing me was one thing, but involving my family escalated this to another level. *I don't care how late it is, I'm calling Ashley now.*

It rang once. Then twice. After the forth ring it went to voicemail.

I tried again. And again. No answer. *Shit.* I started to hyperventilate.

I then remembered that I had Terrance's number and tried him next.

"Hello?" I heard after the third ring.

"Thank God! I'm so sorry to bother you at this time, but are you with Ashley?"

"Mrs. Carlisle?" he asked sleepily and it was obvious that I had woken him. "Uh... is something wrong?"

"I really hope not. But I need to know if you're with Ashley."

"No. Sorry, I'm not."

"She's not answering her phone."

"We have midterms this week, she's probably sleeping."

"Terrance, it's really important that I know she is safe. Please have her call me."

"Um ... Okay. Well if you want, I could walk over to her dorm."

"Yes, could you please? Thank you."

My heart was beating rapidly and increasing by the second. Then the doorbell rang again. This person was really trying hard to scare me. It was working.

I was going to ignore it until the knocking started. Then banging. I had chills running down my spine.

"Victoria? It's Daryl. You there?"

I let my guard down again and was relieved to hear a familiar voice. Maybe I was acting on impulse but finally feeling a sense of relief from the sheer idea of someone safe being on the other side, I rushed over to the door and yanked it open.

I was relieved to find myself in good company. Two officers, who I knew well, from the Alpine Police Department, Daryl Booker and Eugene Conte, stood on my front porch. "Thank God!" I said. Then I realized that the police were at my house in the middle of the night. The worst thoughts flooded my brain and I thought I was going to pass out.

My organs battled as my stomach dropped and heart flew upward. Fear. Relief. Dread. The entire day was a constant emotional battle, for sure, but that moment was by far the worst one.

"What's going on?" I asked nervously; my voice cracked.

"Sorry to bother you at this time," Daryl said.

"I- Is everything okay?"

"Not really..."

"You're not here about Ashley are you?"

"Ashley? No. Why? Is there a problem?"

"Oh, thank God..." I said and felt a little relieved. "I'm not sure, but I hope not."

"The reason I'm here is because I looked into that guy you told Betsy about. Victoria you were right. I ran his name through the police database. His name isn't John Montgomery; it's Christopher Campbell. He's wanted in Colorado for the mysterious disappearance of his wife, Susan Campbell, in two thousand seven. He was supposed to be detained for questioning but fled town the same night before an arrest could be made."

I stared at Daryl speechlessly.

"If he's wanted then why can't you arrest him now?" I asked demandingly.

"We have a warrant. But the address you gave us... are you sure it's current?"

"Yes. I'm a hundred percent sure. Why?"

"We went to the house. It looks like nobody lives there."

"It's completely vacant," Eugene said as he nodded, agreeing.

"What? So you don't know where the hell he is?"

"As of right now... no."

"Great. This is just what I need," I said, then sat down because it really felt like I was going to pass out.

"I can continue to patrol your street and when my shift is over I'll make sure the next officer on duty does the same."

"Thank you for the offer but I'm pretty sure that won't do anything." I exhaled.

Daryl flicked the switch and the light went right on. "Are you okay?" he asked when he noticed my expression.

"Not really. I think he was here... inside the house... just before you came."

Eugene peered over his shoulder then down the hall. "I'll check it out," he said then disappeared towards the kitchen. He walked around as Daryl and I followed close behind him. We checked every room but found nothing. As we scanned the house I filled them in about the time I spent at John's, the weird occurrences around the house, my dog, and Ashley; there was just so much going on it was overwhelming.

"Victoria, I would feel better if you stay at a friend's house for a while. Especially tonight with that storm coming. You know all of Alpine is going to be in the dark if these trees come down. I really don't want you staying here by yourself," Daryl said. "You'll need to go soon. It's supposed to be no joke. Category Four they're saying."

"And don't go to the hurricane shelter zones either," Eugene chimed in. "This guy is definitely dangerous and he will probably try to track you down. He'll definitely take advantage of the situation. Do you have a friend... or a family member?"

By myself in this huge house during a storm? Definitely not. Where could I stay? John knew where Brooke lived and I wasn't going to bring this drama around my son and Debra's family. I had already asked Sue while I was checking on everyone and knew that she had her daughter, son-in-law, and grandchildren staying over. Michelle evacuated the area. Only one other friend came to mind; Britney. I knew it was a long shot but what other choice did I have? I picked up my phone and was completely embarrassed that I had no other option and to be in yet another predicament.

"I could ask Melinda if you could stay with us for a few nights," Daryl said when I seemed to be out of options.

"No. It's okay. I have to take care of my own problems. I appreciate the offer though." The last thing I needed was to be the center of more local housewife gossip. "But, if you could do me one favor, that would be great."

"Sure, what is it?"

"Stay here for a few minutes while I pack a bag," I said sheepishly, but for all I knew my life was in danger.

"Okay. No problem. You found somewhere to go?"

"I think so… or… well… I have a friend in mind."

I stared at my phone then looked at my last text message. Not wanting to keep them waiting on an answer I decided to call. The phone rang twice when I heard Britney's perky "hello" on the other end.

"Hey… uh… I hate to call you to ask for a favor but…"

"What is it?" she asked.

"Where I live… well… the area is a little infamous for the blackouts during these storms. Many of my neighbors are already staying with friends and family. And I'll most likely be without power for a few days."

"Wow… that totally sucks."

"Yeah, I know, right?" I said, then I realized I couldn't bring myself to ask her. How could I even think of such a stupid idea? Then I had nothing else to say either. "Did you have a chance to pick up food?"

"No. I didn't."

"Oh."

"Yeah…"

"Well I should go…"

"Wait! Oh my God, I totally have an idea! Why don't you stay here? I know it sounds a little weird. But I'll be honest; I don't want to stay here by myself."

"I don't know…"

"Aw come on Victoria, please? I was going to ask you earlier but I didn't think you would go for it."

"Okay. I guess that makes sense. I'll bring some food, wine, we'll camp in and make it fun, even if there is a black out."

"Awesome! Sounds good. I'm so excited!" she said. "Wait… what was the favor you needed?"

"Oh, um … nothing. Never mind. So should I come now? Or do you need to find out if it's okay first?"

"If it's okay?" She sounded so confused then she realized what I meant. "No. It's fine."

"Are you sure?"

"Yeah. Just come whenever. I'll be here."

"Thank you so much." I hung up and felt such a sense of relief as I desperately wanted to get out of that house.

So, again, I found myself packing yet another bag. The awkwardness of the situation didn't quite sink in while I was doing it. I only really thought *I'm staying at my friend Britney's house. I'm staying at her place just for a night or two, then everything will sort itself out.*

It's amazing how desperate measures will allow one to believe just about anything.

CHAPTER 13

As I started to drive the rain came down heavily, like a monsoon. I was one of the few cars on the road. I had to pull over three times to avoid getting into an accident. I was sitting, waiting patiently on the side of the road, watching the rain engulf my car, hoping I wouldn't wash away. It was terrifying beyond anything I ever imagined. I wondered if the safer bet would have been to stay in that lonely mansion, knowing that an intruder could possibly be there. Damn, it was a lose/lose, either way I was screwed.

Suddenly my cell phone rang. It was Ashley.

"Mom?" she asked.

"Ashley!" I said, "Thank God! Are you…"

"I'm fine, Mom. Sort of."

"Sort of?"

"I was with the campus police. Someone broke into my room while I was out."

"They stole my phone. And please don't be mad they stole my dog. I'm so worried…"

"Ash, good news, Kiwi is okay," I said. "Someone must have read her collar and returned her to the house." I knew that was a complete lie but I couldn't have her also living in fear. "She's at Morgan's now."

"Oh, okay good. They still don't know who broke into my room."

"That place is crawling with cameras, Ashley. How do they not know?"

"The DVR that records the feeds is broken."

"What number are you calling me from?"

"My friend Luna's. She lives off campus. Between the storm and the incident, I'd rather stay here. You know?"

"Yeah," I said, "I'm not at the house either. I'm at a friend's."

"Oh," said Ashley. "Mom, Luna needs this line open. She's waiting for news on her brother who hasn't checked in yet."

"I understand, Ash, just call me when you can."

"You got it."

I ended the call and was happy to know that my daughter was safe. I just needed to do the same for myself.

I finally had an opportunity when the rain seemed to slow down for a bit to drive straight through the rest of the way.

As I parked my car then stepped out to meet with Sandy and her ferocious winds, I finally admitted to myself; *Victoria, this has to be one of the most ridiculous things you've ever done, and you've done some crazy things.* But who was I kidding? Yes, I was there as a last resort. Of course I was happy to be in Britney's company instead of at my empty mansion, but for whatever lingering reason, part of me was there because I wanted to be closer to Collin. I still couldn't seem to let him go. In distance we weren't any closer, but in theory and feeling, we were.

I missed New York so much... more than I realized. The busy business atmosphere, the air, the noise, Collin's building; which now towered over me. *Here goes nothing.* I walked in and felt like I entered another zone. I was greeted by none other than my favorite doorman, Ian Johnson, and his warm smile.

"My goodness! It has been quite a while!" he said.

"That it has! How are you?"

"I'm good. And yourself? What brings you out here?"

Friendly Ian. This was just like old times.

"Staying for a few nights. The area where I live isn't the safest place to be right now," I explained.

"I hear ya! Crazy storm, better to be safe than sorry!"

"Definitely," I said.

"Well it's great to see you again Ms. Carlisle."

"Thanks," I said then stopped at the second door, adding, "Oh and Ian ... just 'Victoria' will do..."

"Got it!" he said then buzzed me in and I walked to the elevator and ascended the 23 floors to the apartment with all of the memories. I made my way down the hall and had a nervous fluttering as I waited.

Britney opened the door.

"Hey! You're here," she said sounding a bit surprised as she stepped aside to let me in. "Did you get here okay?"

"Yes. No traffic. Actually it was like I was the only car out there. It wasn't easy to drive in."

"I'm glad you made it in one piece," she said as we entered the living room. I was surprised that Collin's apartment wasn't completely feminized yet. Not much changed since the last time I was there. That day was still so clear; five months ago, I was practically breaking down as Britney and I met and talked for the first time. Aside from the few things that she had lying around it was that familiar apartment that used to be my safe haven.

"Thank you for letting me stay here," I said.

"No problem. Make yourself at home."

It *was* like my home not too long ago. And now it's nothing more than a friend's apartment. I was only there by the hands of Mother Nature. I didn't answer with more than a slight smile. I placed my duffle bag on the floor next to the sofa and just stood there awkwardly, not knowing what to do next. Then Britney completely caught me off guard.

"You could put your things in the room if you want," she said pointing her chin towards my bags.

"Uh... Which room?"

"Well there are only two rooms silly..."

"Yeah... I know, "I said cutting her off. "No. It's okay. I could sleep on the sofa. It's fine."

"Wouldn't it be easier for you to stay in the room? That way if I'm up early or coming in late I won't wake you up. And you'll have more privacy."

"Fine, I guess," I agreed, not wanting to be in her way.

I hesitated to walk into Collin's room and when I did, it was an instant nostalgic jolt to my system. Everything was all so familiar and perfectly both in and out of place, as if someone actually lived there, not like the room came out of some magazine. The curtains were still light grey and navy. The bed was made perfectly with the bedding set of the same colors. I crawled onto the bed and rested my head for a few seconds. His wonderful scent lingered lightly on the sheets. *That's a little odd. Actually this whole thing is odd.* I suddenly thought while coming back to reality as I stood up.

I was careful not to touch anything and placed my bag

111

on the side by the closet then rejoined Britney in the living room.

The winds assaulted the windows as whooshing, crashing, threatening noises engulfed the building. The rain really picked up and it seemed as though we were nearing the eye of the storm.

Then the lights flickered more until they finally turned out.

"Don't worry, I totally got it covered," Britney said turning on the lantern and several candles. "I wasn't about to sit by myself in the dark."

"I brought a bunch too," I said as I began helping her set them up.

Britney disappeared into the kitchen and all I heard was "Ow!"

"Are you okay?" I asked.

"Yeah, just burned myself with the candle. Don't worry about it," she said.

I couldn't help but to laugh.

Then she called out, "How long do you think this will last?"

"Most likely into tomorrow. Or longer. Don't think PSE and G will be coming out anytime soon. Or what is it here in New York? Con Ed?"

"Uh...I guess," she laughed then was serious again... "This is my first East Coast hurricane," she said then re-entered the living room and sat next to me. "I'm glad you're here. The funny thing is that I've been through tons of earthquakes but this storm terrified me."

"Really?"

"Yeah. We get them all the time in Cali."

"So I've heard," I said then was quiet for a moment. It was beyond obvious that there was zero chance of me not thinking about Collin while sitting in his apartment with his best friend. Not to mention being in a blackout while talking about California. I figured one of us should address the elephant in the room.

"You know... this is kind of how we met," I said and chuckled at the irony. How long ago *that* was and if I only knew what that one night would lead to.

"Huh?" She asked, obviously not on the same page.

"Me and Collin. We sort of met at my office during a black out."

"Oh. Yeah, I know," she said, then stood up again grabbing the lantern. "We may as well open this bottle I received at the fashion show. I'm not going to drink the whole thing."

"Alright, I'll have a glass, I suppose." Thus, my sober streak was easily broken. But I figured; what harm could I possibly do while stuck in an apartment during a hurricane?

"Wow this is really good," I said, savoring the crisp, semi-sweet white wine. "So was this a party favor?"

"No, this was a thank you gift from a designer that I featured. I put together the whole show you know... it was my first one."

"Aw, I'm so sorry I couldn't make it. I feel like a terrible friend."

"It was amazing! Some big name designers even showed up. You really should have come."

"I know," I said, my voice wrapped in guilt. "To be honest with you, I needed space. I didn't feel like meeting with you to talk about what happened."

"I didn't invite you there so you could to talk to me..."

"I guess I misunderstood."

"Yeah. You really did, Hon."

I stared out the window at the dark city. New York. It was finally asleep. New York... I was here again. I couldn't believe I was that much closer, but yet we still hadn't talked about him. I needed info. I didn't know what to say, and we danced around the topic, so I just sat quietly and wondered how he was doing. And also wondered why she acted like he didn't exist. Then I decided to take the leap and ask, hoping I wouldn't find out anything I wasn't ready to hear.

"So... how is Collin doing?"

"Victoria..." she said with a hint of annoyance in her voice. "I'm not getting in the middle."

"Jeez, I just asked a simple question," I said stiffening in my seat.

"Look, you and I are cool, but there was a point when we

113

almost weren't and it was because I was getting too involved. Don't you think so?"

"I definitely noticed that. But why? It seemed like you had something against me. I just didn't want to say anything."

"Well... You want me to be honest?"

"Of course."

"I had so much respect for you. You weren't afraid to admit your feelings to me or to yourself. That's why I think I felt some sort of responsibility to get you and him to talk. I was the only other person who knew how much both of you still cared for one another.

Cared? Past tense.

"I'm still a little lost as to why that changed," I said.

"One thing I hate is when people play games. And watching my friends get hurt. So when both of those were happening, I decided to leave it alone."

Maybe I should too? I wasn't playing games. Was she referring to him playing games and me getting hurt? No. That wouldn't explain why she was so short with me on and canceled our lunch plans.

"Okay, fair enough," I said feeling unsatisfied with her answer.

Suddenly we had nothing to talk about again so we both quietly sipped our wines.

Just then Britney's phone started to ring.

"Hey you..." she said. "Yeah, I'm good but we lost power like forty minutes ago... Yup she's sitting right here actually... okay, I'll text you tomorrow... Love ya, Boo!"

I looked at her but didn't dare ask. She answered my unspoken query.

"He was just checking on us..."

"Oh... that was nice of him to let me stay here."

"You say that as if you're surprised."

"I am..."

"You shouldn't be."

"I'm exhausted," I said putting my head down. *Was I ever!*

She sighed then softened back to her usual tone. "It sounds like the two of you have a lot of unresolved issues to talk about. With each other; not with me."

"I don't disagree with you. I just don't know what to do."

"Well… it's not really rocket science. The texting thing obviously wasn't working out, and you guys can't use me as a messenger forever. Why don't you just call him?"

"I don't know. I take one step forward and two steps back. Part of me wants to hold on…"

"So then?"

"Well the other part is telling me to move on."

"Yeah… And this is your way of doing that."

I laughed a little then realized that she was right. But it didn't matter. Why torture myself and talk to him when he didn't want to be with me any more anyway? Again I was missing something because she wouldn't gear me in the wrong direction either.

"When did having a relationship become so complicated?"

"I don't think dating has ever been easy. My ex used to mess with my head. She was super jealous because of my traveling and didn't trust me. She would break up with me then apologize afterwards. After spending time moving on, it gets draining. So, I understand exactly what you're saying. But it doesn't mean you don't love the other person. That's why, when you sent him that message, it reminded me so much of her and it made me look at you differently. I didn't mean to get so emotionally involved."

Oh, so when she spoke earlier about one of us playing games she was referring to me.

She sighed then said, "I shouldn't have compared you though, that's not really being a good friend on my part."

"It's okay. You and he are close so I completely understand," I said. "I know you're going to think I'm nuts for saying this but…"

"What is it?" She asked, amused.

"Even in his room I could still smell his cologne in the sheets. It's as if he was just here or something."

She smiled then laughed at me.

"Yeah… I knew you would laugh," I said and couldn't hold back laughing at myself.

"No it's not that. I'm laughing at you because he was here. Last week for a few days.I tried to tell you. When I was at Fiesta he was there with me. I wanted the two of you in the same room so you could talk."

"He was here? I....I should have..."*Should have what, Victoria?* I asked myself. "I screwed up our last communication so much."

"We all make mistakes... it's about what you do after them that matters," she said then stood up using one of the flashlights to navigate through the apartment. She rummaged around in the dark for a minute then came back with her laptop.

"So do you want to watch a movie? I have tons of them."

"What movie?"

"Anything as long as it's not *Citizen Kane*," I said.

"Um... What's that?"

"Exactly," I said. "Nothing. Long story, really."

"We have all the time in the world."

That gave me the opportunity to bring Britney up to speed about the real reason I was no longer staying at John's house and why I felt so much more comfortable being as far away from my house as possible. The power never came back on. We both slept in the living room. The wind whistled, candles flickered, yet I was more at peace laying there than I had been in months. For the first time in months I felt home.

CHAPTER 14

The sun's reflection bounced from one of the high rise buildings and blinded me with its magnificent silver morning rays. *What a way to wake up* I thought, then rolled over so that the sun's warmth now beamed against the back of my head. I wasn't complaining at all. Still safe. Still happier. Still better than being in that oversized dungeon in New Jersey.

Two days had passed since Hurricane Sandy plummeted through the East Coast and things were quite a disaster. Most of New York City below 45th Street was still without power and a lot of it was under water. Thankfully, Britney and I only lost power for a day. I didn't yet know what the condition of my house was, but I planned to check on it soon.

I spoke to Preston who called me as soon as the storm subsided. Obviously, there weren't going to be any houses to show for a while, so he asked me to lunch again which I was still undecided on. Otherwise I hibernated in the apartment, used my laptop, followed up with friends and family again, and had an occasional conversation and glass of wine with Britney.

It was a bit early for my phone to be ringing so it made me extremely curious as to who it was. When I read on my phone's screen that Preston was already calling, I wondered if it was to find out if we were having lunch or not.

I picked up before he was sent to voicemail. "Good morning."

"Good morning," he said sounding wide awake, yet still his relaxed self.

"What's going on?"

"I know you didn't get back to me about lunch yet but..."

"Sorry about that," I said cutting him off. This was maybe the third time he was asking me out and I was beginning to wonder if his intentions were heading in the wrong direction. There wasn't a question in my mind that I wasn't ready for dating of any kind and he was the last person I wanted getting hurt because of my emotions.

"Sorry that I didn't give you an answer, it's just that I

117

don't want you to get the wrong idea."

"Wrong idea? About what? I'm actually not available anymore for lunch. I'm helping a friend out this afternoon. His entire basement is a river."

"Oh. I'm sorry to hear that."

"It's okay. Thankfully it was mostly used for storage," he said and I was relieved that the nature of his call was actually a cancellation.

"But back to what you were saying... What would I get the wrong idea about?"

"I mean about going to lunch... I have to be completely honest... I'm not in the position to be dating or anything like that..."

"Victoria, neither am I. I just wanted to catch up, that's all. It's been a while, you know? Look, if anything we could call it a non-date, if that makes you feel better."

In a weird way it did.

I laughed a bit then said, "A non-date hmm? It would be nice to get out for a bit. Fine...Let's do it."

"I should be free by this evening."

"Sounds good."

"Great!" he said a little too excitedly. "Can I pick you up at eight?"

Uh... pick me up? I had to think that one through; how was that going to work? I couldn't let him come get me in New York. Or risk being seen walking into another guy's car. It seemed like it would be disrespectful, on some level.

"If you don't mind, I could meet you by your place."

"Whatever works best for you is fine by me."

"Okay, sounds like a plan!"

I was actually excited about meeting with Preston. With all the drama over the past few weeks spending time with a friend would be nice.

I rummaged through the few nice outfits that I'd brought with me and chose something dark to match the season and maybe a little of the way I was feeling deep down. But in the end I was able to put together a nice - but not too nice - ensemble.

"I'll see you later Britney!" I yelled from the hallway then escaped unseen. I didn't need her to question my whereabouts. So, now, instead of running out and keeping secrets from Brooke and sneaking around on Frank, I was avoiding Britney so that Collin wouldn't find out what I was up to. If life ever got easier and less scandalous I needed to know when that would be. I was hoping sooner rather than later!

It was a 45-minute drive to Preston's home in Emerson, New Jersey. I followed the GPS along the way. Emerson was such a cute little town with boutiques and cafés in the commercial area and trees and small wildlife in the residential area, as per the norm for Jersey.

I was just parking my car when Preston stepped out of his house wearing a black blazer and slacks. He looked very clean cut and masculine, with his perfectly shaven goatee. I knew it would take some time for me to adjust to seeing him grown and handsome instead of as my friend who was just going through puberty.

I didn't know where we were headed but I let him take over as I relaxed while listening to soft R&B on the way. We drove almost a half hour to Secaucus then pulled into the parking lot of an Olive Garden.

"Hope this is okay," he said questioningly.

"Sure. I've never been here before."

"To this one… or any of them?" he asked and looked at me as if I had 10 heads.

"None of them."

"Really?"

We walked to our table where Preston pulled out my chair for me. The menu seemed okay. I was used to half of my menu being in another language or offering 100 dollar bottles of wine. But that wasn't my life anymore, and that was a good thing, so this worked fine.

"I still can't get over that you've never been here," he said as I glanced over the dinner selections. I was almost certain that I was going to order a grilled chicken salad.

"I know, I know," I said sheepishly. "My husband and I didn't go out much. And when we did it was to some big fancy place. You would think that sounds great and wonderful but it wasn't. It was very artificial. Like a big show. But I'm not sure who we were trying to impress anyway… it obviously was for nothing."

"Don't say that. There is a reason for every relationship we experience, both good and bad. Everyone you meet is for a blessing or for a lesson."

I looked at him questionably.

"Frank Ocean…" he said.

"Oh," I said quietly and nodded.

He was doing a good job masking what he really wanted to say. There was never a question that Preston James was one of the many people in my life who didn't want me involved with Frank. The difference between him and everyone else was his own personal incident with Frank that only strengthened his hatred towards him. Even though we only skimmed the subject, I knew we would eventually have to talk about the real reason we ended our friendship so many years ago.

"To be honest, I don't like being alone," I said.

Actually I *hated* being alone especially knowing that the one person I wanted to be with was still out there, but I wasn't about to share that with Preston.

"I do like that I don't have to be fake anymore," I continued. "Sometimes I wake up and I'm completely lost and think that any moment I'll hear my kid's phones going off, Frank in the shower, or the nanny cleaning. But I have to remind myself that my life is different now. I used to force a smile and even if it was real, it was coated with the anguish of knowing that I had to share the moments with someone I despised. Now, when I smile, it's because I'm actually happy," I said then stopped myself as I caught Preston's fixated glare on me. "Sorry, I'm talking way too much about myself."

"No… You're good," he said then smiled at me which was infectious, as I smiled back at him.

"Ah! So, you *are* happy then."

"Yeah. I think I am."

An older woman with sandy blond and grey hair came over to us. She wore a white button down, black tie, large smile, and held a small notepad.

"Are you two ready?" She asked, her eyes darting from Preston, to me, then back to Preston.

"Uh… yes," I said looking up at him, but our eyes didn't meet. He looked at our waitress and his deep voice overpowered mine.

"Yes. We'll start with the crispy risotto bites, each of us will have a salad. I would like one order of the Mediterranean grilled trout, and she'll have the stuffed Chicken Marsala."

"Okay. And to drink?"

"Um…" I tried unsuccessfully to chime in.

"Two glasses of Malbec."

"Great," she said scribbling on the pad. "I'll be right back with those drinks."

Did he really just order for me? What century are we in? I didn't know people still do that. According to the conversation we had, this was not supposed to be a date! I sat quietly and slumped away from the table into my chair. *Why would he assume that it's okay to order for me?*

"Is something wrong?" he asked catching my scowl.

I shook my head, lying. *Why should I make an uproar? It wasn't that big of a deal. But I would definitely make it a point to mention it because that wasn't my style at all.*

"Tell me more about your business," he said shifting the conversation as he noticed my sudden silence.

"Not much to tell. Most of my clients are older women. The most excitement I'll get is when a client overseas places an order. Or when someone orders in bulk, most likely to resell in their own little shops," I said then went on to tell him how I started the business. We talked about "Little Treasures" for five minutes before we were mildly interrupted again.

The waitress came back and placed a glass of wine in front of each of us.

"Thank you," he said to her then he glanced over at me and smiled.

"What kind of items do you sell?"

"Collectables, gifts, candles, wall sconces, knickknacks. Not much different than Avon or Mary Kay, except we don't really have make-up or beauty products".

"At least that's a nice, calm job."

"It's peaceful now. I used to have an office, which sometimes would become a handful. But now I work from home."

"Why'd you close the office?"

Because I could no longer handle the pressure of being a boss when my world came crashing down last summer. I didn't expect to fall head over heels in love with someone else, on top of it my marriage got worse, then I lost everything, tried to burn my house down, tried to kill myself, and here I am, on a fake date with my old best friend who now has a goatee and orders my meals for me.

"Victoria?" Preston asked then I realized I zoned out.

"Huh? Oh... sorry... um business wasn't doing well."

"What about you?" I asked, deciding that I wasn't ready to talk about myself too much more. "Obviously the real estate, but how did you get into that?"

"After the military I took a little break before I decided to take a real estate course."

"You said you also went to Kean University, right?"

"Yes... Did you go to school?"

"Well I wanted to graduate from high school, and it seemed doable when it was only Thomas, but then Ashley came along... so I got my GED. Never quite got around to college."

"Oh, I see," he said, then we were quiet and the silence stretched.

"How's your mom?" I asked thinking of something that would direct us into a happier conversation.

"She's been having a few issues with her blood pressure and diabetes. We've been in an out of the hospital over the last few months."

"Oh no. I hope she's doing better now."

"She's getting there. You should come visit her. We were talking about you the other day, she would love to see you."

They were talking about me? Why? Either way, I probably should visit Karen. She was amazing support when my mother was arrested, but it started to become too painful to see her as it only reminded me that my own mother wasn't there anymore. Then that reminded me of the other person I needed to visit; my mother.

"How's your grandmother? "He asked.

Boy, were we strolling down memory lane, and it was depressing. My grandmother was the only other person who cared about me and Brooke. At the time I was too young to notice that it was insane for her to let me-- a pregnant naïve teen --and my sister, live with Frank. But I soon found out why she did it.

"She passed away."

"Victoria," he said sympathetically, "I'm so sorry to hear that."

"Thank you. When I moved out she went into a retirement home. She was always sick and they ran tests only to find out she had terminal cancer. She knew it all along, but had no interest in being a... lab rat... were her exact words. She'd seen what chemo did to a few of her friends and family and didn't want to end up like that. She actually went on to live another ten months, just long enough to meet Thomas."

"Wow... I had no idea, I'm sorry."

"It's okay. How would you know? You hated me back then so..."

"Vic... I never hated you!"

"Well, it was hard to tell because you never said one word to me through sophomore or junior years. You never asked about the baby..."

"You already know why..."

"It doesn't matter. We're here now right?"

"Yeah. We are... so... what happened with your relationship? If you don't mind my asking. What went wrong?"

No, I didn't mind. I actually hadn't talked much about my failed marriage which wasn't healthy either. "Come on... you've had the pleasure of meeting Frank, I'm sure you could figure it out."

"Well, I'm sorry that things didn't work out."

"No you're not."

"Okay. I'm not. But I don't think that would be any secret."

"Of course."

Time to change to subject again and I couldn't figure out if our non-date; that seemed exactly like a date, was going well or not. I decided to ask him again about what his original career plans were.

"I wanted to go into engineering. But I needed another

year in the military before I qualified for the hands on training. Unfortunately, I left early…"

"Why? What happened?"

"Actually, I was dismissed after coming home from Iraq."

"How long were you there?"

"A few months. My unit was attacked and we lost seventy percent of our men. It was very… traumatic. Actually I'm surprised to be talking to you about it. I usually don't discuss that with anyone."

"Well, I'm glad you feel comfortable enough to share that with me," I said, reaching across the table to place my hand over his.

"I always did. I'm glad that didn't change. You're very special, Victoria. That hasn't changed either."

Feeling shy and unsure of the unexpected sparks that surrounded us I leaned back against my chair again and glanced away.

"What we had was definitely…something," I admitted.

"I'll raise a glass to that," Preston said then glanced at my full glass. "Hey, you haven't even touched your wine."

"Yes. I just have a lot on my mind to be drinking…"

"Oh."

"Actually, to be honest with you… I don't drink." *Most of the time.*

"Really? You don't? Oh… I had no idea."

"Yeah. Actually, an iced tea would have been great. And I was thinking about ordering a chicken salad but… it's cool, I guess."

"Jeez. I'm such an idiot! I'm so used to ordering that I didn't even think twice about it. Wow, I feel like a complete jerk!"

He was used to ordering for two? Was I the idiot in the situation? Was he married? Did he have a girlfriend? I found myself too scared to ask. Or maybe I didn't want him to say "yes."

"Aw. No. You're not at all," I said, reassuringly.

"Why didn't you say something earlier?"

"I should have. I guess I didn't want to be rude."

"There was a time when we were so close that nothing

would be awkward or rude," he said with such a disdained tone.

"I know…" I said with equal disdain.

"But, despite everything, what are the chances of us crossing paths now? Do you think this was our second chance?"

Second chance? We hardly had a first chance, but the middle of Olive Garden didn't seem like neither the time nor place to have this conversation. Luckily, the waitress returned with our appetizers.

"So, what do you think?"

It was obvious he was referring to the stray "second chance" comment, but I chose to ignore that fact.

"They look great!" I said about the appetizers. "Oh, before I forget, I wanted to ask you if you think taking the house off the market was a bad move. I don't feel right leaving those repairs to someone else knowing that we have the insurance to cover it."

We got into a conversation about people who flip houses then about the buying, selling, and investing that goes into real estate. Preston showed off his expertise and didn't revisit the previous conversation.

With that note the food arrived.

"If you don't like the chicken, it's cool if you order something else."

"Actually, it's really good. Thanks."

"If you don't mind my asking… what made you give up drinking?"

"I wouldn't say I gave it up. The thing is… I can't think of a time that I drank recently and didn't regret my actions afterward. I need to stay focused right now and be in control of my life. For once I am trying to be responsible."

"You weren't dancing on the bars or anything like that?"

I laughed, "No. Nothing like that."

"Okay, good," he said, smiling at me.

We finished dinner and he let me order dessert so that we would be even. I realized that I had to face the inevitable as we started to drive off. I had to face the reality of what I had been avoiding since I started my make believe life in my make believe home. I needed to stop at the house where all my nightmares began.

CHAPTER 15

As we drove up route 17 north I knew we were only twenty minutes from my house and before Preston drove to Emerson I figured I would go out on a whim and check the condition of my house.

"So... I sort of need to ask a huge favor," I said sheepishly.

"Go ahead."

"I know it's out of the way but would we be able to pass by my house?"

"Of course. How's everything there? Is your power on?"

"I have no clue."

"Wow. Really? I'm surprised you haven't gone by yet."

"I'm not."

The further North we drove the less we saw any sign of power or hope. When we turned onto Lilac Lane, it didn't look too promising. The entire street was black, with the large houses silhouetted against the moonlight like square hills. The few trees that had served as ornaments for perfectly manicured lawns were horribly mangled, with branches ripped off in the most unsightly places. Every now and then, I saw a broken window or a wall covered by a tarp marring the houses of our neighbors.

When Preston pulled up to my house, the lawn was the first thing I noticed. Without anyone coming by to clean it, huge tree branches were strewn everywhere between the road and the front door, making my yard look like a veritable death trap. However, looking up, I realized how much worse the house itself was. The roof of the garage had apparently caved in with such force that the garage door was left hanging limply from a single hinge. More shingles than I would have dared to count were missing from the roof of the house. Worst of all, the large maple tree that had proudly dominated the right side of my lawn for about a decade and a half had been uprooted, with treetop having punched through my kitchen window.

We drove back to his house where I had left my car and trusted it would be okay. "Thank you so much for dinner," I said as he walked me to the car.

"It was my pleasure," he said then bent forward and kissed me on the cheek. "Get home safe."

"Goodnight," I said. It was a… nice… night with a glum ending. *Well, what did I expect? I don't know what I expected. I wanted a friend, I got a friend … what more could I want, right?*

While Preston stood next to the car to watch me leave I turned the key and this is when my car decided that it didn't want to start. *Damn. This is so embarrassing. What do I do?* I sat awkwardly still in the driver's seat while Preston stood patiently on the curb. I was hoping he would go away, but of course he didn't. I turned to smile at him. Then found out that I was still able to roll the window down.

He leaned really down and rested his forearm against the car. "Everything okay?"

"Not …" I said sheepishly, "It won't start."

Preston came around to my side and opened my door, gesturing for me to get out. "Let me see. "He turned down all the radio and temperature knobs, waited a few seconds then gave it a try. "I have jumper cables in my trunk … we'll get you started, don't worry." He then flipped open my front end, hooked up the jumper cables and after some hesitation he got the car to start.

"It doesn't like me," I said jokingly.

"Yeah. Or maybe I'm magic," he said with a smile as he stood up, giving me my spot in back. "But, you definitely need a new battery. You'll get home tonight but you may or may not be able to start the car tomorrow."

"Okay."

"Seriously. Don't forget. I don't want you to end up stranded somewhere. I'd suggest taking care of it tomorrow morning."

"Got it. Thanks."

I headed back to New York. I had such mixed feelings about Sandy's damage. Most people would have been devastated, but part of me almost wished she would have taken the whole thing. Just made it all disappear. However, I did count my blessings that nobody was there to get hurt when it happened. If I stayed there I couldn't imagine what would have happened.

Britney was already asleep, I assumed, as it was quiet when I walked in. Finding myself alone for the first time in days, the thoughts in my head continued to swarm. And as my familiar friend insomnia joined me I was face-to-face with everything that had been put on the back burner.

Reaching to my side to feeling nothing but empty space and cool, crinkled up sheets caused that familiar loneliness to bubble to the surface. I was still in Collin's bed. *What am I still doing here?* I'd asked myself that often over the course of the last few days, yet there I was. The absurdity of the situation left a contradictory feeling in my heart. *He's across the country while I'm here...in his apartment...alone. What the hell?* Despite everything, I wondered if he really was still thinking about me as Britney said he was.

I clutched my cell phone longingly in my hand as I scrolled through my saved contacts, the screen displayed each name until approaching the Cs and then came a nervous drop in the pit of my stomach. That rollercoaster ride feeling again, just from looking at his name lit up on my screen. *Unbelievable.* I'd done the exact same thing two nights in a row but couldn't will myself past just staring at the phone. *I can't call him.*

We haven't spoken in -or really spoken-... I sighed at the thought. This had been the longest amount of time ever, since we met. *"Put the phone down, don't be stupid,"* one side of my brain, which felt like logic, tried to tell me. Both hope and fear were known to masquerade as logic and instinct. *Which was this?*

I need water. After burying my phone under my pillow the stroll to the kitchen seemed like a futile distraction, but anything that bought me a few minutes that actually had a purpose was welcome. The walk to the fridge was a tortuous trek down a road of our lost romantic past. I passed the sofa where he and I spent hours cuddled up, the kitchen where we dined and cooked together countless times, oh... and of course... the balcony.

Then back in my bed... Wait...*His bed.* I successfully managed to stall four whole minutes but the fight with my will power was still very one-sided, as my phone's tempting voice begged me to rescue it from its suffocation beneath the pillow.

Back to where I started. Phone in hand, I tipped the king

to his side on the chess board and upon accepting my own dare to myself, I pressed the send button. It rang once. *Shit.*

Second thoughts arose as my heart pounded. *It rings again.* What are you doing? Now pounding harder, my breathing deepens. I did the time difference math in my head as it rang. *He's probably sleeping.* On the third ring I raised my finger to press "end" but then heard an answer.

"Hello...?" He answered partially questioningly and surprised. And I froze. I hadn't heard his voice in months. That sweet, welcoming, sexy voice that I've been yearning for. I don't know why I thought I could do this! *Jeez woman...Say something.*

"Uh... Victoria? You there?"

"Yeah... Sorry. My phone's been ...Hi, Collin... how have you been?"

"Um... I'm fine... What about you? Is everything alright?"

Do I only call people when I have a problem? This was becoming too common a conversational theme lately. Or was he referring to our hurricane situation? It was hard to tell.

"Things could be better, but we're holding up," I said simply. I wasn't sure how else to answer.

"It's almost three in the morning over there..." he said, puzzled.

"Yes. I know. I can't sleep," I said. "I'm sorry is this a bad time for you?"

"No, it's cool."

"Oh, okay...so... um..." and just like that my vocabulary resembled that of a 2-year-old. "Thank you for letting me stay at your apartment," I stammered over my words, "I know it's a little weird but..."

"Victoria, stop. It's fine. And you don't have to thank me."

"Well, either way, I really appreciate it."

"You already know that anything you need..." he said then trailed off mid-sentence.

"Thank you," I said again. Then it was quiet and I closed my eyes and tried to imagine his presence. *Why are we not together? Why?*

"I haven't heard your voice in... a while," he said.

Even though I was just thinking the same thing I

could only utter a simple, "I know." I missed him so much and I was trying hard to fight the small lump in my throat.

"So… is that why you called?" he finally said after a few seconds of shared silence. And there it was. He'd pierced the pretext for me.

"No…" Of course it wasn't. *I'm waiting for some miracle, to wake up one day and not have you on my mind.* But that didn't seem like it was going to happen… ever. "Well yes, but there's more."

"Okay…"

I sighed, thinking about my short, nostalgic night walk earlier. "I can't believe you're really three thousand miles away."

"I know, I still can't believe it myself," he said.

"I… I miss you," the words trembled out accidentally and floated across the country hoping to rekindle the flame of estranged love, yet those words were relieved to be out of my head and into the world.

But then I noticed that he wasn't really saying anything. He didn't sound his usual self at all. I wondered what was going on in his head.

"What's wrong? You're so quiet," I asked.

"I know… I think it's just that…"

"What?"

"You keep catching me off guard, I guess…"

"I'm sorry …It's probably a little unexpected that I called you?"

"A lot unexpected, actually," he said in a softer tone.

"It's just that… we still have so much to talk about… and I figured…"

"Victoria, I don't really think there's anything left to talk about," he said, abruptly cutting me off.

"How could you say that?" I asked.

"We've done this already. We're just going to hit a brick wall again," he retorted.

"I think we need to try…"

"Why should we keep hashing out old issues? What's the point? We both know how this ends." He suddenly sounded angry and almost bitter as if a well of frustration had been tapped. But the situation was so unfair and I was trying so hard for him to understand.

"*What's the point?* Not that long ago we both would have done anything to be together. You used to be so passionate and determined..." This was all so inappropriate for me to pour out all at once, after so long, but it needed to be done. I couldn't stop myself; it was bottled up for too long.

"I know I was," he said then sighed. "Victoria... I wanted to make it work... more than anything... but..."

"*But what?* I'm kind of throwing myself out there and you're dancing around it. I know you don't think there's anything to talk about but I disagree."

"Okay," he said.

His lack of communication was now leaving me feeling frustrated. "*Okay?* What does that mean? I need to know that I'm not holding on to something imaginary," I said.

There was a long pause.

"Well...am I?" I asked dragging out the words apprehensively. I really was putting myself out there, completely unsure of what his response would be or how he felt. Unfortunately, I set the bar too high. My hopes dropped quickly when he didn't reciprocate the way I had hoped.

"Honestly, I'm just not sure anymore...about anything," he said. "You were the one person I would have stayed there for, and you let me go. And now you're calling me in the middle of the night telling me you miss me. I have no idea what you want. "He sounded agitated. Despondent. And everything that I had been feeling was present in his tone.

"Forget what I want for a minute. What do you want?" I asked.

"I don't know."

Part of me was then regretting calling him. What would this accomplish? Nothing. I wanted him here, now, and talking to him knowing he was thousands of miles away was killing me slowly. And now, tapping into his head to find out that he wasn't as zealous about working things out as I was, I felt worse than I did before making the call.

I was now curling with the pillow and a familiar stinging in my eyes grew uncomfortably closer. I held the phone so close with hopes it would bring him closer to me. But deep down; I was also regretting making that call. Every muscle in my belly was aching. The lump in my throat was now the size of a grapefruit. I quietly shed tears while we still held the phones in inaudible agony.

"Please don't cry…" he said changing his tone. "Look, I just mean… I've been here by myself, trying to stay focused. I wasn't really thinking about anything else."

Was that his way of telling me that he wasn't seeing anyone or was that my way of interpreting it?

"All I want is for everything to be right again," I said.

"Victoria," he said again, his voice was low and laced with both softness and control at the same time. "I was so sure that you wanted to get back together," he said then paused for a moment. "But when you sent me that text…ignored my messages…"

"Wait…what do you mean? I never ignored your messages." I didn't mean for it to come out so defensively, but it was unexpected. I practically dove to the phone anytime I thought it could be him.

"Come on, don't do this now. You know exactly what I'm talking about."

"No, really, I don't. I waited for you to call… I felt so stupid… and hurt."

"Don't turn this around on me. I was going to call you… you were the one who said we shouldn't talk anymore. You said it was a mistake… If you were just playing hard to get I'm sorry, I was over it at that point."

"But, I never said that."

"Yes you did… in the message."

What?

"I said that only because you didn't call me…"

"No. It was before."

I was so confused. Was I drinking and didn't remember messaging him? *No. I know I wasn't.* This was so wrong and we were getting nowhere again. What was I missing? The part of me that wanted to give up was starting to have the upper hand. I didn't even know what to say.

"See. You're so mixed up. You really don't really know what you want either," he finally said when I couldn't come up with anything.

"That's not true…" *I know exactly what I want. I want you.*

He sighed and sounded very exhausted from our ping pong-like conversation.

"Let's just not get into this right now," he said.

Too late.

"Fine. If that's what you want."

"I think it's for the best."

"Okay," I said too exhausted to protest.

"Is there anything else? Because I should probably get to bed."

There was so, so much more, but I feared I was the only one who thought so.

"I guess not," I said.

"Okay then."

'Okay then,' I mimicked bitterly.

"Don't be mad at me…"

I exhaled shortly then said, "It's… whatever."

"I had a really long day. I can't think about any of this right now. Can we talk about it another time? Or if you want… call me tomorrow. We can talk-"

Is he serious? I'm going through another conversation like this again.

"I said everything that I needed to say," I said, my tenor very matter-of-fact.

"So where does that leave us?" he asked.

"I don't know. That's on you."

"Um… okay…"

"Good-night," I said.

"Good-night."

That didn't go the way I wanted at all. How is this possible?

I couldn't sleep and just kept thinking and thinking. I went back to early October to replay the details. We messaged each other then I waited for his call. What was I doing? I had my phone… I was at John's… wait… *Oh my God!* Then it hit me. John had my phone! Only for a minute or two. Shit! But would he really? *Yes,* he definitely would! *How could I not have seen it before?*

What now? Do I let it go? I can't. I have no idea how to let him go. But I can't call him back with my crazy what-if theories. But I needed someone to talk to.

I suddenly found myself outside Britney's bedroom door knocking lightly.

"Britney…"

She opened her door with her eyes practically closed.

"Victoria? What time is it?"

"Three thirty…I'm sorry…"

"Is everything okay?"

There's that question again. Then an avalanche of everything I had tucked away came rolling down.

"No. Everything is not okay. Everything is a mess. My life is a mess. Earlier today I saw my house. You should have seen it… it was terrible. And I never see my daughter. I hardly talk to my son… I'm only thirty-three and I'll be divorced already, most women my age are having their beautiful weddings and babies… I'm going to be alone forever… on top of everything else Collin hates me…" I had to stop to breathe. I was completely hyperventilating.

"Victoria, sweetie, calm down," she said leading me to sit.

"You know I haven't seen my sister, who was my best friend, since I left the hospital. That's why I'm here bothering you at almost four in the morning. I haven't been able to really talk to anyone else."

"First of all you're not bothering me at all. Second, I'm sorry about your house but you could stay here as long as you need to."

"Thank you…"

"Okay and lastly, why would you say that Collin hates you? You know that's crazy right?"

"I took your advice. You were wrong. I called him."

"You did?" she asked wide eyed. "What happened?"

"Well…it wasn't what I expected. I think we're over. And I think I know why."

"Why?"

"Well…is it possible to block someone from texting you?"

"Yes. Why?"

"Can you check to see if anyone is already blocked?" I asked handing her my phone.

She navigated through the menu and selected the privacy settings, when she opened the reject list, lo and behold guess whose name was there? One mystery was solved.

"Victoria, I'm confused," she said.

"I think the person I was staying with hacked into my phone. He found an opportunity when I wasn't in the room. He messed up everything."

"Holy crap! But that would explain so much!"

"Do you remember what that message said? Did he ever tell you?"

"Yes. It was something like, I know we were supposed to talk tonight but after some thought I realized this was a huge mistake. It would be best if you don't contact me anymore."

"Wow. I wouldn't blame him for starting to move on. I can't keep playing tug of war anymore."

If I ever got my hands on John he would be the one who was missing. How did I not see it sooner? And now it would be impossible to explain it. He split us up for good. Or... no. Maybe it was me. I couldn't keep pointing fingers. I was so stupid to again worry about my pride and could have figured this out long time ago. What I should have done was never let Collin go in the first place. I was too dumb to realize it then. Was it time to finally accept what I was avoiding for a while?

Was it really over?

CHAPTER 16

Despite wanting to sulk all day I made plans with Preston for Friday evening. I met him by his place then we drove to a pizzeria called Milano. It advertised itself as having "real Italian pizza. "Like the kind from Italy. We both heard good things about it but never tried it.

"So, this is supposed to be like what they actually eat in Italy," I said before biting into what I thought was a good thin crust.

"It depends on the region," Preston said before taking a bite of his. "The type of pizza in Italy varies heavily on the region."

"You've been?" I asked.

"No," he said and laughed. "But I watch Food Network when I have insomnia. Hey, you and I could go. We could take a food tour."

He played it off like a tease. *Is Preston actually imagining a European trip with me?* I shook it off.

He seems like he'd be great to travel with. He'd take me on a trip so I saw things like a traveler, not a tourist. Maybe even better than Collin would on a trip. Why are these thoughts coming up now?

"Well they say Mexican, or I guess, Mexican American food on the West Coast is different than what we have over here. It's more of a cuisine there." *Really Victoria? You couldn't think of a better place in the entire world to say than the west coast!*

"We can head out there too." He was totally unaware of my wandering mind.

We chatted for a few more minutes before concluding our non-date at Milano's.

"Can I steal you away for just a little while longer?" he asked as we sat in his car.

Why not? What else was I doing? "You're not really stealing me away from much," I said.

When he pulled into what looked like a small parking lot, I realized it was the Alpine overlook.

"Just a sec," he said stepping out of the car.

I thought he was checking on something with the car, when I realized he went around to the trunk before I could ask if he'd heard a noise from the car that concerned him. Now his car was having problems too? Being nosey I leaned around to try to look to see what was going on, not that I knew about cars ... but what was taking him so long?

I didn't have the best night vision but as my eyes adjusted it looked like he was pulling something out of the trunk... A tripod?

"What on Earth are you doing?" I asked curiously.

"You'll see..." he said with a mischievous smile.

I stepped out of the car to get a better look. "Are you setting up a camera?" I asked him.

"Yup. Figured we'd do a photo shoot right here in this parking lot. Nothing racy, just maybe get you down to your lingerie. PG-13 stuff."

He saw the look on my face and immediately corrected himself. He didn't realize that my reaction was because of the photo shoot memories I was trying to suppress.

"Victoria, I'm kidding!" he said. "It's not a camera. See..."

He pulled out an expensive looking telescope. There was writing on the side telling what lenses were in it. Probably the name of some brand which would impress me if I knew anything about high end optics.

"A telescope?" I asked.

"This is the best place in Alpine to get away from the light pollution," he said. "Of course there's nowhere out east to really get away from light pollution. Except in some parts of Pennsylvania, you'd really be able to see stars."

"I see..."

"Come here," he said. He put his hands on my shoulders, and positioned me so I was looking through the lens.

It was pointed directly at a star that didn't just look brighter; it looked like an ethereal jewel among the celestial spheres.

"Wow," I said genuinely. It was the clearest, closest view I ever had of the stars. I never took the time to take in the beauty of the world. I never had that opportunity. I was always surrounded by dark clouds and drama. The sky was a deep, black, onyx sheet, with all the little sparkles, like little glimmers of hope.

"Marvelous isn't it?" he asked.

It was only then that I noticed how good Preston's hands felt on my shoulders.

This is Preston, I said to myself.

"What am I looking at?" I asked.

"Orion," he said.

"The belt of Orion?" I asked.

"No," he said, "The belt is the most famous. This is one of the two stars that would be his shoulders."

I look at him straight in the eyes. I smiled deeply, lost in the moment.

"You always were a bit of a science geek," I said.

"Well," he said and returned the smile.

"Do they have names?" I asked.

"What?" he asked.

"The two stars in the shoulders," I said.

"I don't think so."

I looked smug. I picked up my smartphone and in a few seconds had the answer to my own question... "Betelgeuse and Bellatrix," I said.

"You just got that in two seconds on your phone?" he asked with a smile.

"Well," I said.

"You always were the efficient one... when you want to be that is," he joked.

Somehow all our brotherly sisterly banter just seemed to cement our connection more and how much we were only in some ways like siblings and in others... we seemed like something else.

"Preston," I said, "It's late and I'm a little chilly."

"Yes, you're right," he said busying himself with the work of dismantling the telescope, "I have an early showing."

To keep the night good, I leaned in and kissed him on the cheek.

The short ride to his house was quiet. Our energy was calm, and it felt better than when we concluded our last night out.

Then, what happened was a complete Deja vu.

Preston pulled into his driveway and walked me across the street to my car. He smiled at me through the glass of my car's passenger window. *I wish he would have kissed me. Actually I should have kissed him.* My thoughts were random and unexpected, But I knew it was too late to get out of the car anyway as I prepared to drive off. The only problem was, my car wouldn't start again, but this time it wasn't bluffing. It choked and hesitated, but no luck.

"Ah! Still didn't get that battery?" he bantered.

"Err... Oops..." I said.

"Let me give it a look," he said.

I stepped out and it was Preston's turn to attempt to start it but there wasn't even a hesitation this time. Just one click then silence.

"It doesn't like you anymore," I teased.

He popped the hood then messed around with wires and quickly checked a few other parts. I wished I knew what he was checking for. Car maintenance wasn't exactly my thing.

"It's definitely the battery... maybe even the starter."

"You think we could jump start it again?"

"Maybe. But I don't have the jumper cables, a friend needed them ... do you?"

"No," I muttered. *Great.* "I guess I'm not that efficient," I said and laughed.

"Do you want me to give you a ride to your friend's house?"

No. I was still standing by not wanting to involve him with New York in any way. It was back to my double life, but that was my life. The life I had with Collin, even if our relationship was over, the apartment, the friends I met with him; that was separate from my life here. Once the two worlds collided the damage would be worse than that of Hurricane Sandy. I knew it might happen one day, but if I could prolong it as much as possible that's exactly what I was going to do.

I shook my head. "It's really out of the way."

"I don't mind," he said sincerely.

"I know. But, then for me to come all the way back to pick my car up in the morning..."

"Well, I have no problem with you staying here until

the morning. Then I can take you to the parts store tomorrow… If you want."

Spend the night in another man's house? Another house that wasn't mine. How would that look?

"I don't know…"I said with disinclination. "I could just call Triple A."

"It's after midnight…"

"I know," I said.

"Well, just let me know whatever you want to do."

He was right. They usually took an hour to respond and at that point I was so exhausted to wait an hour for a worker to arrive then almost another hour to drive into New York.

"You should have listened to me," he said and chuckled.

"As usual," I said. "You know what. I'm tired. We could deal with this in the morning… if that offer is still on the table."

"Of course," he said then shut my car door, locked it, and handed me the key.

I followed him down a pavestone path that was lit with solar lanterns. The house was a nice size, white and blue on the outside with clean landscaping. Nothing too overwhelming. *Why couldn't he show me a house like this?*

We stepped inside and I was pleased with the instant homely feel to it. It smelled like Bed Bath and Beyond and looked like Ikea. There was life and color, what a pleasant change. A black leather L shaped sofa that seemed to have a recliner in each seat covered two of the living room walls. Throw pillows of red, canary, and charcoal were tossed neatly against the seats. A frosted glass table and complimenting end tables gave the room a crisp modern feel. The walls were painted dark grey and the lighting was dim and sensual.

"Can I get you anything?"

"You don't have tea, do you?"

"Do I have tea?" he scoffed jokingly, as if I asked an outrageous question. He opened a cabinet and exposed an amazing, eclectic collection of what looked like special ordered teas. They were each in little stainless steel containers that were labeled with the names of each tea. He also had fancy infusers, steel tea balls, and cute mugs. I felt like I was in a British tea house.

"Wow. Well which one would you recommend?"

"This one here," he said removing a short steel container, "is a wild berry, blackberry blend with hints of cinnamon."

"Sounds amazing."

He used a small porcelain teapot shaped infuser to brew our tea. Then gave me honey and a cinnamon stick and a pretty orange mug.

"I've obviously been doing this wrong," I laughed. "I can never go back to tea bags again."

"Using the real thing is so much better. It's healthier. And these days it's not hard to find good tea."

"You're right," I said and took another sip, collecting my thoughts.

When I looked up I realized that it was three in the morning and the time had completely escaped us. "Where should I sleep?"

"You can take my bedroom. I'll stay on the couch. Sorry, I don't exactly have a guest room."

I could have asked him to elaborate, but I didn't want to pry. There obviously was an extra room. This time I noticed. Maybe he had a roommate or an office? I definitely wasn't in the position to ask.

"Okay," I said and followed him down the hallway.

He opened the room door then turned on a chrome lamp that had four small shades that coiled outward and were attached to the stainless steel stand. Each shade was black, white, grey, and silver, which matched the striped comforter and solid curtains.

"Let me just grab my sweats and I'll be out of your way," he said then pulled a pair of navy blue cotton pants from the dresser drawer.

"Thank you so much Preston," I said and embraced him. I held onto him for a few extra seconds. I was a little saddened that I let such a good person and friend go. He would have been there for me through so many times that I struggled. He squeezed me tight then slightly leaned back and looked into my eyes.

"Hey... You okay?" he asked.

I nodded. "I'm just so mad at myself."

"Me too," he said. "Mad at myself I mean, not at you."

I gave him a small smile. "Why? You didn't do anything wrong."

"Victoria..." he said then sighed and sat at the edge of the bed.

"Preston, what's wrong?"

"I wanted to tell you this earlier... I didn't want you to run off..."

"What is it?"

He sighed then revealed his secret. "I'm married."

I stepped away from him and studied his features. The look on his face resonated that of remorse.

"Wait... what? *Whoa, the plot always thickens whenever I get involved with something or someone. Can life ever be normal?*

"Well...*separated.* I'm sorry. We were having such a great time catching up. And for once it was nice to have conversations about things other than my failing marriage."

"Actually... I completely understand. *Boy do I understand!*

"There's one more thing...I have an eight-year-old daughter."

"Really?" I asked and had to let it sink in. I wasn't upset about what he revealed to me, I was a little hurt that he felt like he couldn't tell me. "Wow, you could have definitely told me that, you know I have three kids, right?" I felt such a sense of relief getting it all out there.

"I know. Every time I thought about throwing it into the conversation, I wasn't sure how you'd react. I know we're not dating or anything, but I know the drama could even scare friends off."

"Well... It just so happens that I was involuntarily chosen as the queen of Drama Island," I said smiling at him so that he would know that I wasn't upset.

"I think that's a kid's TV show," he said and laughed at me.

"Is it?"

"Total Drama Island... Lacey, my daughter, watches it."

"Hmm. Then I'm...uh...well you get my point," I said, unable to think of something clever. "It doesn't bother me at all. Any of it. As long as you're being honest with me now."

"I am."

"We're good," I said draping my arms around him.

"Okay, good. I couldn't lose you again, Pinky."

"Oh no!" I said pushing him away. "What did you just call me?"

"Pinky... Don't tell me you forgot."

"How could I forget? You sure you want me calling you Blinky?" I said laughing sentimentally. "Wow I haven't said that in...forever..."

"I should have been Clyde instead," he said.

"Hey, do you still have Pac-man?"

"Wow. I don't know. If I have my Nintendo anywhere it's in a box in storage."

"Oh man! Let me know if you ever find it. I'd love to kick your butt in that and in Tetris too!" I said putting my head up and smirking at him.

"You wish!" he said then his words trailed off as my gaze set upon his.

Preston suddenly scooped me into his arms and decided that was the moment he was going to kiss me. It was a nice slow and sweet kiss. It was very short and left me wanting to do it again.

"I was waiting all night for you to do that," I said.

He smiled at me but being a gentleman decided to leave it at that one kiss as he then stood up. "I'm going to change. I'll check on you in a few, see if you need anything."

He disappeared for a few minutes. It gave me some time to think, and breathe. What was going on here? I wasn't sure but when he came back to say goodnight I had made a hasty decision.

"Think of anything else you need?" he asked.

"Yes..." I said. "Come in please and shut the door behind you."

"Oh...okay," he said and obliged.

"Now, come here," I ordered.

He sauntered slowly to the bed.

"Lay with me," I said patting the mattress.

"You want me to stay?" he asked.

"Yes."

He wasn't sure where I was going with it but the truth was simple, I didn't have anything else in mind. It would be just like the old days. "I don't want to sleep alone tonight," I said.

He climbed into the bed close to me but enough to leave space between us. I scooted closer to him, closing the space, and so his arm had nowhere else to go but around me.

"Those two stars we saw earlier..." I said distantly.

"Yeah?"

"Those could be our new nicknames for each other. Bellatrix and Betelgeuse."

"Hmm," he said. "People will think of *Beetlejuice*. They'll compare me to him... didn't they have to say his name three times or something?" Preston laughed.

"Nah," I said turning to face him, "You're Bellatrix," I said jokingly.

"It sounds feminine. And it suits you better anyway."

"How so?"

"Bella...means beautiful..." he said.

I blushed then turned away. "Fine... you win."

"What was that other name you had for me the summer between seventh and eighth grade?" he asked.

"Bumblebee. Cause you were so into Transformers and that was the only one I knew," I said.

"That wasn't the one that summer. I was way too old for Transformers by then."

"Not how I remember," I said then yawned before closing my eyes.

"Good night, Betelgeuse," I said, with my eyes still closed.

"Good night, Bellatrix," he said with a soft chuckle.

I felt Preston reach behind him and click the lamp off then his arm rested over me again. I was so cozy and content. "Good-night, Victoria," he whispered.

It wasn't long before we both drifted away.

CHAPTER 17

I was alone in a large bed and for a moment really had to think hard to find my grounds and figure out where I was. Then I heard the familiar sounds of breakfast being prepared. Is that Britney? *Wait… I'm not in New York*, I reminded myself.

While crawling out of the bed I couldn't believe that I had slept in my snug jeans.

Hmm wonder what Preston's making… but with that thought a loud screeching alarm in the hallway jolted me to my feet.

I ran out to see if everything was okay. Preston was fanning at the stove which was surrounded by a cloud of smoke. The fire alarm was still going off as everything popped and sizzled in the pans. I hurried to his aid turning on the cold water first then removed the first burning mess from the ranges, running it under the hot water. I couldn't even tell what it was that he was trying to make.

"Good Lord! I don't know what's going on with this oven today!" he said.

"I don't think it's the oven, Preston!" I said over my shoulder.

"I have no idea what you're talking about."

"You had the fire on too high," I added smugly.

"Alright. Fine. I have another confession. I don't know how to cook," he said ashamedly. "But I really wanted to make something for you, and I though; how hard could it be?"

"Apparently very," I said and laughed as I used a spatula to scrape a burnt pancake into the garbage. "I'm kidding. It was super sweet."

"My morning client cancelled. I'm having a showing around noon. Maybe we could stop at the diner?"

"No. I really should be getting to the auto parts store."

"Done! I hope you don't mind. I took the liberty of stopping at Auto Zone to pick up your battery. I figured I'd do that while you slept."

"Oh. Wow. I don't know what to say. At least let me pay you back."

"No way. I would never take your money. But if you give

me the key I'll put it in for you. I didn't want to go through your bag."

A real gentleman .I felt giddy and tingly. This is so nice. And this time I didn't have any worries because I already knew him.

"Thank you so much for everything," I said to him. "You're amazing."

"There is something important I do want to talk to you about. Over a coffee and some pancakes would be great."

"Um. Would it be a date or another non-date?" I said lightheartedly.

He brushed my hair out of my face, his eyes fixed in a gaze with mine. "Whichever you'd prefer," he said in a more serious tone than mine.

We connected so well… *maybe I should give him a chance, a real date. He definitely earned it. But am I ready? Is he ready? Am I forcing this so I won't be alone, like I tried to do with John?*

But I couldn't compare what I had with Preston with anyone else. He stood with both of my hands in his waiting for an answer. My palms started to sweat as I felt comfort as his strong hands held mine tight. I looked up at him. He had that serene, yet intense look in his eyes. I knew that he wanted to kiss me again… and I didn't mind if he did. He moved closer to me as my heart drummed rapidly. I closed my eyes and parted my lips…

Then, the melody of my ringtone pierced our connection.

"I should get that…" I said rattled by my growing attraction to him. "And the key…" I added further breaking the trance. I grabbed my car keys from my purse and quickly glanced at my caller ID. I was stunned to see a name on my screen that I wasn't expecting. I was so thrown off that when I heard Preston's voice behind me, asking me if everything was okay, the phone practically leapt from my hand and onto the floor.

"Damn it. I'm so clumsy," I said, as I picked up the strewn pieces from the tiles.

Preston knelt beside me and handed me the phone back then helped me click it into place. Our hands fumbled together and he gave me that look again, but I was already disconnected.

I handed him my car key and quickly stood up.

"Thank you again. Let me know if it starts up okay," I said referring to my car as I scurried into the kitchen and started tidying up. "I'll clean up while you do that," I said. "We'll be even," I added with a smile.

"Okay," he said and headed outside.

He was only gone for 15 minutes before returning with the good news that the new battery fit and my mini problem was solved. *If only all of them could be that simple.*

"So did you decide where we're heading for breakfast?" he asked.

"Can I get a rain check on that? Something came up," I said, feeling guilty. *Something always comes up.* I just couldn't commit any of myself to him when my mind was somewhere else. Or on someone else.

"Oh. Okay. How's tomorrow then?"

"Yes, that should be fine," I said as if I just confirmed a doctor appointment.

Preston looked confused and disappointed. He reached over to kiss me and I kissed him gently on the cheek.

"Hey, is everything okay?" he asked.

"I'm fine ... everything is cool."

After we said our quick good-byes practically ran out of his house and sat in my car for a few moments before driving off.

I wasn't thinking about Preston, where to eat, or what he wanted to discuss as I headed back to the apartment. As usual I could only think about Collin. *Why is he calling me? Are we talking again? Should I call him back?* Why would I even ask myself that? I already knew the answer.

* * * *

I should have been making calls to the insurance company about my house. And to the real estate company. Checking my e-mails. There were a lot of other things for me to do, but instead I sat on the bed, cellphone in hand, and my stomach balled up in knots over my estranged love problem. ..

What's wrong with you? It's not that serious! Just call him back!

What's wrong with me? I answered myself. It could be really good or devastating that he's calling. Collin and I both had time to think and process everything that was said. Sleep on it, so to speak, and now it was time to close with a decision. We couldn't stand still forever. We had to move towards reconciliation or accept defeat and move on.

Reconciliation was my motivation so I called him back.

"Hi. Sorry I missed your call. I was... out," I said.

"Hey. It's okay."

"So, what's up?" I asked casually.

"I've been thinking a lot since the last time we talked."

I've been thinking non-stop since then.

"Me too," I said.

"I need you to help me make sense of a few things."

He asked me why I suddenly suggested that we stop talking so I began to explain the situation to him. I told him about John but left out the details that he was a stalker who was wanted, possibly for murder, and that to this day, still had a collection of my underwear. I told him that I never saw any message he sent to me because he was blocked.

"So...yeah... that's what happened," I said after my explanation.

"I knew something didn't seem right," he said, and I was glad he realized that our relationship was tampered with.

"Now it's my turn to ask you something," I said.

"What is it?"

"Well... What if...What if that never happened? And we actually had the conversation we were supposed to have that night? How would it have gone?"

"I ask myself that every day. But, you're still over there. And I'm over here. That hasn't changed."

"I'm not referring to the distance..." *If you asked me I'd be there with you.*

"You remember when I told you that I was taking time to focus on myself?"

"Yes."

"I was thinking that... well... maybe you should do the same."

Okay, that wasn't what I wanted to hear.

"Is that your nice way of saying it's over?"

My question was answered with a short silence.

"I can handle it, and I sort of saw it coming," I said.

"I don't really know what to do. It was already very hard when we were a state apart... but now we're on the opposite sides of the country."

"Things were more... complicated then. It doesn't have to be that way. Don't you notice that no matter what we end up drawn right back to each other?"

"Yes. You're right. But I also know that we ended abruptly and never really had a chance to talk about it afterwards. Even our last conversation was unproductive. So do you think maybe this is just us needing some kind of closure?"

Closure. That damn word! So, "defeat" won out this time?

"You seriously believe that? Then you didn't listen to a word I said the other night..." I was starting to give up.

"This isn't easy for me either. But shouldn't one of us be honest and admit when it's over?"

"God, you're so damn blind I swear," I said feeling so frustrated with him.

"What?"

"You want honest? I'm still in love with you! "I felt like I exploded when I said it and before he could respond I spoke again. "Fine. It's over, whatever... but don't expect us to be friends. I can't be your friend..."

"Wait...Victoria...I...uh, I really wasn't expecting you to say that. What you just said before..."

"Well, sorry... it's done anyway... I gotta go," I said. My impulse was to hang up on him, but I didn't mean to actually follow through with it. I was just tired Wow, I thought we had something real. Go figure. Six months and 3000 miles was all it took to split us apart. Time and distance.

I didn't want to accept it earlier, I didn't want to come to terms with it, but I was truly, emotionally spent. There was only so much a relationship could handle and we had reached our limit. We finally both had our closure. And it all ended, just like that. So it wasn't real after all. Perhaps losing the moonstone necklace was an omen or a red flag from the universe. I should have listened to the signs I was given back then, in the park, that awful night. Where the fuck was my head? Collin was just a self-centered kid who only cared about himself. He was playing games with me the whole time. That was now obvious.

So, now I know for sure – this is it. No more. Done. *Time to move on with your life, Victoria. Time to move on!*

CHAPTER 18

The wailing of my alarm clock woke me up and after hitting "snooze" five times, I finally shut it off. It was Sunday morning, I had nowhere to be. I was in the only place in the world I cared to be. But feeling quite disheartened as the previous day's conversation started to replay in my mind I had very little will to do much.

I skipped breakfast as I continued intermittent sleep. The clangs of pots and pans were present in the far distance coming from the kitchen as well as the sound of water turning on and off. *Britney must be cooking.* I came to a conclusion that there didn't seem to be anyone in existence that could quietly prepare a meal.

I didn't want to see Britney. I didn't want to see anyone. All I did over the last 24 hours, aside from sleep and cry, was ignore my phone calls and glue to the bed, while listening to songs like XX's "Infinity," Gavin Degraw "Not over you," and Evanescence's "My immortal," on "repeat." When I finally decided to get up for water it was 12:45 p.m.

I walked into the kitchen and immediately smelled faint traces of maple syrup and cinnamon in the air. Britney lit up when I emerged from the bedroom.

"Hey! I was getting worried about you," she said.

"Really? I'm okay…" I muttered.

"You sure? You don't look okay." She pouted at me when she saw my puffy red eyes and messy bed hair.

I tried not to think about why I was so upset, but it was such a fresh wound that was hard to ignore.

"Please eat, I cooked," she said lifting up one plate that was being used as a cover to another plate where several pieces of French toast were piled high.

"Thank you," I said taking a seat at the table. I was still hurting inside and I could hardly touch one slice as I pushed the pieces I had cut around my plate. Britney was still hovering by me.

"I don't like seeing you like this," she said, sounding like a mom.

151

"I'll be okay."

Will I?

"What happened?" she asked.

I gave her a look. "As if you don't already know every detail."

"Actually, I don't. If it has something to do with Collin… he won't talk to me about it either."

I looked at her surprised. "Don't you two talk about everything?"

"Yeah…" she said as if she meant to say "exactly."

"Oh," I said but still couldn't bring myself to open up yet.

"That bad…huh?" she asked softly.

I didn't say another word. I eventually finished half of a French toast and a glass of orange juice before I excused myself, cleaned my plate, and went back into the bedroom. *Now what?* I just wanted to go back to sleep and that's exactly what I did.

*　　*　　*　　*

Preston grew extremely worried about me when I ignored him for two days. When I finally snapped somewhat back into reality I apologized to him for being a ghost. I came to terms with what happened between Collin and me and knew that I couldn't stop living my life. Since the previous weeks were filled with heartache, loss, and unfavorable news I decided to continue spending time with Preston. His presence was comforting and he made me laugh. We eventually did reschedule that breakfast, but we didn't have the important talk. He brushed it off. Maybe it wasn't "important" anymore, or maybe he didn't want to burden me with something big after my disappearing act.

The rest of my week was an array of indoor mini golf, chatting over lattes at the Starbucks in Emerson, eating Paninis at Panera Bread, and strolling around the Paramus Park Mall; all with Preston.

There wasn't a doubt in my mind that Preston and I were both lonely to an extent. *But is this more than that? What exactly are we doing?* I might have complained a lot about being alone but it was actually healthy for me to spend the last and next few months single; getting comfortable in my own skin and not cowering behind Frank's shadows. It was definitely what I needed. So I had to ask myself again; *what were Preston and I doing?* Was he just another distraction? If so, it was working. During the day I was with him, happy, laughing, but most nights, I was still empty.

That's what it was. Two people, two friends, comforting one another, making the days and sometimes the nights, easier to get through. With my divorce court date lurking around the corner as well as the possibility of spending Thanksgiving alone my mood wasn't exactly at its best. It was a good thing I had Preston to reel me out of what would have been a forthcoming depression. It wasn't strange that I was meeting with him for the fifth time over a two week period; he was always my go to person when the roads were rocky. The difference was that after our eighth set of plans this one was to be considered a date.

It was almost 7 o'clock when I pulled up to Preston's house. It was chillier than I expected and I could feel the brisk air through my tights. The heels to my boots clicked along the walkway while I made my way to the front door. I probably put too much thought into my outfit since we were supposed to be staying inside, but I wasn't sure what he had planned. *I sure hope he didn't cook!*

I stood for a minute or two before Preston opened the door and stood wearing a crisp, navy blue button down, and a huge smile.

Preston had such a handsome face complete with a pearly white smile. It was funny how I was slowly noticing how attractive he was. He was like a tall delicious glass of Ovaltine.

"Hey!" he said.

I could just fall in love with that voice. So velvety and deep. He was all man. Not an asshole. Not a stalker. And definitely not a boy. A real man.

"Don't you look nice!" he said taking my hand.

Aw how sweet; he noticed, I thought. I still wasn't sure what the tone of our evening was but I was relieved when I didn't walk in to find jazz music serenading me, or the fire alarm going off. But, I was pleasantly surprised when I saw the effort he put into what he did set up.

'Wow this is amazing!" I gasped. In the living room Preston used sheets, blankets, and chairs to make a homemade fort. "You just brought back so many memories," I said while peeking inside. It was complete with the TV on the floor so we could watch movies from inside. I did notice the smell of popcorn in the air, which I credited to the courtesy of the microwave.

"I figured since Halloween was sort of cancelled this year we could celebrate a little late. I got a bunch of horror movies. I thought you would like it."

"Wow, you know me so well!" I said hanging up my jacket.

"Don't worry… I ordered Thai food…"

"Good thing," I teased.

"And a bottle of iced tea for you," he added.

"Aw you're too thoughtful." I said.

We huddled under the tent and started our classic horror movie marathon, while eating Jiffy popcorn, dumplings and coconut fried rice. It was one of the most simple, yet my favorite, date in a long time. It was nice to be spending time with someone who already knew me. Faults, flaws, and all. I didn't have to worry about what he was going to think or if he wasn't really who he told me he was.

I covered my eyes during every other gory scene and snuggled closer to Preston. "I'm such a big baby now!" I said.

"I don't really mind," he said then put his arm around me.

I looked up at him. "What are we doing?"

"Watching 'Halloween Five,'" he said.

"I know that! I mean with us. Is this a good idea?"

My heartbeat quickened and hands suddenly felt clammy. It was hard to ignore my feelings that were getting stronger by the day, and even more so by the second. Suddenly that promise I had made to myself quickly blurred as the heat from his body closed in on me and he stole my breath with one kiss.

I was lost for a few moments in that kiss. It was wonderful and passionate as his soft lips embraced mine. Then I felt his warm hand on the skin of my side. He caressed gently to my back and sent shivers through me.

I gently broke the spell then looked away feeling a bit modest. I looked up at him again and our eyes met, "This is happening really fast..." I said. "I love spending time with you. But I don't know if I'm ready to go beyond that."

"Is it because I'm married? Or does it have anything to do with your husband?"

"No..." I said and wanted more than anything to be honest with him, and tell him that it wasn't Frank who still had chains on me. But I couldn't bring myself to risk him seeing me as just another unfaithful wife. "I know I might seem complicated sometimes... I don't want you to end up getting hurt in my mess of emotions"

"Victoria, it's not a mess. You've always been an emotional, invested person. I know there has been a lot on your mind this entire time we've been hanging out. That's okay. I know when you're ready you'll open up to me. I'm not going anywhere."

I let the movie finish before ducking away for an intermission. I was having a good time, but it was 10 o'clock and I didn't want to risk getting too tired to drive back. I didn't want to end up in his bed.

"I had a great time. It's getting late," I said.

"You're leaving so soon?"

"Yes..."

"You sure you don't want to stay over?"

"I'm sure," I said and quickly combed through my unraveled hair with my fingers.

Preston was close behind me as I gathered my things. He took me by surprise, wrapping his arm around my waist, whirling me back to him.

"What are you so afraid of?" he asked and melted me with his gaze. The deeper we went following our attractions it was hard to go back to seeing him as just a friend. I wanted to kiss him again... I think I may have wanted to do much more than that. That's what I was afraid of. I made an attempt to answer, or turn away or do something other than stare at him, but it was no use. He drew me in closer and I could feel the current build between us.

I sighed and gently peeled away from him.

"Good-night Blinky," I said.

"Wait... I still have to ask you that thing..."

Please don't ask me anything crazy. Or stupid. Oh please don't mess this up. Things are going well.

I looked at him suspiciously. "Okay..."

"I've been enjoying spending time with you and...whatever this is..."

"Me too..."

"Well, I'm going to Paris next Thursday and I was wondering if you would come with me."

"Paris? As in France?"

"No... Paris, Texas. Of course France! I know it sounds insane and short notice but we talked about the possibility of traveling together, I know it was light and jokingly but let's do it. I don't want to lose you again. I'll be gone for a few weeks. Of course there will be a computer where I'm staying and you could work from there."

"Hmm... I wish you would have told me sooner," I said and frowned.

"No? Okay I understand. It was a long shot."

"No, I mean, I wish you would have told me so I could go shopping. Now I have to go this weekend!"

"Wait.... So... Yes? You'll come?"

"Paris? With you? Are you kidding me? Of course!" I said and threw my arms around his neck. Thursday was perfect. It was Thanksgiving and also two days after my divorce, so instead of sulking and spending it alone I would be with Preston in the city of lights.

"Is that excitement about Paris or going with me?" he asked with a flattered grin.

"Both. But mostly going with you," I said then kissed him on the cheek. He turned his head to catch my lips with his.

Then I stepped away from him. "And that excitement..." I said and he knew exactly what I meant, "is the reason why I have to go now."

He gave me a sly smile. "I can't help it. You're so sexy," he said.

"I hope you still think so when you're stuck in France with

156

me."

"Anything can happen. It's the city of love."

"City of light, Preston, Ville Lumière," I said proud to show off my small knowledge of Paris.

"Oh! Excuse me, Ms. French Connoisseur," he said and laughed. .

"Well Mister City of love, I still need some new clothes. Will you join me for my shopping spree?"

"Of course, Mon Cherie. Saturday or Sunday?"

"Saturday. I'll see you then."

I drove back to New York feeling completely elated. Preston and I? On a trip to Europe? Together as a couple? If I would have figured that out 20 years ago boy would I have saved some heartache.

CHAPTER 19

As I strolled into what began to feel like nothing more than an ex's apartment, I promised myself to do something productive. I needed to get out of there and maybe stay in a hotel. It was probably time to turn to another chapter, one that already seemed to have promise.

"Hey, Girly! How's it going?" Britney asked as soon as I strolled into the living room.

"Good. What are you up to?" *Good* wasn't the word to describe it. I felt like I was glowing. Finally. Paris! I was beyond excited and I couldn't even share the news.

I peered over her shoulder and noticed that she was on the Delta Airlines website.

"Delta? Going somewhere?" I asked, being nosey.

"I was just checking something out," she said.

"Oh. Okay."

"Anyway," she said then casually folded the laptop closed. "There *is* something I want to talk to you about."

Story of my life. "Okay."

"So…I finally spoke to Collin…"

Who? Oh yes. *Him.* After such an amazing week with Preston I didn't want to hear his name. I was starting to slowly feel normal. Finally feeling an ounce of happiness. I didn't want to go backwards.

"I have to stop you there…" I said putting my hand up, "whatever it is I don't want to hear it."

"Oh…but…"

"Please, Brit… not now."

"Are you sure? I kind of have some exclusive information," she said trying to win me over with cuteness. It wasn't working.

"Britney, I'm not kidding. I'm still a little upset about the… break up…" Those words were so painful to say out loud. "And I also had one good thing happen, the first good thing in weeks, I really just want to enjoy that right now."

"Alright…" she said and sighed.

"If you asked me this a few days ago I would have been

here like a high school girl, all excited and gossiping. And for what? To be unsure about what he wants or what I want or where we stand? And I know it's not all on him... I know I'm to blame too. There were, and still are, too many obstacles... including the distance."

"Trust me. I know. Remember, I've been right in the middle hearing both sides of the story this entire time."

"So then you know that it's over. I'm letting it go. You should too," I said. "You don't have to be the messenger anymore."

"Okay. I'll drop it then..." she said slightly putting her hands up as if I was pointing a gun at her. "If that's what you want," she added sounding unsure and hesitant.

"Yes. Thank you."

I walked over to the kitchen and helped myself to a can of ginger ale. I wasn't going to pretend that it wasn't nice being in a familiar apartment, where it always felt like home to me, and being in good company. It definitely beat what I went through being alone or, worse, - at John's. I shuddered at the thought before grabbing a shiny red apple from the fruit basket on the counter.

"What did you do all day?" she asked trying to ease the tension in the room.

"Not much. Stopped over to check on my house again... Went to eat. Ran some errands."

"How's the house situation?"

"Not good. There is a lot of damage, well I told you that already. A lot of the town is starting to come together though, slowly but surely."

"Oh. Well that's good."

"Yeah..." I said then sat next to Britney. "While we're on the topic of homes... I should let you know that I decided to stay at a hotel. I'm actually planning to leave tonight."

"Whoa... Really?"

"Yes. I need a change of environment. I'm sure you understand."

"Of course."

"Thanks for being there for me this whole time."

"No problem."

I noticed that she seemed saddened by me news. "We'll still hang out and what not…" I said when I noticed how quiet she was.

"Yeah," she said then looked at the floor before suddenly looking up at me again and asking, "So… who is he?"

"Who?"

"Your new guy?"

"New guy?" I asked, my voice squeaking.

Oh no! She knows. Was it obvious? Maybe I walked in with Preston's scent clung onto me like white on rice. Then again, so what if it was? *I'm a grown woman. I'm allowed to date!* I thought. *But I'll refrain from saying that to Britney.*

I stiffened in my seat. "Why would you think there is someone else?"

"I could just tell. From the amounts of time you've been out. The way you've been acting. And now suddenly wanting to leave."

"It's not sudden. I've been trying to move on, secretly hoping that I didn't have to. But the other night kind of sealed the deal, and staying here isn't helping that."

"I see where you're coming from. So there isn't someone else?" she asked again.

"Would it be wrong if I said there is?"

"I guess not."

I shook my head. It wasn't official that there was, yet. And if there was I couldn't talk to Britney about it anyway. Accepting a trip to Europe didn't make Preston and I a couple

"There's not. I'm trying to focus on myself," I said but of course she wouldn't know that the comment was somewhat laced with an ounce of spite. But it didn't matter because just as I started to put my guard up she casually ignored then changed the topic.

"Well do you think we could at least do something tonight before you go?"

"What do you have in mind?"

"Maybe go for some drinks?"

"Sure. That sounds okay," I said. I deserved a girl's night anyway.

Britney then stood up, gathered her laptop then started to

head to the room. "It'll be fun! Oh and dress nice!" she said as she trotted down the hallway.

"You're always telling me to look nice. Do I usually dress like a hobo or something?" I called out leaving her laughing as she went into her room.

I washed my face and took all my make-up off only to hop in the shower and do it all over again. But now I would apply my dark colors: black eye liner, light and dark grey eye shadows in a smoky eye, and black mascara. And so my face wasn't overly masked with dark colors, taupe lipstick was the perfect touch. My hair was pulled into a low side pony tail with the top slightly puffed with hairspray.

I didn't know where we were going but I knew one thing; Britney was hot. And young. So, if I was going out as her partner in crime for the night I wanted to dress the part.

I was happy to have my short black cocktail dress in tow. The neck cut into a low V-shape and the sleeves were loose and sheer. Most of my shoes were still in New Jersey, so I had to go with black pumps.

Britney was in the living room, phone in hand, taking pictures of herself and getting a head start on the night's drinking.

"Do I look old?" I asked.

"No! Not at all. Wow, you look gorgeous!" she said hurrying to my side. "Selfies!" she said then squished her face next to mine, held up her camera phone and snapped a photo of us.

"You look so cute!" Britney shrieked approvingly.

"I do? Okay good," I said relieved. "You too!" I said eyeing her up and down. "Stunning!" Britney wore a very low cut powder blue dress and white pointy pumps – and no tights or stockings, just her flawless bare legs. "But, won't you be cold?"

"I got a fur!"

"A fur? That's not politically correct."

"In this weather it is!" she said. "Don't worry it's faux fur," she said then laughed.

She handed me two shot glasses filled with clear liquor, of which I only took one.

"I'm hoping tonight is absolutely amazing…" she said toasting to me.

"Amazing huh? What are you getting me into?" I asked as I grabbed my purse, looping my arm through the straps.

"Well, first, you won't be needing this," she said taking my purse from my shoulder and placing it back on the coat hook.

"Uh. Okay."

"And second…" she stood in front of me then dragged the pony tail holder from my hair so the strands bounced loosely over my chest, shoulder, and down my back.

"That's better," she said. "Oh and I kind of lied. We're not going out."

"Britney! I think I could kill you. I put this whole outfit together…"

"That's fine…" she said with a smile.

"So… if we're not going out… what are we doing then?"

"*We* aren't doing anything…" she said then glanced at her phone. She seemed to be doing some major stalling.

"Okay," I said putting my hands on my hips. "You wanna tell me what's going on or…"

The sound of the door opening and closing interrupted my sentence. Footsteps followed from the hallway… then I was pretty sure it was a mirage.

I fluttered my lashes in disbelief.

But, it wasn't a mirage. He was really there. Standing right there in the entrance of the living room. *Oh my God. Is he really here?*

For the first time in almost six months Collin and I were standing in the same room.

CHAPTER 20

It felt like I was in the middle of a Flash Mob and all eyes were on me. My heart was pounding and I didn't know what to say. So I was a bit relieved when Britney broke the tension. Turning to me she said, "I'm sorry but you're absolutely impossible sometimes." She feigned a look of guilt, but it was obvious she was bursting with excitement. She'd had an agenda the entire time; that was no secret, always playing match-maker.

"Thanks Brit," Collin said.

"No problem sweetie," Britney replied. "I'm glad you got here okay," she said giving him a sisterly hug.

"Well… I guess I'll leave you two to talk." She quickly vanished to her room and I could hear the door shut behind her. Now we were alone.

Moments passed without either of us saying anything, just staring at each other, and I couldn't help wondering if I was hallucinating. *Is he really here? My Collin?*

Collin stood with his sensual gaze fixed on me. He seemed to float across the room suddenly, and just like that, it felt like a ghost was there by my side. As usual, I was speechless. To that day, I was amazed by the instant effect he seemed to have on me.

Despite the fact that he'd been traveling for hours, he looked refreshed and vibrant--not the least bit jet-lagged. He sported a casual light grey blazer over a white shirt and relaxed dark denim jeans. His hair was long and neat but just beginning to unravel the way I used to love it. He was gorgeous as ever.

I panicked momentarily. *Wait. How do I look?*

But I was able to breathe a sigh of relief when I glanced down to find myself in a tight, black cocktail dress. *Oh that's right! I'll have to thank Britney for that later.*It seems she'd thought of everything.

Collin was next to me, not saying anything at first, but he didn't need to. Our connection was still so strong, even then after so much time passed, that I could be in the room with him and feel everything he felt. He turned to face me and I could interpret everything his eyes said. Gently he brought his hands to my cheeks, melting me under his intense burning stare, and yet I could tell he was at ease. Serious, but sweet. It's a wonder how I didn't crumble into a million pieces.

"Hi," he said finally. It's funny how something as simple as *hi* can mean so much.

I opened my mouth and may or may not have responded; it was all so blurry.

He brushed the hair away from my face and said, "God, I missed you," then placed a kiss against my forehead.

I closed my eyes for a second, taking it all in. *Am I dreaming?*

"You're here…" I said hearing the confusion in my own voice. I rested my head against his chest as he wrapped his arms around me, surrounding me with his enchanting presence.

I barely found my voice again and was able to whisper, "But…why? What are you doing here?"

"I thought I lived here," he said jokingly, smiling that heart-stopping half smile of his. He brushed my hair back again.

With his touch my eyes closed and I thought back to those torturous nights alone at John's house. I thought about how I prayed all the while just to experience moments like this one again. And then reality seemed to hit me and all these questions came rushing in: *How could he just leave me then come back and act like everything is okay? It's like he fell off the face of the Earth and now he's* **here** *-just joking around? What the hell?* The enchantment was quickly turning into frustration. "I was being serious," I said then gently pushed him away. I gave him my back, suddenly feeling so conflicted about his impetuous presence.

"I'm sorry. I thought you would be happy to see me…"

So did I. I shrugged as I could feel my cheeks dampening from the tears which we're beginning to fall. I quickly wiped them with the palm of my hand, and hoped he wouldn't notice. "I-I am…I guess," I said, not really sure exactly how I was feeling, but not wanting to shoot him down either.

"Well… You don't seem like you are." He stood close behind me and I could feel the warmth radiate from his body and smell his wonderful scent. The same one that clung to his sheets. He kissed the back of my head and ran his fingers delicately down my arm. "Why won't you look at me?"

I imagined this day a thousand times before. But never quite like this. According to my fantasies, I was supposed to have run into his arms in slow motion, the way it happens in the movies. But this wasn't a movie. This was my life. And this one moment didn't erase everything I had come to feel up to that point. Resentment, anguish, excitement, and relief all twirled together creating the most confusing cyclone within. I was trying to swim through an ocean of emotions, and doing so in his unexpected company, I felt I was sure to drown.

"I don't know how to feel Collin," I uttered in a low voice, guarding the words close to me.

Okay, so he's here. What does it mean? Is he even here because of me? Is he going to stay? Are we back together now?

"Just talk to me…" he said in his usual calm and collected tone, which only frazzled me more.

Just talk to him? Sure, because it's supposed to be that easy to talk to someone who I spent months depressed over. No. More like utterly devastated. And I'll admit that I even became a little obsessed at one point. I started to believe that I would never see him again, yet there he was. I'd had a 20-page speech ready in my mind for this exact moment, but when it came down to it, I felt so unprepared. Maybe I never really thought it would come. I managed to remain calm and collected when I was by myself. But now with him standing right there I was a wreck.

I finally ended up blurting out, "What do you want me to say?" I sounded more agitated than I intended to. Seeing him again was amazing, for sure. But I couldn't just forget all the angst that had seemingly become a routine part of our relationship, or rather, lack of one. I wasn't at all eager about the prospect of returning to that pain and confusion.

He moved close to me again trapping my eyes with his. I stared at him dumbfounded as I waited for his next words.

"The other day…you said that you were still in love with me," he said.

I broke away from him, giving myself enough space while I tried to form the right words. I sighed, my eyes glued to the floor so he couldn't hypnotize me. "That was before," I said.

"Before what?"

Before Preston. Wait-huh... Why did I just think that? Is that why I'm so confused? Because of Preston? Surely my new, uncertain feelings for Preston couldn't affect the way I'd felt for so long about Collin. I just said, "Before you dumped me...I don't know..."

"Victoria?" He obviously wasn't expecting me to be so uncertain. "That's not fair," he said defensively then inched in my direction. "It wasn't even like that. What was I supposed to do?"

"I'm sorry..." I said and felt my lungs tighten. *Breathe,* I reminded myself. "Look. We don't talk to each other... and then when we do it's not good..." I said then sighed. All the feelings I worked so hard to bury were resurfacing. "How could you just go to California, Collin? Didn't you ever think about me? Didn't you ever miss what we had?"

"Of course I did—I mean ...I do... Every day."

"You left me. I never felt so empty... So lost. All I wanted was you, and you weren't here!" The memories of being all alone in that hospital made my lips tremble, and it was only a matter of time before the dam holding back a river of tears would break. I couldn't believe everything that was caged inside my mind was now out in the open. I shook my head. "I needed you."

He looked at me with sadness and sincerity as if he could relate to how I was feeling. "I'm here now," he said reassuringly.

"It's too late..." I stopped again but I could no longer hold back the tears. I wasn't about to stand there while I bawled like a baby either. "I'm sorry... I... I can't have this conversation with you right now," I stammered then turned away again, this time attempting to escape.

His hand grazed my arm and instantly I felt the electricity between us. "Sweetie... wait." He grabbed my hand and drew me back to him.

"No," I said, resisting him. "Don't you get it? I tried everything I could to forget you... but look at me." I threw my hands up realizing how insane the whole thing seemed. "Almost six months later here I am... and do you know why? Not

166

because of some stupid storm or because there's a gigantic hole in the side of my house. I'm here for one reason only. Because this was the closest I could get to you, without actually being next to you. I love that your pillow smells like your shampoo. And even if I'm tortured by them, I love the memories... I miss them..." I said but my voice seemed to disintegrate as the mini waterfall of tears was flowing. This wasn't how it was supposed to be. "I know... maybe I'm a mess, but I can't help the way I feel... then I started to realize that you don't feel the same way..."

"Victoria," he interrupted my tangent. "I just flew all the way here..." he said.

"Why? Why did you come?" I asked, almost resentfully. *I already spent enough time entertaining the idea of living without him, but if he left again I would have to start all over.* I couldn't do it. "You can't just walk in and out of someone's life..." I turned around to face him and, completely unsure of how I ended up in his hold, I stared at him in awe. *Be strong,* I told myself over and over, not wanting to completely break down; resisting the urge to give in to him. His arms felt strong and safe as they kept my body close to his. Both my arms were resting against his chest in some half-assed attempt to keep him away.

I couldn't conceal that I was falling apart on the inside as he held me.

"I'm so sorry that I wasn't here for you when you needed me to be," he said sincerely. "I thought you were back together with..." he stopped and looked away as if it was too painful to finish the sentence. He sighed then brought his eyes back to mine. "I just couldn't keep being the other guy," he said. He bowed his forehead to rest gently against mine and dropped his voice as he repeated, "I'm sorry Victoria. I'm so sorry... but my heart has always been here, *with you.*" He pulled my body even closer to his and stared deeply at me, capturing me yet again with his haunting eyes. "I've thought about you every single day—you have to believe me. How could I ever forget you?"

I was speechless. Why did he have to paralyze me with his words? As it was, I was already at a loss for my own.

He continued, "I was thinking about you then and I'm still thinking about you—even right now."

Tears continued to stream slowly down my cheeks as he stole every ounce of life I had left in me. I held onto him so tight afraid he might disappear any second.

There was nothing I wanted more than to feel his lips against mine. And as I stood there wrapped in apprehension and yet somehow enthralled in anticipation, I thought I would collapse from the suspense.

I brought my hand slowly up through his hair. It was so soft. We stared into each other's eyes and I braced every single part of my body. I was beyond ready to feel what every second of five months, two weeks and four days had kept away from me. "So... what are you thinking now?" I asked but already knew the answer.

He held me tighter. Having his arms wrapped around me sent a chill that surged through my veins. Gently tilting my chin upwards he passionately pressed his lips against mine. I fell quickly under his spell again. And exactly what I was afraid to let happen, happened; I drowned in him.

Eyes closed. Time stood still. *Please let this be real.*

CHAPTER 21

I almost felt too weak to move, still convinced that I was living life's most wonderful dream. Making sure he wouldn't vanish I wrapped my hands behind his head still moving my lips and tongue in rhythm with his.

"Are you really here?" I whispered softly, partially opening my eyes to look up at him.

"I think so," he said smiling. My God, *that smile*. It still had the same effect on me. I enjoyed every second of his lips meshing softly with mine. I couldn't believe how easy it was for me to forget all of my recent woes—it was almost surreal.

"This feels like a dream," I said clinging to him.

"No, Sweetie. It's real," he answered, then before I could say anything else his lips were on me again. Oh how I missed the way he kissed me! Only he could do it so perfectly. I kissed him back with everything I had.

His hands traveled from my hair, down my back, but he stopped suddenly not sure whether or not we were treading those waters yet.

"Is everything okay?" I asked.

"It's perfect, I just—I mean—should we talk about this?"

To quiet his concerns I pressed my lips into his. At that moment I was done talking.

I unbuttoned his jacket and ran my hands over the steel of his shoulders and arms to show him it was okay to keep going. "You've been working out," I said in a hushed tone. Then I took in a sharp breath and bit my bottom lip. A little too hard. "Ouch!" I gasped.

"Are you okay – what happened?" Collin asked concerned.

"I—I bit myself," I said sheepishly.

He chuckled a bit, taking my chin into his hand and tilting my head to see if I'd punctured my lip. I felt a little ridiculous.

"You're okay," he said. I lowered my head, embarrassed, but he just laughed and lifted my face up to kiss me again.

"I'm such a dweeb," I said interrupting our kiss, still feeling a bit silly about breaking the moment.

"What's a 'dweeb?'" Collin asked.

"Oh God—I'm old."

"Yeah but you're beautiful," he teased.

"Shut up!" I shoved him and playfully broke free from his grip, retreating to the couch. He came after me and wrestled me down, falling on top of me. I wriggled underneath him for a bit, pretending to fight him off, before he grabbed both my hands and pinned them above my head. I resisted the urge to bite my own lip again and instead playfully bit his.

"Feisty tonight, eh?" he asked, watching me with blazing eyes. We kissed again and I was elated by how our connection was so strong, knowing that nothing could ruin the moment. Still pinning my wrists with one hand, his other hand was free to roam the rest of my anticipating body. I wanted him so badly right then and there. Lying there with Collin on top of me I could feel him hard against my groin and knew that he was just as hungry for me.

"Take me," I whispered.

"I will," he responded with a look in his eyes that was sinfully delicious. He held my gaze as his free hand caressed my breasts. Pins and needles traveled the length of my being as I let out a moan. He released me from his grip for a moment and began to liberate me from the dress I couldn't wait to get out of. He knelt down in front of me on the floor while I repositioned myself on the couch, sitting up and facing him. With him beneath me, he placed his hands around my ankles and moved sensuously up and up until he reached the hem of my dress at my thighs. He paused for a bit, grabbing and caressing each exposed inch of my legs. His hands moved slowly until he reached my hips. Propping myself up I lifted my hips so he could continue his journey to uncover me completely. I raised my arms towards the ceiling in anticipation when he reached my navel, eager to help him. Finally he raised the garment over my breasts, then shoulders, then gently over my head until I was free.

Sitting on the couch with my panties still on and my breasts exposed, I felt very sexy. Collin admired my body for a moment before standing up. He reached down, sticking out his neck so that I could put my arms around him. As he boosted my bottom off the couch I followed his intimation, reaching my legs up and around his torso. He whisked me away into the bedroom.

He lay me down softly on his bed and I unhooked my arms from around his neck. Standing tall but never removing his eyes from mine he unbuttoned his pants, slid them down to his ankles and kicked off one leg at a time. I propped myself up slightly on my elbows, enjoying watching his every move. I ran my tongue over my teeth, taking in the vision of the wonderful bulge in his boxer briefs. He smiled at me smiling at his cock then seductively removed his underwear.

I was now almost face to face with his erection and all I wanted to do was slip him into my mouth. However, he foiled my plan, moving his focus on me, tracing his fingers over the the rim of my lacey pink panties before hooking his thumb into the sides, then moving them slowly down my legs.

"I want you," I said. I couldn't take another minute of him not being inside me. He knelt down on the bed with one knee, propping himself up with one hand beside my head.

I was fascinated by how his body seemed to fit perfectly over mine. Once again he met my gaze, as his bare chest pressed lightly against my hard nipples. The bundle of butterflies in my stomach was so intense. My heart raced erratically. It was as if it was my first time ever.

He caressed my face and stared into my eyes lovingly; I stared back at him.

The moment was perfect... *almost perfect.*

After a short pause, I whispered, "I need to hear it."

"Hear what?" he whispered back.

"You already know," I said never releasing him from my eyes.

He ran his hand across my cheek and his lip curled into a smile. "Victoria, you are my everything and I am so in love with you."

He lowered his face closer to mine. Our noses touched. Our eyes were locked. As his tongue explored my mouth my body responded instantly to his every touch. Finally he penetrated my awaiting body, filling me slowly inch by inch. I moaned softly against his lips until he was fully inside me. He withdrew slightly then sank even deeper in one strong thrust and I cried out. "Oh! Collin!"

"Victoria," he answered, "I've missed you so much."

The reunion of our bodies after what felt like an eternity apart, was overpowering. The stars were drawn out perfectly over us that night. It was meant to be.

With him inside me his hands moved over my breasts and his mouth met with my sensitive nipple. I whimpered as the warmth and pleasure rushed through my being. Our chemistry was undeniable. I almost forgot to breath and when I finally did it came out ragged.

I took his face in my hands and stared deeply in his eyes as he wrapped one hand behind my waist and pulled me closer to him. My bottom lip trembled as I moaned softly. He drew in a deep breath and pressed his forehead lightly against mine as I rolled my hips into him. Our breathing quickened but our bodies hardly moved.

"Baby, you feel so good," he whispered against my ear as we rocked together slowly, perfectly.

The irrefutable, divine sensations of ecstasy began to build. The tingles and waves were more intense than ever. Maybe it was because it had been so long since I felt those amazing feelings. The connection. The spark. He was the last person who had made love to me and there we were making up for all the lost time.

My breathing... my lips... my body... hell, every single part of me trembled under him as he moved in me with a passion that at once melted and electrified me. I was right there, at my peak. He sensed that I was about to orgasm and began to move feverishly inside me, his moans getting louder. I sang along with him delighting in each sound that escaped his lips. He pumped deeper and deeper until I completely lost myself, crying out blissfully as ripples of pleasure crashed through me. Feeling me tighten and release rhythmically around him he gripped me tighter and let out a throaty groan as he came seconds after me. His body collapsed on top of me and I inhaled the sweet smell of his sweat. Turning his face to mine, tangled together, we kissed again and again. There was one thing I couldn't deny. I completely adored this man.

"I love you," I said to him, and felt complete. It was a night that I would remember forever. I had been waiting for this night for what felt like forever, and now I knew he felt the same.

The bedroom was lit by the city's lights. As we lay there in each other's arms, I was trying to sort through the chorus of happy emotions that had emerged. It seemed like all the problems of the world didn't exist anymore. Normally I would have just wanted to cuddle with Collin for a while, but I needed a moment alone to take it all in; to make sure it was real.

I tried to dislodge myself from our entangled embrace, but Collin wasn't having it.

"And just where do you think you're going missy?" he asked, squeezing me tighter. I squealed and giggled as I wrestled against him a bit.

"May I *please* be excused, Sir? I need to go to the bathroom," I said mockingly.

"Hmmm," he looked at me suspiciously. "I guess if it's *just* going to the bathroom…" He released me from his bear hug. I got up from the bed, threw on a t-shirt and walked away playfully sashaying my hips and turning back to see if he was watching, before disappearing into the bathroom. He called out, "Don't try to escape your cute little ass out the window!"

"I won't," I yelled back. "I promise!"

Looking in the mirror, the radiance I felt inside was reflected back at me. I smiled at myself and thought about how I felt like I was in heaven, to be there with Collin, finally. Even after time had passed he was still so familiar. I loved how playful and doting he was. I loved how he was equally serene and sweet. And with that thought I needed to be in his arms again. Knowing that he was right down the hall was an incredible feeling.

Practically skipping from the bathroom, I got back into bed with Collin and nestled my forehead into his neck. Our legs entwined together like vines of ivy, and both his arms swathed around me. I was in heaven, with the faint traces of city sounds in the background.

"You took too long," he said then placed a kiss against my forehead.

"I'm sorry Baby, I'll make it up to you," I said and smiled.

We were quiet for a few minutes listening to the city and the lulling sounds of each other's breathing and heartbeats.

"You okay?" he asked as his fingers ran up and down my arm.

"Of course I am. Why do you ask?" I said stroking his chest.

"You've just been... quiet is all."

I smiled. "I think I'm in shock that you're here. I keep telling myself not to fall asleep or else I'll wake up and you'll be gone."

He placed a soft kiss against my lips then stared at me for a wonderful eternity.

"What?" I asked him softly.

"You're more beautiful than I remember."

You're as romantic as I remember, I said, but only in my head.

"So what now?" I asked staring up at him.

"'Jimmy Kimmel Live'?" he asked.

I playfully pushed him away, and his joking face became a face of loving serenity as he pulled me tighter saying, "Now you sleep, Baby. I'm going to be right here by your side when you wake up."

I responded by giving him a squeeze. There was nothing else in the world that I would have wanted to hear.

I knew that if Collin and I were going to be together, we would have to fight for what we both wanted. And just like that, I was ready to go to war with the world because nothing was ever taking him away from me again.

CHAPTER 22

Collin and I held each other until he fell asleep before me. I quietly peeled from his hold again, hoping he wouldn't wake up and think I was trying to escape. I giggled to myself at the thought, but the truth was I was simply too wired to sleep.

I crept away into the kitchen and rummaged through the pots and pans in search of a tea kettle. I gave up and opted for a small sauce pan. While I waited for the water to boil my thoughts continued to creep up on me.

We can't keep doing the on and off thing. I need us to be on. I wonder if he's back in New York for good or going back to California... we hadn't discussed anything yet and I knew the conversation needed to happen.

It was 2 a.m. and I sat on the balcony with a blanket draped over my shoulders and cup of chamomile tea in my hands. The night was still. The lights of the city were vibrant and alive as ever, but *my* night was serene and still.

I scrolled through my phone which had been in my purse all night. I only had a missed call from some unsaved phone number and a text message from Preston. Over the past few hours my mind was only on Collin, so everything that happened earlier between Preston and I was suppressed. He was confirming that we were meeting to go shopping for Paris on Saturday.

How do you tell a man that you could no longer go with him to one of the most romantic cities in the world? I wasn't looking forward to breaking that news to him. I didn't write back, since it was so late, but I planned to do so in the morning. I tucked my phone away and continued to sip my tea.

"Look at you. The two girls I love the most and don't get to see enough of." I heard Collin's voice call behind me.

"Two girls?" I asked.

"You and Manhattan," he said.

"Yep. I've come a long way, huh," I said, gazing up at the stars. It wasn't so long ago that I wouldn't have imagined stepping onto that balcony with him, let alone sitting out there by myself. I turned to face him and asked, "Care to join?"

"Of course," he said as he sat behind me. "What are you doing out here anyway?"

"Thinking."

"About what?" he whispered against my ear.

"How beautiful tonight is," I said taking in a slow, deep breath; enjoying the cold early November air that said "winter is coming but fall isn't quite over." These moments were the most dangerous, when I felt so comfortable.

"It's perfect," he said as he gently traced over my hands with his, softly stroking my forearms and shoulder.

"I have to ruin the moment..." I said.

"Hmm... Is that possible?"

"We haven't really discussed what happens next. Are you staying in New York now? I need to know."

"No," he said quietly. "I have to go back tomorrow."

I could feel my reaction in the pit of my stomach. The news broke me a little. "Tomorrow? Really?"

"Yes. I have two days off. I spent one flying here and I'll spend the other one flying home."

"Home?" I asked sadly. "*This* is supposed to be your home."

"Well... pre-production for the film I'm working on now is done. We're halfway through filming. This project will be another three weeks."

"Oh... that's not too bad!"

"Wait... I am already on board for another movie. We start in December and it'll be four months."

"Wow. Four months?"

"Closer to three," he said being an optimist.

"Aw, what happened to never leaving me?" I teased trying not to sound too distraught.

"I know. I'm sorry...But... actually we don't have to be apart. I was kind of hoping that..." he said then ran his hands slowly through his hair unable to finish his statement.

"What?"

"I can't even ask you because I don't want to hear your answer... You'd never go for it."

"You were hoping that I would leave with you to California?"

"Yes." His eyes waited for my answer.

"I can't…"

"I knew you'd say 'no'," he said looking at the ground. "I know it sounds crazy but you'd love it. We'd only be there for a few months…"

"Baby, I would love to go. It's not that I don't want to. But, I have court… so I-I can't leave now."

"Oh," he said then processed my words. "Wait… Court?"

"Yes. We're finalizing the divorce," I explained.

"Really?"

"Yes," I said then absorbed what I just said. *Finalizing the divorce. No more Frank. No more obstacles.* Just like that things were coming together.

"Then, I'm really all yours."

"So… you'll come after?"

"Of course! If your life is over there right now then that's exactly where I'll be too. And you know what? I can't wait."

"Me too," he said hugging me tighter.

"Can't you stay just a few more days? Then we could leave together?" I asked hopefully with my eyes wide like a child.

"I'm sorry Baby but I can't. My boss would *kill* me."

"So… You flew here for one day?"

"I needed to see you."

"There's this little thing called Skype…" I teased.

"True…" he said. "But I can't do this on Skype," he said placing both hands on my cheeks. He then melted me with an intense, passionate kiss.

Wow," I sighed.

"Yeah… wow is right," he said and kissed me again and again.

Every single kiss we shared was more electric than the last. "If only they could figure out how to do that on Skype," I said.

"Let's make an app for that."

"Yeah, you do that," I said and laughed softly.

I missed laughing with him. Kissing him. Having him arms around me. And soon I would be missing it again. My mind shifted back and forth.

"How are we going to get through more time apart?" After the words left my mouth I realized my tone sounded graver than I had intended.

"A few days, Baby. Hopefully it'll go fast," he said.

"We have to talk every single day, no matter what," I said.

"Deal. On the phone though, not through text," he demanded.

"Agreed," I said. "Definitely not by text."

"Victoria, I can come for you when you're ready."

"You don't have to do that."

"I wouldn't make you fly by yourself."

"Okay, fine," I said, and smiled at him.

Lying there in his arms again, it was perfect. Emotions that built from a deep place were awoken. Tears streamed from my eyes and he gently wiped them away with his thumb and kissed my forehead. Our renewed relationship truly started at that moment. Nothing could ruin it. After overcoming so many obstacles, we finally had our chance at happiness. They say it's always darkest before the dawn. But for me, the darkness had passed. The sun had risen. Collin and I were together, and everything else had fallen away like wax dripping from a candle.

The universe was finally... right.

CHAPTER 23

Sitting at the breakfast bar, feeling like the happiest woman in the world, I watched Collin as he started to cook for us. He pulled a frying pan from a lower cabinet then removed eggs, milk, flour, and butter from the refrigerator. While cracking an egg into a bowl he glanced up at me and noticed me watching him. He smiled at me, eyes dancing, and I smiled back before he moved to another cabinet to remove the flour.

Being in Collin's apartment without him was a very different experience for me. Now that he was back everything felt complete again.

I set the table as he mixed the flour, eggs, and milk. When he began to whip vanilla extract and powdered sugar into cream cheese in a separate bowl I finally gave up trying to guess what he was concocting.

Despite there being four chairs which surrounded the table, we shared one seat. I sat on his lap while we fed each other. For those 12 hours that we were together we were inseparable. I hoped I wasn't smothering him, but something as simple as sitting a whole chair away sounded too far.

"So, I can book my next flight to come back," Collin said, suddenly interrupting my thoughts. "If you're a hundred percent sure you're coming."

"Um, I'm like eighty seven percent," I said, taking a bite of my delicious cheesecake stuffed cinnamon pancake. There was silence for a moment. "I'm kidding. I don't know why you think I'll change my mind."

"I don't know. I know it's a big move."

"Collin, I'd follow you to Alaska if that means we'd be together."

"I don't know about that."

"Why?"

"Alaska is way too cold so I'd never be over there."

"Oh I don't know...wrapped in warm blankets, lying in front of open fires. I think you'd come."

"I guess you'd make a really cute Eskimo."

"You're always finding ways to woo me aren't you? Feed me like this every day and we'll be just fine," I said then laughed softly. "Well, what if we did Florida next?" I suggested imagining palm trees and sex on the beach…the drink… both the drink, and the physical act.

"Maybe when we're eighty-five and wrinkled we'll get a little house on the beach in Florida," he said.

"When you're eighty-five I'll be like a hundred and twenty," I said and laughed. I wasn't that much older than him but it was so cute how he got annoyed when I reminded him of our age difference.

"Oh don't start," he warned.

"But seriously I think we deserve a vacation."

"Then seriously, where would you like to go?"

"That's easy… Tahiti."

"You've told me that before. You always said let's run away to Tahiti."

"I'm sure I did. That was always my fantasy."

"Why there?"

"I don't know. I guess I've always seen pictures of the little huts over the water and imagined staring out at clear blue water, frozen drinks in our hands while we sit on soft vanilla sand. Quiet and peaceful. *Paradise.*"

"You sound like a travel agent," he said and laughed.

"Alright that's it. I'm not talking to you anymore." I did my best 6-year-old's pout.

He kissed my cheek and turned my head so our lips would meet. "The world's most beautiful travel agent," he whispered.

"Flatterer," I whispered back, between kisses.

Just then Britney strolled into the kitchen swinging shopping bags. I didn't even hear her come in. I wasn't paying attention to anything else but him.

"Aw, you guys are so freaking cute," Britney said and grinned at us. She had her long blond hair flowing freely with curls on the ends, like how it was when we first met.

"Oh look, if it isn't Miss Matchmaker," I said.

"Yup that's me," she said gleefully. "But aren't you glad I did?"

"Yes Britney, thank you. I guess I was being a little difficult," I admitted.

"Don't I get any credit for flying across the country?"

"Nope," Britney said. She started to brew a cup of coffee and removed a Styrofoam to-go cup from a lower cabinet. "Don't worry guys; I won't be in your way. Just stopping in to drop these off." She held up shopping bags from Mac, Nordstrom, Uniglo, and Urban Outfitters.

"If you could, you'd buy the whole mall," he teased.

"Yes I would," she said proudly.

"Leave Britney alone: it's not her fault she's a shopaholic," I said.

"Hmm I guess you're both right...I have a problem. Maybe I should return this matching couple's gift I got," she said swinging a small Michael Kors bag."

"Ooh hand it over." I said excitedly.

She placed the little beige bag onto the table.

Collin and I opened it together and there was a box for each of us, containing matching Michael Kors watches.

"Oh my God Britney...they're gorgeous."

The bands were adjustable gold links, so I was able to slip it right onto my wrist. Diamonds circled the glass of the face. Collin's was identical to mine, only in the men's version.

"Yeah, but it's too much. We can't accept these," he said.

"Speak for yourself," I said jokingly, while admiring it on my arm. I caught a glimpse of Collin's face and thought maybe it was too much. "No... he's right, Brit," I said placing my dazzling watch back into the box.

"Come on guys it's no big deal," she said as she shrugged her shoulders. "Just think of them as early Christmas presents. I love you guys so much!" she said as she her arms around both of us at the same time.

"When I get to Cali we'll make sure to send you a shot glass," Collin said to Britney and she punched him playfully on the arm.

"Whatever!" she scolded.

Any woman would be insecure with Britney prancing around in her miniskirt and snow boots--I never understood the combination--but I was pretty comfortable with their sibling-esque relationship.

"So what's up?" I asked Britney.

"Well! I just found out that I'll be in Miami next month

doing a photo shoot on the beach. So while you're stuck in the cold I'll be sunbathing. Don't be jealous."

"Normally I would, but I'll be in sunny California then, ha ha!" I said.

"Shut up, no way! You are? Oh my goodness—that's so awesome for you guys," She crooned. "It won't be the same here without you though," she said to me.

"Hmm, Vic, would you like to stay instead and keep ole Brit here company?" Collin joked. "You two seemed to be doing fine without me."

"She's my new bestie!" Britney said. "I was about to steal her away from you if you kept dragging your feet in the mud."

"You'd have to pry her away because I'm never letting this one go," he said wrapping his arms tighter around me.

"Do I have a say in this?" I asked.

"I don't think you do," she said and laughed. "You know what—we should all totally go out and celebrate later!"

"I can't--gotta head back today," Collin said.

"When's your flight?"

"Eight-thirty."

"Aw. That sucks," she said.

"Yeah. I'll be back next Thursday."

"Thursday? The twenty-second?"

"Yeah, I think so," he replied.

"That's Thanksgiving," Britney said sounding surprised that he didn't seem to notice.

"Is it? Okay."

"Wait… I can't ask you to come on Thanksgiving. What about your family?" I said.

"Eh… they'll be alright," he said sounding very indifferent.

"Are you sure? Isn't Thanksgiving a big deal?" I asked.

"Um, I think your mom will have a heart attack if you don't go," Britney said.

"I'll talk to her… she'll be fine…" he responded to her then turned his attention back to me. "Besides my next day off would be the next week and I'm not waiting until December to have you in my arms."

"Sounds like they'll miss you," I said.

"But I'll miss you more." The indifference was gone. There was a look, a longing in his eyes, like he wouldn't be denied.

"Well, when you put it that way…" I said and grinned. "I guess we'll just have to order turkey on the plane."

"Wait, no…why don't we do a dinner together," Britney chimed in. "The three of us."

There was a pause as Collin and I both waited for the other to agree first. Something passed between us, some look that seemed to say, "Yes, sure. Let's spend Thanksgiving with Britney." It all happened in a moment.

"Sure," we said together, and laughed. "But we have to do it properly," I continued.

The three of us came up with a traditional menu of turkey, yams, green beans, mashed potatoes, and corn. I was in charge of the apple pie. No surprise, Britney was in charge of the liquor.

"Yay, I'm excited." Britney had no family on the east coast so we were really making her holiday. As for my family, they all seemed to have their own plans. "Awesome, we'll talk more about it later. I have to get going," she said then went down the hall to her room. She was gone for a minute or two before returning in a new outfit and different purse.

"Alright I'm out of here. Have a safe flight," she said to Collin then looked at me, "I'll see you later."

"So we have about seven more hours together. Anything you want to do while you're here?" I asked.

"Hmm … I'm sure we could think of something."

His lips molded against mine and sweet traces of strawberry syrup and cinnamon danced on our tongues. My breathing became shallow as the kiss deepened and I let myself get lost in him for a moment...

Then he got up abruptly and slid the chair back an inch. He stood me to my feet. I assumed that breakfast was over and we would be taking it to the bedroom, but before I could say anything his hands were around my waist again. He gently lifted me up and propped me onto the table.

"Mmm… I'm still hungry," he said pressing his torso into mine. His arms wrapped around my lower back.

"Here?" I asked, feeling my face flush.

"Right here," he said as he nibbled on my bottom lip.

He scooted me forward so I leaned back against my palms for better balance. This gave him easier access to strip my underwear down my legs. The hard marble was cold against my bare bottom. My eyes explored his face, drinking in his features. His expression was both sensitive and intense. He knew what he wanted, and knew I wanted it too. I bit my lower lip, holding my gaze upon his.

Now standing between my legs he pulled my t-shirt over my head and tossed it haphazardly to the side. With my body completely bare I was quickly being consumed with fiery desire. I felt so sexy being displayed on the table for him like a piece of art, *if that piece of art were waiting to be fucked. Wait, did I just think that?*

"You know some of us actually eat here," I scolded playfully, interrupting my own thoughts.

He looked at me amused, but with voracious eyes, and said, "What did you think I was planning to do?"

I certainly wasn't going to object to that.

Before I even had a chance to respond his tongue was already working its way down the little trail of hairs on my abdomen, his hands at my knees. His tongue reached my navel, I gasped. Then it slipped lower and lower across my body, I could feel his hot breath against me. Just as I anticipated his tongue connecting with me, as if breaking an electrical connection, he backed off. *Was something wrong?* I put a hand on his head, but again, he pulled away. I looked down to see him kiss my inner thigh, just above my knee. He kissed again, a little higher. The next kiss was higher still.

His lips brushed against the soft skin, moving oh so slowly along my inner thigh. My fingers were tangled in his hair eagerly trying to pull him toward my sweet spot, but he teasingly resisted. My heart trilled, beating fast as I felt his breath against my skin.

I gripped the edge of the table and threw my head upward as his tongue finally met with the slit of my sex, barely grazing me. My whole body almost seemed to convulse. "Ooh! Don't stop... mmm yes... f-" I bit my lips to stop my outbursts. *What was he doing to me?* I had never been so wildly vocal before. At that moment I wondered what he would think if I started screaming the things that were beginning to build in my head. I hissed and moaned as his tongue, now as eager as my body, began exploring my innermost being, gliding along my lips, teasing before plunging inside me.

He massaged my sensitive bud with his thumb sending more delicious sensations through my body. I was so receptive to his touch. My breathing quickly became shallow; *is the room spinning?* The hardened bud revealed to him how much I wanted him, needed him. I groaned, "I want you."

"You've got me, baby. What do you want?"

"You know what I want," I said with both my words and eyes.

His other hand disappeared from sight and I knew he was holding himself. My mind turned into a parfait of passion, heat, and want.

"Fuck me," I whispered, giving in to the dark temptation inside my head. My lips tingled and I felt like a different person. A naughty one that was letting hungry lust take over my usual poise.

"Say it again," he said encouraging me. *Okay, good, he likes it.*

"Fuck me, baby. Let me feel you."

He positioned his rock hard tool between my legs and I gasped loudly as I wasn't expecting him to fill me all at once. With one deep, sensuous thrust, my body responded in delight at this most wonderful of invasions. I opened my eyes wide, with my mouth shaping an O, as I accepted him into me. He withdrew much more slowly, and I wrapped my legs around him, wanting to hold him inside me forever. His tip barely brushed my lips when he thrust once more, and offered me again that feeling of fulfillment, of completeness; my whole body electrified, every nerve alive and tingling. Again, I resisted the slow withdrawal, and once more, at the last moment, he thrust forward.

"Oh… yes… it's so good!" I cried out as I threw back my head moaning loudly in pleasure.

He slid in and out of me working me into a frenzy with

185

strong steady thrusts. I shifted my weight forward, wanting my hands around his body, holding him as he sank deeper into me. I shamelessly soaked the table beneath me. My muscles contracted, squeezing him tighter, causing him to gasp and shudder each time. Legs and arms wrapped around him, I never wanted the moment to end. I began kissing his face, his neck, shoulders and chest as his pace increased. I felt his fingers dig into my ass, pulling me onto him, pulling him into me. He punctuated each visceral thrust with a grunt.

"Oh my God, don't stop, don't stop. Give it to me. I love having you inside me," *Is that my voice?*

"You're so wet, baby… so wet for me."

"I can't help what you do to me…"

I knew in our hearts we wanted this moment to last forever, but our bodies were ready to explode any minute.

Was it always this amazing? I quickly remembered what earth shattering chemistry could do to one's body. I was trembling as he held me.

"Mmm, Baby…You're so fucking hot…" he grunted against my lips. "Come for me baby…" And he started pounding me harder and rhythmically. Matching his intensity, feeling like I could take it however he gave it, I started bucking my hips into him.

"Yes! Make me come!" I almost begged. Compliant, he continued to drive into me, his hips moving like a piston.

My sounds of ecstasy rivaled his and before I knew it we were climaxing together; the combination of our wet passion forming a delicious mess on the tabletop.

I clung to him, not yet wanting to move as I continued to experience mini eruptions over and over. Finally my body began to sag in his strong arms. We stayed there like that, entwined in each other for a while until our breaths mutually agreed to slow down. He helped me off the table and with my body still buzzing from the electric pulse of his touch, my legs felt unsteady. His hands met with my skin again, the touch sizzling my senses.

"Wow, that was… amazing…" I said in awe.

"*You're* amazing," he said then exhaled. He placed a soft kiss on my lips.

"Come on, let's get dressed. I have an idea," I said taking his hand.

We showered together before getting dressed and heading out. In typical NYC tourist fashion, I decided that first we would satiate our now ravenous appetites with hotdogs at Gray's Papaya, then wander through Times Square, and end up at the factory. I was excited to replicate one of our perfect first dates. Returning to the apartment with almost two hours to spare, we spent the remainder of our time lazing around watching one of my favorite movies, "Hitch."

That evening loomed near and I was dreading it with every passing minute. Before I knew it our time had expired and I stood quietly by the door as Collin prepared to leave me again.

Collin enveloped me in his arms and kissed my forehead. I hugged him back, gloomily.

"When we met, did you ever imagine that this is where we would end up, in love? About to start a new chapter of our lives together?"

"It's really incredible," I said, beaming at him.

"I love you staying here in my apartment," he said, "It makes me feel closure to you somehow."

We stood with my back against the wall, his body against mine. "I'll miss this face," he said caressing my cheek.

"I'll miss you," I said quietly, my eyes fixed on the ground.

"I'll call you as soon as I land…" he said.

I didn't answer. *He can't leave if I don't say bye.*

He gently tipped my chin up. "Okay, Beautiful?" he said looking into my eyes.

"Okay." I gave in, reluctance lingering on my lips.

He cupped my face into his hands. "I love you, Baby-girl," he said then brushed his lips to mine.

"I love you too."

I kissed him one more time.

He took my hand and gave it a squeeze before turning around to walk out. I held on for a few seconds longer before opening my grip letting our fingers slide slowly against one another's until his hand was gone. I closed the door right afterwards because I couldn't bear to watch him walk down the hallway. I didn't want to cry.

It was hard to let him go again. I knew I would anxiously count down the days until I could end my old life and start my new one. Until then.

CHAPTER 24

Waking up alone without Collin's warm presence, and without his arms around me, it was only a matter of time before I'd be missing him – that dreaded familiar feeling. But something else was on my mind that morning --Saturday. I still had plans to meet with Preston. The where and when were yet to be determined, but I was certain that we would meet. This was it. I needed to end things with him.

I knew the news wasn't going to make him happy, and on top of that I would need to tell him I was moving to California. Still, I wasn't too worried about him being crushed either. See, Preston's the kind of guy who always has a lot on his plate. Too much, in fact, to really be concerned with changing relationship statuses. Besides, it's not like he was in love with me. At least I hoped he wasn't. We shared such an amazing connection, that even I was a little confused at times as to why things hadn't gone farther. But at the same time I was okay that it hadn't, and I wasn't at all confused about my status with Collin. Preston and I shared a great friendship, and at the end of the day we both agreed it was the most important thing to preserve.

As it was on my mind Preston sent a text.

Are we still on for today?

Crap. Yes. I wasn't going to stand him up, but the plan would unfortunately have to change. I let him know I was still free, but asked if we could meet for coffee instead. Sure, it's cliché to break up with someone at a coffee shop, but if I met him for lunch then we'd have to drag out an uncomfortable conversation over a meal. No thanks.

We met at the Westside Café and I could tell Preston knew something was up. It seems like men generally have a sixth sense for these things. We ordered our coffees and found a place to sit. Preston seemed to linger a little too long on the topic of how badly folks along the shore were hit with the hurricane, and as insensitive as it sounds, I was annoyed. It was as if he was trying to hide there, so that maybe what I had to say would never find its' way into our conversation. I waited for a lull and took my chance.

"So…" I said.

"So?" he replied, and smiled.

I tried to think of some kind of segue, but I couldn't. How do you go from the massive destruction of hurricanes to: *So… I was thinking we shouldn't see each other … oh and by the way, I'm also moving to California. Sucks to be you, huh?* Damn. My mind began to wander a bit as I considered how to break it to him, and I dwelled on it a little before finally snapping out of it. I wondered how long I was gone.

"I have something I need to tell you," I said easing into the conversation.

"Okay…"

"I don't really know how to say this."

"Victoria, what's going on?"

"I can't go with you to Paris."

"Is that what you're all worked up about?"

Huh? "I'm not worked up," I said defensively.

"Fine. But you seemed… off… since I walked in."

Maybe I was more apprehensive than I wanted to admit about dropping this bomb on Preston. I really had no idea how he would react.

"I'm sorry. I-I hope you're not mad," I stammered a bit.

"No, I'm not," he said.

Whew! *Wait. Why not?* I thought. I was surprised that he didn't ask me for a reason. I was expecting to make some big apologetic explanatory speech. Now he'd made it even more awkward.

"There's more," I said, swirling the stirrer around in my half empty coffee cup. I couldn't stop staring into it, trying to avoid making eye contact with him. Finally I spit it out. "Preston, we're not gonna be able to do this anymore…"

"Do what?" Preston asked, sounding somewhat innocent. He was killing me.

"This… us… this relationship…" I said and the last word came out as if it were a question. *Was that the word for us? Relationship? Oh, it didn't matter anyway at that point.*

"Oh…" he said as his body language stiffened a little.

He was hurt. *Oh no!* That's the main thing I wanted to

190

avoid. Now I felt like I had to fish for an explanation.

"Preston... Let me explain..."

He didn't prompt me, he just waited. *Awkward.*

"Well... I'm going to California for a while..."

"Oh. Is that all?" he said then smiled slightly. "You're so dramatic," he added. "That sounds great! Don't get me wrong I'm bummed that we can't do our trip, but if opportunities are knocking, you have to answer."

I sure did. But I couldn't bring myself to tell him the opportunity that was knocking, was also knocking my boots. How was I to know that Collin was going to reappear out of the blue? So for the time being I chose to omit those details.

Preston was smiling at me. The stoic in him always seemed to find the silver lining.

"Well," he said, "At least *now* you'll have some stability."

"Mmm-hmm," I said, "Preston, I..."

"No worries," he interrupted me, and thankfully so because I didn't really have an end to the sentence I had just started.

"One caveat," he said, "Two really."

"Okay, shoot," I said.

"Promise me we'll stay in touch this time—I don't care if you go to Australia! Okay?"

"Absolutely," I said without any hesitation. "You have my number. And the second...?"

"That I get to see you at least once more before you go?"

"Yes. You got it," I assured him. I wasn't certain I could keep that one. There was so much I had to do before California, I didn't know if I would really have time.

"Good," he said.

I couldn't tell you where the conversation went from there, mostly small talk and reminiscing. I was so relieved to see that Preston's universe had not in fact imploded after hearing my news. I have to admit, I kind of tuned out after that. *Mission accomplished*, I thought to myself.

The café was so close to the apartment that I had walked there. Preston graciously offered to walk me home which, of course, I turned down. I was a bit anxious for us to part ways.

No sooner had I entered the apartment had Britney dragged me back outside. Clearly she was excited, and as much as I just wanted to relax, I couldn't refuse her. She was making sure to milk every ounce of my company in anticipation of my departure to California. I loved hanging out with Britney; she was so full of life.

The rest of the week kept me very busy. I met with my lawyer a few days shy of the court hearing to go over last minute details. Some important phone calls were made to my insurance company to follow up about the damages to the house. Eventually I started to pack what I imagined I would need for life on the west coast.

Not surprisingly, I spent my final Saturday in the city with Britney, walking around scoping inspiration for her next fashion show. It was such a relief when I was finally able to kick my heels off and relax. Heels were not made for walking around the city.

Every evening since he'd left and as agreed, Collin and I spoke on the phone before we went to sleep, and this evening was no different. We usually spoke around one in the morning, which was a bit late for me, but I was happy to accommodate his crazy schedule any way I could. It was hardly a sacrifice—I could never get enough of hearing his sexy voice.

"What did you do today?" I asked as I laid on my back with the sheets swathed over me.

"Worked all day, went to the gym after. What about you?" he asked.

He went to the gym. I bet he got all sweaty as he worked out that perfect body. Then he went home and showered... with soap...and wetness...and—wait, what am I doing? Oh that's right, what did I do today... Fantasizing about Collin could get out of control at times. "I went into town with Britney to look at dresses," I said lazily as I was so distracted.

"Nice... I'm sure she dragged you around for hours," he said and chuckled.

I smiled picturing his smile and even though it was only days since I'd seen him it felt like forever. "I miss you so much I can't even begin to make you understand," I said. My body was aching for his touch. Having only spent two days with him was such a tease. I wasn't physically prepared to be alone again.

"Five more days, Beautiful."

I sighed dramatically. "Yes. I know. Five more days that I have to be here all by myself...

I could hear him smiling and thinking I was adorable, "It'll be okay—"

"—All... by... myself... in *your* bed..." I repeated changing my tone. "In my light blue, silk nightgown...the one you love."

"Mmm, I wish I was there."

I was unintentionally speaking out loud what I had been thinking privately for days, and I stopped myself, suddenly feeling a little timid. The same thought that I had during our passionate moment on the table resurfaced. I was curious to see where this would go so I closed my eyes and went with it, wondering aloud, "Yeah? What would you do if you were here right now?"

"Well... I'd climb into bed with you..."

I closed my eyes and imagined that he slid under the covers next to me, wearing only his boxers. "Go on..." I said.

"I would hold you close to me, kiss you softly, and make love to you all night," he said. I knew what he was going for, but "making love" wasn't enough to quell the lust building inside me at that moment. The way I was feeling... I knew I couldn't wait five more days.

"I don't want you to make love to me..." I boldly declared, my tone low and deliberate.

"I'm listening..." he teased.

I hesitated wondering just where it was that I was going with my bold little admission.

"Victoria?" Collin said, probably wondering where I'd gone.

"Yes Baby, I'm still here." Then I bit my bottom lip for a few seconds and dared myself to say more. "Collin," I paused, "I want you to tell me what you really want to do to me."

He drew in a deep breath and said, "You don't wanna

know what I really want to do with you..." The way he sounded saying that, nothing could be further from the truth.

"Yes, I do... Please, Baby tell me... will you tell me everything?" I kind of pleaded. I was dying to get something started, but I wanted him to take the lead.

"Well first, I would rip that nightgown right off your body," he said.

I took his sexy suggestion as a demand and eagerly did what I was told; removing my nightgown and tossing it off to the side of the bed along with the covers.

"I took off my nightgown, Collin," I said his name suggestively, "But, I forgot to take off my thong..." I whispered, with an air of feigned ignorance.

"Is that right?" Collin prodded me.

"Yes," I declared a bit more deliberately.

"What color is it, your thong?" he asked, clearly wanting me to describe it to him in more detail. I followed his lead with sheer glee. "A slutty...little...black thong," I let the words drag out one by one.

Hearing him take a deep breath on the other end of the phone made me break out in a rash of goose-bumps.

"Hmm ... slutty, huh?" he sounded both amused and intrigued. "I wish I could see your hot ass in that slutty little black thong."

I was pleasantly shocked at the way it was going. I wanted to continue for sure. "What else do you want me to do for you?" I felt a thrill run through my body as the words left my lips, ready to hear the next sexy thing he could think of.

"I tell you what... " He paused, then continued, "Why don't you keep your slutty little thong on for now."

"Okay, Baby..." I said, a tad reluctantly, but only because I was reeling with anticipation. I had started this game and yet I was already beginning to crave the big finish. "What next?" I prompted him to keep going.

"Massage your breasts nice and slow... I know your nipples are hard... "

I followed his directions and drew in a sharp breath as I fondled my breasts. "Mmm... yes, you know they are," I said. The sensation of my uneven breaths, coupled with the sound of his, made my insides jitter. "I'm imagining you, your lips… I can see your perfect abs, and…" I paused knowing what I wanted to say. But I wasn't sure if I should.

"And?" he asked, prompting me to continue.

Oh hell, I'm going for it, I thought. "And your long, thick cock, ready to pound into me…"

"Damn, Babe… Where did you get such a nasty mouth?" Collin said, but he was clearly loving it and that gave me even more confidence to keep on.

"You like it?" I asked innocently.

"Hell yeah!" he responded emphatically.

"Good," I said.

"Well now I'm thinking about putting something long and thick inside your nasty mouth," Collin asserted.

"Yes!" I said eagerly. The throbbing between my legs wouldn't stop so I positioned the phone between my ear and the pillow, and I began to lower the other hand. "Please tell me more. I—"

"Yes?" he urged me to continue.

"May I take off my thong now?" I practically begged.

"No."

I could feel my head swim as I moaned. I was pouting but compliant. I found his denying my request to be such a turn on.

"I like the thought of you lying there, desperate. You're dying to touch yourself aren't you?" He demanded to know.

"Yes," I admitted. *He is so damn sexy.*

He continued. "I want you to run a fingertip, slowly, from your lips…

"Yes?" I asked, awaiting his next direction.

"Down between your breasts," he continued, "across your navel…

Jagged breaths escaped from my chest. "I'll do whatever you want me to do…"

"Through your trail…" he said, stopping just short.

"Uh-uh. I'm completely smooth down there now. I did it for you…" I confessed, and he let out a husky moan revealing how pleased he was to hear that.

"You're so delicious, Victoria. I can't wait to taste you again…"

He paused and I could just barely hear shallow breaths coming from the receiver. I knew he was as turned on as I was and the thought of it drove me insane. "Please keep going," I begged.

Composing himself, his voice got deeper, "Slide your panties to the side, but do *not* take them off."

"Yes?" I waited in tortured anticipation.

"Slowly massage your clit," he ordered and I immediately obeyed.

"Oh God," I said out loud, what was he doing to me? And I knew we were on the same wavelength.

"You make me so fucking hard," he said in a low husky tone. Then he kind of chuckled to himself, and I could just imagine him on the other end of the phone, shaking his head and biting his lip, while holding himself tightly.

"Oh, Baby, I'm being such a bad girl right now… My hand is right between my thighs… I can't stop touching myself…" I was surprised that I so easily confessed this to him.

"Good… that's what I want to hear from you," he said.

"Anything you want…" I completely surrendered to him.

"Grab my cock and stroke it," he commanded.

"I would give anything to touch you right now."

"I know," he said with an arrogance I found irresistible. "Me too."

I continued, "I want to get down on my knees for you..."

He moaned gruffly. "Yes Baby," he said pleadingly, "Suck me."

Two simple words were never so explicit: *suck me*, I imagined him saying again while I was on my knees in front of him. I knew that he was just holding on – waiting for me to keep going. I couldn't believe the language that was unapologetically spilling from my mouth, but I couldn't stop myself. "Don't come yet, Baby…" I said.

He moaned.

"Not before you take me into the kitchen..." I said. "I... I can't stop thinking about it..."

"About what?" he asked imploringly. He knew damn well what I meant!

"You know..."

"I want to hear you say it."

"You fucking me on the table! I felt like such a... like a slut..." I finally said. *Who the hell was this woman! And where had she been hiding all this time?* "But I loved it... I wish you were inside me right now..." I felt electric as each bold statement spilled free.

"Take off your thong and bend your ass over that damn table right now," he barked at me. I knew his passion was mounting.

"With pleasure." I complied, happy to remove the soaked piece of soft mesh material.

"Spread your legs and take my hard cock," he ordered.

"*Mmm!*" I let out a loud moan as I imagined him entering me roughly. My eyes rolled so far back into my head I thought I would go blind. "Oh Baby, I wish you were really inside me... right now... fucking me hard... making me scream!"

"Put my fingers in your mouth and take me" he directed. I closed my eyes tighter as my fingers disappeared deeper. I pictured what it felt like. What he felt like. I imagined him penetrating me deeply from behind and reaching around to muffle my cries with his fingers in my mouth. I would have sucked them as vigorously as I would like to have sucked his hot tool. I was throbbing and frantic with the need to release. "I wanna come, Baby," I begged. "May I please come?"

"Oh, you want to come – huh?" he teased.

"Yes..." I moaned struggling to hold back.

"Tell me again—tell me what you want!" he said, the base in his voice getting louder and deeper. Usually the sound of a man yelling at me made me panic, but this was so different.

I couldn't take it anymore. "Please!" I screamed, "*Please* let me come!" I circled my clit vigorously with my now drenched fingers.

"I can just feel your body shaking, as I go

deeper...stroke longer—burying my dick inside you..." he continued to tease me.

"I wish I was on top of you right now, facing away so I could grind you... and grind you... Baby, I would grind you so fucking good..."

"Fuck... Babe..." his voice quavered and I knew I had him right at the edge. "I want you so bad..." he whined.

I took the lead, mad with lust, "My sweat dripping all over you, while you hold my hips tight and watch my ass as I roll onto you..."

"You're so sexy... I'm gonna come...," he told me; his voice shaking.

"Oh... I'm so close too..." I whimpered, "I want you to tie me up...pull my hair and pound into me harder and harder until..." My fingers moved furiously under the sheets as I said anything that came to my mind.

"Go ahead Baby... Come. Come for me," he finally said.

"Come with me..." I was barely able to say. I held out momentarily for the sound of his groans 'till I knew we were in sync with one another.

"*Oh... Victoria!* "I loved the way he groaned my name.

"Oh...my!" My orgasm swept through me, cutting my words short as I couldn't hold back anymore. We were both panting and grunting as we released together. Ecstasy's spell took over and my body trembled wonderfully while I squealed against the phone.

As my strained breathing eased I opened my eyes a little disappointed to find myself alone, but the satisfied feeling had my body feeling electrified.

"Wow. I can't believe we just did that," I said quietly as I slowly came back to earth.

"Baby... you're incredible, I swear," he said with his words equally as serrated as mine. "You surprise me every single day..."

"I really surprised myself," I told him.

"Oh yeah?" he asked with curiosity.

"Collin, I've never felt so free with anyone before—until you. It's you..."

"I love you," he answered. "You can always be free with me."

My heart melted with his words. "I love you too," I said. We both exhaled deeply, with the memory of our moment hot on our heels, and the immense love we felt for each other fresh in our minds.

"So..." Collin said, "Do I really get to tie you up or were you just saying that?"

"You can do anything you want to me, Baby. *Anything.*"

"I'll be there tomorrow," he joked. "Nah... I wish could though..."

"Me too," I said and closed my eyes wishing I could fast forward through the next week. Past the trial. Past everything that kept us apart. *Five more days...* I kept telling myself, and then began to zone out.

"Baby?" I heard Collin ask softly. "You're not falling asleep are you?"

"No," I lied. I wasn't exactly ready to hang up yet, but sometime shortly afterwards I fell asleep with the phone still to my ear, and my thoughts heavily revolving around "Five more days."

CHAPTER 25

One more day, I thought as I woke up. I just have to get through this one horrible line up of a day. Driving into Jersey, meeting with my lawyer, facing Frank … I wanted everything done with and to have the band aids ripped off, so to speak.

A black blazer, black slacks and white blouse were suitable for the day. I never wanted to get something over with so much in my life. It was the one outstanding obstacle that stood between my true love and I. Not to mention the tedium and embarrassment of the entire situation. Court. Who woke up excited to go to court? Definitely not me.

To my surprise, I arrived at the Hackensack courthouse nice and early. Unfortunately I was unable to find my lawyer or the court room where I was supposed to be reporting to, and not realizing that I wasn't allowed to park at the bank I had to run out and move my car.

As I came up the steps a second time and was running behind schedule, a voice shouted at me. "Victoria!"

I knew it instantly. I spun on my heels and spotted Brooke.

"Brooke?" I asked with surprise.

"Yes!" She answered loudly. "Did you think I was going to let you go through this alone?"

Yes, I actually did. I mentioned to Brooke where and when my appearance was but she never gave me a response so I didn't expect her to show up. We really never talked, not compared to how our relationship used to be.

It hadn't hit me that I hadn't seen her in months until now, when I noticed a drastic change in her appearance. Her hair, formerly long and beach-blond, now resembled cranberry sauce, and was chopped in super short layers that just barely touched the middle of her neck. She had gained weight, but instead of clinging to her belly or thighs in an unsightly mass, the extra pounds filled out her figure in a flattering manner. Less flattering was the gold ring looped through her left nostril and the several smaller ones that lined her right eyebrow. Even the look in her eyes was different somehow, but I couldn't put my finger on what had changed there. Her appearance was definitely something for me to take in, but I was still happy to see her after so long.

"Brooke... Honey... you really didn't have to come," I said hugging her.

"I know I didn't have to Vic, I wanted to," she said.

"Um, you look... different."

"I know. It was time for a little change," she said simply.

My little sister was dressed in a green ¾ sleeve crop top with black cargo pant. Not appropriate for court but I didn't want to pick on her the first time we were together in months. Even though she went out of her way to be there for me, I felt guilty wishing she hadn't.

"I... I'm late Brooke," I said. "Or I will be... but I think there's some room where I get to consult with my attorney pretrial first. I'm pretty sure you can come with me for that."

"Okay," she said. "So what's up?"

I didn't want to start going into everything that happened since she and I last spoke, but I didn't want to walk silently to the other side of the courthouse either. "Well, I told you already that my house was damaged in the hurricane."

"Yes, you did," she said.

"I was actually house hunting before that. Guess who my real estate agent is?. Preston James. I just saw him a few days ago actually," I said as we headed up the stairs, "Remember him?"

"Oh my God," she said, "I haven't thought of him in so long."

"Yeah, we've been hanging out again." Or we *were* hanging out before I dropped the bomb on him. Who knew what would become of our friendship after that, despite the promises we made to each other.

"Hanging out huh? No one invited me," she said jokingly.

I laughed nervously. Nobody really needed to know about Preston and my short lived fling, especially not while Collin and I were getting back together. "It was unexpected. I think you and I have a lot to catch up on," I said.

"What does that mean?" she asked giving me a suspicious look. "Wait! Are you and Preston fucking around?" She said this loud. Or maybe it sounded loud to me since it seemed to echo through the open space of the court house.

"Brooke! Jeez... no! And keep your voice down," I said then desperately looked around hoping that nobody important to my case was near us.

"What's wrong with you anyway?" I asked annoyed when I realized that she couldn't stop laughing. Suddenly, it was obvious what had changed in my sister's eyes.

"Brooke... are you okay?"

"Yes, I'm just peachy why?"

I gave her a weird look but I couldn't put my finger on it. She wasn't herself. I almost even thought that she was under the influence of something, but I wasn't sure what.

What the hell had happened to Brooke? Was I so caught up in my own world... and in Collin's world? Had I been neglecting her when she needed me? Was it a quarter-life crisis... or had we just grown that much apart?

"Maybe you should wait outside..." I started to say then my focus was reverted.

I saw Daniel Greenburg, my lawyer, waiting right inside the front entrance. Neither Frank or his attorney were present. Maybe they were already in some little room on their own consultation. Daniel motioned me toward a door in the hallway, a dossier already in his hand. As we walked and Brooke followed, I explained her presence to Daniel.

"My sister," I said.

"Ah," he said. "Daniel Greenburg," he said as he extended his hand to Brooke.

"Okay," he began. "So, the good part is this is a no fault divorce…"

"No fault?" Brooke interrupted while looking at me. "Is this dude serious?"

"On paper," he said firmly, shutting her up. "The main focus here is division of assets. That's what this trial will be about. Both we and they have submitted on paper how we feel things should be divided. Nobody is going to get exactly what they want, it will split in the middle, but, how much it goes by our favor, or theirs is what the testimony will decide. Now, I know your husband's attorney, Mike Jackson, and the judge, Robert Dylan. More good news is everybody is going to keep things to just the facts."

"Wait," Brooke said. , "So technically we're going to be in a court room with Michael Jackson and Bob Dylan? That's hilarious."

I saw Mr. Greenburg admonish her with a look.

"Brooke. You should go for coffee or something… I'll be okay…really."

"Not a chance. I'm here for you in case shit gets crazy."

I ignored Brooke's brash comment and turned to Mr. Greenburg. "So, I just need to say the facts, right?"

"Yes," he replied. "And I will step in and object if any line of questioning is inappropriate".

"What if I'm not sure how to answer a question?" I asked.

"I've been doing this a long time," he replied. "But, just pause and make eye contact with me, and I'll throw you a lifeline."

Whatever. As long as this was over, I was a professional person so I liked to think I knew what to expect.

"Is everything else here correct?" he asked as I reviewed the paperwork.

"Yes. I think so."

"Do you have any other concerns?"

"No. Let's just get this over with," I said. I wasn't being completely truthful, but I just wanted to wrap this episode up quickly.

As we entered the courtroom, we had to pass by Frank and his attorney. He wore an expensive suit, nothing out of the norm. His thick black hair was slicked back with gel.

"Frank," I said to him with a nod. *See, I can be cordial... even to you.*

He grabbed my arm, not hard, but enough to stop me so that I made eye contact with him.

"Victoria. I know... I know that..." he lost his thought, "This is a mistake, we shouldn't go through with this."

What? You were the one who served me. On the day of the fucking hurricane. You were the one who...

I didn't end up saying any of those thoughts that were welling up in my head. Mr. Greenburg came in with his promised rescue.

"Mr. Carlisle," Greenburg said, "You can say whatever you want to my client when the judge addresses the two of you."

I sat on one side of the courtroom with my lawyer and Frank sat on the other. I turned around and Brooke gave me a thumbs up and goofy smile. I looked over at Frank again and he glanced at me. We made eye contact shortly again before I looked away. God, this is an absolute nightmare! I would rather be anywhere else than here.

Then my mind wandered for a fleeting second. Wondering what my love was up to in California. Knowing that when this was all over we could really be together my tension eased a bit. Then my name was said in a serious tone and the best second of my day was over.

Greenburg was letting me know that the judge was approaching the bench.

Judge Dylan appeared nothing like his namesake. He looked pretty no nonsense, with eagle-like eyes staring from between a prominent nose and a thinning head of gray hair.

Inside I was fuming. I knew I could get it under control though. I had to regain my center while the attorneys made opening arguments. Greenburg went first. It was much more civilized than how these things were on TV. When the opportunity came for Jackson to stand up, he was silent for a moment. He looked as if something was wrong.

"Permission to address the court," Jackson said.

"Is there something you want to mention other than your opening argument, counselor?" asked Judge Dylan.

"My client would like to reschedule," Jackson said.

"Why is that?" asked the judge.

"To attempt reconciliation with his wife," said Jackson.

"What?" I said, loud, indignantly, and with fire.

All eyes were on me for a moment for breaking the protocol of the court, but Greenburg stepped in again.

"Reschedule of this hearing for attempted reconciliation is not valid unless my client agrees," said Greenburg.

"That is correct, Mr. Greenburg," said the judge, "And does your client agree?"

He looked at me.

"Why are you even looking at me? Of course I don't agree. Would I be here today if I wanted to be married to this man for another second?"

"No, your honor, she does not," Greenburg said quieting me down. "We would like the motion denied and to proceed with testimony."

"Agreed," said Judge Dylan, "Though Mr. Jackson still has opening arguments."

"There is one more thing," said Jackson, "Opposing counsel's asset list is not in total agreement with ours. Permission to approach the bench?"

"Yes," said the judge.

Eternity passed in that moment as the judge took the paper from Jackson and reviewed and scrutinized it.

"There is mismatch," said the judge. "We'll need to adjourn and postpone."

"For when?" I asked out loud, still visibly angry.

The judge did not scold me for breaking protocol, but answered me. "That date will come in the mail, Missus Carlisle," he said sternly. "I can tell you it will be after the holidays at least, in the early part of next year."

"No," I said. "No. He's up to something. He doesn't want to reconcile. We need this done today. Not after what I've been through."

"Mrs. Carlisle…" the judge started to address me but the anger inside me overshadowed my sense to be civil.

"Why are you doing this? There is nothing left for us Frank!" I yelled across the courtroom.

"If you don't compose yourself I will have you escorted out," Judge Dylan threatened.

"How could you tell me that I'm stuck with him? I hate that man and I can't spend another day married to him."

"Mrs. Carlisle! Order in the court," he said interrupting my outburst with a smack of his gavel. "This is your last warning."

Two burly bailiffs drew near to me intimidating. "I could walk myself out, thank you," I said leaving my lawyer to deal with the mess. It was the best thing for me to do to save the embarrassment of being dragged out because I knew I couldn't hold back what I wanted to say.

I sat on the bench just outside the courtroom doors. I waited a few minutes before Mr. Greenburg exited the courtroom.

"What the hell was that?" I asked looking at my lawyer desperately.

"Everything seemed clean and simple until he changed his mind. However, having outburst like that in the courtroom isn't going to help anything lean in your favor either."

"Sorry it's just not right. He's always trying to find ways to screw with me."

Just then Frank and his lawyers walked out of the court room.

"What the hell do you think you're doing?" I demanded.

"We'll talk later," Frank said brushing me off.

"No! Can't you just let me move on with my life?"

"Everything you said back there… that's who I used to be. Like I said, we'll talk privately."

"Did you hear what I said? We will never be together ever again! *I hate you*. Please just sign the damn papers. Let's just end this. I don't care about the money." I didn't. I just wanted to be free, free from the chains that so-called marriage.

"I have to go," he said.

"Don't you dare walk away! If you think I'm going to change my mind you're crazy!"

"Ma'am we need you to lower your voice." I was scolded again by an officer in the corridor.

"This is such bull shit," I muttered as I stormed down the corridor and used a different exit.

"What was that about? I thought everything was settled?" Brooke was standing by the entire time. She didn't make any more crass remarks.

"So did I..." I said. All I saw was red as I stormed toward the elevator.

"What are you going to do?" Brooke trotted along with me, keeping up with my hasty pace.

"I don't know," I said. "Anyway I don't want to talk about this anymore. How are you doing?"

"I'm... good," she said sounding a bit too unsure.

"Thank you for coming out here," I said as we walked to our cars. "Are you okay to drive? I could drop you off..."

"No, I got it," she said and continued small talk as she walked me to my car.

I was so livid I don't remember most of what else was said, but she had to be somewhere and promised to call soon.

As I walked into the apartment, I saw Britney was watching TV. I crept quietly to the bedroom, got my shoes and slacks off, replacing them with pajama pants. Then I draped my jacket on a chair, and normally wouldn't have walked around half dressed like that, but I was in an equal state of internal and external disarray. I plopped on the couch next to her.

"Well?" said Britney raising an eyebrow.

She was hoping to hear me say it was done with. I wished I could say so, as well. I don't know what I should have said then. I don't know if I should have told the truth.

"It's finalized," I said. "The judge will mail his final decision on the division of property".

The only thing that was finalized was that I had a cover story to maintain now, and hope I could maintain it until I could turn it into the truth. And how was that going to happen when I was supposed to be in California at a time I was obliged to be in court in New Jersey?

"That's awesome. Should we celebrate?" She asked.

"Maybe another time."

"Oh. What's wrong? You don't seem too happy about it."

"I'm just exhausted." I really didn't feel like talking, but I needed to buy myself time to think.   "What   are   you watching?" I asked her.

As she explained her T.V. show to me my mind went somewhere else. I thought it was finally my turn to be happy. I desperately wanted to know: *When will my dream finally become a reality; and my nightmare become the past?*

CHAPTER 26

Dawn.

My life wasn't perfect, yet, but at least the day started with
possibility. It was a relief-- after months, or was it years, of the
day breaking with that feeling of inevitable doom. I didn't really
know if I was finally happy again, or if I was just normal. I
didn't care. Release. Unburdened. Lifted weight. That's how I
felt.

I wasn't sure why I'd agreed to meet Collin in Central
Park instead of at La Guardia when we he returned to New
York. His flight arrived in the morning and I wanted nothing
more than to greet him at the airport, but he had other plans.
He made me wait impatiently at the apartment for further
instructions.

Central Park is... okay, I guess, I thought as I changed
my outfit five times, hair style three times, and couldn't quite
get my makeup right. I was definitely nervous. My nerves had
been on edge since I walked out of the courthouse. I gave very
little details to Collin when he called to ask me about the
hearing. I didn't want to lie to him, but I decided it was best to
simply omit certain details. The divorce was essentially final.
Well, it would only be a few months until it was.

I finally received a text message from Collin, despite our
phone calls only rule; he wanted to make sure I had our exact
meeting location. The message read:

Hey Beautiful, We are meeting near the entrance of the
park on 14th Street. Take a taxi to the corner of 14th and CPW
then walk in by the tulip garden. Let me know when you get
here and I'll walk over and meet you. I can't wait to see you!

His message put an instant smile on my face. I hastily
retouched my makeup and looked at myself in the mirror. I still
questioned my outfit of choice; a long sleeved olive colored
shirt, dark denim jeans, an ivory peacoat, and chocolate brown
combat boots, but I didn't want to wait a moment longer. I
wrapped my burgundy scarf around my neck then headed out.

I had another "fun" cab ride on my way there. No, Mr. Cab driver, I don't need a receipt. No, I am not single. No, I can't pay in cash, but I can tip you in cash. If you don't want me to use my debit card to pay you, don't have a machine in the back of your cab that allows me to pay with my card. Besides, you almost killed me on the way here, and I was busy enough thinking about Collin and… everything… and everything… and though you couldn't possibly know it, your story about how awful the tourists treat you was really distracting while I was already trying to make sense of the thoughts in my head. *Oh the joys of the city.* I couldn't get out of that cab quick enough.

The driver let me off at the corner of 14th Street. I walked down the sidewalk to an alternate entrance to the park then double checked my message to follow the directions. I stopped a few feet into the park, not far from the tulip garden, near the first park bench then dialed Collin on my cell phone.

"Hi. I'm here," I said after he answered.

"Okay. I'll be there in five minutes," he said.

"Okay." My voice was small. My heart was racing. I shifted from one leg to the other, placing my hand on my hip then flat against my side, wondering how I should stand. *Do I look okay? Is my hair flat? I should have worn my navy coat instead…*

You would think I was meeting the President, the way I felt. Maybe it was a good sign that Collin still gave me butterflies to that very day. I waited exactly what he said --five minutes -- when I saw him on the path that was paved with orange and purple fallen leaves. My heart felt like it lit up in my chest. I tried to play it cool and resisted the urge to leap over to him. When he took me into his arms I hugged him tight and kissed him eagerly as if I hadn't seen him in years. *So much for playing it cool.*

"Babe, I'm so happy you're here!" I said as I held onto him.

"Me too," he said simply. "Here, these are for you." He handed me a beautiful bouquet of orchids.

"They're beautiful," I said.

"I picked the color combination myself," he said.

I knew he meant it. He hadn't delegated the task to a sales girl, and he wanted the credit for himself.

"Should we walk?" I asked, still unsure of what we were doing. "What exactly did you have in mind? Why couldn't we meet at the apartment?"

"Don't you worry your pretty self about any of that… Just follow my lead," he replied, and he linked his arm into mine.

He had it all planned out, so I deferred to him. As we walked, to our left were children running around with their parents and nannies in a playground. And to the right was an assortment of people enjoying the activities of a brisk fall day. A young, attractive woman wearing tights as pants and an equally tight top, which hardly held her chest in place, jogged by. I caught Collin's glance to see if he'd notice her but he was so distracted in his own world. I felt relieved that he hadn't looked at her, but still a bit anxious because I didn't know what we were doing.

"Oh yeah… Happy Thanksgiving!" I said happily. "I almost forgot."

"Happy Thanksgiving," he said and smiled briefly then continued to move on.

Hmm. What's wrong? Is he upset that he isn't with his family on Thanksgiving?

"How was your flight?" I asked trying to get some conversation out of him.

"It was quick. No stops or delays," he said. We continued to stroll then he turned right where the rows of benches ended and the path split.

"Oh, that's good, right?"

Okay, that was a dumb question.

"Yep."

"How was the airport?"

Another dumb one, what's wrong with you Victoria?

"Completely empty."

"Hmm okay," I said but still smiled.

I hope he's not bringing me here to break up with me…Wait…that wouldn't make sense at all. Would it?

"So…" he said.

Oh no! That was the same opening I used just before gently letting down Preston. I pulled over to a new row of benches, under some trees in the full of their autumn color, fretfully trying to reroute the conversation I was afraid would take place.

"Wow the trees here look amazing right now," I said as I stopped to admire the scene. "Don't you just love autumn?"

I looked over at Collin who was glancing at his watch. I nudged him gently. "Don't you think?"

"Uh huh..." he said but I wasn't convinced that he even knew what the question was.

"Um... Okay..." I said getting a bit annoyed.

"Come on... we should keep walking," he said.

"Fine," I muttered. "Hey... Are you alright?"

"Me?" He sounded surprised. "Yeah. I'm good. Why?"

"I don't know. You seem..." *Distracted* I said again in my mind then realized that I didn't want to start our first day overanalyzing everything. For a walk in the park, Collin seemed so concerned about something. But, maybe he was just tired from the travel, I concluded. "Nothing," I said, dropping the matter.

During our walk, when he wasn't being extremely quiet he was talking about the weather. Specifically the temperature, winds, and that he was glad it didn't rain. Collin was not a small talker. Even when he was on an elevator ride with a stranger he found something relevant to talk about. He only made small talk when he was nervous. I wasn't the only one who was feeling that way.

We suddenly slowed down and he tried to position his body to hide where it was he was leading me, but I saw he was headed to the launch point for hot air balloon rides.

"Oh, Collin... that's incredible," I said. "Are we watching them launch?"

"Yes we're... watching," he said and put air quotes around 'watching,' and I soon knew why as we walked closer to the boarding point.

"Whoa. Wait a second," I said, letting go of his arm. "I know you don't think *I* am riding in one of *those!*"

"Oh my love, I don't think you are... I know you are," he said and his confidence was back.

"You go ahead. If you come back in one piece I'll

think about it."

"Nope, we have to go together."

I looked at him inquisitively.

He continued to explain, "We're starting our day in a way that you'll remember for the rest of your life. It's like the weight of what we've been through since the day we met was lifted and this is our new beginning."

"So... it's symbolic..." I said feeling some sense of obligation to go along with him.

"Exactly."

Then I realized that I couldn't possibly do it. I pouted at him. "Can't we just watch and pretend we're floating away in one." I said trying to get out of it.

"Nope," he said shaking his head. He then clasped my hands gently into his. "It'll be amazing, I promise. You won't regret it," he said with this look in his eyes that I couldn't deny. He was the one person in the world who had the ability to get me to push the forbidden red button. I really would have done anything for him.

I held his hand and rubbed the top of his hand with my thumb a little. How could I say "no?" I smiled, hiding my reservations and said, "Okay."

The group before us prepared to launch, so we stood there waiting to speak with the pilot and his co-worker. While we waited I stared at the grounded balloons in amazement. There were two that had a traditional red, blue, yellow, and green, striped design. One was yellow with colorful '70s looking daisies printed on it. One had an all-American design complete with the white stars and all. Then there was my favorite; a purple, white, and baby blue striped one. Collin stood behind me with his arms wrapped tight around me. He was so quiet again.

"Which one?" I asked him turning my head to the side so he could hear me over the noise of the balloons that were inflating and getting ready to take off.

He kissed me on the cheek then also looked up at all of them. "Which one are we riding?"

"Yes."

"Hmm... the purple one," he said as if he had

213

guessed.

"Really?" I said and smiled. "I like that one the best."

"Yeah, I know," he said. We were summoned over by a staff member.

The operator told us the ride would be about an hour, explained some regulations to us, assured us we were safe, and I think even briefly told us how ballooning and counter-ballast weight worked... but I couldn't take it all in as I was mainly focused on Collin.

At last it was our turn to board. I took a deep breath as my nerves went sky high. "I can't believe you're making me do this," I whined, but couldn't help smiling as it was a super romantic date idea. He stepped aboard first then extended his hand to me.

As I stepped into the basket I found yet more surprises. Rose petals lined the basket interior as well as an arrangement of breads, cheeses, fruit and wine. I couldn't hold back from a gentle kiss on his lips. This seemed to relax him a little. I knew he had set this up for me and that it didn't just come standard with the ride.

He didn't seem upset when a second man besides the pilot got into the basket with us. *Maybe these things have a minimum?* I wondered.

I held on tight as we gradually lifted higher off the ground.

It felt surreal to watch Central Park slowly diminish in size while at the same time looking larger than ever as we could see more of the park, more of the city. It was breathtaking.

I caught Collin noticing me more than the view. He smiled and then resumed watching the city float away with me.

I heard an unexpected noise and was startled for a moment before I realized that the noise I heard behind me was a violin. The other passenger was a violin player. This whole day had been constructed by Collin down to the last detail. For me.

"You planned all this for me?"

"I wanted this day to be perfect," he said while combing his hand through my hair that blew wildly in the wind.

"It is!" I sighed happily and put my head on his chest.

I closed my eyes and smelled the air for a moment.

214

When I opened them, he was dead fixed on me. He was getting ready to speak and had the look of a man who was about to cross the Rubicon. He paused for a moment.

"What is it?" I asked.

He started off serious. "In my life I've had a lot of unforgettable, happy memories…" he said, and when he knew he had my undivided attention he continued. "Three of them I remember perfectly. The first one is when I was eight. I was in Little League, during a game. The bases were loaded… we were down three points. I hit a grand slam… won the game… It was like in the movies, I swear you could even ask my mom."

We laughed together momentarily before he went on.

"Then… there was the day… *actually a dark and stormy night*… I shared a kiss with the most beautiful woman in the world. It was under some desk during a black out *or something like that*," he said in a lighthearted tone, then smiled at me.

"Yeah, that was a pretty memorable night for me too," I said and smiled back. "And the third?" I asked, completely intrigued.

"Well, that one begins like this. I walked into a jewelry store because I wanted to get something for you. I was thinking something simple like a bracelet, or earrings. Then as I told the saleslady about you … your laugh, your eyes, and your smile… I realized that what I feel for you is more intense, more real than anything I ever imagined I could feel for anyone. It's anything but simple."

My throat tightened and I swallowed hard. I wanted to interrupt him and tell him how much I loved him too, but I couldn't even speak.

"I know the feeling isn't temporary, it's something that I'll have with me forever."

I finally found my voice and said, "Babe, I feel the same way about you too."

"I want to create a million more happy memories, I don't care if we're in New York, Jersey, Cali… hell I'd freeze in Alaska with you… as long as I'm with you every second of the way."

I thought he was being his usual sweet self, telling me the kinds of sweet things I loved to hear.

"Victoria, there are so many things I've been unsure about or second guessed in my life, but not this. Not you. When you're in my arms I feel like I have the whole world." He looked me deep in my eyes and took my hands into his. "Victoria, I don't know where the road goes from here but let's travel down and find out together, you and me...forever."

I completely froze. *Did he just ask me to marry him? Or is he about to? Oh. My. God.* My thoughts weren't moving fast enough. I suddenly noticed that he had a small white box in his hand. My mouth dropped as he knelt down onto one knee, my hand still in his. He opened the box and exposed the most amazing ring I'd ever seen; propped upright, in the center. Two smaller diamonds on opposing sides of what looked like a one karat diamond sparkled on a white gold band. Clustered on each side of the smaller diamonds were three pink sapphires.

My own question was answered, but I still had to answer his.

It was so unexpected...So fast. What was the rush? *Yes, Victoria, he's really asking you to marry him! This is what he wants! But wait, is this what I want?* I wasn't even officially divorced yet, but he didn't know that and I was glad. My brain said "maybe," but my heart said "yes."

"Oh, Collin..." I gasped clasping my free hand over my mouth.

"Victoria, will you make a million more memories with me? If you let me, I will dedicate the rest of my life to being the husband you deserve."

The air around us was cool. The balloon lifted even higher as the wind engulfed us. Looking at Collin, so sincere and right there, fully invested in me, I was reminded of how lucky I was, and how lucky we were to be together. When we were apart I wanted nothing more than to have him back, and I finally had what I wanted. Why would I ever want to lose him again? We simply couldn't live without each other. I couldn't hold back the tears that built in my eyes as I realized what I was agreeing to.

My final answer matched that of my heart. I chose happiness.

I nodded slowly, still in shock. I took his face in my

hands, kneeling on both knees in front of him. "Yes," I whispered then smiled as more tears escaped.

"Yes?" he repeated, almost in disbelief.

"Yes," I said again more audibly this time so that the operator and violin player could hear. "Yes, I will marry you! There is nothing I could think of that would make me happier than to be your wife."

His face lit up. Collin took the ring from the box and gently placed it on my finger. It was a perfect fit. The diamonds soaked in the sun and reflected the rays outward. My whole hand glowed, but not as much as my heart.

I believe in all of our time together, this was the happiest I'd ever seen him. Our lips met and the moment couldn't be more magical.

It *was* what I wanted. It was all so sudden, and scary, and intense, and that's what made it *perfect*. It felt right. My life instantly went from a pain filled nightmare to the most romantic dream ever.

When I finally realized that I was wide awake and everything was real I gathered my bearings and we stood up.

I wondered how many New Yorkers actually heard Collin from the ground as he shouted, "The most beautiful woman in the world just agreed to marry me!"

We laughed together and I was so relieved to see that he was completely back to his normal cheerful self.

"Okay, so now I know why you were so nervous earlier," I teased as he held me kissing me all over.

"I wasn't nervous!" he protested.

"Whatever you say," I said and thought he would respond with some smart comment but instead he tickled me until I surrendered to him.

We were both at ease or maybe the word was *"elated."* We enjoyed the remainder of our balloon ride in each other's arms. I could feel his heart beating steadily against my back as he held me. I couldn't stop looking down at my hand in admiration.

"I hope you like it," he said against my ear.

"I love it! It's…"

"I love you," he said, and then kissed my lips.

217

I adored my ring and more than anything; I adored him. What else could I think about? As he promised, it was a day I would remember forever. And there it was -- my perfect dream life began.

CHAPTER 27

It was the morning of my last day on the east coast. I was nervous and excited all at once. Flying was not my thing, but that was only one of my many worries. I hoped that Ashley and Nick would be okay with me so far away. Not that Nick would notice, but the threatening note was still in the back of my mind. Thankfully nothing strange had happened since then so I felt more at ease about being in California. It was so early that the sun wasn't even up yet. Collin was getting dressed and looked amazing as usual shirtless and his hair damp from coming out of the shower.

He climbed into bed and rested his head on my pillow. "Come on, Beautiful, we have a long day ahead of us," he said stroking my cheek.

"I know," I said then closed my eyes while I absorbed the reality of it all. "What time is our flight?"

"Nine."

"Ugh... sooo early!" I complained groggily. "How are you even up right now?"

"Because it's three in the morning over there. By this time I'm already heading to work."

"Yeah, I get that. But how are you up after last night?" I said then stretched my arms out and wrapped them around him. "Five more minutes, Baby," I muttered like a child who was trying to avoid going to school. I pressed my head into his chest. I was being lazy but I couldn't help it. It was perfect just being there with him as the dim morning sky let in a mild blue hue. I needed those few minutes to relish before entering the prismatic madness of the city's daily morning turmoil. Collin hugged and kissed me over and over, and I couldn't imagine peeling away just yet.

"Wanna make that ten?" he said suggestively, his hand trailing up my bare thigh as he kissed my face and chin.

I pushed him away playfully and said something I never thought I'd say to him. "Not now, Baby... You'll have me too exhausted."

"You don't have to do anything..." he said as the kisses

219

trailed to the side of my neck.

"As tempting as that sounds..." I said, escaping from his hold.

"Fine... you're right," he said then hugged me for a few seconds before he rolled away from me then stood up.

I caught sight of his muscular chest, toned arms, and chiseled six-pack. His hair was a mess because of me. Because of the night before. And of course when I saw the massive bulge protruding beneath his boxers I couldn't contain myself.

I reached over and grabbed his hand pulling him back to me. His body collapsed over mine and he placed one hand on either side of my head. We shared a moment and looked deep into each other's eyes. Our lips met and that single kiss managed to wake the animal inside me.

Suddenly my breathing was ragged as my chest expanded against his.

"Mmm... just... can't... get... enough..." he teased, the words staccato between kisses.

"I can't help it," I said pulling his body closer to mine, arching my hips into his. "You're so damn sexy..." *And you're all mine.* The thought drove me wild.

He wrapped his arms under my back and pressed his torso into mine. "You need to make up your mind, Love, a few seconds ago you pushed me away," he said.

"Yeah, well... that was before I got a little preview..."

"Maybe I'll give you what you want..."

"Maybe huh?" I snickered and bit at his ear lobe.

"You know what I liked... hearing your sexy voice begging me the other night."

"Oh you're using that against me? Cheap! That's not happening today," I said as he planted kisses along my jaw line, my face in his hands.

"Come on..." he persuaded.

"Unh-un," I said then bit my bottom lip seductively. "You want it as much as I do."

"You think so?" he said taking my words for a challenge.

My body was aching for him to touch me. As soon as his hand grazed my inner thigh my whole body trembled. His palm ascended until meeting with the heated desire between my legs.

I squirmed against him as a finger sank slowly inside me, my eyes widened.

"Mmm... You're always so wet..." he said as juices trickled down my inner thigh.

A moan involuntarily escaped my lips as a second and third finger teased and tormented me. My body got a wonderful taste of the incredible fullness and what was to come.

"Does that feel good?" he asked with such a delicious dark temptation to his voice. I was soaking the sheets as I waited for him to ravish me.

"Yes..." I breathed, my answer was so obedient. *What did he do to me?*

He withdrew his fingers leaving my body empty and wanting to be filled. He spread my legs wider with his and kissed me deeply before sinking his erection into me slowly, inch by inch as I sighed for more.

"Oh... yes..." I moaned as my muscles clenched instantly. Reflexively my hips leaned toward him for more as he withdrew slowly.

"That's all you're getting," he said leaving me writhing beneath him.

I sighed with frustration. "No...Baby..."

"What's wrong? You want more?" he asked circling his head around my entrance as I desperately arched towards him, my legs shaking.

"Yes..." I whispered; my vocabulary down to that one word which dissolved from my tongue as I gasped it.

"Damn ... Look at you," he said running his hands all over my body, up my sides, over my breasts. My body arched and quivered to each touch. "You want it badly... You're just a little slut aren't you?"

My head was swirling from both his words and actions. So he hadn't forgotten my little confession. *Boy what had I started?*

"Yes, Baby..." I whimpered.

"You love having me deep inside you."

"Yes... I-I love it..."

"Tell me... If I like the way you beg I'll fuck you hard and let you come," he said then devoured my mouth with his. My tongue wanted more. My body wanted more. I was a helpless puppet and he had every string wrapped tight around his fingers.

"I'm so wet, I need you...." I wasn't as boastful as I was over the phone.

Still hovering over me he slid an inch of his cock into me then left me empty again. I whimpered to the torture. He was enjoying every second of watching my needs rise as I panted and squirmed beneath him.

"Fuck..." I said throwing my head back in frustration.

"You know what I want!" He was in complete control. His hand ran up my side over my breasts and he squeezed hard making me whimper to his touch.

"Please..." I said, giving in. "I want it," I pleaded. "I want to feel all of you," I said clenching to him.

"That's my girl, beg for it. Beg me to fuck you," he growled into my ear. I was pinned so tight under him and couldn't move if I wanted to.

"Please... please give it to me..."

"You could to better than that," he groaned.

"Baby, you said you'd fuck me hard and make me scream. I need it now! Please! I'm gonna go crazy."

"Oh I will," he said. His arrogant tone drove me wild. "But first... tell me you're a slut."

Oh, that word was so small but so powerful. What an admission! I was thrown by the person I was becoming, but at the same time I was thriving on it. I loved it. The words fervently poured out of my mouth. I would have said anything—done anything.

"Yes, yes, I'm a slut. I'm a slut for you...only for you. I want you inside me..."

He seemed pleased and rewarded me with a passionate kiss. My tongue found its way into his mouth kissing him back greedily. He locked his arm behind my knee bending it, exposing my sheath to him. I cried out against his lips as he shoved roughly into me. I wrapped my free leg tighter around him and grabbed his ass pulling him closer to me.

Our bodies moved perfectly at a quick, frantic tempo, as the heat and tingling built inside us. Sweat glazed over our bodies, beads trickled across our foreheads.

Each of our rocking motions made my muscles clasp around his shaft which continued to swell inside me. Pleasure charged through me like a thousand volts running though our bodies.

I was moaning like crazy, my volume ascending with each thrust deeper than the previous one. Then I gave up on trying to keep quiet. No longer muffling my noises I screamed out gloriously every time he slammed into me. I screamed his name followed by strings of expletives as well as words that tried to make their way out but were cut off by my own cries of pleasure.

"That's right… you know how I like it, Baby…" I was finally able to utter, no shame, no holding back. I never knew of the filth I was capable of. "I love taking your whole cock inside me," I screamed.

His body trembled with my exclamations. He absolutely loved it too. "Sexy ass. You're gonna make me come if you keep doing that…" he grunted against my ear in an unsteady, breathy tone.

"Do it…" I said finally feeling like I had some control. "Baby, I'm so close…" I whimpered losing my words halfway through as euphoric pleasure took over my body. As his length was squeezed by my contracting muscles I could feel that he was in sync with me. "Oh… Yes… come inside me…" I sunk my nails into his back as a powerful orgasm consumed us. I sang with bliss, pulsating around his throbs as he emptied inside me with long drawn out groans. If any of the neighbors were trying to sleep they definitely hated us at that moment.

I panted heavily feeling like a rung out towel as I lay limp under him. We held onto one another while we descended from our cloud.

"Beautiful girl…" he said kissing my lips, still out of breath. "You're so perfect."

I smiled at him with dazed eyes, brushing my fingers delicately though his hair.

"You're amazing," I said. "I don't know what you do to me!"

"Yeah," he said through his sexy half smile. "I never knew you could be so…"

"Colorful?" I asked and we both laughed.

My heart slowed down and my eyelids felt heavy. I rested my head against his chest and my eyes began to flutter shut as I listened to his heart, which was still beating erratically. I wanted to fall asleep in his arms then I started to come back to sanity. *Fuck! Don't we have a flight to catch?*

CHAPTER 28

"Sweetie, Can't you shower later? We have to get going!" Collin called from the room as I ran the shower water while brushing my teeth and washing my face.

"Easy for you to say... you got to shower!" I said rushing into the room to grab my makeup bag. I wanted to be nice and fresh if the TSA search was really as up close and personal as I heard.

"You should have just come in with me," he said taking me into his arms kissing all over my face.

"Do you really want to make this flight?" I pushed him away playfully.

"Good point," he said.

"Don't worry. We have time, I'll be quick," I said back to him.

"I swear you're going to make us miss our flight," he said.

After what felt like a two minute shower I rushed an outfit together, pulled my damp hair back, and then stared at my suitcases. *Wow, am I really doing this?* The thought shook through me quickly but was dissipated by the pace of the morning.

Collin grabbed my bags and brought them by the door while I checked one more time to make sure I didn't leave anything behind. I figured I could always do some shopping over there if I needed to. Toothbrush? Check. Shampoo and conditioner? Check. The eagerness to spend a few months across the county away from everything I knew? Check, almost.

Of course I couldn't forget that beautiful ring that fit perfectly on my left ring finger. As soon as I was completely dressed, make-up and hair done, and as ready as I was going to be we headed down to the lobby.

Ian helped us hail a taxi and load our suitcases.

"Good luck you guys. Be safe!" He sent us off with a friendly smile.

"Thanks Ian," I said. I stepped into the cab and of

course the driver eyeballed me. I rolled my eyes at him. *What is it about me and cab drivers?* I thought, but decided to cuddle close to my man and ignore the ogling cabbie.

It was 7:45 when we arrived at JFK airport. Collin paid the driver then stepped out and took my hand. "Come on Babe, we have to hurry."

"We're *not* going to miss the flight! We have plenty of time," I assured. At least I thought we did. I took his hand and followed him as we walked through two large glass doors that slid open. We printed our boarding passes at a kiosk, checked our bags, and then waited on a long line that wrapped around roped dividers to get through security. My phone began to ring while we were on line. I got a quick glance at the caller ID and read Frank's name across the screen. Knowing that I had no interest in talking to him, not that early in the morning, and not really ever in general, I rejected the call then shoved the phone back into my pocket.

Collin stood behind me with his arms around me as we approached closer to the metal detectors and two security workers. We placed our phones and wallets into a bin that slid through an x-ray machine, took off shoes and belts, and fussed them back on. I had to throw out a mouthwash container I thought was travel size but was apparently too many ounces over the fluid limit.

It seemed like forever but we finally got to Terminal D and surprisingly had a few minutes to spare. We watched through the large glass as other planes took off.

I was too geared up to relax so I stood at the large window and continued to watch people file into their planes, workers loading the checked bags, and planes roll down the runway then disappear into the sky. My daze was interrupted by my phone.

Frank was calling. Again. I ignored it but when he called a third time I accepted that the responsible thing to do was answer, in case he was calling about the children or house.

I took a few steps away further from the seating area then picked up the call.

"Um…What's going on?" I asked somewhat concerned and equally annoyed.

"Victoria, we need to talk," he said in a grave tone.

"Well... what is it? It isn't really a good time..." I said then stopped as a loudspeaker announcement temporarily drowned out my voice.

"Where are you?" he asked, obviously hearing the noise in the background.

"Is there some kind of emergency or are you calling to interrogate me?"

When he had no answer I knew he was only calling me to get under my skin.

"Please don't call me again," I said and hung up. I was still angry with him for pulling that stunt in the courthouse.

Collin stood from where he was sitting and lightly placed his hand on my arm. "Everything okay?" he asked concerned.

"Yup. Telemarketers," I said simply. I didn't think he was buying it but I stuck to my lie.

I turned my attention back to the planes outside. We watched one that was heading to Vegas taxi out. He gave me a squeeze and I knew he was thinking the same thing I was. Eloping to Vegas would be so cute and so us. Unfortunately, I was still legally married and I hoped that secret would remain nothing but a small inconvenience until it could get taken care of. There was no point in ruining the fun we'd been having discussing our wedding which already had 65 potential guests, both a live band and a DJ, a four tier butter cream cake, an ice sculpture, and CDs with or own handpicked playlist as favors. I hated keeping my secret from him, but I wasn't going to let Frank be the cause of ruining yet another wonderful thing for me.

As Frank crossed my mind as well as the thoughts of how he tarnished everything for me I received a text message that said "There is an emergency."

"Boarding flight one fifty one to Los Angeles rows one through ten," the voice over the PA system said.

I glanced down at my boarding pass. That was our flight. Our seats were in row 32.

"I'll be right back," I said to Collin.

"Wait," he said lightly grabbing my arm. "Our plane just started boarding. Where are you going?"

"To get some water."

"They have water on the plane, Babe."

"I know... but I...uh...want to take a quick walk before we go. I'll be back in two minutes."

"Okay..." he said skeptically, "Hurry, though."

"I will," I said then kissed him quickly before trotting off. I kept a smile plastered on my face until I was far enough out of sight to quickly deal with Frank's nuisances.

I looked over my shoulder before returning his call.

"Frank, what is it?" I asked impatiently.

"A simple hello would have been nice..."

"Are you kidding me? Is there an emergency or not?"

"Not exactly. I had to say something to get to you listen."

"Ugh... I told you I don't have time for this..."

"Look, I'm simply calling because we need to meet to talk. In person."

"No. We don't. If you have anything you want to discuss you can have your lawyer contact mine," I said and knew I sounded a bit harsh.

"That's no way to be with your husband, now is it?"

"Ex-husband, Frank."

"Technically we're still married."

"Yeah, I know. Don't remind me. And I don't know what that was all about but I don't care, I'm not buying it. If you're stalling because of money, or property, or whatever reason you're wasting your time."

Flight announcements blared over the speaker. A flight to Dallas also began boarding.

"I knew it. You're at the airport aren't you? You better not be trying to go anywhere."

"What the hell do you care where I go?"

"I don't like your attitude," he scolded.

"Do you think I give a shit what you think?" *Oh my God why am I still on the phone with this jerk?* "Goodbye..."

"Wait..."

His plea stopped my anger fueled action.

"Don't hang u," he said.

"What?"

"I don't know where you're trying to go but we have court

coming up…"

"So? Let me worry about that."

"Damn it, Victoria!" He started to sound agitated and I was at my wits end with him. I already wasted too many years of my life with his nonsense.

"*You* filed for divorce then you retracted in court and now you're trying to track my every move and asking if we can meet? I don't know what you're trying to pull but just know that you and I are done. Period."

"Listen, you can act tough all you want over the phone, but this isn't over. Keep hiding. Go ahead you can't avoid me forever. I would love to see if you hold up to your tough girl act in person."

"I'm not scared of you anymore," I said.

"Yeah, I've heard that before from you. Do you remember what happened every time? Oh those were the good times," he said sadistically.

"Go to hell," was the only thing I said before ending the call. As I hung up on him I could feel my nerves pricking through my skin. It still haunted me, as if I was going to get it when I went home. *He doesn't control you anymore.* I reminded myself but still felt like I was going to suffer the consequences. I exhaled as tears of frustration grew. I quickly whisked them away then felt a tap on my shoulder.

"I'm sorry Babe…" I said as I turned around expecting it to be Collin. I stopped midsentence as soon as I looked up and realized that it wasn't. *It was Preston!*

"Uh… Hi… Preston?"

Things sure as hell were not going my way.

"Hey. Victoria! What's wrong?"

"Oh… Err, nothing," I said looking away and drying my eyes again with my sleeve. "What are you doing here?" I asked then glanced down at his briefcase. *Traveling, genius.* "Wait, never mind, dumb question," I said then quickly walked deep into the store that was closest to me, now nervous that I was going to end up in an awkward situation if Collin did come searching for me. I figured he would any moment since they called rows 10 through 20 while I was wasting time letting Frank harass me.

"Yeah… the Paris trip…" Preston said, somewhat

awkwardly.

"I remember."

"I missed my flight yesterday… so here I am. And what about you? Are you sure everything is alright?" he said indirectly referring to the phone call.

"It's nothing. Don't worry," I said then aimlessly strolled around the store trying to find a way to shake off Preston. "I'm flying out today too," I said as I pulled a bottle of Poland Spring from the cooler. "Right now actually… I'm kind of in a hurry."

"You here by yourself or…"

"No…" I trailed off leaving my answer vague. "But, I have to get a move on if I'm going to catch my flight…" I said as I handed the clerk a 20 dollar bill.

I took my change and walked out wanting to head back to my gate but Preston was now attached to my hip.

"So, you going to San Diego? Los Angeles? San Fran?" he asked. His interrogation was annoying me.

"L.A.," I answered quickly.

"Which gate are you? I'll walk you."

"No!" I said with a little too much enthusiasm. "It's fine. Thank you."

"Are you sure?"

"Yes," I said and again the speakers overhead called my flight again rows 20 through 30. *Damn, they're moving fast.*

"Shit, that's me and I need to go to the ladies room," I said making a sharp left. Preston walked me right up to the entrance.

"Have a safe flight," I said hugging him in a rush.

"You too," he said as I ducked away to escape.

I hid in the bathroom for a minute and hoped he wasn't waiting for me when I walked out. I washed my hands, counted to 30 then at this point I really was rushing out. Preston was nowhere in sight. I looked over my shoulder as I jogged back to my gate and crashed directly into someone. It was Collin.

I was so relieved to see him. "Oh thank goodness it's you…" I hugged him tight.

"There you are… where'd you go?" he asked obviously worried.

"Water," I said holding up the bottle. "Then the

restroom…"

"Okay…" he said.

"Let's go," I took his hand and headed for the gate as they called rows 30 through 40.

He stopped me in my tracks and held me gently by my shoulders. "Victoria, wait. Are you sure about this? Because… well… if you're having second thoughts or…"

"Baby, please shut up. You're going to make us miss our flight," I said, then smiled at him afterwards so he knew that everything was okay. Because everything was. Frank had me a little shaken up for a moment but I had to learn not to let him get to me anymore. I was safe now.

"Boarding passes?" The woman at the podium said to the elderly couple who were ahead of us.

I reached into the back pocket of my jeans, pulled out my folded pass and grabbed my phone so it wouldn't fall out. It started to vibrate then went to voicemail. I didn't realize that since hanging up on Frank I had accumulated five missed calls.

"Boarding passes and identification please," the pleasant looking young lady said to us, but I just stared blankly at her. My mind was stuck on my phone and the calls and the threats. It was going to continue as soon as we landed in California. The universe was throwing obstacles at me.

I let go of Collin's hand and backed away a few steps. "Uh. I'm sorry. One second."

"Ma'am, they're going to shut the doors," she warned.

"I know," I said, *but this has to be done.*

"Victoria, what are you doing now?" Collin asked me but I ignored both of them as I stared at a waste basket. I took a deep breath then dropped my phone into the metal can. And then I exhaled. *Now I'm ready.*

I rejoined Collin's side and handed the woman my pass. She was looking at me like I was insane.

"Thank you, have a safe flight," she managed to utter.

"Uh… Babe…"

"Yes?" I asked naively.

"You do know that you just threw your phone in the garbage… right?" Collin asked me as we walked toward the plane.

"Yep."

"Um. Why…"

"Shh… don't ruin it."

"Alright," he said dropping the subject.

We walked through a little carpeted closed in area before stepping onto the airplane where we were greeted by a cheerful flight crew.

My heart starting picking up pace. My first time flying. Leaving the only home I'd ever known. Being thousands of miles away from my family. As these thoughts raced through my mind Collin and I found our seats.

"Take the window so you could see everything," he said letting me in first.

"Thank you," I said.

The plane was full and despite the rushing it still seemed to take forever before we actually started to fasten our seatbelts and review the safety procedures.

"Nervous?" he asked glancing over at me.

"A little." The feeling of my heartbeat was strong against my chest.

"You can still turn back. Until they lock the doors. Then you're stuck."

I looked up at Collin and as he gazed down at me, I knew I was right where I was supposed to be. Looking deep into his eyes I said, "I'm not going anywhere, my Love."

He kissed me and took my hands into his as we waited before the plane finally began slowly taxiing into the runway.

"We're going to be fine…" he reassured me as I held his hand tight.

"*Of course*. I'm with you."

There were two planes ahead of us. Before I knew it we were next.

Then just like that we were defying gravity. We were in the air then soon in the clouds. My ears popped furiously, but when I swallowed hard it helped.

"Wow, I'm so excited," I said as I watched the ground shrink below us.

"You are? Good, I have to admit that I was getting worried."

"No, we're fine," I said and knew that it was mostly true. "You have nothing to worry about.

From the day we met Collin and I had to struggle to be together. I didn't expect this day to be easy. The difference was my determination to not let anything come between us. Not even my own secrets and lies. I had very little reservation about leaving the East coast behind us as we literally flew into our new life.

CHAPTER 29

Despite leaving New York at 9 a.m., when our flight landed on the west coast it was only 10a.m. We were in the air for at least three hours. Trying to do the math had my mind spinning. The time change was going to be the first of many things I needed to adjust to.

"This is a little weird. It's like we were only on the plane for an hour," I said to Collin as we stepped into Los Angeles airport.

"You think that's weird... wait until we go back to New York. It'll feel like we were traveling all day," he said taking my hand into his.

"I can imagine," I said.

We walked over to the baggage carousel and waited for the belt to turn on. A few minutes later a variety of luggage began to roll out. After spotting each of our bags, then grabbing them from the revolving belt, we headed outside. Cabs lined up eagerly waiting to heave tourists to their destinations. I noticed unlike JFK, in LA private cars outnumbered yellow cabs.

California initially looked like ... I would never say this out loud; but an overcrowded city. The area immediately around LAX felt like an exaggerated busy city, but as we headed onto the thruway in the little black town car we'd hailed, the main thing I noticed about LA was that there was no central city. There was a downtown area with a skyline, but LA seemed like several smaller cities joined by sections of freeway and highway. This was my east coaster's impression having been on west coast soil less than an hour. It was warm, but fairly dry; the famous California weather I'd heard so much about from Collin and Britney. I was excited with the idea of seeing the desert with my own eyes. Maybe I'd even look at stars out there with Collin. I briefly remembered what Preston said about desert being the best place to see the stars.

I looked around when I noticed we were suddenly at a total stand still. The car had stopped on the highway as if we were in a parking lot.

"Welcome to LA," Collin said jokingly.

I smiled and squeezed his thigh. Though it seemed like forever, eventually traffic did start moving again. Plus, I managed to find another positive: The taxi driver didn't hit on me once. That was a nice change. The traffic was annoying but it didn't bother me because I wasn't in any rush. I was happy regardless of where we were; we actually made it to California together. In my mind Collin and I had beaten the odds.

We were finally dropped off at an apartment complex about 30 minutes from the airport. We started to walk down a path leading to the main gate when Collin stopped first at what looked like the complex's main office. He told me to wait outside with the bags then he ran up a flight of stairs so he could get his mail.

I waited for him and looked around, enjoying the mild weather. I eyed my surroundings already trying to familiarize myself with the area. A little shopping center seemed to be in walking distance but I couldn't quite make out what stores were there.

The trees looked so different and tropical compared to New Jersey's, but not what I imagined Florida palm trees to look like. These LA palms had shorter branches and a much puffier look.

As I continued to scope the view, a young dark-haired guy around Collin's age suddenly approached me. He immediately came off, to me, as a surfer type. I felt bad for already judging Californians.

The surfer kid scanned me from head to toe. "Well hello there…" he said.

"Um … hi," I said shortly. I sighed, annoyed, then I reminded myself not to be rude to the natives. *Maybe he was just trying to be friendly*, I thought, Californian hospitality. Was that even a thing?

"So … Did you just land from Tennessee?" he asked glancing down at my bags with an exaggerated grin.

"No. Why do you ask?"

"Ah, I just figured… because you're the only ten-I-see," he said then laughed hysterically at his own horrible pick up line.

"Wow…" I muttered under my breath. I rolled my eyes

then gave him my back as I tried to ignore him.

"I'm sorry Baby, if I'm coming across as rude…" This kid was still gawking at me with his steel blue eyes. "Your body is cream of the crop and I absolutely need to know your name." He wouldn't give up.

Just as I was ready to tell this kid that I wasn't interested, Collin came down the stairs towards us. I knew he heard the last comment made by this other guy and he was not amused. Then it became obvious that the only reason he held back from lunging at the kid was because he knew him.

"Bro, chill out…that's my girl," Collin said shortly, standing close to me as if to claim me. "Sorry Babe, don't mind my rude co-worker," he said to me then shot a warning look to the kid, who wore a Hawaiian t-shirt and shorts despite it being the end of November. His olive complexion leaned a bit on the orange side and it was obvious that he overdid the tanning beds. All he was missing was a surfboard.

"Oh… my fault," Surfer boy said slightly backing off.

"It's fine." I attempted to let both guys know that there were no hard feelings but I was quickly cut off.

Collin positioned himself between me and the other kid. "Babe, I got it, just give me a second." He obviously didn't want me interacting with Surfer, so I took a step back and kept quiet.

"I'm just saying I didn't know this classy lady was spoken for," Surfer said changing his tone.

"Yeah…" Collin said being somewhat forgiving but still very irritated. "Anyway, what are you doing here?"

"Hey! Relax. I'm here doing *you* a favor…"

I found it to be a ballsy comment coming from the kid, given what just happened, but I realized it wasn't out of character as he continued.

"These are from yesterday." He held up a heavy looking metal case. "I just got off set so I figured I'd drop them off to you. You're welcome."

"Okay. They're for which shoot?" Collin ignored Surfer's sarcasm.

"Sunday. Call time is six a.m. And. don't lose these… there's a couple thousand dollars of film in there."

"Will do."

"Yup. Guess who won't be there tomorrow… yours truly," he said and grinned. "I'm heading to Cancun for a week. But not before grabbing a few drinks at the Starlight."

"Of course…" Collin said as if this wasn't news to him.

"You gonna be there tonight?"

Was there a reason my man would be anywhere near a place called The Starlight?

"Not today," Collin answered simply.

Um. Not today… not tomorrow… not ever. Especially not with this kid. Seriously?

"Aw come on. Bring your lady friend."

"Nah… We actually just flew in from New York… we're kind of exhausted so…"

"Wait… you both just came in?" Surfer boy said. "Hold up… No way bro! Is this the hot married chick you were telling me about?" He said this as if I wasn't standing right there.

I felt compelled to correct Collin's ill-mannered friend, but last time I did that I ended up with my foot in my mouth. But at the same time I felt like a tool just standing there silently.

Collin reluctantly went ahead to introduce me. "Actually…Brad this is…"

Just to show that I could make light of the situation, and that I was very capable of speech, I reached forward and stuck my hand out to Brad. "Hot married chick… or you could call me Victoria," I said and then added a smirk. "Nice to meet you."

"Brad," he said shaking my hand. "If you don't already know, I'm Collin's much more interesting, more attractive friend."

He definitely was not.

"Uh huh…charming," I said.

"So how'd you end up with this loser?" Brad asked half-jokingly.

I rolled my eyes at him then said, "Brad, just a little piece of advice… If you're going to be a smartass, first you have to be smart; otherwise you're just an ass."

"Damn… *burn!*" Brad said then laughed smugly. He seemed amused that I wasn't shaken by his crassness. He was nothing compared to the guys in Frank's entourage. He turned to Collin with raised eyebrows. "Watch out! You've got a feisty one there."

"Yeah, you don't have to tell me that," Collin answered.

"Well… I gotta say…" Brad continued. "You were right about one thing. She's way hotter than…"

"Alright…we'll talk later," Collin quickly cut him off. "We have to go…but thanks for dropping this off," Collin said taking the case from Brad.

"Wait," Brad said trailing behind us. "I sort of need a favor too."

"Yeah. Why am I not surprised?" Collin rolled his eyes.

"So… like I said, I'm looking to party tonight."

"Uh huh. And you want me to do what?"

"Come on … don't hold out on me. You already know," Brad said. They were both on the same page; I was completely lost.

"I'll think about it," Collin replied, but seemed likely to be easily coerced; this kid obviously would never stop asking. Exactly *what* he was asking was a mystery to me.

"Aw come on. I have, like, ten people trying to pop bottles, smoke a little hookah, and just chill out… you know?"

"Fine… whatever… I'll make a call later," Collin said sounding exasperated.

"Awesome. Thanks bro," he said then turned to me. "Nice meeting you, *Victoria*. If things don't work out between you two, get my number from him."

"That's really not helping," Collin said.

"Have fun on your trip," I added and we continued to walk down the path to the apartments. "Wow, your friend is nice," I said sarcastically as we strolled.

"He's not really a friend … and I don't want you talking to him."

"Um, wow, okay. I wasn't talking to him but… okay." I was a bit dumbfounded. I felt like I was indirectly being accused of something.

"Alright. I'm just saying. He's lucky 'cause if any other guy tried to talk to you like that I would have knocked him out."

"Don't even worry about it … it's not worth it."

"Well he'd better not do that again; I don't care if he's kidding or not."

"Come one Babe, stop," I said trying to calm him down. "I've had way worse said to me. Anyway it's nice to know that you're telling all your friends about me. I'm not sure if I should be flattered or offended."

"Hey. That was *his* interpretation. The only reason he knows so much is because we're on set for twelve or fifteen hours sometimes ... we talk when it gets slow."

"I get it," I said. "So... what was that about any way?"

"I was probably going to have to leave early to pick this up on my way tomorrow..."

"No, I'm not talking about the film... He was talking to you like you're some kind of ... I don't know... drug dealer or something."

"Nah, nothing like that," he said then laughed. He still didn't answer my question.

"Okay then," I said and it was obvious that he wasn't going to tell me so I moved on. "Well, on another note ... who am I hotter than?" I said as I squint my eyes at him inquisitively.

"I don't know what he was going to say."

"Aw come on. You could think of something better than that."

"Who cares anyway?"

"Ooh... did you have some other girl I don't know about?" I asked crossing my arms.

"Are we already fighting?" he said gently unfolding my arms. "You've been in Cali for like five minutes," he said with a scowl.

"You're the one who..." I stopped myself. Was this how we wanted to spend our first day? "No," I said loosening up. "No, we're not fighting. I just need to know if there's some chick I need to beat up." I gave him a theatrical wink.

"No, Baby. There is no one else. There will be no fighting... there will be no shoe throwing..." he said, pretending to scold me.

"Hey! Hey! I am not the shoe thrower! Get your facts straight."

"Okay... whatever you say you're right," he said. "You're

always right."

I laughed as he suddenly grabbed me, hugging and kissing me.

"See, I already learned how to be a good husband!"

It was amazing that we were at the point in our relationship where we could joke about something that was once the cause of one of our biggest arguments in the past.

Collin stopped walking and we were in front of apartment eight. "Well... here we are..." He stood twiddling with his key in his hand for a few seconds.

"What's the problem?" I asked noticing his hesitation.

"Okay, look... before you come in. I just have to warn you that it's nothing fancy. And I haven't had a chance to do much to the place since I've been here."

"Aw I don't care about that," I said and smiled at him. I found it cute that for once he was the one being a bit insecure. "You're in luck. It just so happens that I love decorating." I smiled reassuringly at him.

"I'm glad you said that," he said. "Oh...um... and I haven't had a chance to really clean up."

"It's alright Babe, I'll help you tidy up."

He still seemed to hesitate.

I sighed. "I have two sons; I've seen a mess before. Come on already, I'm exhausted!"

He finally unlocked the door. When we walked inside I immediately wished I could retract my previous statements and understood his apprehension. I didn't want to be the nag 15 seconds into being there but "nothing fancy" was an absolute understatement.

"Um... Honey, were you robbed?" I asked bluntly.

In the living room there was only one brown leather sofa, which I could hardly see under the piles of stuff; a small glass TV stand holding what looked like a 32-inch TV, and a glass coffee table.

"Nope. I literally haven't gone to one store since I've been here. These things were in Britney's storage. She let me take them."

"Well... Do you have a roommate?" I asked unable to believe that this was his place.

240

"No."

So this mess was all from him? How could that be? His apartment in New York was always immaculate. I was a little muddled as I took it all in.

"Alright…" I walked around and sighed looking at the clutter

"Sorry, I know it's a little messy, I told you. My schedule is so crazy… I'm always in and out."

"It's okay… We'll get it in order." *Sometime next year.*

The kitchen and living room were basically one big room. The only point of separation was where the tan carpet ended and the light grey tiles began. There was not one painting, picture, or piece of art in the entire apartment. The only decoration was the garbage.

I was afraid to sit. There was no food in the fridge. The stove looked like it hadn't ever been used. Empty pizza boxes towered over on the counter. There were subway wrappers, empty cups, water bottles… I was confused. This didn't look like *my* man's apartment.

I think what shocked me the most was the endless collection of glass bottles. Both empty, half full, and full. Beer, whiskey, vodka. *Should I be concerned?* Or did he recently have a house party? That's exactly what it looked like. Like the aftermath of a teenage house party.

There were enough bags of garbage lined up by the back door for me to safely assume that garbage night came once every few months. I wasn't quite going to compare it to something out of *Hoarders.* No, not quite yet.

I was scared to see the bedroom. It was bad, but not that bad. The bed wasn't made. Laundry hadn't been done in… three…four months?

As if I went right into mom mode I started placing any clothes that weren't in the already full hamper inside a nearby laundry bag. I wanted to make the bed, vacuum, Windex, bleach … or we could just blow the place up and start over.

Collin stopped me from cleaning.

"Babe we'll do that later. I want to show you around. Plus, we need to get to the mall."

"Mall?" *Was I forgetting something?*

"Yeah. You need a new phone now, remember?"

Oh yeah.

Boy was I impulsive. Funny thing was; I didn't regret it. I couldn't imagine starting my California trip with harassing phone calls from my ex. Although it didn't start exactly how I anticipated, it was okay.

"Fine. I guess we'll start cleaning tonight," I said. I placed my bags carefully onto the night table and hoped random critters wouldn't scramble out from anywhere as I quickly claimed one of the dresser drawers, then changed my comfortable traveling clothes into something trendier. *Okay, let's see what California is all about.*

CHAPTER 30

Collin and I were outside again and we walked down the path towards the exit of the complex when he stopped me in my tracks.

"Wait right here," he said. "I'm going to get my car. It's parked in the garage out back."

"Okay," I said.

As he walked away, I wondered if he would come around with some old rusty bucket of metal with no hub caps and drive thru cups strewn about the interior, if the condition of the apartment were at all telling for that of the vehicle. I shook my head at the thought and stood nervously for a few minutes when I heard a deep engine purr from afar. The noise grew closer until a flashy, shiny orange two-door sports car appeared in front of me. Then Collin stepped out.

"Wow! What is *this*?"

"My car," he said proudly.

"Shut up. This is a rental right?"

"Nope. She's all mine. Twenty-twelve Nissan GTR."

"You've got to be kidding me," I said in awe as I inched closer to the impeccably painted and polished sports car.

"Black rims, carbon fiber hood, HIDs..." he continued on naming things that I didn't understand and never heard of.

"It's really nice," I said. I couldn't see the inside through the pitch black windows.

"Come on get in," he said opening the door for me.

The seats were white leather and the entire console was black and white with orange trimmings. It had a touch screen for radio, GPS, and Lord know what other features. I felt like I was in *Fast and the Furious* as I sunk into the low bucket seat.

Collin proudly hopped into the driver's seat and took off.

"You said this is a Nissan...G3 something... uh..." I tried to remember the model. I was never good at car stuff.

"*GTR*," he corrected me.

"Okay, yes. So that's good that you went with a Nissan, at least you probably didn't spend too much..."

"Oh, Sweetie that's cute," he said rubbing my hand with

his but I took offense to his subtle yet condescending actions and tone.

"This is an eighty five thousand dollar car. That doesn't count the customizations," he said.

"Jeez…" I said. "It's definitely a stunning car though." I tried not to roll my eyes at him.

It made absolutely no sense. He lived in this tiny, dark, messy hole in the wall apartment but drove a gorgeous expensive sports car? I knew firsthand he wasn't compensating for the obvious most men are with such a car, and he was far too young for midlife crisis, so was he just trying to show off? Or was this one of the dumb young things I had to deal with while he was still in his 20s. Oh well. After my annoyance passed I realized that I could definitely get used to being a passenger in a flashy sports car. That was one expensive thing Frank and I never had.

This ride along the broad and shiny streets was nothing like the previous one in the taxi. Everything zoomed by whenever Collin had a green. My heart held on tight inside my chest as the adrenaline built. We were going so fast, I was scared to look at the odometer as we flew down the highway which was empty due to the later hour of the day.

We arrived at the Beverly Center Mall in one piece. It was nice. Nothing out of the ordinary, though. We stopped first at the mobile store. I told them I lost my phone at the airport because I wasn't sure how they'd react if I said I purposely threw it in the garbage because my soon to be ex-husband was harassing me. I decided on the new iPhone. My original plan was linked to my account, but Collin had a different idea.

"Why don't we add a second line to my account?" he asked as we stood at the counter.

"I don't see the point. I already have a line."

"Actually if you get a new phone on a new line it'll only be a hundred dollars for the phone today, as opposed to the retail price of five ninety nine," the salesman said convincingly.

"I mean, I figured if we're getting married shouldn't we start putting some of our things together anyway?" Collin said.

"Uh… I guess."

"Besides, you won't have to worry about those telemarketers bothering you," he said and I knew by his tone that he knew it wasn't a telemarketer earlier at the airport.

"Okay," I agreed. I wasn't sure why I was so reluctant about combining our phone plans. He was right, that we would eventually have most of our bills joint anyway. I guess I wasn't expecting it to be so soon. Things were happening so fast.

We spent another half hour in the mobile store adding a line, choosing a few phone accessories, and finalizing the details. We eventually left the mall, but not before hours of browsing and shopping; being sweet together just as we were in New York. He treated me to bags of clothes from whatever boutiques I chose. He also picked up a few outfits for himself, some of which I selected. I really enjoyed the attention we received as we toured LA in his GTR. He took me to the Sunset Strip where I spotted at least six or seven celebrities. A quiet dinner at Musso & Frank's Grill, a survival of old Hollywood, was just the thing to settle in the first night, before the faster pace of sports cars and LA became my new routine.

We had a good first day together but I was drained because even though the clock on the west coast said 8 p.m., my body still felt like it was 11 p.m. When we got back to the hole in the wall aka "the apartment," I was too spent to care about the mess.

The day ended too soon as Collin and I climbed into bed early since he had to be up in the middle of the night for work, or early morning, or whatever it's considered. I figured he would just want to sleep but when he started to run his fingers through my hair and pull my body close to his I could only wonder where he found the energy. But of course there were no complaints on my end.

Even though our day was full of obstacles we made it. We were finally together, happily engaged, and living together on the west coast. In my mind we beat the odds.

*   *   *   *

My almost perfect first day in California was interrupted in the middle of the night. *Ding-dong,* was the sound that woke me up while the moon was still shining. But it wasn't the doorbell. It was the incessant sound of Collin's phone. I wasn't sure if it was an alarm or a text message or what this time.

"Is that a text?" I muttered groggily as I turned to face him.

"Ugh… Yeah," he said, phone already in hand.

Don't freak out. It's only two in the morning.

"Who is it?" I asked nonchalantly.

Before he could answer me the phone went off again, but this time a happy melody playing in a loop and I knew that a call was coming through.

"Hey what's going on?" He sounded concerned. "No… I'm not working today, why what happened… Oh wow… no, sorry I really can't… what about your brother… oh." There was a pause and he looked over at me and seemed to contemplate for a moment before he sighed and gave in to the person on the other line. "Alright I'll be right there…"

"Everything okay?"

"Yeah," he said as he pulled on his t-shirt then reached over for his sneakers. "Um … okay so don't be mad," he said.

"Why would I be mad? Do you have to go into work now?" I said and knew my tone carried a hint of agitation. This demanding job was going to take him away from me for 12 to 16 hours a day for five days a week. Was it so much that I asked for one more day together before that happened?

"No… that actually wasn't my job."

"Oh…" I said, now with peaked curiosity. "Well, where are you going then?"

He sighed again and approached me as if I was going to swing a bat at him.

"Well…Vanessa's car broke down on the highway… she just needs a ride home."

And the mention of *her* name made me wish I had a bat. I was instantly wide awake. I knew while being in California that she would pop up sooner or later… I was just hoping it wasn't going to be on my first night there!

"I'm going to pretend you didn't just say that and you're going to come back to bed…"

"Babe, I'm sorry I know how it looks but she's asking

246

me for this one favor. What am I supposed to do?"

"Tell her to take a bus," I said bitterly.

"There are no busses at this time where she is."

"That's not your problem. It sure as hell isn't mine."

"Please don't put me in this situation…What if your sister was stranded in the middle of the night?"

Somehow I could imagine that, the way Brooke was acting lately. I was also able to imagine it happening to me since it just did a month earlier in front of Preston's house. I wouldn't admit to Collin though that Vanessa and I even had the slightest imperfection in common. I sure as hell wasn't going to sympathize with her circumstances since it was still very disrespectful for her to call my man at two in the morning.

"Please don't go there… It's not even the same thing," I protested. "She's not your sister, she's your fucking ex-girlfriend and why the hell is she calling you at this time anyway?" I was starting to feel myself get worked up.

"She thought I was going into work already. If I didn't take the day off I would have been heading out around this time."

And Vanessa had his work schedule memorized? Why? I didn't say this though; I tried to keep the small flame of a discussion from erupting into a volcano. I didn't want to sound as if I was jealous of that whore.

"You're mad…" he said when he noticed my pensive state.

"I'm not mad."

"Really?"

I could understand his skepticism but I wasn't letting this become a problem. "If you really feel like you have to go then I'm not going to stop you. As long as this won't be an ongoing issue…"

"It won't. She doesn't know that you're here yet. I'll let her know today," he said.

Of course, deep down, I was livid. How dare this skank interrupt my night with Collin! At the same token my ex also attempted to ruin my day, but I didn't let him. I didn't argue with him because I didn't want to let her get to me or be the cause of an argument, I wouldn't give her that kind of satisfaction. I trusted him and I already knew he would never leave her outside in the middle of the night -- his constant need to try to help everyone -- I was well aware of this when we started dating.

As he walked out I was proud of myself for handling the situation maturely. It was starting to become apparent that our time apart may have ultimately been beneficial for Collin and me. Our love felt stronger than it ever was especially as I ironed away some of my insecurities. I wasn't even worried because I knew he was mine.

CHAPTER 31

Saturday. Our first full day in California and all I wanted to do was clean and unpack. Collin wanted us to go watch the sunrise and have breakfast on the beach. But instead we spend the entire morning in bed and we didn't start getting dressed, ready, and out of the apartment until two in the afternoon.

Collin didn't inform me as to what the rest of the day had in store for us. He always wanted to surprise me in one way or another. I didn't mind but I always loved trying to guess anyway.

What a gorgeous day it was as the car raced down the interstate. I could barely make out the signs as they seemed to fly past.

"Hmm... I got it. We're going back to New York," I said as I was able to spot that we were headed towards the Long Beach airport.

"Why would he do that?" he asked and laughed.

"You're kicking me out already," I said and pouted.

"Nah, not yet..."

He received a playful punch in the arm for his comment.

"There's a lot more in Long Beach than just the airport," Collin said.

"Yeah," I said. "I'm sure there's a beach... I assume it's long," I said jokingly.

"There are beaches, but we won't be going to any of them," he said.

"Why not?"

"Just trust me on that."

"Well if you won't tell me I'm sure Google will."

"Okay, see what it says," he said and laughed.

I ran a search for the beaches in Long Beach in my phone and found mostly low two and three star reviews with comments, their focus varying from the unfavorable water color, sand that was flooded with trash, mostly condom wrappers and syringe needles, and the not so friendly groups of people hanging around the area. Good call on his part that we were avoiding that beach, he knew his stuff.

"Ew," I said out loud as I read a review about empty prescription bottles, random shoes, and dirty diapers in the sand.

"Yeah… exactly," he said.

"Alright then, let's see where you're really taking me…"

I did a little detective work and in the search engine I found the most popular tourist attractions in Long Beach. "The Aquarium of the Pacific" sounded amazing, home to over 1100 animals; penguins, and sharks which visitors were able to safely touch. The aquarium even offered an exhibit where we could feed the sea otters. It was gorgeous, looked clean, and had rave reviews. I was hoping it was where we were going.

Then I soon realized there were hundreds of attractions that sounded equally fun. A site seeing tour which explored around the area, highlighting major tourist attractions and celebrity homes was an option. Disneyland would have been magical, but I wasn't dressed for Disneyland since I had on low sandal heels and a sundress, so I knew we couldn't be heading there. The list went on and on from helicopter rides and cruises to farms and museums. Many of the "things to do" were on boats and along the shoreline.

"There is so much around here I can't even guess," I said forfeiting.

"I know. I wish I had the whole week off, we would do everything."

"It's okay, I'm just happy to be here with you," I said placing my hand over his. "Well I give up which one are we headed to?"

"We're going to the Queen Mary," he said.

"Ah!" I said, "So we *are* sailing back to New York."

"No. You're thinking of the Queen Mary Two. This is the original. It's been docked in Long Beach since the sixties. I think."

I did see it within the top 10 attractions. The Queen Mary was a giant cruise ship that was active during the 1930s and World War II. The Queen Mary was very popular as even Hollywood celebrities and royalty would set sail on her cruises. The final sail was in 1967 and afterwards it was docked and became a floating attraction and hotel.

The day tours included a tea room, brunch, cafés, and a market area. It was all fun, romance and history by day, but what caught my attention was the paranormal and spiritual themes of the night. The legends behind the ship claimed it to be haunted and tourists had supposedly spotted spirits roaming around at night. Some of the late tours included walking through the areas of the ship that were believed to be the most haunted. My heart raced at the thought and the thrill.

"I'm reading about it now and it sounds amazing!" I said. "But shouldn't we be going there when it's dark?"

"I didn't know if you would want to, I figured we'd have a late lunch there then head somewhere else afterwards."

"No. Can we go at night? It sounds fun."

"You're not too scared are you?"

"No. Are you?" I challenged.

"No! Of course not," he said.

"Sounds awesome."

"Okay… so then where should we go now?" he asked as the car hummed, patiently waiting to be operated.

I chose the attraction that caught my attention the most: the aquarium. We had an incredible time exploring the many exhibits.

I had to buy flip flops because my feet were hurting from walking around in the heels and we both bought t-shirts because we got splashed by the dolphins. Collin bought us matching Long Beach CA hats to be cute, so we really looked like tourists.

When the sun was just about setting we headed back to our original destination. We parked in front of the massive ship which had a white and black colored exterior and was bigger than what I imagined it to look like in person. It was enormous! The interior of the ship's main reception area was like something out of *Titanic* and my eyes settled on a grand staircase out of a fairy tale.

"Oh… my," I said.

"Yeah," he said. "I love it here. The cabin is used as though you can just come for dinner. And of course the ghost tours if you didn't change your mind," he said.

"Nope…"

"Alright," he said and went to grab his wallet to pay for the tickets.

"Babe, I got it," I said. My debit card was already in my hand.

"Victoria. don't be silly…"

"No, seriously. You've been paying for everything since we got here. The mall, the aquarium. Please let me treat you for once."

"Um, I guess," he said reluctantly.

I went to a clerk and presented my debit card.

She swiped it through then I heard a beep. The machine printed a receipt but the clerk carefully scrutinized it before returning her attention to me.

"I'm sorry Miss, it was declined," the clerk said.

"Hmm… It might be the magnetic strip," I said inspecting my card. I wiped it with the bottom of my shirt the handed it back to her.

Again -- that beep.

"No," the girl said sympathetically and shook her head.

I handed her my credit card and the same thing happened. I felt like my face was the color of a tomato. Collin came to my rescue and handed the girl cash to pay for our entrance.

"It's alright Babe, maybe it's just because you're in another state. Safety precautions against identity theft?" he guessed trying to make me feel better.

I wished he was right. Somehow I was very doubtful and in the back of my mind I felt like…or knew… that Frank was responsible for the mishap.

I was able to get passed the embarrassing situation and I washed Frank out of my thoughts, at least for the moment as Collin and I found our way to the dining area. Dinner was amazing and in a beautiful ballroom on the top deck. All through dinner Collin kept checking his phone. His text alert kept going off every few minutes. He responded to a few of them, and it was a bit annoying, but it wasn't excessive enough for me to feel too left out.

"Is everything okay?" I asked.

"Yes, sorry… work stuff," he said simply.

I wasn't mad but I still wanted him all to myself. At least

while we were on a date. "Could you let whoever know that you're busy?" I asked.

"You're right," he said. He seemed to put his phone either in silent mode or airplane mode then he tucked it away into his pocket.

We enjoyed dessert and wine —without interruption. By the time we finished dinner, the sky was a solid onyx-colored sheet and I was ready for the ghost tour.

As we walked through the splendid corridors I held onto Collin's arm. It was creepier than I had expected. First we ventured into the boiler room. It was dark and musky and smelled like old rusty pipes. It obviously was kept in its original condition and was quite run down, everything corroded, cob webs everywhere. If there were ghosts on that ship, that's where they would be hanging out.

"See anything yet?" Collin voice suddenly pierced the silence as he grabbed me from behind, causing me to almost jump out of my skin.

"Ugh! I'll get you back," I said shoving him playfully.

"Aw come on its kind of romantic," he said grabbing me then placing a kiss against my lips. I kissed him back but felt the eeriest chill as if little ghost eyes were enjoying the show.

"Come on let's get out of here," I said clinging to him again as we clambered up a creaky set of stairs that lead back to the main deck.

We searched the main floor again when the figure of a woman suddenly appeared out of the shadows. I screamed and covered my eyes -- to what turned out to be a drunken girl coming back from the bar.

Collin laughed hysterically at me then I eventually joined him laughing at myself.

We didn't see any actual ghosts but we still had an amazing time and it was a thrilling experience nonetheless. Any excuse I had to adhere myself close to Collin was good enough for me.

"This place is fantastic," I said. "I wish I could see one of the rooms."

He got a coy look on his face. "Well," he said "the third floor is supposed to be the most haunted."

I knew he was up to something and wanted to lure me to the third floor so I followed behind him.

As we passed room 312, he removed a key from his coat.

"Well, you wanted to see a room," he said.

"Oh, you're so sneaky!" I said and rewarded him with a kiss on the cheek. I figured he made the reservation earlier and must have picked up the key when I wasn't paying attention.

The room was a beautiful suite with period furniture, a king bed, and fabrics all of deep autumn reds and gold. I felt like a movie star of old Hollywood or a travelling woman from the first part of the twentieth century. A bottle of champagne chilled in an ice bucket, no doubt a touch of Collin's arranging.

"They don't rent by the hour," he said. "So we may as well stay for the night."

I kicked off my heels, and tiptoed to reach up and kiss him deeply.

"We're going to need more than an hour anyway Mister," I said as I closed the door to the suite behind us.

CHAPTER 32

Collin and I ended up leaving The Queen Mary early in the morning so we could both get back to the apartment and get started on each of our busy days. I had to figure out what was going on with my bank. I still needed to unpack and get that apartment to look at least half decent by the end of the day. He needed to get to work at nine in the morning and would be gone all day.

After coming out of the shower Collin returned into the bedroom to get dressed. He brought a wonderful, coastal, clean scent trailing in with him. He dressed in a simple blue tee and dark jeans. His hair was done up with mousse this morning and looked more luxurious than usual. After three whole days together I was going to miss having him to stare at all day.

"I have to go, Baby," Collin said.

"Alright," I said wrapping my arms around him.

He kissed my lips softly and hugged me back. "Text me if you need anything," he said. "I'll try to call you on my break if I get one."

"Okay…What time will you be home?"

"What's today? Sunday? It'll be a little late tonight. Around nine, maybe."

That's a long day. He did warn me though and also it was only temporary. I didn't want to complain so I just smiled weakly and said, "Okay" as he kissed my forehead.

I was alone. But that was acceptable. It was back to reality. Still adjusting to a new time zone and Collin's interchanging hectic schedule was going to take some time. After he left I wanted to make coffee but I couldn't do it around the mess that still cluttered the kitchen. And there was no coffee. Or coffee pot.

More important than the lack of coffee in the apartment I had to deal with the issues with my bank. When I called and spoke to an agent they confirmed that my account was frozen. They couldn't disclose too many details over the phone. The issue was the same with my credit cards. Frank didn't know of one reloadable prepaid card that I bought a few months back as a suggestion from, surprisingly enough, John. So I wasn't completely broke but I needed to be very careful because I only had a limited amount on it.

I knew Frank was trying to force me to have to contact him, since he didn't have my new number, and he had no idea of my whereabouts, but I wasn't falling for it. I decided I would address the issue in court and I was sure his actions would definitely cause the judge to lean in my favor so I wasn't letting it stress me out.

Then the next thought on my mind was *I need to clean.* Clean like crazy. I remembered the little shopping center and figured it would be a good time to explore my surroundings. It was mostly residential. The complex had uniform designed short buildings and looked almost like a hotel down the shore in New Jersey. It was pleasantly mild out, especially for a November day. The walk to the store wasn't far.

I spent a half hour staring at different multi-purpose cleaners, bleaches, and disinfectants. *What the heck is the difference?* Galina always did the cleaning in my old house. She also did the shopping, cooking, errands. I had no idea what to buy. Sometimes I felt like a failure of a wife, then I remembered that this was my second chance to figure out what being a "good wife" meant.

After reading the uses of each product I finally bought one bottle of each spray, sponges, and gloves, as well as enough meat and side dishes for that night's dinner. Good thing I knew how to cook, at least.

I placed my headphones on, put up the music as I stood in the middle of the living room. I didn't even know where to start. *What happened here?* I wondered again. His place in New York was immaculate, well, before Britney came along. But that was just one thing that changed. Then again, as I thought about it, there were a few other changes as well, like having his phone glued to his side, his jerky acquaintance compared to his nice friends in New York, and the need to blow money unnecessarily. Unless I just didn't spend enough time with him before to notice those traits were always there. Either way, I would help him get things in order; especially if I was going to be living there. I began trying to organize everything, starting with the living room. I knew it would take all day and I was right.

I was on all fours in the kitchen, scrubbing with my headphones on and planning my next moves. The bathroom was done. The bedroom was done. I made several trips bringing bags to the dumpster in the back of the complex. Dinner was brewing in the crock pot that I walked back to the store to buy... *once this floor is clean I can shower, change, and then have an hour or two to relax.* It sounded like a good plan. Other than the Dido song that was playing through my headphones, I became distracted when I thought I heard a noise in the room. I paused the Pandora app, but heard nothing else. That eerie feeling that I wasn't alone returned a few moments later.

Is someone here? No, enough Victoria! Don't bring that paranoia shit with you here! I calmed myself down and ignored the feeling, raising the volume of the music. I tried to re-focus myself on every last detail of the tiles. But the feeling quickly crept back in and I felt that someone was standing behind me. Or maybe I really was going crazy? *You seriously need help, Victoria, get a hold of yourself!* So, I forced myself to close my eyes and take a deep breath. *I can't live like this. Not here.* But my instincts were right this time. I wasn't crazy or paranoid. There was in fact someone in the room with me.

I couldn't think or react fast enough as I felt someone's arms wrap around me. My heart stopped, I jumped, and screamed; either simultaneously or somewhat in that order.

"Hey... hey, it's just me."

I was relieved at the sound of Collin's comforting voice. "Oh my God ... you scared me!"

"I'm sorry, I thought you heard me. You okay? Since when are you so jumpy?"

"I wasn't expecting you here," I said clutching my hand to my chest and breathing in and out deeply.

"Oh ... you sure you aren't scared from our little ghost adventure?

"Yes, I'm sure," I said and smiled at him. "Wait, I just realized something ... why are you here?" *Had I lost track of time while cooking and cleaning and freaking out about sounds?*

"We wrapped a little early. I wanted to surprise you."

I was happy he was home early, but I also kind of wished he wasn't. I was in absolute disarray. My hair was pulled up high into a messy ponytail. The t-shirt I stole from his drawer sagged unflatteringly off my body. But worst of all was the pair of yellow, rubber cleaning gloves that encased my hands. The little blush and foundation I applied before heading out earlier in the day had long wore away.

"Ugh, don't look at me. I'm a mess," I said covering my face with my arms.

"Well … I think you look sexy."

"Stop. There is nothing sexy about me right now."

"That's impossible," he said leaning forward brushing his lips again mine. As we kissed our incredible chemistry ignited.

"But look at what I'm wearing," I protested, still opposed to my not-so-sexy attire. "I look like Missus Clean!" I said and we both laughed.

"The last thing on my mind is what you have on," he said. He grabbed the bottom of the shirt and pulled it over my head then dropped it on the floor. "Problem solved," he said then he stood to his feet. "Don't move."

"What are you doing?" I turned my head to look at him.

"I want to play a little game," he said. "But no peeking."

A game? Interesting.

"Okay." I played along and looked forward.

He disappeared to the table and it sounded like he removed items from a grocery bag. When he returned he stood in front of me, holding a silky black blindfold in his hands.

"Are you okay with this?" he asked.

I bit my lip and was immediately aroused. My heart stuttered in my chest as I imagined the possibilities. We had never done anything like this before. I nodded my head. He fastened the blindfold over my eyes, and I couldn't see a thing!

He helped me to a kneeling position, and peeled each glove from my hands, before binding my wrists together behind my back. I couldn't tell what he'd used because it wasn't too tight and wriggling my wrists a bit, I knew I could break free if I wanted to. *Was it a thin rope? A shoe lace?* I had no clue, but I knew for sure I wouldn't be trying to escape any time soon.

"So a game huh, like Monopoly?" I asked innocently then

giggled. I was tied up, blindfolded and half naked in the middle of the kitchen floor; *of course I knew he wasn't talking about a board game.*

"Okay. You're not allowed to talk anymore unless you have my permission," he said firmly, obviously trying to sound intimidating. "Be quiet and wait for me to come back."

"Oh *sorry* … or I mean, um … yes, sir," I said then burst out in laughter.

"What's so funny?"

"I'm sorry; you're just so cute, trying to sound authorative."

"Authorative isn't a real word," he said.

"I know *you're* not correcting *me* on *my* grammar," I said.

I heard him walk away again and I wondered what he was doing.

"This isn't very sexy," I teased.

"Well … I'm trying but you're ruining it," he said.

"Okay, I promise I'll be good," I said, then added suggestively, "Or maybe I won't."

He disappeared for a few seconds. I waited patiently for him to return. I could hear him at the kitchen table behind me; it sounded like he was rummaging through those grocery bags again. But I played along, never once turning my head or speaking out of turn.

I felt so exposed; I couldn't hide my breasts with my hands behind my back, and all I was wearing was a pair of light cotton shorts. What kind of game? I turned my head slightly to try to make out the next sound. Was that a soda can opening?

I had the sense that Collin was right in front of me; could I hear him drinking? Then I felt his lips against mine, and his mouth opening. I opened mine and reciprocated his kiss. But suddenly there was a cold, bubbly liquid filling my mouth! Soda? He had kissed me a mouthful of soda! I spluttered a little, but swallowed it down, delighting in the sweetness of the fizzy drink, and the nastiness of my man.

"Well done," Collin said after he pulled away from my mouth. He chuckled then I felt something cold against my breast. "A nice cold can of…?" he waited for me to fill in the blank.

"Soda?" I asked.

"What kind?"

"Pepsi?"

"Hmm …" he sounded displeased.

"What's wrong?"

"It's actually Coke, but I'll let that one slide," he said.

"Oh is that right?" I asked and smirked. "So … what happens if I guess wrong?"

"Umm ... hmm ... I haven't really thought about that."

"That's not really a fair game for you then."

"It's okay I've been dying to tie you up ever since that night, when we were on the phone," he said then laughed. "Why? Is there something else you want me to do?" he asked suggestively.

I think he knew what I wanted, but he would never take it further on his own. I was really coming to enjoy exploring the wilder sides of myself with Collin.

I bit my lip then said in a low voice, "Well … you could spank me … if you want."

There was a pause.

I never thought those words would come out of my mouth. I've read about *sensation play* in my romance novels. It sounded really erotic, and I felt our little "game" was a safe way to continue exploring.

"Really?" he asked excitedly, but then, "I don't know…"

I guess he felt a little apprehensive given what he knew about my past. But it just wasn't the same thing to me. And my past didn't need to define my every move anymore. I was letting it go. I knew Collin would never hurt me and it was an incredible feeling that I could trust him completely.

"It's okay … I …I wanna try it."

"Hmm … we'll see," he said.

It didn't take long for my breathing to become thin at the thought.

I heard the silverware drawer open before he returned to me.

"Something on a spoon next," he said. "Open up!"

I smiled and opened my mouth, when I felt the spoon against my lower lip I closed my lips around it, expecting something sweet, but in a matter of seconds I was surprised to find that my mouth was burning! I did my best to swallow down the tangy liquid, coughing and choking. "Argh! You…" I didn't know what to call him. "You ass!" There it was. "Is that Tabasco sauce!?" I could feel my face flush, and my tongue continued to tingle.

"Too easy, huh?" he asked arrogantly, unfazed by my shock, and probably a little amused.

I frowned and then growled at him, but just before I could call him another name I felt his finger rubbing something wet on my nipple. I knew Collin had just dabbed a little Tabasco on my nipple because it started to warm immediately. The heat radiated all the way through my body and in between my legs. Suddenly I wasn't frowning or growling, and felt myself leaning forward a bit, wanting him to keep rubbing.

"Mmm … what else you got?" I asked eager for the next quiz.

"I'm pretty sure I said you're not allowed to talk."

"What are you gonna do about it?"

I felt a swat on my ass.

"You're only to speak when you have my permission," Collin said firmly.

"Mmm … okay," My ass stung and the delicious tingling had my senses awakened; they liked what was happening. I wanted more. My insides were unraveling from listening to him take charge of me in a silly, yet erotic, game.

"Good…" Collin said, "A quick learner." Then he went to grab the next object. "Well, you're pretty good with your mouth, I wonder if you can make three in a row."

There was a pause and the rustling of the grocery bag; then I felt him by my side. His voice was right in my ear, whispering, "Open up, Sweetie."

"It better not be Tabasco again!" I said doing my best to sound threatening.

"You know you liked it," he responded.

I did. He was catching on. I very much liked how Collin could be so sweet to me in one moment, and yet so naughty in the next. I didn't always need sweet in the bedroom, or on the kitchen floor for that matter.

I opened my mouth and felt something soft and warm on my tongue. I closed my mouth around it; he had peeled a banana. This was fun. My heart was racing. I imagined what else he might have placed on my tongue and pretended that he had. I rocked back and forth, sucking it, my tongue pressed against it, groaning softly to show how much I was enjoying his banana. It became slick as I continued and Collin withdrew it from my mouth. Next I felt it touch my chin, then slide down my neck, and down between my breasts.

"Well?"

"A banana."

"Very good, my dirty girl."

"But…"

"What?"

"I wish it was something else," I said seductively.

What did he bring out in me? I felt flushed; seriously hot and wet between my legs.

"Patience, my eager little slut, patience," he said.

And oh boy — there was that word again. Why did it excite me so much?

"Now it's time for round two." Collin helped me to my feet. He was standing behind me and I felt his hands on my hips. His thumbs went under the waistband of my shorts and he slipped them down, taking my panties with them. My heart started to pound. I couldn't see a thing through the blindfold, but I could almost sense where Collin was; as if shadows passed in front of me, or his heat, or small sounds. I moved my head left and right trying to locate him; I thought he was circling me. Then I felt the palm of his hand brushing my nipple. I gasped — he hadn't been where I thought at all. I turned again and he pinched my other nipple. I exhaled hard. The room went still. Then I couldn't hear him moving at all. He was like a phantom. Something suddenly touched me between my knees and my body jerked a little. Too cold to be Collin. I bit my lip as I felt it slide upwards; higher and higher, this cold, firm object, until it brushed both my thighs.

"Not your mouth this time, dirty girl. What is this?"

The almost rubbery object slid higher and touched me, brushing against my sex. I hesitated, it was either a zucchini or a cucumber, I decided in my mind.

I was so disoriented I wasn't even sure that I wanted to guess right.

"A zucchini?" I guessed.

Slap!

My insides clenched. I was soaked between my thighs, my breathing increased. I wanted him badly.

"Nope," he said, then leaned in and whispered, "Cucumber."

"Jeez you got the hang of that fast," I said. "I think I might guess the next one wrong on purpose."

"Baby, you're too much," he said amused.

When I heard him walk away I worked the ties off my wrist and held them in my hand so he wouldn't know I was free. When he stepped in front of me again I pulled down the blindfold to see what he had next -- a can of whipped cream. I snatched it from his hand.

"Ha! Now it's my turn to have some fun," I said.

"Bad girl ... I wasn't done with you!"

"Well you are now," I said then impatiently peeled his shirt over his head.

I ran my hand over his chest and abdomen. I was so obsessed with his body. With my palms firmly against his chest I backed him into the wall.

"You're so sexy," I said I pressed my breasts against his chest as I kissed him fiercely. My tongue exploring his mouth as my hands ran down to the rim of his jeans. I unbuttoned them and worked them off then knelt to the floor dragging them down with me.

I stood to my feet again and pressed my body against his again. I nibbled his earlobe then whispered, "So you think I'm good with my mouth... do you want to know how good?"

I placed the nozzle of the whipped cream onto the tip of my tongue and squeezed a small amount into my mouth.

"Mmm ... that's so good," I said in an exaggeratedly sexy tone. "Do you remember when you asked me to do that? Is it because you like watching things go into my mouth?"

"Yes," he said, his voice strained, as if he just ran a marathon. I pressed my lips against his and plunged my tongue into his mouth creating a sweet and messy kiss. I withdrew from him then, and with the bottle of whipped cream, drew a frothy white line from the middle of his six-pack all the way down to his shaft and down the tip. I slid my tongue down the line then stopped, knowing he was quivering with anticipation.

I then squeezed another dap of whipped cream, this time onto his finger then licked it clean. "You feel that? Doesn't that feel so good? You want me to lick it off of your cock don't you?"

"Yes, Baby," he whispered.

I then dropped to my knees so that I was eye level with my treat.

I moved my mouth closer and lapped up some of the cream then stopped.

"You want more?" I asked, looking up at him. He leaned against the wall behind him and gasped loud as I closed my lips around his head, slowly working in every inch I could swallow. He groaned with great pleasure as I bobbed up and down his shaft using my hand to follow my mouth.

I peered up at him, his reaction sending a triumphant satisfaction tingling through my body. He looked down at me and our eyes met as I worked hard to make him groan. Doing what I loved to do; pleasing him.

"Ooh ... Mmm ... yeah..." Words and sounds escaped his lips encouraging me more.

I knew how he liked it and with long, steady motions I filled my mouth and throat letting my tongue do some of the work moving in circles as I came down leaving him twitching in my grip. I repeated the process bringing my lips up to meet with the base of my hand.

"That feels so fucking good baby... *Fuck* ..."

I moved closer to him so I could use my other hand to reach up and massage his balls. This nearly sent him over. I was on my knees doing whatever I could to please him, yet I was the one in full control. It was fucking amazing.

I could feel the throbbing between my legs. My thighs were soaked and my insides shook as I listened to his erratic

264

breathing and as he hummed with pleasure and said my name in a mix of expletives and moans.

Then I had that urge again. Knowing he was ready to explode I inched my mouth away, but my hand continued stroking in tight, slow pumps. The crazy took over. *The slut* came out to play.

"You like when I suck you off like a dirty little slut don't you?"

He wasn't expecting my dirty talk any more than I was and his answer was hasty between breaths.

"Oh ... God ...Yes..."

"I know you want to come in my mouth."

He groaned and nodded.

"I want to hear it," I said.

His voice trembled as I continued to steadily move my hand up and down. "Baby I need to come ... I want to come in your mouth," he said half pleading with me.

All I wanted was to hear his were the sounds of his pleasure and know that I was the cause. It was exhilarating in the sexiest way possible. Not only was I greedy for my own orgasm, I was greedy for his too! I caved like a chump even though I knew he wouldn't have been so easy on me.

I repositioned my lips over his head, this time bobbing quickly. I blindly fished for his hand then positioned it on the back of my head, letting him grab a fistful of my hair as he finished.

"Oh shit! Yes! Victoria ... I'm gonna come..." He groaned loud and hard. At last, his cock began to pulsate, and as I felt the warm liquid spew and coat the back of my throat. I had what I was waiting for. I was satisfied.

His grip eased off my hair and his body sagged sluggishly against the wall, as I stood to my feet. He lazily pulled me close to him.

"Babe... that was..." his words disappeared into my hair. "Undescribible."

My thoughts exactly. I kissed his neck and nestled against him. "I love the way you taste," I whispered.

I was so happy that I could have him whenever I wanted. He'd be my breakfast, lunch and dinner. Or the other way around. Or both.

I felt sharp slap against my ass.

"Hey! What was that for?" I objected.

"That's for the foul of turning the tables," he said. "You're the worst sub ever," he said jokingly.

"I didn't see you complaining," I said and smirked.

He exhaled then said, "Come on." Finding his grounds he lifted me up and I wrapped my arms around his neck, legs around his body. "It's your turn," he said as he carried me to the sofa where we collapsed together and started all over again.

CHAPTER 33

Trees, road, and the wonderful energy between Collin and I were the only three things that I noticed on our short road trip on the second Saturday of December. Otherwise, I was too anxious to notice the mundane landmarks. As amazing as it was to see my new surroundings, there was something more important on my mind that day.

During a short conversation Collin and I had the night before, he sprung the news on me. I had just finished making his -- or was it *our*-- apartment presentable. I spent hours shopping online for wall art, lamps, furniture, towels, bedding, dishes, and about everything a place needed to look like a home. While he was at work I set everything up. He hugged me tight, said I was "the best" and he couldn't wait for me to meet everyone.

Everyone?

"Who's 'everyone'?" I asked.

"My whole family will be there," he said then began to tell me about his little cousin Sophia's birthday party. Apparently I would be meeting his parents as well!

Wow, was I ready to meet his family? That was a huge step. But we weren't exactly a new couple and I didn't have much of a choice.

The 40-minute ride to Newport Beach felt quick and our conversation consisted mostly of the names and details of the family members whom I would be meeting.

"We're here," he said suddenly pulling up to a gated property. He rolled down his window and typed a code into a keypad.

"Wait ... where?" All I saw was the gate in front of us, and land behind the gate.

"Here," he repeated. I looked up in awe as the tall black gate slowly opened. "This is where my parents live."

We drove up a hill and arrived in front of the most gorgeous property in the world. As if we were parking at a valet, a well-dressed man walked up to the car and opened the door for me, then went around and took Collin's keys from him. I grabbed the pink and yellow gift bag from the back seat. As I stepped out of the car the heat hit me; it was a beautiful day — perfect for a garden party, with hardly a cloud in the sky.

"Wonderful to see you Mister Turner," said the middle-aged man who wore a white button-down, black vest, and black slacks.

"Thanks, Jimmy," Collin said. "This is Victoria."

"It's a pleasure to meet you, Madam," Jimmy said with a warm smile and courteous nod.

Madam? My mind was stumped for a moment but shook it off.

"Thank you," I said returning the smile. Collin took my hand as we walked to the front door. "Uh… Babe… this isn't exactly what I was expecting," I whispered to him.

Wow. I thought I lived in a big house. "Big" wasn't the word to describe the Turner's home. "Mansion" didn't quite cut it either. "Estate," maybe. A curved white brick driveway led us right to the front door. There were a few cars already parked ahead of us.

"You never told me…" I didn't even know what to say.

"What?" he asked nonchalantly.

What? That you're parents are millionaires… and probably have a jet… and a yacht…a collection of expensive cars… and possibly even their own zip code. How could he have omitted these details? I knew his family had money, and that finances never fazed him, but this seemed to be something worth mentioning. At least I thought it was.

"Nothing. I wish I could have at least met your parents first," I said feeling my nerves wreck.

"You'll be fine. My mom is a little intense but she'll lighten up after talking to you for a bit. My dad is cool as hell; you don't have to worry about him at all. Not sure if he'll even be here… he works a lot."

I was so nervous. I also felt completely underdressed. It was an 8-year-old's birthday party! But thankfully I hadn't worn jeans. I was sporting a pair of khaki Capri pants and a white polo shirt.

Not knowing how much information he disclosed to his parents about me wasn't calming my nerves either. He obviously left out pertinent information to me; maybe he did the same with them. Were they even expecting me?

"Wait…" I said. My apprehension was palpable.

"What's wrong?"

"Why didn't you tell me about your parents?"

"What about them?"

"*You know what I mean.*"

"Because it doesn't matter. I want you to meet them, and for them to meet you… and well, everyone else of course."

"Okay, I guess."

I surely was missing something. *If they have all this space then why wouldn't he stay here instead of at that dinky apartment?*

"Don't worry," he said. "If this doesn't go well, or if you're still uncomfortable, let me know and we'll leave." He rang the bell then looked over at me again and smiled reassuringly. *Wait… If it doesn't go well? Was he subtly joking around or was his comment to be taken seriously?* But it was too late for me to address it so I smiled back trying to hide my anxiety and in an instant the door opened.

This time we were greeted by a tall, lanky butler. "Good afternoon. Welcome," he said.

"Who is it?" I heard a woman's voice croon from behind him. The pretty older woman, whom I'd seen before in photos, began walking towards us. She looked better in person. Her outfit looked as if it came out of a Burberry catalog. She wore a pair of beige slacks and a plaid top. She was draped with sparkling diamonds from head to toe. Diamond stud earrings, necklace, bracelets and rings. I immediately noticed that Collin had her eyes.

Her face lit up when she saw Collin. "My Goodness. You came!" she said with enthusiasm and her pace doubled from a stroll to a slow jog. "Come here," she said and immediately scooped him into her arms. He let go of my hand to hug her back. I stood there patiently waiting to be introduced.

"I'm happy to see you too, Mom," he said as she continued to hold onto him forever.

"Oh, it is so wonderful to finally see you! *My baby.* How are you?"

"I'm great…" he said releasing himself from her bear hug.

"Of course you are! Oh, with your big job and all. Too busy to visit your mother," she said. "But I am so proud of you, Honey."

"I'm sorry, Mom, I've been busy." he said simply.

He's been back since May and he's just now seeing his mother? That's a little strange. I made a note to ask him about it later.

Their never ending reunion was starting to make me feel very uneasy as I stood by, feeling invisible.

I lightly cleared my throat.

"Oh," Collin said suddenly remembering my existence. "Mom, this is Victoria," he said stepping aside. "Victoria, this is my mom."

I smiled my biggest most charming smile. I passed the gift bag I was holding over to Collin then I leaned in to hug her. "Hi, Mom!" I said, trying to be cute.

She gave me a very stiff, dry pat on the back before stepping away. With a fake smile she said, "You could call me Margaret."

"Oh. Okay," I said instantly feeling rejected. "It's great to finally meet you." I still managed to muster the words with a smile.

"Likewise," Margaret said to me quickly then turned her attention back to Collin. "Shall we join everyone? Your Aunt Edith is here, she is absolutely dying to see you." Margaret turned around with Collin, and I followed behind them.

Damn, does she hate me already? I looked at him questioningly. He shook his head trying to reassure me, as if he could read my thoughts. He wasn't worried about it.

Margaret reminded me of Meryl Streep's character in "The Devil wears Prada"; poised and debonair. She was beautiful but intimidating as hell. As we walked into the kitchen the workers quickly straightened up and made sure they looked busy. She made a show of checking their work: tasting this, approving that.

We walked through a bright, spacious, hallway; I could hear the party of guests as we neared an entertaining area. The room was massive, with cathedral ceilings, gold toned walls, and elaborate crown moldings bordering the ceilings. A glass door led to an enormous backyard where even more guests gathered outside.

"Oh my!" I heard then turned to see a super cute, gray-haired, elderly lady approach us. Her eyes lit up. "Look at my little Collin. You're so tall now!"

"Hi, Aunt Edith," he said hugging her gingerly. "How are you?"

"I'm wonderful and it's so nice to see you. Who is this beautiful young lady accompanying you?"

"This is my fiancé, Victoria," he said.

Whoa. *Fiancé?* It was the first time I heard him use that word to refer to me. It was a bit of a reality check but I beamed inside and out, realizing that I was completely comfortable with it, and happy that he was, also.

"Lovely to meet you," I said to her.

"You too, Dear. You are a delightful young woman." She looked me up and down as she held my hands then smiled softly. "Please keep him out of trouble," she added.

"I will," I said and smiled. *Did his family get the memo that he was an adult?* They all acted like he was 4 instead of 24.

A distinguished looking man sauntered passed us, holding a cell phone to his ear. Suddenly there was laughter and turmoil as a parade of children whirled through the house like mini tornadoes. "Hey... hey... outside you guys!" The man said to them.

"Hey, Dad!" Collin waved trying to get his attention. He glanced at Collin, smiled broadly and held up his finger mouthing "one minute," and then he walked over to the den closing the door behind him.

Being shooed out by one of the maids the majority of the children began to stampede their way outside.

"Wait. Nobody said 'hi' to me!" Collin managed to round up a few of them up while the others escaped. Two of the girls were very excited to see him. They looked close to 7- or 8-years-old. Their long hair had been plaited and pinned as if they had circlets on top of their heads; it had taken someone hours.

"This is Ariana and Giana," Collin said to me.

"We're sisters," Giana said, very matter-of-fact.

"I'm older," Ariana chimed in with a smug grin.

"Well I think you both look glamorous," I said.

"Thank you!" Ariana beamed. "This is Noah. He doesn't say much." A little blond boy dressed in a plaid button down and dark jeans started at me with wide eyes. "Come on Noah let's play outside," she said to him.

A new little group zoomed by as the previous ones went outside.

"Ah and here is the lady of the hour," Collin said picking up a brown-haired, bright-eyed little girl who was wearing a white, flower-print dress. She was wearing a string of pearls, which were clearly out of place, but, to this little girl it made her seem to feel all grown up.

"Oh, hi!" she said hugging him tight. "Yay, I didn't know you were here! Today's my birthday." She seemed to be Collin's number one fan.

"I know," he said with a smile. "That's why I'm here. I wouldn't miss your party for all the ice cream in the world!"

She giggled and hugged him. "Did you bring me a present?"

"Of course," he said then glanced over at me.

Her eyes lit up but her smile quickly dropped she noticed me.

"Who's *she*?" She asked pointing her finger at me. She had a scowl as she narrowed her tiny eyes at me.

"Hi, you must be Sophia. My name is Victoria," I said to her in a soft voice. "Happy Birthday, thank you for inviting us to your birthday party," I said handing her the pink and yellow bag.

She cautiously took it from me. *"Are you his girlfriend?"* she asked making a disapproving face.

"Um… yes, I am." I said.

"Yuck," she said and made a funny face. Sophia suddenly lost interest in us. Collin placed her down and she sprung off to join the other children. "Come on guys lets go back outside!" Sophia led the remaining children to the yard. Collin shrugged at me and laughed at the same time. I simply shook my head and smiled. It was *fine*; I was used to not being the favorite amongst children.

Collin's father reappeared from the den. I wondered whether that's what Collin would look like in another 30 years. He still had a full head of salt and pepper hair, and not a lot else showing his age—maybe a few laugh lines around his eyes. He stood straight and seemed in great shape, with no middle-age spread. A quick mental calculation and I assured myself I was closer to Collin's age than his father's.

I was only briefly introduced to William Turner before he pulled Collin aside. They needed to "discuss something privately" so I didn't tag along as they disappeared away from the festivities.

After we split up I wandered around conversing on my own. I met a few more aunts that had nothing but good things to say, as well as several uncles, and cousins. I continued to navigate through the large house where tons of family members awaited greetings, including tons of energetic children.

I wanted to offer to help in the kitchen but there were already too many workers in there doing exactly that.

I made my way outside and sat on the stairs of the deck where Collin eventually found me. We watched as the children ran around in the grass.

"Everything alright?" I asked him as he sat with me.

"Yep … just had to talk about a few things."

"Oh…"

"What about you? How are you making out?" he asked me brushing a few strands of hair away from my face.

"Good. Everyone is so nice. I haven't had a long enough conversation with anyone yet, though."

"I'm sure you'll get to know everyone," he said.

Suddenly, Ariana and Giana ran up to us and appeared to be arguing. "Do you want to do a tea party with me?" Ariana asked Collin.

"No! I want to play pirates!" Giana, who was holding a plastic sword, objected, and scrambled onto Collin's lap.

"No! Go away we're doing a tea party!" Ariana said.

"I don't care, *I* want to play with Collin," Giana objected while trying to push her sister off his lap.

"Hey, that's not nice," he warned in a soft tone. Giana pouted immediately. "What if we play pirates then do a tea party after?" he suggested.

"That's not fair I asked first!" Ariana whined and crossed her arms in protest.

Now they both didn't look too happy. He looked at me and I shrugged my shoulders. But I had to admit I was enjoying watching him in the sticky situation and was curious to see him attempt to get out of it.

He thought for a few seconds then said, "I got it. But you both have to promise, no fighting, okay?"

"We promise," they said in unison.

"We can do a super cool pirate tea party!" he said excitedly to them and they both lit up.

"Awesome!" Giana approved.

Ariana pulled his hand and jumped up and down. "Yay! Let's go! Let's go! Let's go!"

"Alright, sweetie, give me five minutes. Set it up and invite a few party guests. I'll be right there okay?"

"Okay!" they both said and scurried off.

He turned to me again. "I love them. They're so cute," he said and I smiled.

I had to admit that I was very impressed. I didn't know it was possible but I think I fell even deeper in love with him in those moments.

"You're the one that's cute. You're so good with the kids," I said.

"I grew up with all of them. My Aunt Tina and Uncle Leonard have six kids."

"I remember you were telling me."

"And my Aunt Rebecca has four,"

"Ariana, Giana… Jacob and Justin, right?"

"Yup. You're good," he said. He put his arm around me as we watched the girls play. "So… you think that's a lot… four kids?" he asked randomly.

"I guess if that's what they wanted," I said not putting too much thought to where his question was going.

"Have you ever thought about a fourth?"

This was a little out of left field. My stomach felt leaden. But I couldn't say that it was completely unexpected. His parent's backyard wasn't exactly the place where I wanted to have that conversation with him. I would have loved to have children with him. It was obvious that he would be an amazing dad, unfortunately it wasn't in our future and he didn't know this yet.

"I ... I thought about it," I said uneasily.

"Well so have I and you know what I think?"

"What?"

"We would have some really good looking kids," he said then hugged and kissed me playfully.

"We definitely would," I said trying to keep my spirits up. Would it be a complete deal breaker for him if he knew that kids weren't going to happen with me? Suddenly Noah joined us also turning his attention to Collin who seemed to be a magnet to these children.

Noah said something in baby talk that sounded like, "Ken you hawp me tie my soo?"

"I would buddy, but... I have a tea party to attend!" Collin said and stood up. He picked up Noah then placed him next to me. "Do you remember Victoria?"

Noah nodded looking at me with big, innocent, blue eyes.

He turned to Collin and shyly said, "She's pwetty,"

"I know. And, I'm going to tell you a secret. The reason why she's so pretty is because she's actually a princess and she has magical powers."

Noah's mouth dropped. "Whoa! Cool!"

"Shh, you can't tell anyone. But she knows a really cool trick. In fact, she taught me how to tie my shoes. Isn't that right?" he said winking at me.

"That's right," I said convincingly to Noah. Collin smiled at us then walked away to join the girls.

"So aw you weally a pwincess?" Noah asked, his blue eyes twinkling.

"Mmm-hmm," I said nodding my head.

Noah had straight blond hair, long eye lashes, and looked almost exactly like what I pictured our son would look like, if Collin and I had one. Except he would have inherited the light hair and eye color from my father, like Brooke did. But I didn't know why I was putting so much thought into it since it was the baby that would never be anyway. Just another of my many

275

fantasies.

I took Noah's foot onto my lap and used the bunny technique I had used to teach my children how to tie their shoes. It had been a while. We practiced for a few minutes then had a silly conversation that mostly consisted of me answering about 450 questions. I finally sent him off and he ran around with the other kids. A young woman, who I hadn't been introduced to yet, sat next to me.

"Thank you so much," she said. "He really likes you!" she added. "Noah, I mean. He doesn't like too many strangers."

"Oh, no problem. He's adorable," I said, and safely assumed she was Noah's mother.

"Collin has told me so much about you. I'm so happy the two of you were able to make things work out," she said.

"Thank you. Me too. He's amazing." I said. I watched him and Gianna chase Arianna and the other children who joined in on the fun.

"And I hear you're engaged!" she said excitedly.

"Yes. We are," I said showing her my ring.

She held my hand in hers, her touch soft as she examined my ring; "Congratulations! It's absolutely beautiful!" she said. "Wow where are my manners? I'm Eliza, by the way."

Eliza. One of the mystery female names that I found in Collin's phone one year prior. It was nice to know that all of those names turned out to be friends, family members, and of course Britney, who falls into a category all her own.

"So, where are you staying?" she asked.

"We're in LA."

"I'm only a few minutes out west. Get my number from Collin. If you get bored you could always stop by. I'll show you the area. That is if you don't mind a four-year-old tagging along."

"Not at all. Thank you. And I definitely will ask him for your number."

In the distance I could hear the unmistakable sound of the dreaded Captain Collin of the Spanish Main as he chased two squealing girls towards the plank.

CHAPTER 34

The Turner family and I gathered around the long, white, marble table for dinner. Every children's birthday party I ever attended served one thing: pizza. Not at a party in the Turner's home ... no. They served tilapia, chateaubriand with wild mushrooms, chicken Française, roasted potatoes, grilled mixed vegetables, and brown rice. It was a good thing I didn't eat before the party.

Collin and I sat next to each other, two seats away from the head of the table, where William took his place. Margaret sat next to her husband and across from us. Next to her was Aunt Edith; then Aunt Tina, Aunt Rebecca, Uncle Leonard, and Eliza. Several other family members I hadn't been introduced to also joined us. Sophia, Noah, Ariana, Giana, and the other children sat at a smaller table next to ours. Ariana was still sporting a pirate's eye patch and Giana had a burnt cork beard.

As we sat at the table, everyone seemed to be intrigued by Collin and me.

"What do you do dear?" Aunt Edith asked me.

"I run an online shopping website."

"Oh! That's nice," she replied. It was that generic answer that older people can give to sound positive and encouraging, but your answer has gone completely above their head.

"We just recently downsized and I closed the space we were using. It was an unnecessary use of space."

"That's great. It never makes sense to pay a bunch of employees for what you could do yourself, I always say," Leonard said.

"Figured it would be easier to keep up with, since Collin and I have plans to travel. We actually just applied for our passports last week," I said.

"Good for you guys. Margie and I have done our share of traveling," William added. "The two of you should definitely check out the island St. Lucia. We have an excellent timeshare and tons of properties all around the world. Just let us know where and when."

"Thank you so much, that's so generous of you," I said,

happy that our relationship was approved by at least one of his parents. I smiled and turned back to Collin who returned my grin. I was still getting used to his family's wealth.

Then Collin went ahead and decided to say, "Awesome, cause we actually thought about getting married on the beach."

Almost everyone smiled approvingly or said "aw" … everyone except for Margaret. She looked like she was going to be sick.

Margaret stiffened in her chair. "Oh?" she said once she found her voice. She sounded completely shocked as if this were the first time she was hearing about it.

"Mom, I told you this already," Collin said sounding a little annoyed.

"I didn't imagine that you were actually serious … and maybe this shows that you're not! I have never thought a beach an appropriate place to exchange vows," she said.

Then it was suddenly awkwardly quiet. Thank Goodness Collin stood up for me. "Well I *am* very serious," he said. She ignored his comment and everyone continued to eat as nobody knew what to say. Little side conversations continued but Margaret drew the attention right back to herself again.

"Remind me again of how old you are," Margaret said to me.

"*Mom!*" Collin objected immediately. But we had everyone's attention even the pirates and the rest of the children were engrossed.

"Marge I don't know if that's the most appropriate question," Aunt Rebecca said, also coming to my defense as I shifted around awkwardly, not knowing what to do or say. I wasn't that much older than him. Did I look old? What was the purpose of the question anyway?

"What?" Margaret asked innocently. "We're amongst family here, are we not? We are all adults. I'm proud to say that I'm fifty-two. I don't see the big deal."

"*Well it is…*" Eliza rebuked.

"No. It's okay," I said not wanting to be the reason that anyone else ended up in the dog house. "I'm thirty-two." In the pause that followed it felt like everyone was doing the mental math.

"You have children, correct?" Margaret continued.

"Yes. Three. Thomas, Nicholas and Ashley."

"I'm curious as to how all of you get along. How do they feel about this?" she asked directing the question to Collin. Another pause.

"Actually…" he said. "I haven't met them yet."

"The timing hasn't been right," I chimed in defensively.

"Really?" Margaret asked sitting back a bit, as if she got me. "Your children haven't met Collin? And the two of you plan to get married?" She had such a smug look on her face. Was it because she was making me feel so uncomfortable, or was she thinking that maybe Collin and I wouldn't end up married? Suddenly our plans seemed so flimsy.

"Alright Marge, that's enough. Why don't we just let the kids eat," William said.

Funny he said that because I wasn't so hungry any more.

Margaret wasn't having it. "I haven't seen my son in months and I'm meeting Veronica for the first time…"

"Her name is *Victoria*," Eliza said and seemed to be outraged by Mrs. Turner's poor hosting etiquette. She turned to smile at me in support.

"Indeed, Victoria," she corrected. "As I was saying, I think I have every right to be brought up to date about this relationship. Do I not?"

No one disagreed. Not even Eliza. I didn't because in a way she was right. I couldn't imagine what I would do if Thomas or Nick brought home a woman they already had intentions on marrying and I hadn't even met the girl yet. I just would have been less vulgar about getting to know one of my sons' future bride.

Thus, Margaret's inappropriate interrogation continued freely, "And when is this *wedding* supposed to take place?" she asked putting a sarcastic emphasis on the word "wedding."

Collin and I looked at each other. The spotlight really was on us. He wanted me to answer and I wanted him to. Finally I simply said, "We haven't really locked in a date. It's still very new. The details are all up in the air."

He looked over at his mother agreeably. "Don't worry

Mom, we're not getting married tomorrow," he said then reached over for my hand. "But it will be soon," he added smiling at me. I smiled back and hoped he knew I had no hard feelings towards him. I actually felt bad for him because he was in the center of the fire. He had to be careful to keep both of us happy.

"So, what about any more children?" Margaret asked. *This woman didn't hold back at all!*

"We already talked about that," Collin said confidently.

We did? Now *this* was news to me. That little 10 second conversation we just had earlier in the day was his idea of family planning?

"Well sort of…" I quickly added. My heart was in my throat. I felt my face flushing.

"Do you feel as though having another child would be an inconvenience?" she asked towards me. "You mentioned travelling and all."

"No," I said. "But I guess that's amongst one of the many things he and I still need to discuss."

"I see. I only ask because, I know we would all love to see Collin have a family of his own. I'm sure you can see that we already have quite a large family."

"Don't worry Mom! I know what you're getting at. You'll get your grandkids." I think I almost fell out of my chair. Then he turned to me and said, "Right, Babe?"

"Collin…" I said feeling really uncomfortable. My stomach felt like it was being weighed by an anchor. I just wanted to sink into a hole in the ground.

"What?" he asked obliviously.

"Uh… c-could we not talk about this here…" Now my face was burning red.

"Um … alright…" he sounded confused.

"Hmm … Maybe you two aren't as united as you thought," Margaret said finding the great opportunity to jump in at the first moment he and I weren't in sync with each other.

"It's not that…" I objected.

"Will the two of you be living in California or New York?" Uncle Leonard asked obviously trying to helpfully change the subject, but unfortunately we didn't know how to answer that one either.

Collin and I looked at each other unsure again. *Were we on the same page?*

I felt funny and everyone was staring at us. Or at me.

"Uh … I guess Cali for a little while then New York …" I looked to Collin for help.

"Can we talk about something else?" he asked. "Like … did we decide what we're doing for Christmas this year?"

"Of course we did," Margaret said stuffily. "We decided on the cruise. You would know this if you were actually with your family on Thanksgiving Day instead of parading around New York City…"

I couldn't sit there and listen to her any more. "Excuse me," I said in a tiny voice as I placed my fork down. I couldn't look at anyone; I knew they were all looking at me. I scurried away from the table. I didn't even know which direction to go. I walked down the long hallway where we came from and sat at the bottom of the staircase, my chest pounding. Collin was a few seconds behind me.

"Hey!" he said sitting next to me. He put his arm around me and kept me snug against his body. "Baby, I'm so sorry about that."

I shook my head, too embarrassed to talk. I wanted to sort through everything by myself but he took my hand and led me up the stairs. "Come on," he said.

We walked up the large staircase and on the top floor there were two hallways, one on either side of us, several doors on both sides. He led me to the right and opened the second door. The bedroom we entered was all mint green and white and I assumed was used as a spare bedroom.

"Talk to me," he said cupping my hands into his.

"I'm trying so hard but I don't think your family likes me."

"Don't say that. They love you."

"Not all of them." I didn't want to come right out and say it.

"Aw, Babe," he said hugging me. "I told you my mom is a little tough. Don't worry about it."

"A little tough? Collin that was an understatement.

281

She's…" A monster, an overprotective psycho, a nightmare… We were talking about his *mom* so I simply said, "really intimidating."

He exhaled and dropped his shoulders in resignation. "I know. I'm sorry. What else did you want me to say? I tried but she was on my case too. I was hoping she wouldn't do this."

"It's not your fault. She's obviously floored by the idea of us being together. I don't want to get married unless we have everyone's blessing."

"We will," he said. "She knows about our break up so she's a little wary. She's just being a mom. She'll get over it. Don't let her get to you." He kissed my forehead but must have sensed my tension.

"That's not all… is it?" he asked.

"No … I hate to say it but she was right … There is so much we don't know; so much we haven't talked about yet. Maybe we announced too soon?" *Was that a question or a statement?* Part of me really wondered whether we were moving too fast; another part wanted to go ahead — even more just to show Collin's mom.

"We both know what we want, don't we?" Collin whispered reassuringly. He gave me a squeeze. "Don't we?"

"Yes. But …"

"But, what? What is it? Are you having second thoughts?"

"No," I said then sighed. "Collin, why are we talking about children? It's very sudden and uncomfortable."

"It was a little weird at the table. But you were fine with it when we were outside."

"I wasn't fine … I think I was surprised."

"I didn't know it was a big deal. I mean if it's something we both want. And if you really want to win my mom over …"

"Collin, just stop. We're not having kids so your mom could like me."

"That's not what I meant."

"Just drop it," I said and realized I finally had to tell him. "We can't have kids anyway," I said while looking down at my hands.

I looked up at him and he looked a bit surprised. "Why?"

"We just can't."

"Is it because you think I'm too young? You think I can't handle it don't you?"

"No. That's not it. You'd be a wonderful father," I said and was as hurt to admit it aloud as I was afraid to finally confess one of my deepest secrets to him. "We can't have kids because ... well ... *I* can't ... physically." As the words left me I was relieved and scared. I buried this secret for years and never thought I would have to relive the pain. "I never told you this ... but ... I was pregnant, once, after Nick. It was when the abuse was at its worst. I lost the baby at six months." The pain of talking about it was palpable. But Collin deserved to know. "The doctors said the possibility of me becoming pregnant again is less than one percent."

"You should have told me," he said, but there was no accusation in his voice; he wrapped his arms around me again. "You've gone through so much in your life and I would do anything if I could take away even an ounce of the pain you've ever felt."

"You can ... just like this," I said. I closed my eyes as he held me. "You always know what to say," I whispered. I was instantly reminded of why I chose him. And why I chose to leave everything I knew to be with him.

"I'm sorry to have put all that on you before," he said.

"It's okay. You didn't know."

"Come, I want to show you something," he said.

He took my hand and led me down the hall into another bedroom.

A brown and cream comforter covered a queen bed. A black desk sat in the corner with a laptop propped in the middle. Café colored curtains matched the comforter. A bulletin board with several pictures push pinned to it hung above the desk. I immediately recognized a peppy teenage Britney in pigtails and a varsity jacket, with Collin and two other kids, at what looked like a football game. The other pictures were also of him with family or friends.

I realized that I stood in a room full of Collin's past. And everything was intact.

"There's no way they left this room alone this whole

time."

"Are you surprised?"

"Not really," I said with a chuckle.

It was like an exclusive behind the scenes glimpse into the Collin I didn't know. The amount of what I didn't know was still quite vast.

CDs sat on a shelf. I traced the titles with my index finger. The variety was similar to the playlists from when I went through his MP3 player when we met. CD singles. *Wow I remember singles!* The chrome tower held a large collection that included Blink 182 "All the Small Things," Red Hot Chili Peppers "Rollercoaster,", Bowling for Soup "1985,", Offspring "Pretty Fly For a White Guy" ...

He showed me his yearbook and a few souvenirs he had from high-school. He let me keep his class ring and a picture I thought was cute.

"I guess we should go back downstairs?" I asked when I realized that I stole him away for about a half an hour.

"Do you want to go back to the table or head home?"

"I think I'm all partied out." I felt guilty. I knew he didn't see his family often. "Unless you want to stay," I added.

"No. I'm ready to go too."

Collin and I returned to the dining room where everyone was beginning to clear their plates. We said our good-byes and he lied on my account and said that he had to be up early the next day. His mom gave me the fakest farewell before we headed out. I felt like her eyes were shooting me with daggers.

Back at the apartment Collin and I still didn't say much. We changed out of our party clothes and curled into bed next to each other. All my worries seemed to dissolve when I was in his arms in the quiet of the night. We were face-to-face with our bodies close. He kissed me passionately as I moved my hand slowly through his hair.

"No matter what our day is like this is my favorite part," I said looking into his eyes.

"Me too," he said kissing my forehead. "Goodnight, Baby, I love you."

"I love you too," I said and closed my eyes.

Internally I worried deeply about how our relationship

would change. Hoping that what I revealed to him wouldn't chase him away. It hurt me that we wouldn't ever have our own mini versions of ourselves running around. Not to mention the tension between his mother and I was a time bomb waiting to explode.

Despite it all we still seemed to be going strong.

CHAPTER 35

Life went back to its routine after the birthday dinner incident. Collin and I still hadn't talked about it, or about what I confessed to him. I concluded there was nothing else to talk about and it was best to leave it alone.

Six a.m. became my new waking time so that our sleep schedules would be somewhat in sync. This particular December morning the elated feeling I had since Collin and I arrived in California was absent. I wasn't sure if I was homesick or if the novelty had worn off. My mixed feelings about being across the country, was putting a damper on the experience but at least they weren't getting in the way of our relationship. I was gritting through the unfamiliar setting, my future mother-in-law, long hours by myself while I waited for my fiancé to get home, and of course there were those little things that were bugging me that I chose to believe were just my imagination, until they became impossible to ignore.

I was already starting to adjust to new Collin's schedule, when it changed again. Most of the time he left the house at 3:30 in the morning and worked a long day but was usually home at least to have a late dinner with me.

We spent the first two Thursdays and Fridays together, and he worked weekends. Barely a month into our move he started disappearing on Thursday and Friday nights as well. Then it started to feel like he was only home to sleep.

I hadn't brought up my concerns to him yet, but I started to question his priorities. Feeling a little stir crazy since I'd been in the house I considered taking Eliza up on her offer to meet, then I backed out not wanting to bother her — or was that just an excuse? What did we have in common except Collin? Instead I walked over to the little convenience store down the street to buy a few groceries; I wanted to cook something that took a while to make.

As I stood at the stove staring a risotto and homemade apple pie I realized that I was turning into a housewife. Even though I still spent time managing my business online I was always home, cooking, and cleaning. I wanted to be around people again and receive a steady paycheck. I didn't move to California to become a housewife! As I sat around and reflected I also realized that my social life was fading away. I'd only spoken once to Brooke, who was still surprised about my decision to temporarily relocate. I talked to the kids as often as they were able to; they were busier than I was.

Since I left for California I only spoke to Preston recently as he returned from Paris. I had to message him first since I had a new number. He kept me company, in a sense, during the long hours while I was alone. I was chatting with him on the phone as I waited for Collin to return from work.

What time is it? I wondered when I woke up alone. The phone was inches from my head and I knew I must have fallen asleep on it.

That's weird; Collin never came home last night. I reached over sleepily and lifted up my phone to check the time: 6 a.m. No missed calls. With one eye still squint-shut I typed a message to him.

Me: Hi Babe... Is everything okay?

Collin: Yeah. I'm on my way.

Me: Hey. What happened? I thought you were getting out at seven.

Collin: I did. I went out after work. I'm actually right around the corner I'll see you in two minutes.

Did he really just say that? I couldn't believe that I had a flashback of Frank, despite my efforts not to. The night we sat in the dark with Brooke and I asked Frank where he was. He simply replied "I went out." Feeling a bit agitated I couldn't lay down any more. I sprung out of bed and went into the kitchen. I didn't want to fight with him but I needed him to understand the difference between being single and being in a relationship.

While my thoughts were still racing, Collin casually walked through the door. At first I tried to put on a happy face, but I

287

just couldn't hold in my anger. He leaned in to kiss me and I instinctively turned my head.

"What's wrong?" he asked surprised by my taciturnity.

I sighed not knowing exactly what to say. This is how it started ... This is exactly how it started ... *with Frank.*

"Are you mad at me?" he asked. His tone indicated that he was slightly confused about the reason.

"What do you think?" My tone was gruff, my body language stiff.

"Why? Because I went out?"

"No. I don't care if you go out. You know that." I was hurt that he would even think that was the issue. "You never once thought to call or text me?"

It seemed so unlike him.

"I figured you were already sleeping," he said.

"Well I wasn't. And it really only takes two seconds to send me a message anyway."

Now it was his turn to sigh, interrupting me as he walked away. "Jeez, alright, *sorry,*" he said. He obviously didn't mean it.

"What?" I asked noticing his equally annoyed reaction.

"I didn't know that I have to report everything I do now," he said as he placed his keys on the counter.

"Don't make me sound like the bad guy! All I'm saying is that it's common courtesy to tell me ahead of time that you're not coming home."

"Okay. And I said I was sorry."

"You didn't mean it."

"Look, Babe," he said shortly. "I've been working sixteen hours every day for five days straight. My mom's on my case, my dad is on my case, and my boss is on my case. I come home, where it's supposed to be peaceful and now you're on my case too. I went out for a few fucking hours. I think I deserve that much."

"Don't curse at me," I said. I was hurt that we were having that argument. We weren't like that. That was all behind me... *wasn't it?*

"Sorry," he said but meant it this time. "But seriously, coming home to being nagged is just too tiring right now."

"Being nagged?"

"Well…"

"Me caring about you is 'nagging'? Wow. Real nice…"
Stop, I urged myself. But the argument felt like it was on auto-pilot.

"Great. So this is what being married is like?" he said.

"No, it's not. Because married people don't spend all night out without having the decency to call or even send a text. You're behaving like a rebellious teenager, not a married man."

"I'm too tired to argue with you. You're right. Whatever." This time he wasn't saying it jokingly. "I'm going to sleep," he said then stopped before walking into the bedroom then added, "If that's okay with you…"

Okay with me? How could he sleep while we were in the middle of an argument? Men! But I didn't want him to turn into Frank. I didn't want us to turn into me and Frank. Was it inevitable?

"Maybe… maybe I shouldn't be here," I blurted out. I'll admit that at that point I was nit-picking; but the argument wasn't resolved and the fact that it wasn't even moving him the least bit annoyed me more.

He stopped in the frame of the door for a moment before turning to look at me.

"Why would you say that?"

"I sit here all day. I do nothing. I'm not used to this life. All I have to look forward to in the end is the little time we do spend together. And you couldn't care less about that time."

"Is that what it is? You feel trapped?"

"That's not what I said." He completely misunderstood me. Any other time he would have gone to the end of the world to understand, to make me happy. But it wasn't just his behavior, the arguments: his mom, my kids, the prospect of a childless marriage—none of it was resolved and it all hung heavily over our heads. This was supposed to be the exact moment when he would quiet my fears and take me into his arms and promise me that we were fine. He reached for his keys and slid them across the counter to me.

"Look, I'll let you use my car. Why don't you get some air? Go shopping. Buy something for yourself. Put the mall in the GPS. Just be back by two this afternoon I have to be at work at three today."

I had to decide if he was trying to be nice or arrogant. Whichever it was, I felt insulted. I didn't know if I should be offended or appreciative. No, it definitely wasn't meant as a nice gesture. I knew this when he took a stack of 50s and 100s from his wallet and placed them on the counter. It was as if he was trying to show off and shut me up with money and things. That was familiar.

He didn't even say anything else before returning to the bedroom. All I wanted was for him to take my hand and lead me to the room to lay with him. But he seemed to have lost sight of that. Maybe he really didn't need me anymore. The fantasy was old and dead. Annoyed and a little upset at myself for not being able to control my temper I slid his keys across the counter hard enough for them to slide straight across and to the tiled floor with a clatter. A bit immature yes, but maybe all I wanted was a reaction. And I didn't even get that. He ignored my mini tantrum and slammed the door behind him.

So I went out too. But not with his car. I went for a walk to my new favorite little convenience store then I went to a café in the same shopping center where I worked for a few hours on my laptop. I didn't go back to the apartment until after 2 p.m. when I knew he would be gone already.

While I was on my computer I received a message:

Blinky: Guess what?

I always giggled that I saved his name into my new phone that way. It was between Blinky or Betelgeuse but I stuck with the classic.

Me: You won a million dollars?

Blinky: Better

Me: You won a million and five dollars...

Blinky: No! I'll be in California next month!

Me: Oh. Wow. Cool.

I knew I would be happy to see Preston, but I was equally curious as to why he was traveling across the country.

Me: I hope not on my account…

Blinky: I'm helping with a presentation. But you were definitely some of my motivation. I really want to see you.

Me: That sounds great. Let me know when you're in town.

Later that evening I was in bed early on a three-way phone call with Thomas and Ashley. They caught me up on recent happenings and wanted to know what California was like. All three of us were in a different time zone so the call was only several minutes long before we had to say our good-byes.

I heard the front door open and was surprised that Collin was actually home before midnight for once. I heard him in the kitchen for a few minutes before he entered the bedroom.

"Hey…" he said as he stood sheepishly and ran his hands through his hair.

"Hi," I said.

He sat by my side. "About earlier," he said starting off apologetically.

"It's okay," I said almost automatically. I was in the habit of being very forgiving right away.

"No, it's not. I'm sorry, I've been a little stressed out, but I shouldn't have taken it out on you."

"I understand. You've been running on three hours of sleep or less lately," I said sympathetically. "I don't know how you do it."

"It's still no excuse. You didn't do anything wrong."

"You mentioned that everyone has been getting to you including your mom? You didn't say anything to me about that earlier. Was it about what happened at Sophia's party?

"She's just being ridiculous. I know if she got to know you she would feel better."

"We didn't get a chance to talk, except over dinner and

you already know how that went," I said.

"Well, she mentioned going to brunch tomorrow."

"All three of us?"

"Just you and her," he said.

"Oh," I said. "I guess so." Did I have a choice?

"Okay, great. I'll tell her. I'd feel so much better if you two could get along," he said. "I'm off tomorrow so we'll spend the rest of the day doing whatever you want, okay?"

"Deal. But I am looking forward to the day with you, more than brunch with your mom."

"I should hope so," he replied and smiled.

He and I really did need to talk about kids and weddings and not having our own kids. The thought of meeting Margaret again before we'd talked it all out, was unnerving. My heart yearned for the moments when we were okay so I was happy that we weren't arguing any more. I still wasn't very confident about our time together in California, but I was happy that it was only temporary.

The next morning I woke up alone and with a note next to my bed:

"I'm so sorry my love. Something came up. I'll make it up to you."

It seemed as though disappointment was going to become a new trend in my seemingly hazy life.

CHAPTER 36

Lucky me… Margaret was still available and willing to meet me for brunch. "What should I wear?" was always my famous question before leaving to meet with anyone, but this time I really meant it. *What should I wear?* She was obviously judging me. There was a feeling of extra pressure knowing that she didn't care for me. I wanted her to like me. Being fully accepted into the family was important to me.

Margaret and I met at The Hard Rock Café in Hollywood. I soon found out that transportation around LA was similar to New York. There were so many busses and rails it made getting around without a car manageable.

I arrived at the Hard Rock early and waited for Margaret at the entrance. She spotted me and headed in my direction. She wore beige slacks and a frilly white blouse.

"Pleasure to see you again," I said. I noticed how I suddenly turned on my super proper demeanor in her presence.

"Shall we?" she asked letting me lead the way to the hostess.

"So … Collin told me that you wanted to meet with me," I said once we were seated.

"Yes. As I mentioned the other day … I am uncomfortable with how very little I know about you."

"I think it's a great idea that we get to know each other," I said then my eyes dropped down to scan at the menu.

"Victoria, I'm going to get straight to the point," she said.

Was I supposed to be scared? I couldn't get past the fact that she got my name right.

She started, "You may or may not know that my daughter was the victim in a violent relationship. I am also aware of what you've been through and I'm sorry about that."

I acknowledged her comment with a weak smile. "I appreciate that," I said and thought that maybe we would start off on the right foot. We had something unfortunate in common. She continued, hardening her tone.

"Ava would still be here today if I had intervened when my maternal instincts told me I ought. But I didn't."

"Oh, Missus Turner, I could never imagine the pain you went through losing Ava, but you can't blame yourself either. If you could have protected her you would have."

"Thank you," she said. "However aside from William, my son is now all I have left. I love Collin more than anything in the world."

She paused her lecture when the waiter came over to our table to take our orders. I was surprised when she ordered a glass of Merlot and wondered if it would be inappropriate to order a glass...or bottle... of their strongest vodka. I resisted the temptation and selected a simple glass of Prosecco instead.

Margaret looked up at me again and appeared to collect her thoughts before she continued. "My son seems to be infatuated with you. He's very serious about you; I hope you're aware of this."

"I am." *Obviously.* I secretly glowed on the inside because if his mother was saying this then Collin must have raved about me and about us.

My glow didn't last long as Margaret made sure to dim its strength. "Although I simply cannot imagine what the two of you could possibly have in common," she said.

Oh, Margaret you don't want to know what Collin and I have in common, I thought. But other than the sexual chemistry, he and I been through so much and when it came down to it we wanted to be together no matter what obstacles came our way.

"I don't know if the word *infatuation* suits our feelings," I said.

"Oh I am well aware. I've expressed my concerns to Collin about the two of you getting engaged; unfortunately he didn't receive my advice very well. I'm not going to say anything more to him. You see, my son has always preferred to do what he could to avoid conflict."

"I know." I tried to keep my annoyed tone at bay. *Why did she talk to me as if I didn't know him? Why would I travel across the country to be with him?*

"No. You don't. You've only been in his life for, oh what, about a year or two? That's not long enough to really know

294

someone."

"I think I know everything I need to know," I said.

"It's absolutely not long enough to get married!"

"Is that what this whole thing is about?"

"William and I were together for three and engaged for four years before tying the knot."

"Margaret, trust me I understand, I have two sons ... I get it. I understand what it is like to be the mother and to ..."

"I don't think you do," she interrupted and I had to work very hard to keep from rolling my eyes. "I'll tolerate this little charade. Because it's what he wants..."

"With all due respect Missus Turner, Collin and I have been through a lot together. And I'm not letting him go. Not for anyone. Not ever. We're getting married and I'll be a great wife. I love him very much and I know we'll be happy together. I would love to have your blessing by the time we are ready, but we *are* getting married, with or without it."

I didn't mean to go so hard on her but I was glad I did. I meant every word of what I said to my future mother in law.

"Love is a wonderful thing, Dear, but it isn't everything. And, well, I hope for your sake he doesn't change his mind about wanting children."

"He told you about that too?" I asked.

"He didn't need to. I knew right away when the conversation came up at the table."

"That's one of the many things that we will figure out between the two of us. You have to understand that he's an adult and is very capable of making his own decisions. Right now we both feel that it's best that we go back to New York after his current project. You will always be the number one woman in his life. And I'm not trying to take that from you."

She sighed. "I didn't want to have to do this."

"Do what?"

"You say you're so in love. You're both planning to have this wonderful life together. When exactly were you planning to tell him that you're still married?"

She dropped this bomb on me, and the waiter chose that moment to bring our meals. I sat there, as he presented our plates, cheeks burning, eager to respond, but not knowing what to say. Finally, he left.

I still didn't know what to say, and finally stammered, "H-how di-did you know?"

"I have my ways."

That wasn't good enough. "I would appreciate it if you told me how you know about my personal life," I said firmly. Yes it was bold, but what did I have to lose? Besides I was outraged. The woman practically told me to my face that she didn't like me and she seemed to respond to the directness anyway.

"When I found out about this engagement I wanted to find out for myself who my son was rushing to marry."

She did a background check on me? I wondered what that looked like. Did my hospitalizations come up? What an invasion of my privacy!

"I know how it looks ... but ... it's a small bump in the road. Nothing I needed to mention to him."

"But something you felt important enough to keep from him?" she asked and then frowned at the matter.

"I'm just sick and tired of my ex being an issue."

"Well is he?"

"No! Not at all. That's why I didn't bother getting Collin all worried about it. I'll be divorced in four months. We're not getting married before that anyway. I don't see the problem."

She raised her eyebrows, but didn't say a word, waiting for me to continue. Waiting for me to dig a deeper hole?

"Margaret, why don't you tell me what the real issue is here. You would do anything you could to keep me from marrying your son ... why is that?"

"I want to like you Victoria, I really do. You seem sweet. You're attractive enough. I just can't shake the feeling that he is going to end up being hurt by you."

"Well then ... I guess only time could prove you wrong," I said.

"I'm letting you know right now that if anything happens to him because of your nonsense I'm ending this thing between you two," she said.

I didn't have much of a response without it coming across as combative so I quietly let her continue.

"You're already being dishonest with him. Is that how you want to start your marriage?"

She was right but what were her intentions? However, I had just finished getting on his case about communication. *Maybe I should practice what I preach?*

I sighed then said, "You're right ... I'll tell him today ... I'm glad we had this talk."

"Indeed. This went well," she said then politely flagged the waiter over for our check.

That went well? I would love to know what a bad conversation with Margaret Turner looked like. Then again, maybe I didn't.

Neither of us had done more than push our food around our plates. I was still famished but eager to get out of there.

I wanted to tell Collin about my divorce situation. I wanted to be honest with him. It seemed like every time I kept secrets in the past they blew up in my face. But when I returned to the apartment I had yet another surprise. I received a giant bouquet of lilies and red and pink roses. Collin had it delivered to me with an apology card attached to it. How ironic. *He was apologizing to me.*

That night we went out to Hollywood. We walked along Hollywood Boulevard and down the walk of fame where various celebrities' names are written in gold stars. We also went to the wax museum then had dinner at the Boa Steakhouse. I couldn't quite find the opportunity to sneak in, "Hey, by the way I'm technically still married." It would have ruined the evening.

I eventually decided that I didn't want to cause any rift in our relationship. I wanted to deal with, and iron out, our differences over time and to adding another deal breaker to the equation wasn't an option yet.

As the weeks flew by, "Jingle Bells" began to play in the stores. Santas appeared at the malls. The holiday season without snow was something of a different experience. Refreshing, because it fit in with the new life I was aiming for, and equally dismaying to be away from my familiar holiday environment and family. I was way ahead of myself and did my shopping. Gifts were already shipped to all the kids.

"When are we heading out?" I asked as I placed my new earrings on. It was Christmas Eve and I was so happy to get to spend it with Collin unlike the previous year where I was stuck entertaining Frank and his friends and his family at our huge house party. All I could think about then was being somewhere else with someone else, and finally there I was. *Just me and Collin.* It was amazing how much I didn't miss the material things after all.

"In a few minutes Babe," Collin said. "Let me call and find out if we should drive there or take a cab to the dock."

"Hey Mom, Merry Christmas ...yeah almost ready ... we're leaving in fifteen minutes ... yes... uh, me and Victoria ... of course ... why would you even ask ..." He glanced at me then trailed off mid-sentence. He kissed me on the cheek then walked away to finish the call. He returned with unfavorable news.

"Change of plans," he said.

"Why? What happened?"

"We're not going on the cruise anymore."

"What? But, why?"

"Well, it's completely sold out and my mom said she bought the tickets before you were here."

"But she got a ticket for you?" I asked.

"Yeah."

"Well then... if you want... you could go," I said reluctantly.

"No way! I'm staying right here," he said.

"Aw, but ... we have all these gifts. I can't ask you to miss a Christmas cruise with your family. You already missed Thanksgiving. Your mom is going to be so upset. The kids are probably dying to see you ..."

"It's my mom's own fault. You and I will just do our own thing. I'm not going without you. We'll drop off the gifts to the kids when they get back."

I reluctantly agreed to let Collin stay with me. I secretly felt selfish to enjoy having him all to myself for once. We needed the break and we had an amazing time together opening gifts, drinking wine, and watching "A Christmas Story."

New Year's wasn't as fun for us. Unfortunately he ended

298

up having to work. When it was 9 p.m. by us, I knew the ball had dropped in New York. I received a ton of happy New Year text messages; however, I was still in 2012 on the other side of the country.

It had only been several weeks but I was ready to go home. I couldn't find myself calling California "home." I hoped Collin and I would leave that upcoming May, still wanting the same things and moving forward with our dreams together.

I really hoped we would.

CHAPTER 37

It was a beautiful January evening for Collin and me to meet with his family for dinner.

We were both getting ready and I was relieved to finally spend a full evening with him. Dividing his time between work, sleep and the club where he seemed to live, I was getting a very small piece of his left over time. It was leaving me eager for April to come around when we would finally go back to New York together.

"Babe, do you know where my phone is?" Collin asked me.

That was the other thing; *he was always on that damn phone.* I felt like I was in the dark about so many things but I was doing everything in my power not to argue with him. I let so many things slide since the first day we arrived in L.A. -- no matter how much they bothered me.

"I'm not sure," I called from the bathroom while trying to apply my mascara. I heard him rummaging around for a minute. *He could never find anything!* It drove me crazy that the bedroom was already a mess again.

"Can you call it?" he asked.

My hands were occupied, my face was in the mirror as I was then in the middle of applying eye liner and he couldn't possibly realize how annoying it was trying to juggle the task while talking to him at the same time. "My phone is on the dresser," I said.

"Got it," he answered.

I finished my hair and unplugged the straightening iron. I was putting my makeup away when he checked on my progress.

"Are you almost ready? Reservations are for seven." His tone was off. He suddenly sounded as if we were going to a funeral.

"Well don't sound so excited," I teased. "How do I look?" I twirled around in my new black and white Escada dress.

"Um, fine. Come on, let's go."

"Hey! I didn't spend all this time doing my hair and

300

makeup … not to mention all the time it took me to find this at Saks, for a simple *'fine'*," I said then playfully threw my arms around him.

"Yes, you look really nice," he said shortly. He shrugged out of my embrace then handed me my phone. "Here, don't forget this," he said.

"Wait is something wrong?" I asked.

"No, it's nothing." It was the kind of "nothing" that actually meant "something."

"Come on … What is it?"

"I should have known that I can't use your phone without finding something," he said under his breath.

"What is that supposed to mean?"

"It doesn't matter," he said, following behind me to walk out.

"No," I said stepping back into the apartment. I gently closed the door. "I want to talk about this first. What could you have possibly found that made you this angry?"

"Alright, fine…You know I would never go through your phone. I don't do that…"

"Right, so then…?"

"When I used it just before to call mine a message came through."

I glanced to see my last incoming message. Preston randomly decided to say, "Miss you."

"Oh." I sort of understood his concern.

"Is there something I should know about?" he asked.

"It's from a friend back in Jersey."

"Yeah, okay, a friend named Blinky…"

"Well it's Preston actually. He's just an old friend…"

"I don't get it… Why do you have fake names for guys saved in your phone?"

Fake names? It was only one name.

"It's not a fake name, it's just a nickname," I said. Seeing how skeptical he was I was hoping an explanation would help. "Babe, it's nothing. One year when we were kids Preston, Brooke, and I dressed up as the little ghosts from Pac-man for Halloween. I was Pinky, Preston was Blinky… the red one … and Brooke was Inky the blue one. It was so cute. The names kinda stuck…" I said then smiled. Somehow he didn't find my story as cute as I did.

"Whatever. You've never mentioned him before."

"I haven't … Sorry."

"I don't know if I'm comfortable with you talking to this guy…"

"Babe, you have to understand that the same way you have friends so do I."

"I have no idea what you were doing while we were split up and now this guy who's supposedly your friend is messaging you."

"It's none of your business what I was doing because like you said we were split up. And FYI I wasn't doing anything but trying to focus on myself and thinking about you."

I didn't mean to sound so brash, but if he only knew how depressed I was over losing him we wouldn't be having the conversation. The main reason I spent time with Preston was to distract myself. I thought we were past this?

"Whatever. I don't even feel like going anymore. I'm not in a partying kind of mood," he said.

"Oh, that's interesting," I said and scoffed.

"What?"

"You've only spent every other night at that damn club. And every other night you're walking in here at two in the morning. But the one night we are supposed to go out together you're not in the mood to party."

"First of all, I'm not partying when I'm over there…"

"Sure. Whatever." There was a pause. You could have cut the atmosphere with a knife. Eventually, I continued, "Are you really this mad? Preston and I are just friends. He was helping me look for a house actually. Do you want me to call him and prove it to you?" I was pissed! My heart was beating, my face flushed. How could he not trust me?

"No, it's fine…" With his keys in his hand he was already ahead of me. "What kind of name is Preston anyway?" he said and sounded like a little boy trying to get in the last word.

"Oh, don't be immature!" I scolded. "I don't want to go if you're going to be giving me an attitude the whole time either."

"I'm not… I don't even care. Let's go."

He didn't care? Was this really about Preston, or something else?

While we drove, the tension in the air was still thick. I didn't know if I should talk about something else as if nothing ever happened, or reassure him again that Preston wasn't a threat. All I wanted was to be with Collin, by his side, yet there we were sitting in an uncomfortable silence until he turned the radio on. I sighed and stared out the window.

"You really don't trust me?" I muttered. I was hurt. My eyes still fixed on the passing sites outside the window.

"What I sometimes worry about is the same thing most of my friends and family always tell me."

"And what is that?"

"Well ... look how we started off," he said.

"Okay, so what's your point?"

"What happens when you get bored with me?"

"That's so unfair!"

I didn't cheat because I was bored! Is that what he thought of me? Or was he saying things out of anger? When we met I saw something in him. I thought I did. At the moment I couldn't even remember what it was. All I could see in those moments was red and I was only aware of the increasingly burning feeling in my face. I never in a million years thought he would throw it in my face or hold that against me.

He didn't say anything else. He just continued to drive. What was going on inside his head?

My heart was racing and I tried to fight back tears; somehow his words really got to me. I shifted in the seat and felt something hard under my thigh. I reached under and grabbed the tube shaped object. Then I stared at the object I held in my hand. Woman's lip gloss.

"Great ... look what Vanessa left behind," I said bitterly.

"Just throw it out when we get to the restaurant."

"Yeah. Whatever. She probably left it on purpose." It felt like the lip gloss was burning through my hand. Lip gloss ... pink leopard print thong ... what's the difference? Collin was never home and he was accusing me of something. Was he feeling guilty about something? Was Collin just another Frank? Suddenly a blinding rush of anger took over.

"Here, why don't you just give it back to her yourself," I said throwing the lip gloss tube at him.

"Why are you getting mad at me? It's not my fault she left something in my car."

"How am I so sure that it's hers anyway? It could be one of your other girlfriends that I don't know about."

"What are you talking about?"

"You ran out in the middle of the night to pick up your ex-girlfriend! I said I was fine with it but you know what -- I'm not fine. If you could do that I can't imagine what you would do that I don't know about."

An animalistic fury crept out from a deep cave where it was hiding. I was pretending to be okay with everything when in fact I was just burying my feelings -- habits of the past.

Suddenly the thought of being in the car with him was making my skin crawl. I couldn't continue to sit like a passenger to my life and watch myself turn into the woman who was supposed to be in my past. The fury grew and began to possess me. "Pull over. I want to get out!"

"What?"

"I said I want to get out of the car," I repeated.

"We're almost there…"

"No! I'm not going anywhere with you. I just realized how stupid I am! Your fucking ex shouldn't be in your car in the first place. I don't care what the circumstances are. And you have the nerve to question me about who I'm talking to …"

"I already told you I don't care about what you do … just don't be mad when I'm doing the same thing."

His words caused the blood to boil within my veins and I couldn't see past the blinding red tones that replaced my normal vision. Whenever I was this angry rationalization wasn't an option.

"Stop the damn car!" I demanded again. When he ignored me I grabbed the steering wheel, pulling it hard to the right. "Let me out right now!" I started hitting him, my little fists flying into his arm and side. It was as if I suddenly snapped. The car zigzagged as we then fought over the wheel.

"Victoria what the hell are you doing? Get off!" He jerked the wheel back to the left but the car swerved almost into oncoming traffic. The cars coming towards us held down their horns. He pushed me away and blocked my attack and used that opportunity to bring the car to pull over abruptly.

"What's wrong with you?" he snapped once we were safely stopped.

I was wrong, but at the time I didn't care. I couldn't think of the danger or that I may have almost caused an accident. I yanked at the door handle.

As I started to storm down the side of the highway I knew I had no idea where I was headed. I couldn't seem to get it together. Collin followed behind me.

"What the hell are you doing?" he asked taking a hold of my arms.

"Get off me!" I ripped free from his grasp and pushed him away. Between his comments, his not trusting me, and the thought of him with Vanessa I wasn't even sure where the root of most of the anger was coming from. It was a full blown storm of rage at that point.

"Victoria you're acting crazy! You almost crashed my car!"

"Fuck your car. That's all you care about. Your precious race car, your job, and that stupid night club. Why the hell am I here then?"

"I thought you're here because you wanted to be," he said.

"I thought so too." It wasn't going as smoothly as I had planned. "You're never home..."

"You can't be mad at me because. I'm working a lot and trying to save for us!"

"It's not just that..."

"Well then talk to me, but you definitely can't do crazy shit like this every time you're mad about something!"

I stood on the sidewalk with my arms crossed. It was definitely chillier than I expected outside.

"Come on ... let's go back to the car ..." he said in a calmer voice. "Look at you, you're freezing."

"I'm fine."

He stepped over to me and gently grabbed my bicep to steer me towards the car. "Victoria, just get in the car I'm not leaving you out here by yourself."

We drew quite some attention as other cars were looking

to see what was going on. One car even pulled over a few feet ahead of us.

I put my head down embarrassed and didn't make eye contact with the strangers as I quietly clambered back into his car. Needless to say the rest of the ride was ridged and silent.

We pulled up to the restaurant and he turned the engine off. But neither of us moved. It seemed like an eternity before he turned to face me.

"Are you okay?" he asked.

I nodded.

"Look, I didn't mean anything I said earlier. I'm sorry I got mad at you over something so stupid," he said in a low voice.

"I'm sorry too. Sometimes my anger and emotions get out of hand ..."

"You acted like you understood about Vanessa ... you have to believe there is nothing going on between me and her," he said.

"Well it bothered me more than I realized. And more so the fact that you're never around ... even if you are working, I still need you to make time for me ..."

Our conversation was cut short when Eliza pulled into the parking space next to us and waved to us with an enthusiastic smile.

"I guess we have a few things to talk about when we get home," he said.

"I think so," I agreed and nodded. He stepped out of the car and followed behind him. I wished we could ditch the dinner but we both put on a happy face for his family as we greeted the others at the door. Good thing I hadn't started crying, or I'd have looked like a raccoon.

A much smaller group of Collin's family were in attendance than the last time we were together. Sophia's party was flooded with children, whereas only Noah joined us for this dinner. This time around it was only Margaret, Eliza, Rebecca, Leonard. William was absent. Business trip. He always seemed quite consumed by work.

"Is everything okay?" Eliza asks us; her eyes darting from me to Collin then back to me again. We must have looked like two children who were just sent to time out. I was quiet. He was quiet. We didn't make eye contact with each other. It must have been obvious to everyone that there was a rift between us.

"Yes," I answered quietly.

"Yeah, just a little tired," Collin answered.

"That's because you're working too hard, Honey," Margaret said to her beloved son. "On your next day off you should come over and relax. I'll make some fresh squeezed lemonade and we could sit out by the garden or stay in and watch movies all afternoon. Doesn't that sound wonderful?"

She forgot the video games and bagel bites. A 16-year-old's dream.

"Sure, Mom, one of these days, maybe," Collin said.

Then Margaret turned her attention to me. "Victoria, I am simply mortified about what happened at Christmas. Please accept my apologies."

"It's okay. We would have loved to join everyone but Collin and I didn't mind having some time alone anyway."

"Glad there are no hard feelings," Margaret said to me and gave me a smile that I just knew was fake.

"None at all," I said then returned the smile.

Margaret went on. "I wasn't sure that you would still be in California by then. But I'm glad the two of you were able to resolve your issues."

Of course she didn't think I'd be there. She thought she would have already succeeded in voting me off the island.

"Actually we're fine mom," he said defensively.

"That's very mature of you," she replied. "I'm not sure how I would have felt in your situation."

"What situation?" He sounded confused.

My mind was equally muddled by her comment. There was only one "situation" she could have been referring to and I knew -- or hoped -- she wasn't about to bring that up. I looked at her, my eyes pleading, but she wasn't looking at me.

"Well, with Victoria still being married and all."

I think I died inside a little. I wasn't expecting her to blow up my universe just yet. Was it intentional? Now what? Everything in my head seemed to pause and fast forward at the same time. My ears felt hot. My stomach churned.

"Mom, she's not married I told you this already. Why are we talking about this right now anyway?" Collin asked irritably.

Margaret pursed her lips then looked at me then back at Collin whose eyes were now set on me for an answer.

"Babe, please tell her," he said exhaustedly.

"Oh, Dear," Margaret said feigning innocence. "I'm sorry, I've said too much."

Collin's mood was already off from our argument. And now was when I had to come clean? I wasn't sure what this was going to do to us but I was convinced it was part of Margaret's plan. The rest of the table was silent. All eyes on me.

"Um…" I chimed in.

"Well?" Collin urged.

"I don't think this is the place to talk about this," my voice quavered.

It was the birthday party incident all over again …

"There's nothing to talk about. It's simple … tell my mother you're not married so we could drop it and move on," Collin said.

I opened my mouth but nothing came out. My eyes stung.

"Victoria?" He sounded confused when I couldn't answer. First he looked hurt. Then as the silence prolonged it quickly changed into fury. "You're kidding right?"

"I … I can explain," I stammered. *Could I?*

His icy glare shot to his mom next. "And you knew about this?"

"It's not her fault!" I was surprised at how fast I jumped in to defend Margaret. But in all reality no matter how inappropriate it was for her to expose my secret at the table that way, it was my fault for owning the secret in the first place.

"You know what … I'm done." He escaped from the table.

I scanned the outraged faces of Collin's family before shamefully excusing myself and following behind him.

"Wait!" I called out to Collin once I had caught up to him outside.

He stopped several feet from the entrance of the

308

restaurant with his back to me.

"Please listen…" I said. I wasn't sure how I would approach my explanation but he deserved something. I didn't put much thought into keeping the fact that I was still married from him … I just didn't want it to ruin anything. I was pretending. Pretending that everything was fine. And it was … until now.

He turned around to face me and the pain in his eyes was profound. My betrayal hurt him more than I imagined it would.

"You're still married …" he said in disbelief. It came out as both a statement and a question.

At this point tears already formed behind my lids. My words were all choked up between sobs.

"Technically … yes … but …"

"So, what the hell was all this then? Us being engaged … planning a future … just more of your lies?"

"No! Of course not. It doesn't change anything."

"It changes everything! How can I ever trust you?"

Tears flowed down my cheeks. I slowly took a few steps toward him until our bodies were only inches apart. Now that I stood closer to him I could see tears in his eyes as well.

"I would never do anything to intentionally hurt you." I placed my hand against the side of his face. "I love you…"

"Stop." The tone in the one word said so much on its own. He didn't believe me. He didn't want to hear anything I had to say.

"Baby, please…" I tried desperately to bring him back to me. I needed him to understand my reasons for withholding the truth.

He turned away from my touch. "I can't," he said shaking his head.

"I'm sorry," I whispered.

"I can't be here right now," he said and quickly turned away from me. I didn't chase after him. No matter what I said I wouldn't get through. It was broken, all broken — and all because I had this impulse to keep secrets. *When would I learn? When would I learn?*

I sat outside on a bench just outside the restaurant. I

couldn't bring myself to face Collin's family. Eventually, Eliza found me there and offered me a ride home.

"Just a left over here," I said as we entered the apartment complex.

Thankfully, Eliza hadn't tried to make conversation, and though the silence was awkward, any conversation would have been more awkward still. I was very embarrassed and hoped Eliza and the rest of the family didn't view me differently.

"I really didn't mean for it to be this way," I said as we pulled in front of the apartment.

"Give him some time. I think you two will be okay," she assured.

"Thank you for the ride," I said as I got out of the car. I said bye to her and Noah and watched them drive off.

I walked into the apartment and to my dismay, but not quite surprised, Collin wasn't there.

I couldn't even pinpoint my emotions while I sat alone in the quiet apartment. I curled onto the sofa and checked my phone to see if he had called or texted. Nothing. I was exhausted from crying, I had a headache, and couldn't sleep. I turned on the TV as a distraction and found the movie "You've Got Mail." Watching the main characters, played by Tom Hanks and Meg Ryan, fall in love in a New York setting, and watching them explore the city and stop at Gray's Papaya and walk through Central Park, brought back fonder memories. I really missed New York and our life there. I fell asleep curled under a blanket feeling more alone than I'd felt in months.

CHAPTER 38

For three days Collin and I didn't talk. It was 72 hours of complete agony. The morning after the argument I woke up to find a note to let me know that he would be staying at his mom's for a night. I guess he took her up on the offer. I hoped he just needed space and we could talk things over when he came home. That was my best interpretation. I wasn't good at relationships, it was at that moment I was well aware of this sad truth.

One night at his mom's became two then three. I called and texted him all weekend but, no response. When I finally gave up was when he let me know that he would be home that evening.

It was early in the evening when Collin walked in. My heart was pounding when I saw him. I feared what his views of me would be after a three day anti-Victoria fest at his mother's house.

I inched carefully closer to him as I was so unsure of what was going through his mind.

"Collin, please talk to me…" I said; my voice small.

"What exactly are we supposed to talk about?" He didn't sound angry which was some sort of consolation, but we were obviously so far from where we needed to be.

"Are we … um …" I searched for the right words.

"I'm just trying to figure things out …"

"Can we please do that together?" Every time I moved closer to him he moved further away from me.

He looked down and was quiet for a moment then it seemed like all of his thoughts suddenly exploded into real form.

"Victoria … you lied to me."

"I know. I didn't mean for you to get hurt," I said.

"No. You didn't mean for me to find out. Fuck … when were you going to tell me?"

"I …"

"Or were you planning on never telling me?"

He had a wall up and I couldn't get through. I felt helpless and wished I could undo all my mistakes. My sweet lover was absent, our chemistry was dampened, and it was my fault.

"I didn't think it mattered …"

"Are you serious? You didn't think it would matter to me that you're still married?" His voice escaladed as the latter words thundered out.

"We were still going to be together regardless … I … I wanted to tell you," I said, then paused while fighting back tears. "But then you proposed so unexpectedly and I didn't want to ruin everything by dropping that on you."

"I think you made the wrong choice."

"The divorce was supposed to be finalized in November. Things got a little complicated and the court date was pushed back, only until May. But there is absolutely nothing else left with my marriage …"

"You have no idea what I go through to be with you. I'm going against friends and family. Everyone thinks that maybe we rushed into this," he said.

"Everyone?"

"Not everyone … but you know what I mean."

"Well … Do *you*?"

"I don't know … I can't be wrong about us," he said shaking his head. "Or I thought I knew…"

"You're not wrong." I moved closer to him again wanting to feel some sort of connection. Wanting to rekindle our flame. "Baby, I'm right here … I came here for you, for us …"

"Trying to get over you was one of the hardest things I ever had to do. I don't want to go through that again."

His comment threw me. *Getting over me? Why was he going there?*

"You won't ever have to."

"What happens when you go back to New York and he ropes you back in? Where the hell does that leave me?"

Why … how … could his thoughts even go there? Go back to Frank? I would never in a million years. How could he not know this?

"That won't happen…"

"Well, it's exactly what happened last time."

"It won't. I'm not going backwards … ever. All I'm

looking to is my future and only you and I are in it."

"Victoria …" He said my name with such a heavy weight and I felt like I should sit down, but I didn't. I waited. I anticipated, and knew because of the look in his eyes, and because I knew him, that he was going to say something that might devastate me.

And I was right.

"I'm not going back to New York," he said.

"Wait … what?"

"I … I accepted another job over here."

"So what does that mean for us?"

"I don't know," he said. "It's another six month project on a feature film … another step up in my field. I feel like it's what I need to concentrate on."

Our relationship couldn't handle another six months on the west coast. Even if I wanted to stay I couldn't … It was only supposed to be temporary, I wasn't going to just abandon my kids and the other parts of my life.

"I can't stay…"

"I know," he said.

"So are we…?" The lump in my throat wouldn't allow me to finish the sentence, but I didn't need to because he knew what I was going to say.

"No … I mean that's not what I want. I just need some time."

That was where the conversation ended. One of the heaviest discussions we've ever had was cut short because he had "something to take care of." He was living a double life. We both were. Every time he walked out the door we grew further and further apart.

*   *   *   *

What began as a three-day argument stretched into a four-week coldness. For an entire month I watched my relationship deteriorate. Despite the fact that we both wanted to work things out, Collin and I hardly spoke to each other. He wouldn't come home for days at a time. The late nights he did come to bed I would wrap my arm around him only to be rejected, or we slept in separate rooms. Even both my birthday and Valentine's Day came and left, my best company being my phone on both occasions. He said he'd make it up to me -- it was added to my collection of empty promises. I tried everything I could think of to fix us, but nothing was working. It was a two-way street. Even though the fuse was initially lit during our first set of arguments, all I could see was the bomb ahead ready to detonate. We lost our spark and simply put, we weren't happy anymore.

I often thought about going back to New Jersey. I questioned my presence in California as I seemed to serve as nothing more than a maid and a cook. I spent more time chatting with Preston than I did with my own fiancé. It was mostly because I didn't want the loneliness to consume me. I found myself back and forth between the store and apartment, refilling the liquor collection as I began turning to the bottle again, only to help get through the nights. I wasn't supposed to be lonely. Things were supposed to be perfect.

"Hey? Are you sure you're okay over there? You sound so glum."

My mind came back from where it wandered to when I heard Preston's voice on the other end of the phone. I stared at the ceiling of the dark bedroom. I realized that last time I was paying attention the sun was still up.

"Huh? Oh … I guess so. I … I don't even know …" I replied to Preston.

"Well, I have some news that might cheer you up," he said.

I don't think anything could cheer me up.

"What's that?" I asked.

"Remember when I said I would be up there? My trip is actually this weekend. I'll be in LA."

I shouldn't be meeting with Preston. I shouldn't even be talking to him, but somehow Collin's loss of interest in me was making me reciprocate the feelings about our relationship. As much as I knew it wasn't true deep down inside it still hurt me and felt like I was holding on to the memory of what was.

"I … I don't know. I'll let you know Preston …"

"Aw, come on… what's the big deal? I miss you."

"Yes, I know. You said that in the text message you

314

sent me."

The message that started everything...

"What?" He was so clueless. He wouldn't remember because it was something so small in his mind.

"Look, I wasn't completely honest with you when I came out here. I am actually seeing somebody. I'm sorry, I feel like a shitty friend." I was so blunt about it. What was the point of dancing around the truth?

"Oh, you are? Well, I can't say that I'm entirely surprised either. You haven't mentioned anything else about you and me so I kind of put two and two together."

"Really? And you still want to see me?"

"Didn't we agree to keep our friendship going no matter what?"

He was right. There was no reason two people couldn't be in a relationship and not have friends of the opposite sex. I had no friends while I was with Frank. I wasn't going to repeat history. And at least Preston actually wanted to spend time with me.

"I'll let you think about it," he said. "You can text me a location of where you think we can meet. No big deal either way."

"Okay. I'll let you know," I said.

After hanging up with Preston I closed my eyes and left the dark room only to get lost in the darkness inside my head.

CHAPTER 39

As the warm California version of March rolled in, and my circumstances with Collin weren't improving, I knew we were in trouble. I made another attempt to "save" us as I left him a sweet note in the morning letting him know that I wanted us to have a date night, something simple -- dinner and a movie. Or anything really. On Saturday nights he was usually home early enough.

My thoughts were hopeful and a feeling of contentment brewed in my mind as I imagined Collin and me finally spending a few hours together. But my fantasy left abruptly when he walked through the door passing by me with a brief, dry greeting before vanishing into the bedroom.

I walked into the room behind him and he was at his dresser. He moved as if he was in a hurry, removing clothes from the drawers and closet, assembling a new outfit together, placing the garments onto the bed.

"Hey ... did you get my note?" I asked.

"Oh ... yeah. I can't tonight," he said.

"Going somewhere?" I asked as I stared at the bed noticing his white button down, lined up next to a pair of dark gray pants. He was getting dressed up to do whatever while I got to sit around in the apartment alone.

"Yeah, I thought I mentioned it to you," he said.

"When? We never talk."

"My friend Edwin is getting married ..."

"Oh. Okay. I remember," I said recalling one of the few conversations we had a few weeks prior.

"Well me and a few friends are going out to celebrate," he said while gathering his things together.

"Yeah. A bachelor party. Great," I said. I really didn't want to fight, I just missed him. We spent more time together when we lived in different states.

"I already told you it's not a bachelor party. We're just all getting together before he gets married."

"I'm not stupid. That's called a bachelor party," I said.

His phone rang and he glanced at it. "Hold on," he said to

me before stepping away to answer it.

"Yeah what's up? I know, I'll be there by nine-forty-five ... relax ... of course we're in VIP did you seriously just ask me that ... tell them to have everything on the table before we get there .... Don Perignon, Belvedere, and Grey Goose ... definitely ... the girls want Malibu ... alright let me go ... I'll see you in a few," he said and hung up, then turned to me and asked, "What were you saying?"

"Nothing, Babe ... I was actually just going to ask you if we could do something together soon. I know you're so busy so whenever ..."

His phone rang again. He looked really annoyed and answered it again. "Hey? Why does everyone keep calling me? It's really not that complicated ... Yes, the VIP fits fifteen people ... didn't I just finish telling Mauricio all this ... I'm not driving so I can't pick anyone up ... I'll send Duane out in a car ... yeah ... whatever, that's fine ... If you guys have any more questions ask your brother it's his party anyway ... I gotta go."

He brought his attention to me again.

"Wow, Mister Popular," I said.

"Yeah, it's really annoying," he said. "Um, can we talk later? I really have to get ready."

For some reason I was suddenly able to remember the detail that Edwin was Vanessa's brother, so unless this was a different Edwin, or he had a brother, then the last phone call was from the skank herself.

"So is *she* going to be there too?" I asked.

"A lot of people are going to be there."

"Can't you ever just answer a question?" I suddenly snapped.

"Yes, Vanessa, and Edwin's fiancé, and a lot of other people are going to be there. Do you have a problem with that?"

"Obviously it doesn't matter how I feel. What kind of bachelor party has girls there anyway?"

"It's not a damn bachelor party," he said then sighed. He then grabbed a towel before escaping into the bathroom. "I have to take a shower.

I sat at the counter feeling defeated. I wasn't even sure

why I was holding on anymore. I did the same thing I did for the last few weeks -- filled a glass with ice and straight tequila.

Collin and I were becoming roommates and no matter how much we held on, that didn't seem to be changing. It was heavy on my mind when I heard the squeaky sound the shower made when it was shut off. Shortly afterwards Collin emerged and passed through the kitchen again, his fresh scent mixing with that of my tequila on the rocks. His wet hair clung against his head before he used a towel to tousle it, leaving it messy and wavy.

I walked into the bedroom after him. He had a towel wrapped around his waist.

"Babe…" I said and enfolded my arms around him.

He hugged me back a moment. I closed my eyes, wanting to stay there forever. It had been a while since we were intimate with each other. I never thought I'd see the day.

"Instead of going to that party … I can think of a few things we can do here … I don't mean dinner and a movie," I said then pressed my body into his as I kissed his neck. I missed the feeling of my lips against his skin.

"Victoria … you're gonna make me late."

"Since when was that ever a problem?" My hand traveled down his chest, down his abs, then stopped at the towel. I tugged on it gently. "I want you," I whispered.

He seemed to react adversely to my touch as he peeled away from me. "Not now," he said.

I looked up at him shocked. I stepped away and he began to get dressed. I sat on the bed with my back to him.

"Are we … are we okay?" I asked as I stared at my hand and my dazzling engagement ring. But at that moment it just felt like a piece of jewelry. The promises behind it were absent.

"Jeez… why do you choose when I'm leaving to talk about this?"

"You're always leaving!"

"Look, if you're still up when I get home we'll talk then." He completed his attire with a gray jacket and a matching fedora hat. He looked gorgeous and I was resentful to the fact that he was really going out. Our relationship was going in the opposite direction as time passed.

"I know things aren't perfect right now but we're going to be fine..." he assured me as I stood solemnly.

"No, I don't think we are ... I'm not happy anymore and I think it would be best if I go back home."

"Well ... if that's the way you feel ... fine then," he said. It was obvious that he didn't mean it. I didn't mean it either. *What the hell is wrong with us?* We were supposed to be in love and put all the pride, fear, and insecurities aside, but we both were too scared to be the bigger person and put everything on the line.

"Fine. I guess I don't need this." Again letting my emotions and impulse control my actions I twirled off my ring and shoved it at him.

He took the ring in his hand. "Come on, don't be like this," he said.

"I don't want it ... not now anyway ... I don't understand how you could go out drinking and partying with your friends while you and I are falling apart."

"I don't know what you want me to do."

"This is what we've turned into? I've never had to explain what I was feeling to you -- you just knew," I said and just about gave up. "You know what? Just go..."

He stood for a few seconds, sighed and actually seemed to have contemplated the situation. Then at that moment he had a choice. We both needed to make sacrifices for each other. He knew this, and at that moment I needed him to make the right decision.

He walked over to me and touched my face, staring at me longingly. His eyes seemed to carry the same look of dismay as mine did. We wanted to go back to the way we used to be, but maybe neither of us knew what to do anymore. We drifted so far away.

It was only about seven seconds that he was completely mine again. Just for those seven seconds we reconnected and a strange serenity was there. I took in a slow deep breath. Then he broke the spell when he kissed my forehead and took a step away from me.

"Victoria, I'm sorry I have to go..."

My mouth dropped open. I silently watched him leave

319

and shut the door behind him.

I knew that I tried. I also knew that I needed to accept when it was over. The truth was we weren't ready for marriage. We were nowhere near that point. We weren't even ready for a relationship.

Maybe I'll just be alone forever. Less drama. Less pain. I couldn't keep fighting. Fighting to be with him. Fighting with him. Fighting for his attention. It was very exhausting.

At some point between drinking and venting to Britney on the phone I began packing my suitcase.

"I'm so sorry," Britney said. "I wish I knew what's going on with him."

"Me too," I said then took a break from packing to re-fill my glass.

"Britney, tell me now if there is someone else! I know you know!"

"Jeez. Why are you yelling at me?"

"I'm not yelling." *Was I yelling?*

"Britney, I hate it here," I said and began rambling on and on about our drama, my future monster-in-law, and Vanessa, and the argument and my stupid mistakes.

"He talked to his ex, right in front of me, she's gonna be at that damn party with him while I'm here."

"No!" she gasped. "What kind of bachelor party has girls there anyway?"

"That's what I said!" I was happy someone agreed with me. "That's not all. Could you believe he left in the middle of the night to pick her up? What kind of shit is that?"

"What? When did that happen?"

"That was back in December."

"You never told me about that."

"I know. There is a lot I haven't told you. I wanted to pretend everything was great. It's all blowing up in my face now."

"Well, what are you going to do?"

"I don't know any more," I said and sighed and then stared at my half packed suitcase and empty glass. *How did I get here?*

"You guys really need to talk," she said.

"I tried! So many times. We either end up arguing or he walks out. I don't think I could do this anymore."

"Sweetie, I'm so sorry. You could always come back to New York to take a breather. I'll get tubs of ice cream and movies …"

"Aw. Thank you Britney, you're so sweet. But you know if I left I wouldn't be able to stay with you …"

"Why? Because it's his place? Yeah, right, I'd like to see him try to say something to me. This is my place now," she said trying to add authority to her voice.

I smiled for a moment at Britney's attempt to amuse me. I continued to catch her up about all the details she missed over the recent months. She was shocked to hear about us. But as I verbally relived everything I went through I grew angrier by the second. "Wait this isn't fair. I came to California for him! I left my life behind to be with him. And he's out at a fucking club!"

"Victoria … Calm down…"

"No. I'm so stupid. I let Frank get away with whatever he wanted. Now he's doing the same damn thing. This is my first marriage all over again."

"I don't know about that…"

"I'm going over there!" I declared. This is what my drunken self wanted to do and my sober self was exhausted and all cried out, so I deterred to the first one.

"Don't be hasty Vic. That's probably not the best idea …"

"Whose side are you on?"

"I'm on both, Sweetie. Just hear me out … you're mad. Wait it out and talk to him when he gets home."

"I'm done waiting on him. I'll talk to you later."

By the time I hung up the phone not only was I fully intoxicated but I was also certain that I wanted to go to the night club and confront Collin. I gathered an outfit, changed, and then tossed my suit cases aside.

I took his keys from the counter and staggered out of the apartment. I knew exactly where to find him. I got into his car and programmed "Starlight Night Club" into the GPS.I was completely unaware of what I was getting into.

CHAPTER 40

I arrived at the front of the Starlight Night Club. I didn't end up driving there, I called a cab. When I attempted to drive Collin's car I realized two things, I was way too drunk to drive, and that I wasn't great at driving stick. I paid the cabbie and when I took a step out I stumbled on my heels, almost falling out of the cab. *I hope they let me into the club. I should never be allowed to drink.* My thoughts stumbled through my mind, as much as my feet did the same against the pavement.

The security guards weren't going to let me in until I told them I was there for Edwin's party. At least I'm at the right place, I thought, as I walked into the club and was blasted away by the bass of blaring music.

Why am I here? What am I doing?

Blinking against my hazy vision and the flashing of multicolored lights, I looked around at the dancers: couples, groups of guys, groups of girls and guys ... but I couldn't see Collin anywhere. *Fuck*, I thought, *I know he's here somewhere.* It seemed like it was mostly guys over by the bar, but it was too far away and my eyesight was too clouded. I couldn't make out what anyone looked like. On another side a dozen girls with unnaturally colored hair and wearing nothing but bras, panties, and stiletto heels, danced on the bar. I almost became overwhelmed with the idea of looking for Collin then I remembered he and his friends were in a VIP section.

I was about to try to find which area when a security guard tapped me on the shoulder. "Miss?" he said.

I blinked in mild surprise. "Huh?"

"The party you're looking for is over there," he pointed me in the right direction.

With a rushed word of "thanks," I hurriedly tottered forward.

I found the VIP area with a group made up of about eight guys and five ladies. I couldn't tell which one was the bride and groom, it was always obvious in parties like these. I recognized one of the guys then after a few seconds I realized it was the surfer guy, Brad. The group sat around a large cocktail table that was covered with hors d'oeuvres, grapes, cheeses, buckets of ice, and endless bottles of Moet, Hennessey, Belvedere, and other top shelf liquors. I don't know why the table was the first thing I noticed. Maybe because it felt like I was surrounded by complete strangers. Or surrounded by Frank and his friends. At this point, the difference was becoming increasingly difficult to distinguish.

And then there was the icing on the cake: as I glanced up again at the faces around the table there was one female whom I realized I did in fact recognize, the last person I wanted to see -- Vanessa. Then I noticed that Vanessa happened to be wearing a hat. But she wasn't wearing just any hat, no. She was wearing my man's gray fedora hat.

None of the guests realized that I was standing there, as they all laughed and drank while my internal battle was between ripping that hat off Vanessa's disgusting head or confronting Collin first.

Brad happened to glance over in my direction and was first to notice me. He looked a little like he'd seen a ghost before leaning over a friend to tap Collin who was taking shots with the other party guests. Collin looked up at me and his demeanor immediately changed. He quickly scrambled around the table.

"Victoria? What are you doing here?" He looked shocked to see me.

"I could ask you the exact same thing," I said.

Just then some of the guests, including Vanessa noticed our drama. "Oh, great," she mouthed rolling her eyes.

"You have a problem?" I took a few swaying steps in her direction to challenge her.

"Nope … no problem," she said shaking her head. She wasn't being the loud mouth that she was last time. I was surprised, especially since she had her entourage surrounding her.

Collin grabbed my arm, turning my attention back to him. "I can't believe you came here," he said to me.

"If this is the only way for me to talk to you …"

"You're not talking to me … you're screaming at me," he said.

"What the hell do you expect?"

323

"Don't worry about me," she said then placed the hat on the table. "I was just about to leave anyway," Vanessa called out over the music.

"Nice to know that this is what you're doing all these nights when you're not home!" I said with disgust.

"What are you talking about? You knew I was coming here," Collin said defensively.

"But I don't know how many other times you're with this whore at this fucking club…"

"Aw… *pobrecita,* you have no idea do you?" Vanessa said condescendingly to me. She directed her next comment to him, "I don't know why you put up with this shit…"

Collin positioned his body between me and Vanessa to block our views of each other. "Both of you stop," he said to us, then to me, "We're not doing this here. Victoria, go back to the apartment."

"Are you kidding me? I'm not going to leave while you stay here with her."

"She's not staying anyway …"

"You need to calm your insecure ass down," she said to me, pointing and waving her finger from where she sat.

Suddenly, feeling like a wild animal, I almost dove across the table at Vanessa, but Collin blocked me with his arms before I reached it. I settled for saying, "Go ahead. Keep making fucking comments. You think I'm scared of you?"

She rolled her eyes again.

"Go ahead … roll your eyes at me one more fucking time, little girl, I'll rip them right out of your head!"

She didn't roll them again, but just the sight of her made me want to take a bottle from the table and smash it across her face. I hated my jealous rage because she was right, I was jealous and he gave me every reason to be. I hated this bitch so much and I just wanted to finish the first fight that was broken up.

"Come on, what are you going to throw at me this time? Another shoe? Stupid bitch … calling my man all hours of the night … you have no respect …"

"Yeah, I'm supposed to respect you?" she said with a snarl. "Ha … sure whatever, *Grandma!*"

"Come on, why don't you come over here and say that?" I realized I sounded trashy and immature ... I sounded like her ... but I didn't care.

The entire time I was yelling at her, Collin was holding me back. "Victoria ... calm the fuck down!" Collin tried again to use his presence to deter me from my argument with Vanessa. "You're out of control!" he said steering me in another direction.

"Fuck you. You're just another asshole too," I snapped, pushing him away from me. "You two deserve each other."

Just like the last time we were in a squabble, Collin sided with her, or at least I felt like he did, as he held me. During my ferocious attempt to break away, I managed to slip free from his hold long enough to advance in Vanessa's direction. I was only a few inches from her when Collin caught me by the waist and pulled me back -- harder than I think he meant to. I was flung to the ground as if a taut rubber band was around me the entire time and then released.

The various faces at the party gazed at me, jaws dropped, wide-eyed, in astonishment. There I was, sitting on the ground, embarrassed, my palms stinging from the hard landing, but none of that mattered when I realized why he did it. I glanced up at Vanessa, who was now standing up. My fury seized and turned into sheer, utter confusion as her large round belly, which was previously hidden by the table, was now visible.

My head spun. "What the fuck..." I said and was lost in a dumbfounded state.

"Shit ... I'm so sorry, Babe..." Collin said and immediately he lowered his hand to help me up from the floor, but I refused his aid. I was mad, humiliated, disoriented, and just plain done.

I couldn't address it. I almost pretended that I didn't see anything. *Vanessa is pregnant?* If I let that anger unleash in the club, at that moment, it would have been a dark, angry unstoppable force that nobody needed to see. I bottled it, hard, and gritted my teeth as I pushed myself up from the ground.

"Let's go. I'm going with you," Collin said to me as if his words were supposed to be comforting.

"No … Damn it, just get away from me. I can't even look at you," I said feeling my eyes instantly begin to sting.

"Victoria, it's not what you think …"

"Just let me go."

"I told you I'm leaving with you. How did you even get here?"

I didn't say anything. *Shit I was really drunk. How did I get there?*

"Whatever … come on," he said.

Collin turned around to let his friends know that we were leaving then returned to me and we started to head out.

Timing is definitely everything in situations. There is never a good time to be a smart ass, but Brad chose the worst. I saw from the corner of my eye as he stood up and began an exaggerated applause. He staggered a little, and then laughed like a crazed hyena, yelling, "Yeah! It's about fucking time you get her out of here!"

Collin stopped in his tracks and spun around. *Great this is the last thing we need, more drama.*

"Fucking dickhead…" I said over my shoulder; Collin, though, did something louder and even more belligerent.

"You got something to say?" he demanded, confronting his friend.

Brad, obviously the typical can't-handle-his-liquor type, continued to instigate. All eyes were on him and he wanted to put on a show. "Come on Dude, I'm just saying that you've got to learn to get your *bitch* on a *leash!*" he said then may as well have taken a bow afterwards.

I thought I was shocked but when I saw the look on Collin's face my reaction was miniscule. I had enough for the night and wanted to tell him to let it go, we already had our own shit to deal with. But he was too fast. Collin's face contorted almost beyond recognition as he spun around faster than a top to confront his friend.

I looked around the table at everyone there. The guy I assumed to be Edwin stood up and looked as if he was ready to intervene. All the eyes of the girls at the table had gone wide, and they were shifting uncomfortably from Collin to Brad and back. Brad, on the other hand, was wearing a rough smile.

"What the fuck did you say?" Collin thundered at Brad.

"Come on, Bro," Brad said in a haughty tone then set his focus on me. "Victoria ... I'm sorry, you're hot as shit, but you're still a fucking bi-"

Brad didn't get to finish his sentence. Collin lunged at him but Edwin and another guy in a red shirt quickly broke it up. Edwin grabbed Collin by the waist and a split second later, Red Shirt caught hold of Brad's arms.

Brad wouldn't let up. "Well," he exclaimed mockingly, "It's all good ... Collin here forgot that it's bros before hoes!"

"Brad, knock it off!" Edwin said through gritted teeth, straining against Collin as he redoubled his efforts.

I could already feel the situation spiraling out of control. As much as my insides burned with fury at Brad's crass comments, I dreaded what would happen next. Collin still seemed ready to do something he'd regret later. Red Shirt was doing his best to keep Brad under control, but I knew that he had already crossed a very important line as far as Collin was concerned. I doubted that Collin would back down now even if Brad had gotten on his knees to beg for forgiveness.

"Forget it," I chimed in, and had to put all my own anger aside so there would be some control in the room. My hand lightly clasped his arm, "Come on. Just let it go. I don't care what he said, "Let's just get out of here!"

"Victoria ... I got this," Collin said cutting me off, turning briefly to face me.

"No ... you don't. You guys are making a scene. Could we just go?" My words seemed to calm him down enough to control his temper. He relaxed enough to prompt Edwin to release him, while across the table, Red Shirt let go of Brad, still watching him out of the corner of his eye.

Still, I thought it best to get out of there before the situation reached a boiling point again. Collin was annoyed at me, or my comment, or that I was getting involved ... I wasn't sure which one but while his focus was on me we were blindsided by something.

I felt a couple of wet, slimy objects impact my face. Next to me, I saw Collin clap his hand over his eye, teeth clenched as he grimaced. Brad laughed his maniacal laugh again. After a shocked glance at Collin, I looked down, and I realized that the objects were shrimp covered in a spicy salsa which had left spots of sauce on my face and shirt. Collin had been even less lucky, having been hit in the eye. *This isn't going to end well,* I thought.

Feeling like I had to do something, I tried grabbing hold of Collin's arm again. However, I'd barely moved an inch when he upended the table, attempting to smash the rim into Brad's ribs. Everyone at the table jumped back, screaming. Startled by the commotion, a few scantily clad girls nearby stopped dancing to watch.

"For fuck's sake, you two," yelled Edwin, stepping between the two of them. "Calm the hell down!"

But Collin didn't hear anything. He was like a lion ready to pounce on the gazelle.

"You're fucking dead!" shouted Collin, who completely wasn't hearing any of us, as he blinked hard, trying to clear the salsa from his burning eye. With those last few words, he bounded over the fallen table, swinging his right fist into Brad's jaw.

I saw Brad mouth out something before Collin swung his other fist at his face. Brad dodged to the side; he only just managed to avoid getting hit. Spinning out of Collin's reach, Brad got in a shot that landed against Collin's jaw.

Caught in his own momentum, Collin collided with the table, giving Brad the chance he needed. Rushing up behind his adversary, he bear-hugged Collin from behind, pinning his arms to his sides.

Watching helplessly, I could only scream at both of them as Collin wriggled, trying to break free of Brad's grip. I hoped some of his friends would intervene, pulling Brad off, but none of them moved an inch. They just shot each other nervous glances as Collin struggled. Finally, with seemingly superhuman strength, Collin twisted forward, grabbed Brad with his newly freed hands, and shoulder-threw him onto another table. The only thing that cushioned Brad was the plate of grapes on the table. Bottles rolled off and spilled over everywhere.

"You son of a bitch!" Brad snarled, pushing himself upright again then reached over and attempted to strike Collin with a fallen bottle. Collin avoided the would-be weapon and threw himself onto Brad. They fell backward, Collin on top, both of them grappling furiously at each other.

Taking a couple of steps forward, I saw that Brad's face was showing tiredness. Collin was clearly winning this contest of brute strength, and it was only a matter of time before Brad gave out. Recalling the time in New York when Collin had beaten Juan Carlos almost to death in the middle of Central Park, I continued to call out, "Alright, guys that's enough! Please ... stop!"

Neither Collin nor Brad gave any sign of hearing me, though. Fists flew between the guys as the severity of the fight escalated.

I wished I could somehow break them up. I couldn't find any solace in Collin's friends either. They were discussing amongst each other; contemplating whether to call security, maybe? Or the cops?

Edwin, with disgust written all over his face, barreled through the line of spectators and disappeared in the crowd. Finally, Red Shirt, his jaw clenched in a resigned, yet determined grimace, stomped forward to break up the two fighting guys again.

Just then, four burly men in security uniforms burst through the crowd. Two of them grabbed Collin's arms, hoisting him off Brad while the other two knelt over Brad, asking if he was alright.

The two men on Collin looked like they meant business when they grabbed him until a third large man rushed over to them and said something frantically.

"Get the fuck off!" Collin shouted yanking his arms free from each guard. "Don't fucking touch me! Are you crazy? Do you know who the hell I am?" Both men let him go as if he were some famous rock star. Shame was etched on both of their faces.

I was a little dumbfounded. If this were New Jersey they would have dragged both Collin and Brad out and dropped them on the pavement already.

Yet they all cowered as Collin went on. "I swear if anyone touches me again I'll have all four of your asses fired."

"I'm sorry... they're new," the larger guard with a deep voice said apologetically to Collin while shooting each of the men a disapproving look.

Collin trudged with tunnel vision to the exit, grabbing me along way while uttering a stern, yet exhausted, "Let's go."

The men followed close behind us to ensure that the scuffle wouldn't continue inside the club but they were adamantly careful not to grab either of us.

Collin and I stood outside of the club trying to gather our bearings.

The deep voiced guard came outside and approached Collin. "What happened in there?" the guard asked.

"What else is fucking new ... Brad acting like a piece of shit again," Collin said and obviously was still worked up.

"You guys have to try and keep that shit outside."

"I know; my bad." Collin said unmoved.

"The bartender saw the fight and called the cops. He had no idea you were in the middle of it. I'll never hear the end of it ..."

"You and me both, Duane, I'll take care of it," Collin said nonchalantly waving him off. Then he turned to me. We stood there realizing we needed to get home. But he was one step ahead of me. He turned again to Duane. "We need a ride," he said.

"I'm on it," Duane said, and like an obedient dog, quickly disappeared inside. He returned with one of the two guards from earlier. "Greg can drop both of you home," Duane said.

"That's fine, thanks," Collin said then signaled me to follow him.

We stepped up to a black Chevy Blazer. Even though we weren't on the best terms Collin still managed to think to open the door for me. We clambered inside the large SUV but sat on opposing sides of the roomy backseat area.

Greg turned out to be one of the bouncers from earlier. He spoke to us, glancing through the rearview mirror. "Um... Yo, man... I'm so sorry about before ... I really didn't know…"

"Don't worry about it Greg," Collin said. "You were just doing your job."

He looked exhausted and if he just gotten out of a one round UFC fight. Meanwhile I'm sitting there, my head trying to grasp around everything that was going on. I was beyond confused.

"Okay," I said not knowing where to start as I stared out the window.

Collin didn't say anything.

"Thank you for defending me," I said. There was so much more I wanted to say and wanted to know. The truth was, I didn't really know Collin at all … did I?

He had no response for a minute or two then he eventually said, "He was out of line." That was it, nothing more. And I was too exhausted to keep prying. I knew our argument would continue on both sides when we were out of that car so I just accepted the cold silence as we were driven to the apartment. The lights were bright on the freeway; every time I closed my eyes, all I could see was the fight with Brad, large security guards cowering from my man, and of course Vanessa, pregnant.

CHAPTER 41

Back at the apartment after another relationship shattering night, Collin and I stood on opposing sides of the living room, one waiting for the other to speak. Finally, he caved first.

I demanded an explanation about everything. Collin shared that he was unhappy about a side of me I was showing; one that I would have preferred to keep hidden myself. On the other hand my head was spinning and I felt I had no choice but to let that side of me out

Then Collin became distant again as I watched him maneuver around the kitchen, taking a bottle of water from the refrigerator, then sitting to answer texts that were coming through non-stop since we left the club. I couldn't believe how long I went on holding my tongue, but it was probably because I wasn't ready to know the truth. I didn't know where to start. I was in shock. But I needed to know; and it was now or never.

Sitting adjacent to Collin, I waited for him to acknowledge me, but at this point he was wrapped up, still exchanging messages, probably with his friends who were at the club. It was also obvious he was intentionally rebuffing me.

"Don't you think we have a lot to talk about?" I finally asked cutting through the silence.

He finished the message he was in the middle of writing, placed the phone on the table, and then looked up at me. "Yeah…" he said.

Okay, good. We could do this without arguing. Our relationship couldn't handle another argument. But, where do I start?

"First of all … what happened at the club …" I began to explain, but he quickly cut me off.

"You were completely out of line showing up like that! What the hell were you thinking?"

"Whoa … I know you are not seriously turning this shit around on me!"

"Victoria, you showed up, completely drunk out of your mind, just to check up on me at my friend's bachelor party. You know how crazy is?"

"I thought it wasn't a bachelor party!"

"Whatever ... that's not the fucking point right now."

"Well, my showing up was because I was sick and tired of you walking out on me!"

He ignored my comment and went on. "Not to mention you almost fought Vanessa, who's seven months pregnant ..."

"Yeah I noticed! When, exactly, were you planning to tell me about that?"

"Why would I tell you? You two hate each other."

"Then why the hell do you spend time with her?"

"I already know what you're thinking. Why don't you go ahead and say it ..."

"Don't play games. If you have something to tell me then do it ..." I looked at him but felt so disgusted and betrayed that as he opened his mouth to speak again, I quickly shut him down. "You always do this! Since the beginning of our relationship ... Everything is my fucking fault!"

"I never said that ..."

"No. Fuck this. I'm tired of it!" I felt my blood begin to boil as my heart drummed furiously in my chest.

"Victoria, it's not you ..."

"I swear ... don't you dare finish that fucking sentence with 'it's me'..." I said through gritted teeth. I had him cornered; I didn't want him to use such a poor excuse in this heated of a situation.

He sighed and looked away.

"I thought so. Just forget it. You don't get to make excuses," I said putting my hand up. "I've been there before. Not this time. No. You're not going to make me look like a dumb piece of shit while you go out and do whatever you want!"

"I'm out doing whatever I want? Really? I'm working like eighty hours a week to save for us."

"I never asked you to ... so don't throw it in my face now."

We were arguing about a hundred different things at the same time and I could no longer pinpoint the root of it. I couldn't see beyond my rage as I stormed into the bedroom with him at my heels.

"I'm sure you'll be glad that I packed all my shit

already," I said as I did a once over in the bedroom. "I'll be out of your way."

He glanced down at my suitcases and disheveled dresser drawers then laughed mockingly. "Oh I see. We're doing *this* now?" He rolled his eyes.

"I'm serious. I'm so over this."

"Why don't you stop the drama act and put the bags down," he said. "You know you're not going anywhere."

"Yeah? Watch me. " I wasn't feeding into his patronizing comments.

"It's three in the morning. Where are you gonna go?" he asked narrowing his eyes at me. This wasn't a question of concern as much as it was one of distrust. He really thought I was seeing someone else? He blocked the doorway with his body awaiting my answer. Keeping the tight bounds he had on me, both physically and emotionally.

"Wouldn't you like to know?" I waited for him to move but he stood his grounds. "Get out of my way," I said, in the firmest tone I could manage. I momentarily swallowed my anger to let him know how serious I was. At this point I only took two of my duffle bags and both of them sat on one shoulder. I continued a futile attempt to escape; our plummeting relationship.

"Come on … put the bags down," he said in a quieter, yet still demanding tone. He held onto the straps so I couldn't move forward.

He didn't realize that he was only challenging me. This was my chance to see if I could finally stand up for myself, even if it meant walking out with nothing but my dignity. "And why would I stay here?"

"Because it's what we both want. And we still need to talk …"

"Talk?" I scoffed. "Oh, now you're ready to talk? It's too fucking late for that," I said putting emphasis on each word. I let go of my bags and managed to push my way past him.

I had barely taken two steps before I felt his hand clasp around my wrist. Yanking hard, he brought me around to face him. "Babe, don't do this," he said. I couldn't comprehend the look on his face, whether his insistence was based on remorse or possessiveness.

Maybe it's remorse? I thought. Or hoped. *I don't want to leave. I don't. But I also don't want to become a doormat ... again.*

"Please," he said in a much softer voice. Then, taking control again, he steered me toward the couch, and continued, "Look, we're gonna sit down, and we're not getting up until we've talked this over."

My anger was finally subsiding enough for me to hear him out, and I hesitated before sitting on the sofa to take a breather. Still angry, but guilty for my previous outbursts, I let him sit down next to me and put his arm around my seat. That was when the tears began to erupt and I felt sick from it all. I sat there and sobbed; sobbed so hard I could hardly catch my breath. I sobbed out my anger, my mistrust, the months of frustration, of separation, of uncertainly.

Finally, wiping the tears from my eyes, I said, "I hate what we've become."

"Me too," he said. He sighed and ran his hands through his hair.

"I know I was wrong for lying about my divorce ... and I told you that I'm sorry, but you can't keep holding it against me either."

"I know. It's not only that," he said simply.

I looked over at him, wondering if he'd say anything else, but he just sat there with the same penetrating expression on his face. *Fuck. He has no intention of actually talking. He just wants to get his way. Keep me here just for the hell of it.*

"That's it? You have nothing else to say?" I asked, trying to prompt him. Finally, giving up, I turned away and leaned forward, showing him my back. "Asshole," I muttered under my breath.

"Victoria, I'm sorry..." he finally said. But what I had desperately tried to avoid was happening.

"You're sorry? That's it? " *Of course.* A deep breath and my raging thoughts cut off my own sentence. That's how it always starts. *They're always fucking sorry. All these nights I spent wondering what he was doing and who he was with! Wasting my time! I'm not doing this again.* "I'm not perfect but I deserve better," I said through streaming hot tears. I thought I was all cried out, but

335

here I was again, crying over this fucked up relationship.

"Baby," he said again, trying to subdue me.

I felt his hand gently touching my arm, and like magic, my thoughts changed into words and actions. "Don't you dare touch me!" I shouted reflexively, shoving his hand away. I quickly shot up from my seat, and reattempted what I knew I needed to do. Even if it was to prove a point. Or maybe I really did want to leave. It was hard to think clearly. I grabbed my bags from the floor. "I can't believe how stupid I am. I'm fucking done!" I screamed as I stomped away, making my way to the door; it was all I could do to keep from letting my rage take control of my body. But he intervened, blocking and grabbing me. He wouldn't let me leave. I would never win this battle. My sorrow and my tears had transformed into anger.

"Stop trying to leave. Just calm down."

"Excuse me? *Calm down?*" I asked shooting him an irritated glare.

"Yeah! You've been acting like a fucking psycho all night!"

"And?" I gave a drunken, sarcastic, sardonic laugh. Then continued, "Look who's talking! You've probably been buying all the fucking baby clothes for that *slut* of yours for months now!"

"Are you serious?"

"Well?" I said demanding an answer.

"You really *would* think that! The baby isn't mine..." he said.

I was relieved but I felt equally stupid, then again he could by lying. Or I had just completely lost my mind.

"Shit, I just about fucked Brad up for what he said about you."

"I didn't ask you to."

"Well whatever ... now I'm starting to think he was right."

His words drove more tears and more actions as I completely lost control. I could barely even feel my face contorting as I shoved him in the chest. The angry monster inside me took over completely. Striking him with my hands and spitting acidic words with my mouth. The person I didn't

336

want to become began to possess me anyway. "You think you could play these games and then apologize and everything will be okay!" I yelled, hitting him hard in the chest. "And now you're siding with that douche bag friend of yours!" I shrieked, punching him even harder. "I hate you! I swear! I wish I never came here!"

He grabbed hold of both of my swinging arms, but I continued to shout as he pushed me back.

"Damn it, Victoria, you really need to calm the hell down."

"Let go of me!" I shouted trying to rip free from his grasp but he wouldn't let up. Each of my wrists was caught in his tight grasp and the more I fought him off the tighter he held. "You're hurting me!" I shouted, resorting to weakness.

His expression changed as he released me then slowly took a few steps away realizing the dangerous red zone our argument had entered. I then had my opportunity, the one I was looking for to walk out, as he backed away, forfeiting.

"I can't fucking do this anymore," he said. "Maybe we are too fucked up to be together. Go ahead … just go…"

"Yeah …well … I guess you forgot how my last relationship was," I said bitterly.

He scoffed. "Now, I get why … yet you're always the fucking victim."

"What the hell is that supposed to mean?"

"You know exactly what I mean. *You're fucking crazy.* I think you love the drama. You probably asked for it," he said spitefully. He was so done with me at that point. I could tell by his tone and the vile look he gave me. His eyes were dark and he looked exhausted and as if he would snap at me if I mustered even another ounce of the argument. Being aware of this, a normal person would have walked away.

"Really? Is that what you think?" I asked and found myself challenging him again. "So … What? You want to hit me now too?" I hit him in the chest with both palms, roughly shoving him away from me, but he closed the space as quickly. I aimlessly swung at him, most of the blows were blocked and some of them landed against his face, chest, and arms. I wasn't mad at him for his comment, or even entirely for that night, it was all the anger I had over the months that were kept bottled up. In my drunken rage it made sense. I wanted a reaction. I felt like he didn't care anymore.

"Victoria, I'm not fucking kidding, stop hitting me," he growled then pinned me against the wall.

"Or you'll do what?" I challenged. My body was suddenly suffocated between him and the wall, but even with nowhere to go my anger continued to egg him on. "I'm not afraid of you! Do it! Fucking do it. Hit me then. Go ahead ...you're so fucking tough? Fucking hit me!"

I stopped, mid-outburst, at the force of my back bumping against the wall. He used this opportunity to take hold of my sides, pinning my arms. Catching the sight of his blazing eyes I knew the fire inside him ignited. I felt my arms released and his left hand pressing me against the wall. His right fist came in—

I closed my eyes. A rush of fear mingled with my anger was enough to tame the beast inside of me. *He was actually going to do it.* I could take a hit. I wasn't surprised that it escalated to that; it always did in arguments with Frank ... even with John ... why wouldn't it with Collin? But with those passing moments I realized that I wasn't struck. The sound of the drywall crunching made me open my eyes and look over to see his fist smashed into the wall beside my head.

Was he going to hit me? I thought, suddenly aware of my hard breathing. This mix of thoughts and emotions coursed through my blood. I looked up just in time to see his head drop onto my shoulder, and both anger and fear receded slightly. No. He couldn't do it. Of course he couldn't. *Shit. What the hell was I doing?* Coming back to my senses my thoughts whirled through my mind like a tornado. *Was I actually testing him? To see if he was like the rest of them? Maybe it wasn't the men ... maybe it was me? He's right, I am fucking crazy!* Nothing made sense anymore.

"Damn it, Baby," he said softly, raising his eyes to meet mine.

With my realization I settled down a bit. My chest expanded and flattened rapidly with my breathing. I placed my hand against his cheek as he looked up into my eyes, the blaze was still there but it wasn't because of me, it was for me.

Suddenly, as the feeling continued to come back into my body, I began to sense his torso pressing me into the wall and his left hand fall to my hip. Then he backed away slowly, and my frustration resurfaced; this time in a different form. I could feel my chest expand and hear my heartbeat in my head. I kept looking into the deep dark wells of his eyes, pleading, and he moved forward again, and we met, torso to torso, arms to waists, lips to lips.

His voice was shaky as he whispered, "You really are…"

"I'm what? I'm fucking crazy … I know," I whispered, against his lips. *Yes, I also just realized this myself.*

He lowered his mouth to my neck, kissing the side and front. "Victoria … I swear … no one could ever get to me the way you do … You cloud my mind to no return and make me go to a dark place that I hate."

"Do I?" I asked in a low voice as I held onto him. I pulled him closer to me. "It's okay, Baby … just take me with you," I said, turning my head so our lips would meet. It seemed as though I should be running and never looking back but I couldn't. I would never run. I wasn't afraid of the dark, especially not if I was there with him.

His body closed in on me, pinning me harder. His bulge was in full contact with the throbbing between my legs. I whimpered against his lips. It had been weeks since I felt him.

I wrestled my tongue against his, raising my right leg to meet his hand. After what seemed like hours, I felt him break the kiss.

"Victoria … I …"

Hearing his voice trail off, I reversed our positions. Pushing a shoulder with each hand, now it was my turn to shove him into the wall. I pressed myself roughly against him, grabbing his jaw. "Shut up," I growled and unable to contain myself, seeing his eyes glaze over and his mouth salivate, I went in for the kill, plunging my tongue into his mouth. Our heartbeats drummed together and the adrenaline in our veins continued to meld into a heated passion.

I tugged on his bottom lip with my teeth, my hands on either side of his face. "Baby, you're my most dangerous drug,"

I said, my voice low and hoarse. "The kind they don't have meetings for." My palm traveled slowly down his abs and into his pants. I brought my lips to his earlobe, then I whispered, "I'm completely addicted and desperately need a fix."

He wrestled my tongue and switched our positions again, pushing every part of his body into mine. He dominated my mouth with his and pinned me so tight that it almost hurt.

I gasped and broke the kiss when I felt him pull my hair. I looked up into his eyes which were still dark and now very possessive.

"Victoria… you're mine … you're all mine … don't you ever forget that," his words unshaken, his lips hovered over my mouth; his free hand caressing up my inner thigh.

"Yes, Collin … I'm all yours," I whimpered, in a ragged breath.

His lips lingered over my last words leaving me in a fiery suspense until I couldn't take it anymore. "Well … what are you waiting for?" The words were carried out through my harsh breathing.

He kissed me hard and I suddenly felt both weak and strong. I wanted to collapse into his arms as he completely possessed my body. I don't know why but it felt so amazing to be wrapped up in our own anger and desire. I'd been yearning for him for so long. We were playing a cat and mouse game all night, and it only ended one way.

Collin's mouth went to my neck. He kissed, sucked and bit hungrily until I gasped. He had hold of one of my wrists, but with his other hand he grabbed at my breast, mauling it through my clothes. My sadness, my anger was evaporating with the heat and spiraling into lust. Lust like I had never felt before. And Collin felt it too. He ripped open my shirt, and the buttons flew across the room; fabric tore. I tried to help, to shrug it from my shoulders but it caught at my wrists, almost like I was handcuffed behind my back.

My bra was the next casualty; he yanked at the cups, exposing my breasts. Open mouthed he attacked my nipple, biting and pulling at it with his teeth. I still couldn't free my hands. He pulled my bra from my shoulders and the straps held my arms too; I was entangled in my own clothes.

340

Dropping to his knees, he popped the button on my pants and dragged them and my panties to the floor. Now I couldn't run, couldn't defend myself. Nor did I want to. I was giving myself to him completely, to his desire, while fulfilling my own as well.

With his hand against my stomach, he pushed me against the wall and attacked me with his mouth, kissing my belly, then further down. His tongue against my sex, thrusting into me. I shook one foot free of my pants and lifted my leg up, exposing myself to him. I hooked my leg over his shoulder and felt his tongue jab at my pussy. I arched my back, zealous moans escaping my lips. My body wanting more. Craving more.

As he attacked my clit with his tongue, sucking and licking, it felt like thousands of electric shocks bolting through me. I almost lost my balance completely. Finally I got a hand free from the entanglement behind my back. I grabbed a handful of his hair. I pulled him on to me, urging him on. But he pulled away. I looked at him quizzically, until he unzipped his fly and pulled out his cock, already hard and throbbing. He wrapped his arms around me and lifted me like I was light as a feather, my pants still dangling from one foot, my shirt from my hand. But his cock found its mark: he impaled me, claimed me as his, with a single thrust. I could feel his fingernails dig into my ass which made me cry out, "Oh, Collin. Oh...." I gasped. "Yes, fuck me Baby," Those last words more like a growl.

He got the message. My body held up by his hands, the wall, and his cock, he continued to slam into me. My arms wrapped around him, never wanting to let him go; wanting to be lost in that moment forever; without everything that had happened in the last few months. All I wanted was that moment.

I leaned into his neck and kissed him as he fucked me. He didn't make love to me: he fucked me, *hard.*

My screams of pleasure encouraged his strong thrusts as I clung onto him. My heart pounded in my chest, and I felt the drywall giving way behind me as he pounded into me. Sweat dripped from my body to his and from his to mine. Lights were flashing in front of my eyes, and the room started to spin; I felt light headed. My orgasm hit me like a freight train.

"Yeah… that's right, Baby, come for me." His voice husky and commanding. His thrusts became deeper, slower strokes as my body convulsed against his, my mind shattering like glass.

I crooned and moaned; every shake and shudder seemed to be magnified. The most intense experience ever. While I was still holding tightly onto him, panting heavily, and him still inside of me, he lowered me to my feet. My body trembled slightly as he withdrew from me leaving me feeling empty too soon.

His eyes were fixed on me. I stared back at him, ready to ask what was wrong but he grabbed me hard by the biceps and abruptly spun me around. He positioned my hands against the wall and used his foot to spread my feet apart so I had a wider stance. His chest was pressed against my back, his breath warm on my neck, and hands firmly at my hips. I felt his head graze my entrance briefly before he bucked his hips into me, penetrating me with dominating force. My mind went blank. I let out a loud shriek and felt my knees shake. I felt every inch of him swell deep within me.

"Take me, dirty girl!" He grunted the words.

I squealed and screamed but Collin kept going. He slapped the side of my ass and I felt myself tighten around him. Tingles rippled through my body. The intensity of the pleasure and pain was sure to onset another spell of ecstasy.

"God, Baby, I love fucking you…" His admission sent me over. He fisted my hair and yanked down hard, bringing my head up. I opened my mouth to cry out and felt his tongue plunge into my mouth. I kissed him back feverishly.

Then his pounding increased, I couldn't even move with him so I kept my hands planted firmly against the wall and took every punishing thrust. Each one became more erratic then the last. My legs wobbled; the electric waves shot through me again.

My nails dug into the wall as another orgasm ripped through me. I felt the familiar pulsating of his cock and moments later he erupted inside me; every muscle in his body taut as he groaned and grunted his release.

He sank to the floor, and I with him; a tangle of

342

clothes and sweat and Collin and me. Our bodies were slumped against the wall for a few moments; the only sounds were that of our heavy breathing. We eventually made our way to the bed where he pushed me hard onto the mattress. I knew right away that he wasn't finished with me yet.

CHAPTER 42

What now?

That was the only question I could ask myself over and over as I sat silently while Collin finished getting ready for work in the morning. Long after the physical satisfaction was over and the drunken madness had passed, different emotions swam through me. Instead of the usual euphoric and relaxed feelings, I felt guilty, confused, and foolish. *What are we doing? Are we okay? Of course we aren't.* Yet for weeks neither of us could address it. When did our relationship become so dysfunctional?

Collin walked over to me and kissed my forehead. Was he still mad? Indifferent? Or had he let it go? It bothered me that I was no longer able to read him.

"I'll see you later..." he said, almost as a question.

I couldn't even respond. I didn't want him to go. Suddenly a wave of other unwelcome sadness snuck up on me and I was soaking my hands and face with salty tears.

"Victoria?" He sat next to me on end of the bed.

"I'm sorry ... I'll be okay... I-I know you have to go," I said through sobs.

"No..." he inched closer to me. "What is it?"

"You're going to be late," I warned drying my eyes, and sitting up straight, as I attempted to give a plausible performance of nonchalance.

"I don't care," he said. There was a long pause.

"I'm upset because ... I mean last night was amazing ... but it doesn't change anything," I said through sniffles and tears. "We're still a mess and you'll leave for work and everything will be the same as it has been ..."

"No ... I really think we'll be okay..."

"You said that last time," I cut him off. My heart couldn't handle any more empty promises.

"I'm sorry; I have my own ways of dealing with things. I didn't realize how much I was hurting you," he said.

"We haven't talked about what's really going on."

"I wanted to talk but talking ... drinking ... it's not a good mix," he said.

"I know."

"Well ... first ... I know you're mad that I still talk to Vanessa, but you have to understand my side."

I gave him my attention. *This should be interesting.*

"When you and I broke up last May she was the one that was there for me the most and pushed me to go to the interview that got me the job I have today. She took time out of her day to be there for me when all I wanted to do was sit here and sleep or drink all day."

"Really?"

"There are some things you don't know about me."

"And I guess Vanessa does? So she came to the rescue ..."

"No ... I'm sure she had her motives, but I haven't been interested in her in that way for a really long time," he said. He noticed my tension and the look I was giving him. "I was too hung up over you," he added reassuringly.

"I really had no idea," I said. I couldn't imagine him being depressed over me. He always appeared to me like he was so held together. Then again it would explain the messy apartment, the bottles when I arrived. *Why didn't I think of that?*

"Yeah ... So when you came here I didn't feel right just cutting her off," he explained.

Damn I hated when he was right about things I didn't agree with. Especially when that *thing* was Vanessa.

"But why would she need your help? What about her brother?" I asked.

"He's been wrapped up with wedding stuff."

"And the father of her baby?"

"He's locked up."

"Oh ..."

"Yeah. But I know it's not fair to you either and that it really bothers you ... so if you want me to stop talking to her I will."

"No, only if that's what you want," I said. Vanessa wasn't an actual threat and I wasn't going to try and control his every move.

"I really need to know what going on with that club. I mean you're there almost every night and what happened with the security guards was really strange to me."

He ran his hands through his hair and sighed. "I guess I knew you were going to ask me that sooner or later."

"You work there?" I asked.

"Uh, yeah, you could say that."

"Are you bartending? Or security? Valet?"

"No…" he said shaking his head to all three. "Do you remember when my dad pulled me aside at Sophia's party?"

"Yes," I said.

"Well he asked me to take over the club for a few months while he's been traveling for business. Starlight is actually his… and my mom's… club."

"Really?"

I completely missed that detail. Then again nobody ever told me anything anyway.

"Before you came here, I told him to let me help with any of their businesses to keep me busy. And of course I wanted to make more money on top of what I get from my other job. I always told you that you wouldn't need to worry about money if you were with me. I had to keep my end of that deal."

"I don't understand why you didn't tell me this?"

"I wanted to. I thought I could somehow juggle everything without it cutting into our time … but I had no idea how many hours I was going to have to invest. Managing a club is a lot harder than it sounds."

"I know that. My ex owns a club …"

"Yes, I know. You were already starting to compare me to him, and we've been fighting all the time …"

Then suddenly his reasons for keeping everything from me made sense. If he told me about the drinking and that he was running a night club, the comparisons I was making between him and Frank would have actually had depth.

"I was mad when I said that. I should have never compared you to my ex and I'm sorry," I said. "You're absolutely nothing like him."

"I'm really sorry I didn't tell you earlier. It seemed easier to keep everything to myself and try to deal with it. I didn't want to fight with you and the exact opposite ended up happening."

"But, that's not how a marriage … or relationship … works at all. If something affects you then it affects me. We deal with everything together," I said.

"I still want to work on … uh …" he was fumbling for the words. "Us," he said with the sincerity I had missed.

"I want the same thing," I said. "We can finish talking later." I didn't want him to be any later for work than he already was. Not to mention my head was pounding, my bones felt achy, and I couldn't wait to get to the gallon of water that was in the refrigerator.

Some of the heaviness I had been feeling was gone. The load I was carrying had just gotten a little lighter. Collin and I still had so much to work on, but it was a start. He left for work, and I had my own agenda. Even if it didn't seem like I had my priorities straight, I wanted to make sure I didn't lose myself in being in a relationship. Rather than considering the 18 years I spent with Frank a waste of time, I thought of it as a learning experience. While in that long, confining relationship I lost all of my friends, interests, and hobbies. I basically lost myself. I wasn't about to repeat history so it was important to me that I kept my plans.

Preston landed in Los Angeles the night before and asked me where we should meet. I chose a cute little frozen yogurt place that I often stopped at in the Beverly Center Mall. We met in the early afternoon later that same day.

When Preston found me I was so happy to see a familiar face from Jersey. I threw my arms around him and he squeezed me tight.

"Wow, Victoria you look great," Preston said. He was dressed down, wearing a corn-silk blue t-shirt, brown cargo shorts, and tan flip flops.

"Thanks. Don't you look comfortable," I said and smiled at him.

"I'm enjoying being away from Jersey. Don't worry: you're not missing much, it's pretty cold over there!"

"I think I might take the cold and snow over LA."

"Really?"

"I've just been a little lonely over here." I said aloud what meant to be thoughts inside my head. I looked up at him catching my slip. "Oh … uh … never mind. I shouldn't be telling you that."

"It's okay, that's what friends are for."

"You have no idea how these last few months have been … like a crazy rollercoaster ride."

"I do. I can hear it in your voice every time we talk. Even the tones of your text, I can still sense how you're feeling," he said.

"I was so happy to finally have what I want. I thought it was going to be a dream come true. Yet my bags are packed and sitting on my bedroom floor. Sometimes I just want to go home … sometimes I figure I'll wait it out until this feel like home … but I think things are getting better."

"I think you need to do what's healthy for you," he said.

"I'm going to wait it out. I'm being positive."

"Of course," he said. "But I hope you know that I'm always here for you." He then reached his hands across the table for mine. I placed my hands into his then noticed the expression on his face change. His warm smile dropped. He took my wrists gently and rotated them slowly. I looked down and both of my wrists had multiple rosy, deep blue and purple marks. They didn't hurt so I hadn't even noticed, but I had forgotten how physical the argument was the night before. I pulled me hands away from his, embarrassed, and shoved them into my lap where he couldn't see the scrapes and bruises.

"What happened?" he asked concerned.

"Um…" *How do I explain?* "It's nothing," I said disappointed with my lame answer.

Preston's eyebrows furrowed, his features glowering. "So this is the kind of guy you're with?" he asked.

"No! It's not like that," I said defensively.

"Again, Victoria? That's fucking bullshit! Excuse my language but …"

"Preston, it's really not what it looks like …" I knew he wouldn't understand but I felt so guilty for letting my relationship appear worse than it was to an outsider.

"I think it's exactly what it looks like."

"No …really … I-I started it …" I stopped realizing my explanation sounded better in my head.

"That's the most bullshit excuse I've ever heard! You must have these memorized, huh? Next time I see you you're going to tell me you fell down the stairs?"

"Preston, you're blowing it out of proportion."

He stood up then moved from across the table to take the seat next to me, his expression pensive.

"Victoria, I care about you a lot, and I can't understand why you keep doing this to yourself."

"I know what you're thinking but ..." I felt like there was nothing I could say. "He would never hurt me."

"Then what do you call this?" he said taking my forearm into his hand. The bright lights of the mall illuminated the marks. "You're in another abusive relationship and you don't even realize it. Or you're in serious denial."

"Preston, I'm fine. Honestly." I said retracting my arms again. "Maybe I shouldn't have come here to meet with you. This ... this was a mistake," I turned away from him to grab my purse.

"Wait ... before you go ... there has been something I need to say."

I was ready to bolt but he placed his hand over mine pleadingly.

"Please ... just two minutes ..."

"Okay," I said.

"Victoria, before you left Alpine in November, when you declined my Paris invitation ..."

Wow way to make me feel even guiltier!

"I already apologized about that," I said.

"I know. But I sort of thought there was something between us then. I know you felt it too. I wasn't going to say anything but now I have to. I kicked myself for years for not telling you how I felt when we were young. It took you getting stolen away from me for me to realize everything I wanted to say to you. I regretted it every day. I don't want to have any regrets this time."

"Um ... I love having you as a friend as well ...but ..."

"Victoria, we reconnected after all those years. We're amazing together ..." His words trailed off. Anonymous Californians walked by in the mall, as we sat in silence for a moment, just the two of us, a tiny corner of Jersey.

"I think you're awesome," I said, "We're the same age, we love the same kinds of movies and music, and I agree that we have a great time together. Maybe you are perfect for me," I said.

"So then what's the problem?"

"All I want is him," I said.

"Even though he isn't treating you right?"

"There are accountabilities on both sides." *Preston should understand, he's been married so I'm sure it wasn't all fun and games.* "I can't do anything to further jeopardize my relationship."

"Wow," he said. He sounded outraged.

"What?"

"Nothing … just … lucky guy is all."

I shrugged. "It's not really luck; it's love."

"I completely understand, Vic," he said. "I understand because it wasn't *luck* that brought me here …" he said suggestively.

Then it was love? Oh no. Not this again.

"I'm sorry, Preston," I said. "If the circumstances had been different…"

I'm not sure how or when he ended up right in front of me inches from my face. He caressed my cheek and I gently lowered his hand with mine. He then slowly leaned forward to kiss me.

"No," I said turning my head to the side and towards the ground. *Did he not hear anything I said?*

"You know. You're telling me you're so in love with this guy. Then why are you here with me?" he asked sounding frustrated.

"I promised you that we'd meet. And I cherish our friendship," I said.

"Maybe … or maybe there is a part of you that wanted to tell me all this. You want me to know that you're not really happy …"

"I don't think I had an ulterior motive." Now I was getting frustrated.

"Then let me ask you this. When he asks you where you were today, what do you plan on telling him? You and I both know that you're not going to tell him the truth. You're very good at keeping your secrets, Victoria, I've known you since we were kids remember? But you can't hide the way you feel from me. I know you too well."

He was probably right. I wasn't exactly planning to run and tell Collin that I had spent time with the friend that we were just arguing about. But this was *my* life and *my* decision. I was sick and tired of the lying and secrets. Someone always ended up getting hurt. I didn't answer Preston because my mind was fixated on his last statement but he continued.

"Vic, I came here to see you … not because of work."

"Wow … I didn't know."

"I did. I know you're ready to go but all I'm asking from you is one kiss. If you don't feel anything then I'll never bring it up again. I'll just go right back to being your friend, no hard feelings. I just ask that you do me that one favor; kiss me and tell me that you don't feel anything."

I rubbed my thumb along the top of his hand. What a deal to make. I understood his wild theory but I was way in over my head meeting with him in the first place, while my relationship was already on the rocks.

"Alright," I said.

He looked stunned for a moment that I had agreed but the same cockiness it took for him to make the bold request took over just as quickly. He leaned forward and as his lips inched closer to mine I turned my head so they would land on my cheek. I reciprocated, kissing him on the cheek. Then I pulled away and smiled faintly at him.

"Thank you for everything," I said. "I have to go."

Preston slumped back into his chair with a disappointed expression seeping onto his features.

"Friends it is then," he said almost bitterly.

I didn't say anything. I just gathered my purse, frozen yogurt cup and water bottle from the table.

"Take care of yourself," I said then walked away with a lot to think about. I threw away the half full yogurt cup then glanced over at Preston one last time before leaving the store. He wouldn't know it, but I thanked him because he really had helped me. Although I'm sure it wasn't his intention at all, after everything he said, I realized more than I had expected — much more. What I thought was going to be a simple meeting with a friend turned out to be a real eye opener.

While I waited for the bus, I erased Preston's number from my phone. I would have stayed friends with him if we were just friends, but he wanted more. He was entitled to his opinion about my relationship, but he crossed the line when he asked me to kiss him knowing how I felt. That wasn't a real friend.

When I arrived at the apartment I was so relieved to find Collin already home, lounging on the sofa. It was nice to see him relaxing and not on his phone or running out the door.

"Hi," I said as I strolled in.

"Hey," he said looking up to make eye contact with me. "I'm glad to see that you're enjoying Cali a little more."

"A little," I agreed. I moved towards him but wasn't sure if I should kiss him or hug him or not. Unfortunately the energy between us was still slightly rigid but we were still trying. I simply joined him on the sofa, but sat by his legs and wondered if he would move further away from me or not.

"What did you do all day?" he asked.

I cleaned? I shopped? Worked on my computer? No... those were all lies.

"I went to that yogurt shop in the mall."

"You went there by yourself? You should have told me, I would have met up with you," he said.

"I didn't know you were getting out early today," I said.

"Yeah, me either. Half of the time I never know what to expect with my schedule," he said. He leaned forward and snaked his arm around my waist then slid me closer to him so that my body was against his. I curled my fingers through his hair.

He was being so sweet with me. I didn't want to ruin it. I really didn't want us in the middle of another argument, but I wasn't going to continue to make excuses for keeping secrets anymore. If I ever wanted our relationship to work, or for us to grow, so that the prospect of marriage would be a possibility again, I had to be honest with him.

"And I ... uh ... actually I wasn't by myself," I said then

swallowed over the lump in my throat.

"Oh ... okay," he said then waited for me to elaborate.

"I met with my friend ... Preston. He was in the area and wanted to talk," I said then waited for him to say something.

Silence.

I figured I'd continue. "It probably wasn't the best idea, I know. I don't have too many people over here to talk to and I don't want to cut all my friends and family off. I've been there before ..."

"So how did you get to the mall?"

That's his reaction? Or is he hiding it? Was he trying to get all the facts together before flipping out on me?

"The transit around here isn't too hard to figure out," I said.

"Yeah, it's not too bad. LA is like number eight in the top ten most walkable cities, or something like that."

"Is it? What's number one? Let me guess, New York."

"Of course," he said casually.

I was a bit disoriented. Did he not hear me before? Was he purposely ignoring what I said?

"You're not mad?" I asked.

"No. Babe, I'm not with you to tell you what to do or who to be friends with. We agreed to make this relationship work so I'm going to stick that promise. I trust you."

"Thank you," I whispered then gently kissed his lips.

"I actually won't be hanging out with him again," I added hoping it would still be somewhat reassuring news.

"Did something happen?" he asked concerned.

"No." I kept my answer simple. I didn't want to talk about Preston anymore. "Do you want to do something tonight?"

"I know we haven't spent any time together. I'm sorry. Tonight I'll be at Starlight ... but that's it after that. It's too much drama over there. I wish I didn't even have to go today."

"Me too," I said in a low voice. We so desperately needed time together.

"My dad gets back tomorrow," Collin said offering some good news. "So he and his business partner could deal with it. I'm done. I don't care how good the money is."

"It's a lot of responsibility, trust me, I know."

"I'm going to take this weekend off for us." He was reading my thoughts. Or he simply just knew what I also knew.

I've heard that before, I thought, but was hopeful.

"Okay," I answered. "Well, do you at least have time for a movie?"

"Of course," he said.

We spend the rest of our afternoon simply cuddled on the sofa and had time to watch two movies. I wasn't too upset when he left later that evening. I felt such an amazing relief to know where we stood. I could be honest with him, even if I made a mistake, and not cause a fight; who knew?

Before I went to bed I called to check on my kids, deleted a ton of spam E-mails, and then started reading a novel. Turns out I didn't need Preston, or alcohol, or anyone else to keep me occupied after all. I was doing just fine keeping myself company.

CHAPTER 43

I woke up to find Collin's side of the bed empty. *So much for spending the weekend together.* I sighed and rolled around to face the other side then noticed a note on my night table. I reached over and blinked my eyes into focus. The note read:

"Be dressed and wait outside at 10 a.m."

I looked at the clock; I had time, and I needed a shower. A half hour later, my hair and body, both wrapped in towels, I realized I needed something to wear. My bags were still packed from the night of our argument so I searched for them since all of my clothes were inside, but there was a problem. The bags were gone. Everything except my purse was gone. I looked in the closet as well as in the living room. I panicked a little then I noticed draped over my dresser was a brand new halter-top, sea-shell colored sundress; a dress that I had admired from the window of a store that was closed when Collin and I went shopping. *How sweet, he must have picked it up for me!* And it was my size. I was thrilled and eager to try it on. I wasn't worried any more. I figured my missing clothes must all be part of this obviously well thought out plan.

I dried my hair first then shimmied into the dress; it fit perfectly. I beamed at my reflection but realized that I needed a bit of make-up. I only had eyeliner and blush in my purse to apply. I left my hair down and wavy. I slipped my feet into a pair of cute peach sandals; another surprise present from Collin. I was ready.

I waited anxiously on the curb at 9:59 a.m. The beating of my heart was faster than usual. I went along with following the instruction, but I had no idea what was going on. In one minute the same black navigator from the club pulled up. I recognized the driver, Duane, so I knew it was okay to get inside.

He was dressed in a black suit with white gloves and a black chauffer hat. He came around and opened my door for me.

"Good morning, Victoria," he said.

"Morning, Duane. Nice to see you again."

I climbed into the vehicle and held my purse on my lap. The music was playing low and he turned it up slightly before pulling off. The Beatles, "Magical Mystery Tour," played and I thought: it couldn't be a coincidence.

"May I ask where we are going?" I asked.

"I was instructed to pick you up and drop you off. I am not supposed to disclose any details," he said sounding very professional.

"Okay then," I said, then sighed but could help smirking too.

I sat back and prepared to sit through some traffic. The possibilities of where I was heading raced through my mind. I thought of everything from a surprise park picnic to a simple mall stroll. Or was it something bad? What if he already sent for my things and wanted me gone? He was mad at me for seeing Preston? I looked at the road and tried to anticipate our destination; then I noticed that we started to head near LAX. The next song played. Talking Heads, "Road to Nowhere."

I smiled.

As the route we followed started to match every sign which read LAX, I knew that's where I was being taken. *Am I right?* I wondered eagerly as we neared.

Duane pulled the large vehicle over at the departure's drop off area and again stepped out to open the door for me.

"Thank you," I said, scrambling out of the SUV. "Uh…" *Now what?* I wondered. Before I could ask him I felt someone hug me. I turned around and found myself in Collin's arms.

"Hey you," I said with a relieved smile.

"Were you expecting someone else?" he said jokingly.

"No, but I swear you're always plotting something!" I said pushing him playfully.

"You have no idea," he said then he was serious. "You look really pretty." He took my face in his hands and kissed me softly.

"Thank you," I said and gave him a loving smile.

"Well, come on, Gorgeous, we have an agenda." He took my hand and led me into the madness of the airport.

"So what are we doing here?" I asked as we stood on the security line and started the tedious shoe removing, phones and bags in bins process.

"I promised you an entire weekend together," he said. "We start today."

"Okay," I said shrugging agreeably. *Finally.* "A bit extreme," I teased.

He handed the boarding passes to the TSA agent, and I tried to peek at them but he wouldn't let me see them.

"I'm hoping my bags are already checked?"

"What bags?" he asked.

I stopped in my tracks and crossed my arms, "You'd better be kidding!"

"Yes, Baby, I'm joking," he said then laughed. "Don't worry, everything is already taken care of," he said.

We stopped for an $8 cup of coffee when his phone rang. It was his boss, Erica.

"I'm so sorry, Babe..." he said almost as if he was asking my permission to answer.

"Go ahead," I said and found a seat for us while he answered the call.

"Hey Erica, what's going on? Yes, I'm off today, I got Mark to cover ... No I'm already off. Tomorrow I can't come in either ... he knows what to do ... I'm sorry if you're short-handed but I'm not available ... I'm at the airport with Victoria, we're going away for the weekend but I'll be there Monday ..."

He placed the phone back in his pocket then turned to face me.

"I hope this trip isn't going to get you in trouble," I said.

"I haven't taken any days off since November. Two days isn't going to hurt anyone. I really don't want to end up being like my dad with work. He's always on the phone or on a trip..."

"If you're sure that ..."

His phone rang again. He rejected the call then put it in his pocket.

"That was the last call I'm taking until we get back."

I took my cell phone then also turned it off. No interruptions. Sounded wonderful.

"Wow, I see you discovered the 'off' button," he said.

"Huh?" I said then realized he was teasing me about tossing my phone away. "Shut up," I said, pushing him in the arm.

As we left the airport café I noticed how leisurely this travel was compared to our last one. We weren't rushing or running or being distracted by everything else. We strolled through while everyone around us rushed.

"So can you tell me where we're going?" I asked.

"What do you mean? We just came here for coffee ... let's go home now."

"Stop messing with me!" I said but couldn't help laughing with him.

He looked at his watch. "Alright fine ... Come on, let's go to the gate," he said taking my hand.

I didn't mind wherever it was; but I secretly hoped it wasn't Vegas. I was sure he knew we couldn't actually tie the knot yet. I wasn't sure if we were at that point, nor was I sure if we were still engaged anymore. I stared down at my bare hand. I missed my ring. I was so comfortable knowing that every single time I looked at it I knew I was his.

There were many uncertainties, but I was sure about one thing; we needed the mini vacation, regardless of the destination. I hoped we could find the spark that was smothered through the stressful times.

We inched our way closer to the departure gates. I continued guessing both in my head and aloud, reading as we walked along. Guam? Washington? Mexico? But it was none of those. Then we finally stopped walking. "You better not be taking me to Alaska!" I said and laughed.

He stopped then waited for me to look up. Gate 245. International flight. Hawaiian Air to Bora Bora, Tahiti. I spun around on my heels.

"Seriously? Is this us?"

He smiled then nodded.

I couldn't believe it and looked at him skeptically. "Really? You're not messing with me again are you?" I narrowed my eyes at him.

He pulled the boarding passes from his pocket and

handed them to me. And yes; they were two international boarding passes for us to escape to the one place I had fantasized about for the longest. He knew me. He really was paying attention.

"Oh my God, you're unbelievable! I don't even know what to say!" I felt tears of joy emerge as I threw my arms around him. He squeezed me tight.

"Don't say anything," he said. "Let's just walk onto that plane and leave all this behind us. We can fly to paradise together. That's all I want. You and paradise. Little huts over the water … clear blue skies, vanilla sand … quiet and peaceful paradise."

I smiled at him and took his hand. We walked away from the storm cloud that we'd been trapped under. We walked into an opportunity for a relationship with clear skies. I, too, would have what I wanted all along; him and paradise.

CHAPTER 44

Never in my life did I imagine what it would feel like to be standing inside a real life tropical postcard. Perfection. The most radiant blue sky. Crystal sparking blue water. Clean air. Heaven. It was exactly how it looked in pictures, better. The air smelled amazing. My life went from one extreme to the other. The previous weeks were no walk in the park. Yet, again, we weathered through the storm.

I woke up to the sound of a wave crashing into the sand. It gently hissed away as the water receded then the process repeated. The water was so close, only several feet away from where we slept comfortably. Earlier in the afternoon Collin and I walked to the beach with picnic baskets, blankets, and towels. At some point we had fallen asleep under the sun.

Only a thin sliver of sun was left in the now purple sky. I woke up right in time to catch the sunset. Collin's arms were around me as he slept peacefully on the beach towel. Every single time I looked at him my heart stuttered. Awake. Asleep. It didn't matter. His presence made me feel something indescribable. I touched his face then kissed him softly in attempt to wake him up.

"Baby, you're gonna miss it," I whispered to him.

"Hmm?" he asked slowly opening his eyes.

"Look how gorgeous the sunset is."

He stretched out his arms then placed them around me. We repositioned our bodies so we were upright, but still comfortable. I leaned my body into his and we stared out as thick masses of clouds invaded the sky, soaking in the fiery glow behind their cottony fullness. A slight lavender hue remained above the descending ball of fire. The turquoise bed of water was a brilliant sheet covered by a million sparkling diamonds. I had never seen anything like it. Not even in my dreams.

"Isn't it the most beautiful thing you've ever seen?" I said; my stare fixated on the breathtaking display.

Collin brought his hand to my chin turning my face so our eyes would meet. "My Love, it doesn't even come close," he said. He pulled me closer to him and pressed his lips against mine.

He reached over then pulled a white sheet out from our beach bag. He stood up and unfolded it, shaking it open letting it sweep in the breeze. It looked like a parachute for a few seconds before it flattened over and encased us. We were in our own little love cocoon. He was positioned over my body and my senses responded to him. I equally wanted and needed him in so many ways possible. I shifted my weight from under him so that I was straddling his hips. Both of my palms were pressed against his abs, then they slid up over his chest then higher until my fingers were tangled in his hair as I lowered my forehead against his. I licked my lips before tracing my tongue delicately over his lips.

His hands also explored my body, outlining my back, passing over the curves of my waist, and then over my ass. His touch left my skin and I lifted my hips as he lowered his shorts. He held my hips tight lowering me slowly down onto him. My moans were quieted by his kisses, as I felt him slowly fill me.

It couldn't have been more different than the last time. The same chemistry, but entirely different. His hands enfolded me as I lay onto of him, my breasts pressed against his chest, gently rocking backward and forward, feeling whole, feeling complete. I placed kisses everywhere, starting at his shoulder, moving over his neck, jaw, chin and then finally his lips.

There was no urgency, this was no race; the warmth of Collin's body against mine, the feeling of him inside me, completing me, was wonderful, and I wanted this wonderful moment to last forever. I sat up and Collin held my waist as I lifted myself up and slid down once more, my back arching gracefully, as the sheet fell off of us and I looked up to the darkening sky.

How could it be any better than this? This man knew me, knew my needs and reflected them back to me in his lovemaking. Always giving me just what I wanted, what I needed. I felt his hands, his fingertips tracing shapes on my back and I closed my eyes to the sensation.

While still under me Collin sat upright then wrapped his arms around me. We clung to each other tight. Our lips molded as out tongues slow-danced together. Our bodies moved effortlessly and passionately, in sync with the waves. Our love making sounds were like a song with the winds and the resonance of nature. In harmony, we climaxed together and it was simply beautiful.

Afterward, we continued lying on the beach, which was absent of color as night fully settled in. Navy blue and indigo washed across the water and sky creating a dark globe of endless blue. We watched as the stars twinkled the same way the water did earlier.

"Look at us now," I said. It was amazing, as if we weren't just having problems a few days prior.

"I know. Perfect, right? Maybe it's something in the air," he said.

I smiled then snuggled my body closer against his. "Stay with me forever," I whispered.

"Forever, my love, I promise." He kissed my head and intertwined his fingers with mine.

"And I promise that I'll never leave you. No matter what. Whatever we go through in the future it will be together. Us against the world," I said, stroking his hand with my thumb.

His kiss was gentle but his hold was strong. We listened to the waves roll and crash.

"I have something to tell you," he said.

"What is it?"

"When you go to New York next month, I'm going with you."

"Thank you Babe, that means a lot. I could definitely use the support for those days."

"You're so cute," he said then chuckled at me.

"What?" I asked. *Did I miss something?*

"Not just for a few days! I mean I'm going back with you for good."

"But ... What about that summer project? Wasn't that a big deal?"

"I told my boss I couldn't do it."

"Why?"

"Because I want to be with you more than anything," he said.

"I don't want to be what kept you from your dream. Or for you to mess up your future."

"Victoria, *you* are my future. And I don't care about what comes my way if you're not by my side. Or if you're unhappy. There are just as many amazing opportunities in New York. I'm not going to lose you."

I kissed him and it felt like we had set off fireworks. He broke the magic and turned away from me reaching into the beach bag. He pulled something out then placed it into my hand. It was my engagement ring.

"I know things haven't been great lately, but I hope you'd still consider…"

He didn't have to say any more. I gave him my hand and he replaced my ring where it belonged.

"There's nothing I can say that you haven't heard already, so I'll just show you no matter how long it takes," he said.

I'd always been looking for perfect. I was obsessed with perfect. *But why?* Our flaws were what made us unique as individuals; and accepting them and working through our differences was what made us stronger as a couple.

It took a while for me to realize that "perfect" meant that we would have our ups and downs. No matter what we fought through we always wanted the same thing in the end -- to be together. So, yes, our love was as flawless, sublime, and unique as the diamond that was on my finger.

The tide was at its highest point and if I reached over my head my fingers could almost graze the next oncoming wave.

"You think it's too cold to go in?" I asked.

"I don't think so, but there's only one way to find out," he said. He removed his watch and placed it on the towel before heading towards the water.

I propped my chin onto my palm and enjoyed watching Collin disappear into the ocean. Then in an instant he was gone, diving beneath the surface. When he came back up his hair clung to his forehead and curled slightly into his eyes. Then he swam out a bit with slow, easy stokes and then lay over floating on his back.

"So … you gonna watch me or you coming in?" he called from the water.

"Hmm ... I think I'm just gonna watch you." *I could lay there and watch him all night.*

"Aw, just come in. I miss you already!"

"Okay, I'm coming," I said. I didn't need any more convincing. I strolled slowly to the water, the soft sand running between my toes. I stuck my toes into the rising water and was surprised to feel the lukewarm liquid wash over my ankles. It wasn't what I expected for April. The water receded then came back up over my calves.

I drew into Collin with what seemed like the identical gravitational effect the earth had on the tide. My hands folded behind his neck as he stared down at me.

"You're so beautiful!" he said then showered me with kisses.

The water was dark and the moon was high in its place shining luminously above us. The triangular pale white beam seemed to illuminate directly over us.

"I wish we could just stay right here," I said to him.

The only sound that could be heard was the gentle lapping of the waves rolling into the beach. We spent an eternity on the beach before returning to our hut. We had an hour of sleep before going out to watch the sunrise. The rest of our weekend was amazing, just like the start. White sand, subtle waves, cocktails at the tiki bar, breathtaking sunrises and sunsets, passionate nights, and most importantly; spending undivided quality time with each other.

After our paradise mini-vacation came to an end we returned to Los Angeles where the undeniable love we shared was still present and thriving. The weeks of the spring flew by and our relationship only grew stronger.

During my last month in California I joined the gym Collin had a membership to. While he was at work I walked on the treadmill and attended the kick-boxing, yoga, and Zumba classes. I kept myself busy and was really enjoying life.

It was May again. One year after our 2012 break up. This time we were on the other end of the spectrum. I was ready to sign those divorce papers and move on from Frank. Collin and I spent a lot of time discussing areas where we would move and to meet each other half way we were narrowing the choices down to several areas in New Jersey that were closest to Manhattan. We finally agreed to buy a house in Edgewater, New Jersey and begin to plan our wedding. We were ready for our forever. Of course we needed to overcome many obstacles, but this time it would always be together. Nothing could prepare us for what those obstacles would be.

Collin and I stood by our plan to return to New York together and I never thought life could look so promising. Our flight arrived on a Tuesday morning. It was a long non-stop, rainy flight to La Guardia. Not my best flying experience. The turbulence actually made me sick. The entire flight made me sick. *I should have gotten Airborne,* I thought as I threw up in the tiny bathroom of the aircraft.

After a typical jerky, zigzagging cab ride through Manhattan we finally arrived at the apartment, which was going to be our temporary home.

"That flight got me really tired," I said as I staggered down the hallway and through the door. "I have no idea how you did this so many times! I never wanted to see a plane again."

Britney greeted us at the door and I must have looked as green as I felt.

"Oh no ... what's wrong?"

"Motion sickness and jet lag," Collin explained.

"Aw, I'm sorry," she said.

"Maybe, but it feels like I'm coming down with something," I said bringing my hand to my forehead to feel if it seemed warmer than usual. "Ugh, people are so disgusting," I complained, feeling extra irritable.

"Er ... I was going to tell you about this concert but I'll just let you know the details later," Britney said.

"Okay."

Britney then disappeared down the hall. We placed all the bags in the middle of the living room. The thought of traveling, unpacking, or doing anything for that matter was exhausting.

"My poor Baby," Collin said to me then scooped me off my feet. "You should rest." He carried me to the bedroom and placed me gently onto the bed. He pulled the covers over me, brought me a glass of water, and handed me the T.V. remote. "What else do you need?"

"I should be fine after a nap. Thanks, Baby."

He snuggled next to me and I fell asleep in his hold again. The way he softly caressed my head always pacified me. I had wonderful dreams of our dream get away before waking up. I was alone. And still tired. *What time is it?* I wondered while stretching then scooting to the edge of the bed. The curtains were drawn and the lamp was on. I rubbed my eyes and stayed for several moments longer before searching for Collin.

The hallway of the apartment carried a thick ambrosial aroma. Spices and herbs marinated through the air, the scents growing stronger as I neared the kitchen. Collin was busy attending to a large pot. He noticed me as I entered the kitchen.

"Look who's up," he said smiling at me. "How do you feel?"

"Um, still a little tired. What are you making?" I asked looking into the pot.

"Chicken noodle soup and balsamic rice."

"You really are so sweet," I said hugging him. "I'm very lucky."

He sent me back to bed and brought my soup and tea and took care of me all night. I sat with my laptop on my thighs and cell phone against my ear. Coming down with the flu or whatever it was, wasn't going to stop me. I needed to contact my lawyer as we executed several phone meetings and e-mails to make sure my statements and documents were fool proof. Another rescheduling wasn't an option. I had one week to get focused before the official court date. There was absolutely nothing Frank could do to stop this divorce from being finalized ... or so I hoped.

CHAPTER 45

I couldn't believe it was final. I was a free woman for only five hours but it felt like the shackles of a lifetime prison sentence were removed. When I was younger I always had mixed feelings and worried that I wouldn't know how to be without Frank, then it turned out being my own person and making my own decisions ended up leading me to the happiest I'd ever been.

I really wanted to celebrate that night, especially since it was the same evening of the Electric Daisy concert: We had four tickets that Britney bought and she invited me and Collin. I invited Brooke hoping to pull her out of the strange phase she was going through. I thought someone energetic and happy, like Britney, would be the ideal person for Brooke to associate with.

I unfortunately had to decline the tickets. I was still feeling so sick and I absolutely couldn't keep putting off cleaning the house. I had another cause for celebration since a family closed a deal on the house with the real estate company. It was all over. The marriage, the house; they were going to be nothing more than a chapter of my past.

I felt so lucky to have Collin by my side the entire time, with exception to the divorce court, which I chose to exclude him from.

I was apprehensive about bringing him to my house, letting him peer into the window of the other part of my life. But I caved. He really wanted to be there for me and of course I equally wanted him there.

So, there we were, in the middle of the dining room floor, surrounded by the mess of moving out leftovers. Collin sat next to me and ignored his calls while he helped me make four piles: keep, storage, donate, garbage. We spent a majority of the late afternoon in boxes and bins and before I knew it I was turning on another lamp where the sun had previously given light.

"Are you sure you're fine here? I could stay," Collin said, after I mentioned for the third time that he was going to miss the concert on my account.

"No. You go have fun. I'll only be another hour or so," I said

"Why don't we leave now and come back for everything else tomorrow? I don't feel comfortable leaving you by yourself." He brushed his fingers against the stray strands of hair that fell over my eyes.

"You're being paranoid," I said, also tangling through his locks. "Don't worry. It's always quiet and creepy around this part of Jersey… you're just not used to it."

"It's not the quiet or area that's bothering me."

"I know, Baby. But I'm tired. And I could use a little bit of this quiet. These last few days have been hectic. Besides, after this you're completely stuck with me so enjoy it."

"I can't wait to be stuck," he said then kissed my forehead.

There were only a few items I wanted to pack. My kid's baby books were in a box as well as a few other important documents. The rest would go to the curb. I tried to move as fast as possible, but I was so inexplicably exhausted. It wasn't like I hadn't had 11 hours of sleep the last few nights. It was so strange.

I told him I didn't mind being there alone yet Collin still didn't budge. I looked over at him.

"What's the problem?" I asked.

"I can't explain it…" he said and ran his fingers through my hair. "I just have a bad feeling…"

"Stop, Babe. I think it's only because you associate my house with me being unsafe. Nobody even knows that we're here. I'll only take another hour or so," I reassured.

"Are you sure?" he asked.

"Yes. Then I'm done here forever."

"Call me when you get home? I won't be too late. Okay?"

"Okay," I said as he wrapped his arms around me.

"I love you so much," he said with his face buried in my hair.

"I love you too," I said squeezing him tight. We suddenly acted like two people who would never see each other again. Feeling a funny stinging in my eyes with the passing thought I took a deep breath and pushed him away gently. "This is silly," I said and chuckled. "I'll see you soon."

"You're right," he said, his eyes gleaming at me. We stared at each other until our connection was broken by the abrupt ceasing of the music.

"Great," I said in a huff. "My iPod died."

"Here," he said reaching into his pocket and pulling his iPod out. He placed the ear buds in my ears scrolled through the songs. "I have the perfect song for you," he kissed me on the nose and left me listening to "(Everything I Do) I Do it For You."

I felt his apprehension tangible in the air as I watched him walk out. I almost wanted to leave with him but I also couldn't put off the stuff in the house. It had to get done. I really couldn't wait to start our lives together. This was the one last thing holding us back so I ignored my gut feeling and got back to work.

It only took about 45 minutes before my triumphant victory. The last item in the entire house was in a box. I was officially all packed up!

When I stood up I felt a little dizzy. Wait ... nauseous, actually. I dashed to the bathroom and cursed the city's germs as I lost my lunch in the toilet.

Nothing sounded more amazing then getting back to the apartment, taking a warm bath, two ibuprofens, and of course a cup of chamomile tea. Then I would wait patiently for my three favorite people to return.

I piled the six medium boxes by the front door when the ringing of my phone interrupted Snow Patrol's "Chasing Cars." It was Brooke. I paused the music, and then answered the call.

"Hey, what's up?"

"Nothing. How's it going over there?"

"Not bad ... I'm actually just finishing up. How's the concert? Didn't it start already?"

"Yes. I came outside to call you. Tell Collin that if he doesn't hurry he'll never find us. Both of our phones are dying too."

"What do you mean? He should have been there a long time ago."

"You sure?"

"Yeah, he left here an hour ago." There could have been traffic. But at this time? He could have made a stop. My sixth sense feelings kicked in and I just knew something was wrong.

I peered outside then noticed Collin's car still in the driveway.

"He never left," I whispered to myself. *Did he stay here this whole time because he didn't want to leave me alone? Or was it something else?* An uneasy feeling flooded my veins.

"Victoria? Is everything okay?" Brooke's voice was laced with concern. "What's going on?"

"I'm not really sure," I said. Then, before I could even try to wrap my mind around what was happening, my train of thought was startled by a knocking at the front door. I was suddenly reminded of what happened a few months earlier. *Could it possibly be John harassing me, now that I'm back?* I thought as I checked the front door. But I was dead wrong. It was Frank.

"Victoria? Hello? You still there?" I heard Brooke's pressing voice on the other end of the phone I forgot I was holding.

"Don't hang up okay?" I said to Brooke and could hear the dread in my own voice.

"I won't ...I'm here," she spoke over the music blaring in the background. "My phone is going to die any second ... is something wrong?"

I stepped back in shock as Frank stood in the doorframe. He wore all black and looked messy and rugged, a complete 360 of how he appeared earlier that day at the courthouse.

"Frank? Uh ... What are you doing here?" I asked; my tone as surprised as I'm sure my expression was.

The phone was still to my ear and Brooke heard me. *"Frank is there?"*

"You're going to need to hang that up now," he said in a serious tone, abruptly snatching the phone from me. He took a step into the house. The old familiar stench of his heavy drinking was thick in the air as he neared.

I knew I couldn't show him any fear. No more living like a child who's scared of the dark. My new confidence was like a shining a light; and I no longer needed to cower from any darkness.

"I don't remember saying you could come in," I said, blocking the small space of the entrance with my body. My foot was anchored behind the door, my hand clutched onto the inside door knob.

"I don't need permission to come into my own fucking house."

"Technically, it's not our house anymore. As of midnight tomorrow," I said trying to remain calm but firm. "And it's getting late so you need to go." I attempted to push him out.

"That's not happening," he said as he shoved his weight against mine ultimately winning the short battle. We were now alone in the house and I needed to do something to quickly change that. I needed to get out. "I'm only here to talk."

"Well ... now is not a good time," I said; my tone still steadfast. I knew immediately that he wasn't there to talk. What could he possibly say that couldn't have been said earlier with lawyers present in the safety of the courthouse? He wasn't there for anything productive and all I could think about was getting out of there and finding Collin.

"I have somewhere to be," the words trailed behind me as I passed Frank and headed for the open door.

"Victoria," he said trying to sound sincere. "You know we can't do this."

"Do what?"

"You know what I mean. You can't be serious about this divorce."

"No, Frank. I just spent all that time in and out of court as a big joke. You got me!" I said sarcastically throwing my hands up.

"What about the kids?"

"Yes, we'll always have them in common. But they're grown and don't need their parents in a dysfunctional relationship either. You and I are done." I stared straight into his dark eyes as I said it making sure to emphasize on the word "done." "Now if you don't mind," I said, still trying to maneuver around him.

"I do mind," he said then slammed and locked the door behind him. He stood in front of me, menacingly. I matched him and stood as tall as possible, with my shoulders back and head held high.

"Let's stop this now. You're not getting your way. I'm a

371

stronger woman than the person you used to be married to, Frank!"

"So it's really over?" he asked.

His expression changed and he turned away slowly, as if to back down. He pressed his palm against the wall and dropped his head into his other hand, covering his eyes as if he was crying. "Figures! You just don't care about me or our family anymore," he said trying to make me feel guilty.

I care about my family.

While he sulked in his drunken sorrow and regrets it was my opportunity to escape. I turned to the door then glanced over my shoulder. My keys were on the table.

We were in the same position one year prior. I was a mess sitting alone in the bedroom that I ended up charring. That day Frank stopped to get my phone and call my sister, and she was the one who called the police, otherwise I might be dead.

"Look ... Frank ... it wasn't always bad. We just grew apart. I don't blame you." *Okay that's a lie.* I swallowed hard and tried to think of something else. "The pressures of raising kids while we were so young took a toll on both of us."

He said nothing and I moved closer to the table.

"Anyway aren't you already with someone else."

While Frank was looking down I grabbed my keys from the table.

I inched carefully to the door. I was almost free, but the same coward he was, he turned and sucker punched me as I had my guard down.

He laughed an exaggerated, vindictive laugh as he towered over me, "Hmm ... that's funny, you still seem like the same weak piece of shit I remember," he said and then he magically regained his composure with a sinister grin on his face.

I was on the floor, but nowhere near defeated. He was only getting started, as was I, waiting for him to get closer, so ready for the coming combat. Deep down, I had been waiting, and almost wanting this moment. I knew he wouldn't ever just leave me alone. Each item, knife, gun, I didn't pack wasn't by accident. They were all meticulously placed around the house, hidden in drawers and closets, in case of a situation exactly like the one I was in.

I lifted my head and egged him on. "Go ahead. I know what comes next … I would love to see you try…"

"And you'll do what? There ain't shit for you to throw at me this time."

That's okay; I'm not planning on throwing anything at you.

I just looked at him and waited.

"Yeah, you think I forgot about that? Your little tantrum, last summer, was real fuckin' cute. But not again. I told you if you ever tried to leave me I'd kill you. Do you remember that?" he said as he paced in a semicircle around me, inching closer. I stayed on the ground and waited patiently for the perfect shot.

"Yes, I do. But, I'm not scared of you, Frank," I said challenging him.

"Oh … Is that right…?"

I pulled my foot back and, like a missile, launched my heel directly into his shin. He keeled over. I wasted no time to turn to my hands and knees to retreat.

He grabbed my ankle but I kicked free and headed for a drawer containing my gun. There was no room for error.

Frank watched me from the other side of the room. I was in control now. I held the gun straight up, pointing dead at him. This was where I messed up last time. But not now, he wasn't going to follow me for the rest of my life, clouding over every bit of light I had. I was given a second chance and this time with an advantage. My mind was clear.

But despite my unwavering confidence, my firm hand, and the merciless look on my face, something still wasn't right. Frank didn't even flinch.

"Go ahead shoot me," he dared.

"I *will* do it, Frank!"

"That's funny because just a year ago you tried to fucking kill yourself over me. Over our marriage."

I chuckled smugly, amusement briefly washed over me at his big-headedness. "Oh you poor fool," I said shaking my head in pity. "It wasn't over you." I was surprisingly relieved to have it out there.

All the confidence in the world that I had and it only took him to say three words for it to vanish.

"Yeah, I know."

Wait what? "You … you do?" *He knew? Since when? Was that why he was really there?*

"You must think I'm so fucking stupid. I'll admit, you had me for a while," he said.

"W-What do you mean?"

"You came here alone?"

"Yes," I lied right away but wondered if he already knew the truth.

"You sure about that?"

My confidence started to diminish. Fuck, why is he asking these questions? My mind was becoming cloudy. I wasn't the one with a gun pointed at me yet I was more scared than he was.

"Yeah, that's what I thought," he said when I couldn't answer. He then reached into his pocket.

"Hey!" I barked, toughening up again. I gave him a warning glare, re-pointing the pistol. "Hands where I can see them!" I said, sounding like a cop, except I felt far from one.

"I just have a little present for you," Frank said as he put one hand up and grabbled something small from his pocket. He then slowly lowered it to the floor before sliding the metal item across the room to me. I stopped it with my shoe then bent down to pick up the object. I immediately recognized it: *Collin's watch.*

"W-where did you get this?" I asked but his answer was silence and a cold glare. "What the hell did you do?" I whispered aloud.

"I'm sorry it had to be this way. You left me no other choice. Wouldn't want anyone else getting hurt, now would we?"

His ominous words were already burned into my mind and I knew exactly where I knew them from. "You left me that note?" I said my voice shaky. "*You?*" I repeated, still in disbelief.

"Now that you know I mean business, I'll need you to put the gun down."

I stood there, petrified.

"Put down the gun … or you'll never see him again. Now!"

"Okay … okay," I said. I emerged from my reverie; placed

the gun on the floor and slid it across to Frank. For moments everything seemed surreal. I couldn't move. Numbness seemed to take over not only my body, but my thoughts and emotions as well. Then reality hit me like a bus.

I broke down into a muddle of nothingness, dropping to my knees as I lost it, my body curled into a ball, as I cried and screamed as if someone had ripped out my insides. I clung desperately onto the watch and I couldn't stop sobbing. While I cried I prayed and hoped.

I heard Frank's footsteps and felt that he was standing over me. I looked up to face him and a hard blow, I wasn't expecting, thrashed across my face.

"That's for pointing that fucking gun at me!" he thundered.

Now, I was defenseless again. His human demeanor vanished as the monster returned in full force. The second hit caused a gash across my cheek and I could feel blood sliding down. "That's for being a lying cheating cunt!" He continued to kick and hit my limp body screaming at me the entire time. Then he dragged my listless body across the floor to the rec room and forced me to kneel by the built in barstool. Then he proceeded to duct tape my hands around the base.

"Why are you doing this?" I said. I continued to bawl. He ignored my plea and continued to roll layers of the silver tape around my wrists. "You couldn't just let me live in peace? I gave you eighteen years of my life!" I said. "Haven't you already taken enough from me?" I cried and cried as my insides knotted.

Frank laughed cynically, with a dark brew in his eyes. I was familiar with that look. I was screwed. "Oh, Victoria, my wife," he said grimly. "I'm only just getting started."

To Be Continued...

Acknowledgements

I am truly blessed to have so much love and encouragement while embarking on this journey! My book's reviews and the positive messages I receive bring tears to my eyes! I am eternally grateful for all of my supporters and "gems"!

Thank you to my endlessly supportive mother who is there for me every step of the way, with every single dream I follow. And to my family Caroll, Monique, Papi, Carmen, Alex, JP, Andrea, Cheryl, Cindy, Michael, Sherri, and Johnny.

I would like to send A special thank you to Cathy Tamburello and the Montclair book club for being the first book club to read and discuss Moonstone Dreams! Thank you for your support.

Jessica Gilbert, I am honored to have been a guest of The Fantastic Ladies Book Club. It was a pleasure meeting each and every one of your club. The discussion was enthusiastic and fun and was an experience that I'll never forget.

Thank you Pat for joining me on said road trip and for your ongoing support!

To my wonderful editor Maryanne Mistretta; you deserve 10 pages of thanks for believing in me, encouraging me to be my best, and not only being incredible to work with but being a great friend as well. You are super positive, full of light, and you inspire me to reach for the stars. I definitely couldn't have done any of this if you weren't there to push me along the way! It was a pleasure and I can't wait to work together again.

I have the best beta team ever! My novels would not be possible without my wonderful, amazing, awesome team: Suraiyah, Nicki, Chris, Andrew, Rachel, Melina, Darrius, Celeste, Tammy, as well as all my many author promoters out in the social media world!

To my partner in crime, Nikki, you hear the most of my rants both good and bad, you help me keep my sanity! You are my Britney!

Immanuel Smith you are awesome and a real inspiration. I look forward to working on many more amazing projects together.

Theodore Gibbons, although you'd never imagine I'd be thanking you in my book, it was the opportunity you gave me on the set of Spiderman 2 where I met some amazing people. It opened many doors while I was simply doing research for my novel. You are one of the coolest people to work and I thank you for including me on the project.

Heather Corrigan, you are my walking street team! Thanks for helping out and showing me so much love!

There are soooo many loved ones and friends to name so thank you a million to each and every one of you for your continued support.

I love to hear from you! Message me @ smiotto23@gmail.com

Like/follow @ www.facebook.com/scmiotto. for updates on latest and upcoming works, to ask questions, or leave comments.